Halon-Seven

Xander Weaver

Halon Seven

For Jamie, Wenzel, and everyone in Cheryl's book club.

You make the realm of writing extremely fulfilling.

Prologue

Near the Podkamennaya River, Russia
June 30, 1908

Colonel Rumsfeld Pellagrin, USMC made his way down the dimly lit concrete corridor. Fighting the urge to glance over his shoulder and struggling to maintain an even gait, he was careful to avoid drawing suspicion. He navigated hallway after hallway of the underground labyrinth with precision and practiced skill. Pellagrin had crossed continents, even infiltrated a foreign military compound just to make it this far. He wouldn't allow a foolish mistake to give him away now. Not when he was so close to completing his mission and seeing his life's work become a reality.

Rounding yet another corner of the utilitarian corridor he came upon a pair of Russian soldiers moving in the opposite direction. Pellagrin struggled to control himself. It was critical to avoid anything that might draw undue attention. With relief he noticed the pair were not officers and were deeply engaged in conversation. They paid him little regard. He, in turn, passed them without so much as a nod of his head. This was Russia and these men were soldiers, they had no time or interest in common pleasantries. It was so unlike the American schools and laboratories where Pellagrin normally spent his time.

One more turn and Pellagrin entered a long hallway bordered on the right by a series of service doors. This passage was much wider than the earlier corridors. He'd reached Central Research, the heart of the military facility.

Passing a few steel services doors on his right, he moved on. These entrances were marked in Cyrillic, denoting them as supply closets and utility access stations. Next he reached a larger steel door mounted on heavy industrial hinges. The handle was a mechanism with a large rotary wheel which controlled a heavy rubber gasket protruding from the lip of the door to create a powerful air-tight seal. The wall to the left and right of the doorframe was made of glass that was several inches thick. It allowed observation of the lab from the safety and security of the hallway. A sure indication that the work conducted within was hazardous.

Checking the placard beside the airlock entrance, Pellagrin noted the room's designation as High Security Laboratory #3. According to information provided by the US SIS (Signals Intelligence Service) and the work order he'd forged earlier, the stolen American technology should be located in High Security Lab #1.

Moving down the corridor, Pellagrin found a duplicate lab located across that hall. Continuing further still he found his destination, Laboratory #1. A quick glance left, then right, confirmed he was alone. Taking the large wheeled handle in both hands he gave it a muscle wrenching spin. The force required to break the seal was surprising. Some of the scientists he'd observed while undercover for the past week were quite slight in stature. How some of them would contend with the doors heavy-handed control system was a mystery to Pellagrin.

Freeing the latch, Pellagrin stepped through the hatch and pulled the bulky slab shut behind. The door must have been outrageously heavy yet it moved silently on its heavy steel hinges. Spinning the latching wheel until it came to a stop, he reached under his long white lab coat and retrieved an eighteen-inch long crescent wrench. He'd secured the wrench under his left arm by looping a spare shoelace through the close end of the wrench and tying the lace up over his shoulder. As he pulled the end of the shoelace and released the knot he considered how lucky he'd been, not needing to use the blunt force weapon to gain access to the lab. Jamming the wrench between the crosshatch supports securing the outer ring of the door's release wheel to the mechanical gears that operated the seal, he ensured the door could not be opened from the outside.

Stepping across the small airlock, Pellagrin spun the wheel of the second door, a duplicate of the first, located on the opposite side of the tiny vestibule. He stepped through and pulled it closed. This time he used the shoelace from his improvised wrench sling to tie off the door's control wheel. It was unlikely anyone would defeat the wrench in the outer door, but Pellagrin knew he was too close to the finish line to take unnecessary chances.

He was finally alone in the dimly lit Russian lab. Everything he'd risked to make it this far had paid off. Looking back, he was shocked that the hastily assembled plan had actually worked. Infiltrating Russia's borders was easy enough. Backstopping the credentials necessary to gain access to the facility had been the real gamble. Without proper documentation, the operation was dead in the water. Fortunately, well-placed bribes and creative fiction secured his access to the facility in the end. Corruption didn't make espionage possible, but sure made things easier. All of that was behind him now, and it was game time.

Crossing the darkened lab, Pellagrin found a pile of large wooden crates stacked in the back corner of the room. Each crate was stamped with Cyrillic lettering, Russian script, indicating the contents to be Top Secret. His breath caught in his throat as he made a quick count of the containers only to find two missing. Looking closer, he found the missing pair stashed behind some larger boxes and wedged tight against the wall. Breathing a sigh of relief, Pellagrin wiped the sweat from his brow.

Such a mistake would cost him his life.

Moving on to the next stage of his plan, Pellagrin looked around the lab more carefully. A large locked steel cabinet took up the center of the labs back wall. Etched into the thick plate doors in Cyrillic text were the words:

Огонь звезды

In English, this translated to *Fire Star*. And if the reports he'd read were accurate, the name was extremely appropriate.

The heavy steel doors were locked with three industrial grade padlocks the likes of which Pellagrin had never seen before. At least this was a problem he'd anticipated. His source inside the royal palace of Nicholas II, the ruling monarch of

Russia, had explained that it was impossible to make copies of the three keys required to access the Fire Star cabinet.

A quick glance around the room revealed a large cabinet stocked with a wide range of glass jars and vials. As he suspected, the lab was well equipped with chemicals and solutions for just about any scientific test imaginable. Looking at the steel doors now, Pellagrin was more confident than ever that those keys would not be an issue.

It took him several minutes to sort through the jars before he selected the four he needed. Translating Cyrillic on the fly wasn't Pellagrin's strong suit. Regrettably he'd had little more than a month to prepare for this mission. Just a single month to learn to speak Russian like a native as well as read the language and acquire a passable knowledge of the countries political and military hierarchy.

Taking the four jars to the sink in the far right corner of the room, he removed the screw-on cap from the largest of the containers. It took only moments to dump the contents down the drain. Next he removed the lid from one of the other containers and poured a measure of its crystalline substance into the large empty glass jar. Setting the container of crystal powder aside, he took the third container and added a generous dose of its clear fluid to the large jar.

Placing the cap on the glass jar, Pellagrin set it in the sink and proceeded to wait sixty seconds. The timing was critical so he made use of his cheap Russian wristwatch. Being under a time pinch, he knew better than to count the seconds off in his head. He was sure to count too quickly. Finally, he took up the large glass jar and shook it vigorously for thirty seconds. This time there was no benefit of the watch. His hands were full.

Setting the jar back in the sink, Pellagrin took a step back, turning his face as far away as possible. With one quick motion, removed the bottle's cap. The horrible smell that escaped threatened to pull the air from his lungs. Knowing his body would respond with the urge to cough, maybe even vomit, didn't make it easier to fight. He raised the fourth and final bottle before quickly adding a very small measure to the mix. Replacing the cap and screwing it tightly, he stepped away desperate for fresh air.

Grabbing a pry-bar from a nearby tool cart, Pellagrin began popping the lids from each of the wooden crates. After disassembling the boxes and removing their contents, he spread the components out across the floor. Even in the dim light cast into the lab through the thick glass walls on either sides of the airlock, he was already doing a mental inventory of the components. Another big relief—everything was accounted for. Nothing had been lost when the Russians stole the device from his facility in the United States.

Without delay, Pellagrin set about reassembling the device. This was a painstaking process done without schematics, completely from memory. His infiltration of the secret Russian military installation was risky enough. Were he to be captured with the plans for the machine, there would have been no way to explain himself. Worse yet, if the Russians recovered the plans for properly assembling the device, they would discover that it was not a modular energy weapon as they'd been lead to believe. Allowing the Russians to abscond with the device was one thing. They knew nothing of its true design. But if they were to learn of its true purpose—its true potential—it would forever shift the balance of power on a global scale. Just the thought of this caused Pellagrin to double his efforts assembling the device. Morning was approaching far too quickly. If he didn't complete the platform in time, his mission would yet fail.

Three hours later, the bulk of the work had been completed. Pellagrin had stripped down to his undershirt and trousers and was covered in sweat. But his work was nearly finished. He'd worked nonstop, assembling the seemingly disparate components into larger more substantial portions of the device. In doing so, the primary platform had taken shape.

In the center of the darkened lab's concrete floor stood a small raised circular platform, four feet in diameter. Two small steps led onto the raised deck of the device. Behind those steps and tucked beneath the raised platform were tangles of heavy gauged wire. Off to the side of the platform, Pellagrin was working on the last portion of the system. The command and control box was a critical component. The low light of the room hampered him. The wires behind the crude control panel were color-coded, but in the dimly lit room he couldn't tell one wire from the next.

Wiping the perspiration from his eyes, he squinted down at the series of loose wires once more. Pellagrin jumped at the sudden sound as someone ponded on the observation window. His heart racing, Pellagrin spun to see a pair of armed Russian soldiers glaring at him from the hallway.

One of the soldiers bellowed at Pellagrin, instructing him to open the airlock door immediately. Beside him, the second armed officer was trying desperately to spin the door's wheeled lock. It would be no use. With the long heavy wrench jammed into the mechanism ,the solider had no chance of freeing the latch.

"Well, I guess the cat's out of the bag," Pellagrin muttered to himself. No longer concerned with stealth and no longer having to hide from security patrols, he walked across the room and flipped the series of switches on the wall.

The light banks anchored to the concrete ceiling sprang to life driving a stabbing pain into Pellagrin's eyes. He'd been working for hours in the muted light of the lab. Now the room was lit with what felt like the full power of the sun. Shaking off the eyestrain, he returned to his improvised workbench. He'd been discovered and time was running out, but at least he could see the color of the damn wires.

The two soldiers outside were joined by four more. One of them, clearly an officer, took charge and began barking orders. Moments later a security klaxon rang out through the facility. Despite his improvised door locks it was only a matter of time before the lab was breached. Pellagrin paid the soldiers only peripheral attention as he finished attaching the last of the color-coded leads. Time was of the essence and he had a mission to complete.

Flipping the control panel right side up, Pellagrin glanced at the three controls. He turned the large power toggle knob back and forth between the on and off position. The knob was large, black, and industrial. It was the kind of thick exaggerated control a person could use even while wearing a heavy insulated glove. The other two controls shared a similar industrial look. One was an oversized toggle switch covered by a hinged glass cap designed to prevent the switch from being accidentally triggered. The last control, the most obvious of the three, was a massive red button larger than a man's fist. It took up the entire left end of the control panel.

Pellagrin clicked the large on-off switch back and forth several times; satisfied with the healthy mechanical click he heard when the switch reached either of the two positions. With a sweep of his arm, he knocked the tools from the top of the cart and gently set the control box upon its top shelf. Wheeling the cart to the side of the platform, he was careful not to kink or fray the heavy black cable stretching between the platform and the control box.

Gunshots rang out drawing Pellagrin's attention back to the six soldiers gathered in the hallway. Dark bullet smears pockmarked the glass wall. Even through the heavy transparent layer he could hear the ricochets bouncing between the glass and the concrete walls of the hall.

"Not smart," Pellagrin muttered with a grin. He made eye contact with the commanding officer on the far side of the glass. The Russian was furious. Pellagrin's grin only deepened as he shook his head in a knowing manner. The man was a fool.

Pellagrin had done the calculations. Barring any structural flaw in the glass barrier, there was no way the soldiers were getting through it with anything less than three full sticks of TNT. The thought made him look back to the commanding officer. The man was once again shouting orders at someone out of Pellagrin's field of view. *TNT...* Pellagrin didn't like the thought of it. For some reason he had a feeling it was only a matter of time before the guards did something foolish. But would they risk damaging, even destroying Fire Star?

Of course they would—these were the same men thoughtless enough to fire rifles at a glass surface several inches thick while standing in a concrete-lined box! There was also a very good chance the officer in charge had no knowledge of Fire Star let alone its residence in this lab.

It's time to get the hell out of there.

Returning to the sink, Pellagrin grabbed the large jar and set about another thirty seconds of vigorous shaking. He put the bottle down on the counter and pulled the largest pipette from a stand near the sink. After removing the cap from the glass jar, Pellagrin was instantly confident he'd attained the proper chemical reaction. The caustic smell had been reduced to a mild, easily tolerable, pungent aroma.

The pipette was essentially a glass version of a drinking straw. Dipping the pipette into the bottle, he placed a finger over the top end. This trapped a measure of the solution in the hollow core of the long glass wand. Turning to the fortified plate steel box marked 'Fire Star,' Pellagrin placed the bottom end of the glass pipette over the top edge of the heavy steel hinge along one side of the cabinet. When he removed his finger from atop the pipette it allowed the solution trapped inside to drain out the bottom, washing over the massive hinge.

Pellagrin returned to the bottle three more times, each time drawing another measure of the caustic liquid and dispersing it over each of the remaining hinges. Once finished, he placed the pipette in the sink the returned the cap to the jar before placing it, too, in the sink. It was a volatile mixture and something he didn't dare spill by mistake. Just dispersing the material with the pipette made him twitchy.

Funny, he thought. He'd infiltrated a foreign nations most secure military installation and locked himself inside one of their most secret laboratories after a month long cram session to learn anything and everything he could about Russian culture. Even after all that, he was concerned about spilling a bottle of chemicals for fear of burning his face off. That bottle should be the very least of his concerns.

Speaking of which… turning back to the glass wall, he'd just realized the soldiers outside had become disturbingly quiet. Now they were nowhere to be seen. Somehow that was even more troubling than his caustic chemical brew.

Cautiously, Pellagrin approached the glass wall. Glancing to the left he found the troops gathered around a satchel on the hallway floor. One of the men reached into the bag and pulled out a spool of wire. Setting it aside, he retrieved a three-stick bundle of TNT.

Dynamite…

Dammit!

Pellagrin darted back across the room. He grabbed the pry-bar from the wreckage of the crates and headed for the steel Fire Star locker. Wasting not a single step, he wound up and smashed the pry-bar across one of the cabinet's top hinges. The hinge exploded as if made of porcelain. He followed this with another powerful swing that reduced the second top hinge to dust. Pellagrin stepped back as the weight of the doors and gravity did the rest. The plate steel doors tipped forward as the lower hinges shattered under the stress of their load. The doors smashed to the floor. Amusingly, the doors were still intact, their locks still securely in place.

Inside the cabinet was a large two-foot wide glass cube. This was Fire Star. Looking closely at the craftsmanship of the glasswork, Pellagrin was impressed. The flawless transparent glass box had no visible seams. Surely the cube was an assembly of six individual panes fused along their perimeters, but for the life of him he couldn't find a hint of a joint. This leant credence to the intelligence SIS had gathered. The report indicated that the glass box was air tight and under vacuum…containing absolutely no atmosphere.

A small innocuous looking rock sat on the bottom of the cube. It was irregularly shaped, dark gray in color, and about the size of a baseball. A thick black cable ran to the left wall of the cube and was affixed to the exact center of the cube's left wall. A mirror opposite of that cable was attached to the right wall of the cube. So far all of the intelligence was absolutely correct.

Looking over his shoulder, Pellagrin saw two soldiers taping three sticks of TNT to the outside corner of the glass wall. *This was good*, he thought. They were placing the TNT at the corner of the glass where it met the base of the wall. If they were smart, they would've placed the dynamite in the center of the pane. There was a chance, however remote, that the TNT wouldn't breach the wall on the first try.

Gotta love the Russians!

His work almost done, Pellagrin returned to the glass cube. To the right of the cube, also mounted inside the cabinet was a large metal switch box. It had heavy gauge wire leads affixed to each side and a large red handled circuit breaker lever in the center. With a deep breath and one final prayer for luck, he pulled the power lever down engaging the circuit and sending a rush of electricity into the vacuum-sealed cube.

There was a distinctive hum of electricity that instantly made his skin tingle. Pellagrin felt the hair on his arms and the back of his neck stand at attention. Even through the oily moisture of his perspiration, the surge of power in the air was unmistakable.

His eyes went wide as the chunk of ore rose from the bottom of the cube and floated freely in mid air. It took up a stationary location, vertically and horizontally, at the exact center of the cube. Then, after floating for several seconds without movement, the stone began to turn slowly on its axis.

The stone spun slowly for almost a minute before Pellagrin realized he'd been holding his breath. Intelligence reports hadn't detailed this phenomenon. He was unprepared for a reaction of this nature. He'd never seen anything like it. After another minute he realized the size of the stone had changed. Somehow the chunk of ore was growing smaller.

His mind swam as he considered the possibilities. Was the density of the object increasing? But as he looked closer, he realized that an ultra fine particulate matter was beginning to spread inside the cube. It seemed the stone was somehow shedding its outer layers in the form of microscopic granules that floated freely inside the cube. They quickly began to gather in small foggy clouds.

As a scientist, Pellagrin found this amazing. He'd never read of such a thing. A hundred questions collided in his mind. What was the strange ore? Why was it reacting to electric current in such a way? If it reacted to the present power flow in this way, how might it react to current of different voltage—or a different amperage? He'd come here to use the Russian's Fire Star because intelligence suggested the device could power his platform. Reportedly, Fire Star was capable of generating massive amounts of electricity by amplifying a relatively small current when it was fed into the device. But what Pellagrin was seeing was beyond anything he'd ever imagined. Whatever the Russians developed defied explanation.

A tapping sound drew Pellagrin's attention away from the contents of the cube. The sound was coming from the gauge mounted on the back of the cabinet. Rapid tapping was made by the gauge's display needle slamming against the right most wall of the device's display, well beyond its maximum value. The power level had surpassed the max reading so quickly that the needle slammed against the end of the display area so hard that it bounced several times before coming to rest solidly against the display's wall. Whatever was happening here, the device truly was generating a massive level of energy. This was encouraging! His gamble might pay off. If anything was able to generate the power level needed to fuel his platform, surely it was Fire Star.

Pellagrin's eyes jumped back to the cube just as the last layers of dust separated from the object that had been buried at the core of the stone. While whisking clouds of fine particulate matter continued to circulate inside the cube, at its absolute center now floated a perfectly spherical black orb about the size of a child's marble. It was so perfectly shaped and uniform in color that Pellagrin found it impossible to tell whether the object was spinning as the stone had been.

Pellagrin wanted to observe the process further. He wanted to take notes. He wanted to understand what he was seeing. In all his years of scientific endeavor, he'd never conceived of such a thing. Where in the hell had the Russians found this? Or worse—had they built it?

The thought of spending time watching the strange orb snapped him back to the present. His concerns jumping back to the soldiers still working to breach his fortified position. They could detonate the TNT at any moment. In fact, why hadn't they done it already? He spun around to assess the soldiers' progress.

To his horror, he found that a soldier had just attached a second, three-stick bundle of TNT to the opposite corner of the glass wall. No wonder they hadn't stuck their first bundle to the center of the glass—the crazy bastards were going to detonate six sticks simultaneously! That much TNT would not only breach the wall, but the back pressure in the confined space would turn every one of them into human stew.

That's it, time to get the holy hell out of there...

Pellagrin knelt down before the cabinet containing the glass cube and pulled open a heavy steel drawer. Inside was just what he expected, a pair of very heavily insulated power leads. With no time to waste, he pulled both cables out at the same time. Each cable was as big around as his wrist and had a heavy industrial alligator clip on the end.

Pulling the wires the short distance to the platform, he dropped to his knees. Very carefully, he removed a metal panel from the back of the platform to reveal a pair of stout metal flanges—one marked with a plus and the other marked with a minus. Taking great care as to not cause a spark, he connected the lead wires; one to each terminal on the platform.

Jumping upright, Pellagrin returned to the cube. Giving it another fateful glance, he pressed the large green button located under the large red circuit lever beside the cube. As soon as the button was pressed he could hear the surge of power reach the capacitors on the transport platform. Glancing once again at the TNT strapped to the glass wall, he knew it was now or never.

Stepping to the transport platform's small control panel still atop the small-wheeled cart, Pellagrin turned the ignition key and flipped up the glass cap protecting the toggle switch. He flicked the heavy switch, then slammed his fist down on the big red button. Without so much as a breath, he spun on his heel and stepped onto the platform. With great care and precision, he took a position at the very center of the raised circle.

A five second delay had been built into the system. It was designed to give him enough time to activate the device and move into position before it engaged. But now he was very concerned those five seconds would cost him his life. As he stood waiting for the device to engage, his eyes were glued to the sticks of TNT taped against the outside of the glass less than ten yards away.

Finally, just before he thought something had gone wrong with the platform, a small flash of light filled the room. It was follow almost immediately by another flash, this one stronger and brighter. Pellagrin couldn't figure out where the light was coming from. It seemed to form all around him. Another flash and he felt a pull on his body—a strange force—as if he were suddenly twice his normal weight.

There was one more final blinding flash and then Pellagrin was gone.

––––––––––

The platform stood empty in the brightly lit laboratory. Electricity hummed as it coursed through the transformer in the cabinet at the back of the lab. The components inside the platform buzzed as they began to power down. Aside from that, there was eerie silence. The marble size sphere continued to hover at the center of the vacuum-sealed cube.

Finally, the fuse ran out on the two bundles of TNT. The dynamite detonated, obliterating the glass wall and sending shards of glass the size of grains of sand blasting through the laboratory. The fiery explosion ignited a gas line in the wall of the lab, engulfing everything in an instant inferno. The detonation's percussive blast rocketed backward through the breached lab wall and down the concrete corridors pulverizing the six nearby Russian soldiers. They never felt a thing.

The force of the blast would have been enough to collapse the concrete structure of the hallway and the lab itself if the blast wave and shrapnel from the wall had not already breached the vacuum seal of the Fire Star cube. With a hiss, the strange composition of the vaporous clouds and black orb contained within instantly mixed with the atmosphere. The electrified conflagration caused a cascading breakdown in the strange element. The resulting detonation that made the eruption of the TNT and natural gas look like a hiccup by comparison.

When the strange black sphere went critical, its resulting detonation wiped out not only the lab, it removed every trace of the Russian military facility from the face of the planet. Along with it, destroyed in an instant, were 770 square miles of Russian wilderness.

Chapter 1

London, England
Two Months Ago

The chill from the day's ceaseless rain penetrated Professor Walter Meade's old bones. He stared out the taxi window as historic London passed the rain-streaked windows. The afternoon had grown late but it was impossible to gauge the time—the sky had remained the same persistent dreary gray since the moment he arrived in the city early that morning. He had planned to spend the evening trading stories with his old friend Allan and Allan's wife, Helen. It was their custom whenever Walter came to town. But an unexpected email had arrived on Walter's phone and change the course of his afternoon.

The nature of the message had Walter deeply concerned. A rare book dealer was reaching out and claiming to have located the lost, privately published copy of J.K. Holloway's *Den Dschinn*. This was troubling because it was completely unexpected. Walter's contact, Heinrich was the owner of the bookstore which specialized in rare manuscripts, maps, and journals but more importantly he was also a highly regarded smuggler who traded in exotic gems and ores. The J.K. Holloway book that Heinrich mentioned was actually a code. It meant he'd located a supply of an extremely rare mineral known as Halon-Seven. The news was alarming because, to the best of Walter's knowledge, he already possessed the entire known supply of the substance. If a new source had been discovered, Walter needed to know about it immediately.

It was this news that brought Walter's relaxing evening to an end and sent the 80-year-old man out into the pouring rain for a clandestine meeting with an old German smuggler. Walter's eyes watched the scenery pass without really noticing. His mind was swimming with the implications of Heinrich's discovery. A new source of Halon-Seven would open a great many doors for his research. This might very well be the break he'd been hoping for. The limited supply of the substance was preventing him from completing his project, satisfying his life's work. He had spared no expense scouring the globe in search of another source of the ore, only to find nothing. But if Heinrich's message was accurate, he'd missed something. Unlikely, but not impossible. And if this were the case there was hope for *Meridian*, after all. He could yet fulfill his life's ambition and leave a mark that would forever change the world.

The taxi pulled to the curb before the quaint old London bookstore. The large glass front window offered little view of the warmly lit interior. It, too, was streaked by the unending rain. Walter pulled the collar of his wool coat tight around his neck, stepped carefully over a large puddle, and pushed his way through the shop's door.

The silence of the bookstore struck him as odd but it took him a moment to realize what was out of place. The door chime, normally triggered when the front door opened, was missing. It was unusual, but not strikingly so. It had been nearly a year since Walter last stopped to visit old Heinrich. But there was something more. It was the silence. The bookstore was normally nearly as quiet as a library, but Heinrich always kept a small portable radio tucked under the front counter. It was perpetually tuned to a London talk station. Heinrich kept the volume very low, but the lack of the constant droning of voices emanating from beneath the counter was the second item out of place.

"Heinrich?" Walter called quietly. There was a tickling sense at the back of his mind telling him something was wrong. But the rational part of his mind overruled that sensation. He rounded the counter and walked deeper into the small bookstore.

Walter passed row after row of floor to ceiling bookshelves breaking the body of the store into aisles. The shelves were packed end to end with old but interesting books. Every one was completely unique and a rare literary find. As he passed each aisle, Walter cast an expectant glance toward the back of the store. Each time he was surprised not to find his friend cataloging the eclectic collection of old tomes.

He reached the far wall but still found no sign of Heinrich. His concern was growing. He made his way to the back of the store. When he got there, he found the old wooden door leading to the back office slightly ajar. Walter smiled. Of course, Heinrich was in back. There was no need for alarm.

"Heinrich," he called through the door. "It's Walter. I hope you haven't fallen asleep my friend! It's not even—"

Walter pushed through the door and into the small office. His breath caught in his throat. There, sprawled face down on the floor was Heinrich. A bullet hole was clearly visible in the back of his head, as was the blood and brain matter that coated the floor and the wall just beyond. Walter knew at once he was in danger. He would make for the street, find the nearest public place and call the authorities. As he spun on his heel to make his escape he realized he would never have the opportunity.

The cold dark barrel of a silenced pistol was the first sight to catch Walter's eye. The gun was leveled squarely at his face.

"Not a sound, old man!" the armed man commanded. About six feet tall, the man wore a black watch cap, a black coat, and dark trousers. He had dark penetrating eyes that left no doubt in Walter's mind, this man was perfectly willing to pull the trigger.

As Walter fought down the panic, he studied the gunman's face. He had a long healed over burn scar on the left side of his face, about the size of a large fist. Walter decided the man's lack of regard to hide his identity or the distinguishing mark didn't speak well for him getting out of this with his life.

"Get back in there," the man instructed. His voice was low and threatening, almost a growl. Walter wasn't sure if the man was trying to be intimidating or if that was just his way. Likely it was both. The man had the look of an experienced killer. Heinrich was proof enough of that.

His observations reinforced the analysis, as Walter was forced into the office. Looking at Heinrich's body on the floor, the man had been shot in the head. His proximity to the back wall and the blood splatter indicated he was on his knees when he'd been shot—when he was executed. The bloodstain on the wall told Walter even more. The blood had congealed and dried to a large degree. Heinrich had been killed some time ago. He was not the one who sent the email Walter had read. Walter had walked into a trap set specifically for him.

The gunman put his hand on Walter's shoulder and guided him at gunpoint past the body and around the corner of the desk. They passed through a doorway and down a short hall before coming to a small worn out old kitchen. Sitting on a rickety wooden chair beside the kitchen table was a thin lanky man wearing a very expensive Italian suit. Walter recognized him immediately. His bird-like build and oddly egg shaped head meant he could be only one man. As dire as the situation was a moment ago, the stakes had just gotten worse.

"Good evening, Professor Meade," Nil Bayer said with a toothy smile.

A chill ran through Walter. The man's grin did nothing to belie the rock hard indifference that shown in his eyes. His smile was as cold as poor Heinrich's corpse.

Walter's panic went up by several degrees when he considered the man before him and the coded message used to lure him to the bookstore. If Nil Bayer was here, Walter knew his situation was critical. If Bayer knew about the Halon-Seven, the situation was far graver than he'd dared speculate. This man had the reckless ambition and the limitless greed that constituted Walter's worst-case scenario.

Walter felt a painful tightening of his chest when he thought of the damage Bayer would do if he had control of Meridian. Though Walter was not prone to panic, if ever there was a time, this was it. He'd walked into this trap. He could already foresee the situation spiraling out of control. Walter needed to get the upper hand and to find out how much Bayer knew. But he was short of breath. He felt weak in the knees and put his hand on the kitchen counter to steady himself. Was this what a panic attack felt like? He needed to keep his head. He had to keep thinking.

"Take a deep breath, Professor. You don't look well." Though the words sounded like concern, Walter knew better. He knew Bayer's reputation well. The man was gloating. His trap had worked; Walter had walked right into it. Hell, given the circumstance, he'd almost come running into the snare. He'd been so concerned with the discovery of a new source of Halon-Seven that he failed to take precautions.

"Tell me what you want." These were Walter's first words to the man and the sound of his own voice surprised him. His voice was sickly and hollow. The room was spinning as well. There was a constricting pain in his left shoulder. It had been there for some time but he was so distracted he'd only just realized it. As he struggled to take another breath, the truth of his situation dawned on him.

Bayer nodded to the gunman behind Walter. The man placed the barrel of the suppressor at the base of Walter's skull, pressing it just behind his right ear. He applied pressure until Walter cried out in pain. Walter felt his knees threatening to buckle but fought to keep his footing.

"You know very well what I want!" Bayer spat. "You call it Meridian. Your predecessor, Rumsfeld Pellagrin referred to it as 'Silent River.' Whatever the name, you know well its power. Give me what I want and I'll make you a very rich man."

Despite his pain, Walter couldn't help laughing. Bayer had wealth beyond compare, but his only interest was more money and more power. Anything he could hold over the heads of others. "You see yourself as Alexander the Great? You would use Meridian to conquer the modern world? It's short sighted and pathetic! Meridian holds far more power than you realize. It is the power to unite *the entire world.* To bring people together, to join them in a way few have ever dared to imagine."

Walter now felt the pain in his chest and across his back. His left arm had grown numb. It was a struggle just to remain standing. He could feel the perspiration forming across his chest and down his back. "I'll never give you Meridian," his words came out as little more than a raspy whisper.

The gunman must've taken them as a challenge because Meade immediately felt the press of the gun driving into the base of his skull. Walter was forced to his knees.

Bayer looked down his nose at Walter, distain clear in his eyes. Bayer studied him with detachment. Walter's resistance was something he couldn't understand. "You'll give me what I want," he said confidently. "In the end, Meridian is *not* worth your life!"

Walter smiled and met the man's eye. So all was not lost. Bayer understood how Meridian could be used toward his own ends for power and wealth but he had no understanding of its true value to the world. If he did, he would know that Meridian was most definitely worth his life. Walter had believed this since the fateful day in 1955 when Rumsfeld Pellagrin invited him to join Silent River. With this understanding, Walter could look proudly on the fact that his heart was now failing. Not only was he willing to die to protect the project, he would go to the grave before allowing someone like Bayer take it from him. He only wished he knew for certain whether Bayer knew about Halon-Seven.

Greater pressure was applied to the gun at the back of Walter's head. The room was spinning. Everything was growing dim. Halon-Seven was all that Walter could think of. He needed to be sure. If Bayer knew the secret, he would surely execute the research team and take the project for himself. As much as Walter didn't want to see the project perverted, the thought of those kids being gunned down somehow seemed more tragic.

"The book!" Bayer bellowed into Meade's face. The man was squatting down in front of him but Walter was so lost in his thoughts that he hadn't heard a word Bayer was saying.

"Where is the book?" Bayer demanded once more.

The man was growing red in the face. Walter took a measure of pride in that. His vision was growing more dim and clouded but he could still see the rage in Bayer's visage. "What book?" Walter finally managed in a hoarse whisper.

"Your contact told us about the book! We emailed you about it. Just as he promised, you responded immediately. He said you've been searching for the book for many years. He told us you hired him to locate it for you…"

Walter's mind was spinning. His head was pounding and he couldn't breath. Why was Bayer asking him about the book? What had Heinrich told— That was it! Heinrich told Bayer about the book! That was their code, their cover story. Heinrich referred to Halon-Seven as if it were a book in all of his communications. That was their arrangement. But when Bayer showed up with his gun-toting goon, Heinrich had maintained the deception. Bayer didn't know about Halon-Seven. Heinrich, ever the crafty smuggler, spun a yarn about being hired to locate a copy of J.K. Holloway's lost novel.

That was it. Walter had received his dying wish. The heartless bastard, Bayer was still in the dark. Walter knew his team would be safe for the time being. Thankfully, there was a contingency plan in place. Arrangements had already been made. In the event of his death, the Meridian project would land in capable hands.

One last surge of pain coursed through Walter's body. He felt it from head to toe. The next thing he knew he was lying face down on the filthy linoleum floor. He heard Bayer and the gunman yelling but their voices were miles distant. With some satisfaction, Walter knew there was nothing more they could do to hurt him. He realized his end had come, as he had feared, with his heart giving out before it was time. He had the Russians to thank for that. If they had just left well enough alone. Strangely, though, he now felt ready. His physical pain was slipping away, replaced by a sense of calm as his mind adjusted and accepted the inevitable.

There was just one thing left undone. One thing that he cared about before he moved on. He knew he was dying of a heart attack. As such, no one would ever know he'd fallen victim to Bayer's ambition. He wanted to leave a message, point a finger at Bayer and let someone know what had happened. But that time was passed. There was no way left to communicate.

A smile crossed Meade's lips in the last moments of his life. There, curled in the fetal position on that horrible floor, he thought of a way to communicate. He couldn't tell anyone who had led him to this point, but he could leave a clue indicating his death was not entirely due to natural causes.

Struggling for one last breath of air, Meade clasped his hands together. He wrapped the pointer and middle finger of his left tightly in the grip of his right hand. Prying on his fingers, he twisted with all of his remaining strength. The last sound he heard in life was the snapping of the bones in these two fingers.

Strangely, there was no pain. Only relief. His message was sent. He only hoped the warning would not go unnoticed. It was up to Cyrus now.

Chapter 2

The Gold Coast, Chicago, Illinois
Present Day
Saturday, 4:11 pm

With no subtle show of reluctance, Tyler Alcot lead the two detectives into the large sitting room of his penthouse apartment. He didn't care to encourage the men to stay any longer than absolutely necessary. Unfortunately, before Tyler had a chance to get down to business, his aging Spanish maid entered carrying a large serving tray complete with a carafe of coffee and three cups. She looked expectantly at Tyler and his two guests.

So much for forgoing informality. He had fallen victim to Esmeralda's practiced efficiency.

Tyler motioned for the pair of police detectives to join him before taking a place on the sofa. His back was to a massive picture window with an expansive view of the Chicago skyline. It was mid-afternoon and the city was cast in crisp detail. Both detectives reluctantly took places on the sofa opposite Tyler. They obviously intend this to be no more of a social call than Tyler.

Moving swiftly, Esmeralda served the coffee in short cups set upon saucers before leaving the carafe at the end of the coffee table between the two sofas. Without a word she exited the room. Quiet, efficient, and never underfoot. Tyler only wished he had thought to mention the expected arrival of his guests and asked her to forgo to usual pleasantries.

The officers were veteran Chicago police detectives, and they looked the part. Both dressed in cheap blandly colored suits, one was tall and rail thin with short sandy colored hair while the other might have been 5' 8" if he wore thickly soled shoes. The short detective must have weighed close to two hundred pounds but he didn't carry it low on his torso like most overweight men. His girth was evenly distributed between his belt and his chin making him look like a giant billiard ball dressed in drab attire. His prematurely bald pate further contributed to his cue ball like appearance. The tall detective's name was Marsh and the short one went by, appropriately enough, Stubbs. No joke, you didn't need Tyler's eidetic memory to remember a name like that. Still, while he had no trouble with their names, Tyler preferred to think of them as Detective Stretch and Detective Cue Ball.

"What's the problem?" Tyler asked, anxious to conclude the visit. "I though we had a deal. You said the next time I saw you I should have the rest of the money ready—the job would be done."

Detective Stretch leaned forward on the couch doing his best to be intimidating in the opulent surroundings of the spacious penthouse living room. "When we do a job, we like to take a close look at the guy doing the hiring. We gotta be sure the job's on the level."

The look on the detective's face implied Tyler was expected to say something even though no question had been asked. Tyler remained silent and looked on expectantly. He knew experienced detectives favored this approach. The idea was to say something pointed before letting the statement hang, waiting to see what the suspect said to fill the silence. It could be very effective, but he wasn't falling for it.

"*The problem*," Cue Ball said, finally picking up where his partner left off. "Is that you asked us to provide a service and we agreed, acting in good faith. *The problem* is that you weren't on the level with us."

"Good faith," Tyler said with a laugh. "Provide a service? You make it sound like I hired you to resurface my dining room floor! I hired you to murder my wife!

"What's the problem? You're businessmen. I offered the money and you accepted payment—half down and half upon completion of the job. You took the job and you took the down payment. Now quit screwing around. I want her dead!"

"That's just it," Stretch growled through clenched teeth. "You're the problem. It's your fancy watch and your penthouse apartment. Your golf club membership and your big investment firm…they're all bullshit! We did a little digging and none of it stands up!"

Crap, Tyler thought. That wasn't part of the plan. He hadn't expected these guys to perform any sort of due diligence let alone dig that far into his life. This life was only a veneer. He hadn't backstopped his credentials at the firm. These guys were supposed to be thugs, here to do the job, collect a fat wad of cash and move on. He had clearly underestimated the sophistication of their operation.

"Sure," Stretch continued, still sitting on the edge of the sofa. His eyes burrowed into Tyler as he spoke. "The golf club membership is real. But you only joined two months back. Same for this fancy ass apartment! There's no lease—you have a month-to-month rental agreement. The last owner was some douche bag defense attorney that went missing." He laughed to himself, apparently amused with the thought.

"Can't say we're too sorry about that," Detective Cue Ball said with a matching chuckle. He was sitting back on the couch letting his partner handle the confrontation. The stout man seemed content to watch Tyler squirm.

"Even your position with Rollins, Cussler, and Robinson is a total sham. Sure, we can call the switchboard. They'll even put us through to your voicemail. But when I show up and ask for you in person, it's the damnedest thing—no one's even heard of Tyler Alcot!"

As Stretch hammered away a Tyler's cover, Tyler was becoming more and more uncomfortable. His entire backstory had unraveled. They knew he wasn't who he claimed. These were hardcore bad cops. There was no way they were letting him walk away from this. But there was some hope. They hadn't killed him yet. It could be because Esmeralda was somewhere in the house and they didn't want a witness but he was pretty sure there was more to it than that.

Stretch continued and Tyler got his answer. "So when we know that Tyler Alcot ain't who he claims to be, the question becomes who is he and why'd he really hire us?" He let the comment hang in the air for intimidation sake. It was effective.

"So we did more digging. You know what? We found some disturbing stuff. Sure, you did a pretty fair job of hiding your identity—even hiding your real name. So we put a tail on you. Sure, you slept here in the penthouse. I guess I'd stay here too, if I had the chance." He looked around the apartment, taking it in as if seeing it for the first time. "You came and went— the gym, the market, the bar down the street. You actually have a talent. You were *very* convincing. You went on as if you really were Tyler Alcot and never broke character. Not in the entire week we were watching you.

"But there's one thing you can't hide. One thing you can't change—no matter how hard you try. While we were tailing you, we lifted your fingerprints. Running prints is pretty easy for a cop, you know."

At this revelation Tyler virtually deflated, physically and mentally. He slouched back into the sofa, exhaling in defeat. They had him. They hadn't just broken his cover ID, they had his real name. Along with it, they knew everything there was to know. If there was a worst-case scenario, this was it.

"Mister Cooper, isn't it?" Stretch continued. "Cyrus Cooper?" His eyes searched Tyler's, or Cyrus's, as was the case.

Cue Ball leaned forward, apparently ready to participate. The look on his face made it obvious he was enjoying the exchange. They had Tyler—Cyrus, dead to rights. He was screwed. Cue Ball pulled a small leather bound notebook from the inner pocket of his suit coat, flipped through a series of pages, and consulted his notes.

"Cyrus Cooper," he said in that way seasoned police detectives do as they run through the facts of a case. "Twenty-eight years old, white male, 6 foot no inches tall, one hundred eighty pounds. Half a dozen unpaid parking tickets, two moving violations on his record, no known felonies, no known aliases. No wife, no children."

Cue Ball lowered his notebook and looked Cyrus right in the eye before he continued without the benefit of his notes. "Freelance reporter for a number of news publications including the Chicago Tribune and the New York Times."

"And therein lies our real problem." Stretch was seething. "We know you didn't go to the authorities. Mostly because, well, *we are the authorities.* But also because you're a reporter—a good reporter from what I read. Good reporters won't risk getting scooped. So you've obviously been keeping our arrangement quiet—at least while you're writing the story. Unfortunately, it's a safe bet someone else knows about the story. Maybe someone at one of the papers?"

"We wanna know who you talked to at the paper," Cue Ball remarked. "We wanna know who's aware of the story and we want all your notes. Give us that and you get to walk away from this."

Cyrus had been sitting slouched on the sofa while they metaphorically pummeled him with the facts of his situation. He struggled to listen to their words. Paying attention to the sound of their voices would help keep the panic away and it might offer some slim chance of finding a away out of this mess alive. No story was worth his life.

But hearing that last statement from Cue Ball, Cyrus was thrown for a loop—Shocked to the point he found it possible to push his panic aside for the moment. They were offering a way out? Give up his notes and Gary at the Tribune and he could walk. Could it be that easy? Really?

Hardly.

It was an offer far too good to be true. Those notes were the only reason he was still breathing. That and the suspicion he may have talked with someone at the paper. If he gave up the notes he was a dead man. If he so much as mentioned Gary, Gary would be dead too. That flicker of hope quickly faded. There was no way out.

Cue Ball looked at Stretch. "I told you, he's not one to go the easy way."

"That's okay," Stretch said with a shrug. "It's more fun when they won't talk. Then we get to make em' talk."

At this threat, rather than collapse entirely under the stress of the situation, Cyrus's eyes cleared as if his mind had cut through the confusion and come to a decisive conclusion. He slowly pushed himself up from the couch. There was no need to make any fast moves. The two detectives were most certainly armed and he didn't need to get himself shot before he could put the next stage of his plan in motion.

Taking a moment, Cyrus looked at the pair of police officers. Starting to say something, he stopped before the words came. He began to pace slowly, back and forth before the massive picture window as he gathered his thoughts. The skyline was the last thing on his mind. The officers remained seated. Cyrus wasn't a threat. They held all the cards and Cyrus knew it.

"You got something to say?" Stretch questioned, puzzled at what was going through Cyrus's mind. "Go ahead, spit it out."

Cyrus stopped pacing and looked back at both men. He gave an embarrassed half smile. "I know it's crazy, but I'm standing here knowing I'm gonna die and all I keep thinking is, 'I wish I'd made better coffee.'"

Cue Ball cocked his head at the absurdity of the statement while Stretch just busted out laughing. The two men just stared at Cyrus. Cyrus just stood there, as if waiting for something to happen.

The awkward moment stretched on, Cyrus waiting for something and the two detectives waiting for Cyrus. Finally Cyrus glanced at his watch. He looked back at the detectives. A look of concern had returned to Cyrus. Something had gone wrong. He looked back at his watch. Absentmindedly, he scratched at the center of his chest.

Stretch laughed again, and rose to his feet. "So, right now you're wondering what happened to your backup…"

Cyrus's head snapped around and his eyes met those of Stretch.

Oh, shit.

"That's right. You used the GO word! You said 'better coffee' and when you did, the door was supposed to bust open and a SWAT team was supposed to come crashing in and arrest us."

Stretch scrunched up his face, leaned across the coffee table, and glared at Cyrus. "But, like I said, *we are the cops!* There's no SWAT team. Hell, the two guys monitoring the wire taped to your chest? They're sitting in an apartment one floor down laughing their asses off right now!"

The color drained from Cyrus's face. He looked like he was going to be sick. His shoulders rolled forward as his eyes droped to the floor.

Shit…

Shit! Shit! Shit!

Finally he looked back at Stretch. He tried to look the man in the eye, but couldn't. Cyrus's eyes dropped back to the floor. He was beaten. He'd gotten the two detectives to admit to their murder for hire scheme, but it was all for nothing. Literally nothing! The guys on the other end of his wire probably weren't even recording their conversation. Stretch was right. They were downstairs laughing right now.

Cue Ball pulled his girth from the sofa, drawing a snub nose revolver from inside his cheap suit coat. With some disappointment, Cyrus realized his work on the story was drawing to a close. It had been fun playing the part of Tyler Alcot. Gallivanting around town, hitting the clubs, putting on a show, all the while knowing he was being tailed. But that was over now.

"Ok," Cyrus muttered. He knew the detectives had been through this before. They had killed a lot of people and made a lot of money in the process. They thought they'd done a good job hiding the money but they were mistaken. Unfortunately, while these two had been sloppy with their finances, clearly others were involved. Officers who'd been more circumspect with their ill-gotten goods. Obviously the two cops running surveillance downstairs were in on it. He'd actually suspected as much but there had been no anomalies in their financial histories. He knew because he'd run a thorough check. The burning questions in his reporter's mind were simple. How many cops were a part of this, and who were they?

"Ok," Cyrus repeated, still running through his next move. "What happens next? You stick me in a steel drum and dump me in a landfill somewhere?"

The idea made Cue Ball chuckle. "Hardly. This isn't a mob outfit. We've got more class than that. You'll be glad to know you're going to a great little place not too far from the Wisconsin border. Out in the middle of nowhere, really. A place where no one will ever look for you. You'll be fertilizing a cornfield before you know what hit you."

Cyrus resumed his slow pacing before the picturesque skyline. It had already become habit in this brief but intense time of stress. It was a habit that wouldn't trouble him for long. "You make it sound almost pleasant," he muttered mostly to himself. "Judging by the research I did on you two, I'm sure I won't be lonely. How many guys like me have you got planted out there?"

Cue Ball shook his head and waggled his gun at Cyrus, discouraging any thoughts of making a break for it. "Son, you're a reporter to the bitter end, aren't you?"

"It's my nature—can't help it."

"No, you're not going to be hurting for company. Must be fifty or sixty bodies buried out there by now," Stretch said, pride in his grin.

Cyrus first though Stretch might be boasting, but a glance at Cue Ball led him to believe otherwise. These guys had been busy.

Shit…

Shit! Shit! Shit!

He had most of what he needed. But he still didn't have a full idea of how deep the corruption went. How many cops were involved? In order to fully wrap this up, he needed to know who was in on it.

"Ok," Cyrus said dropping his hands back to his side and facing the detectives. They were both pointing guns now.

41

"There's still one thing I don't understand. You two are bent, I knew that. But your cohorts downstairs, I didn't see that coming. They're obviously much better at hiding the money. You might want to get some tips on that, if you want my opinion…

"Anyway, I thought there were only two of you in on this 'murder for hire' thing." He held up his fingers to make air quotes as he said 'murder for hire.' "But now I see that officers Neal and Bob downstairs," he waited a beat to see if they caught the slight. Nothing, so he moved on, "are in on it too. It cost me fifteen thousand dollars to kill my wife—"

"Kill your fictitious wife," Cue Ball corrected.

"Fine, fifteen thousand dollars to kill my *fictitious* wife. That's not bad money if you're splitting it two ways. But cutting that four ways? That's not even four grand apiece. And that's assuming you're not cutting anyone else in. That's not a lot of—"

"Hey—Hey! Don't trouble yourself with the math, buddy!" Stretch had lost his temper. Apparently questioning their moral code wasn't a hot button issue but looking at the risk versus reward merits of their after hours work? That was something over which to get bent out of shape. "Fifteen grand split five ways works out just fine. The only downside here is that we only got your down payment. I got kids to put through school! And here you are wasting my time. I'm gonna put an extra bullet in you just for that."

And there it was. Their crew consisted of *five*. Cyrus knew he could draw this out a little longer and try for the name of their fifth but Stretch was already starting to get suspicious. Or maybe he was just getting defensive—it was hard to be sure. Cyrus was pretty sure Cue Ball hadn't picked up on anything. The man didn't appear to be a deep thinker.

Better to put an end to this before things got out of control, Cyrus thought. After all, guns were drawn and presently pointed at his abdomen. That changed things a bit and would require contingency plan number three. It meant the Go Code was 'sick.'

"Ok!" Cyrus held up both hands in capitulation. "Ok. Look I'm sorry. I know you're pissed. Just let me use the bathroom. I think I'm going to be *sick*."

Stretch cocked his head and looked at Cyrus as if he was insane. "Bathroom? Sick? Do you think I care? I'm about to shoot you, you dumb son-of-a-bitch! Do you think I care if you're gonna—"

A loud knock at the door silenced Stretch, mid rant. Both officers' shot looks over their shoulders in the direction of the front door. In doing so, as is human nature, both of their guns veered slightly to the right. Expecting the knock, and at the sight of the guns being drawn off target, Cyrus leveraged the momentary gap in the detective's attention. He grabbed the coffee carafe and smashed it against the gun of the nearest cop. In his clumsy attempt to maintain control of the weapon, Stretch shifted his weight and was knocked into Cue Ball. The clumsy move threw them both off balance.

Cyrus stepped on the coffee table and took a flying dive over the couch the detectives had been sitting on just as the double front doors exploded in a shower of splinters. A dozen men dressed head to toe in black battle armor rushed in leveling short assault rifles.

The FBI Hostage Rescue Team (HRT) had both detectives face down on the floor before they knew what hit them. Their hands were cuffed and they were searched for additional weapons. Moments later, the two Chicago detectives were escorted from the apartment and hustled down the hall.

Through it all, Cyrus stood silently behind the sofa. He watched the FBI HRT team sweep through the apartment before departing with practiced efficiency.

Once the tactical team had pulled out, only a single FBI agent remained. It was Special Agent Mindy Shaw, a dour white woman about five foot eight wearing a dark FBI branded windbreaker. She was holding a walkie-talkie in one hand and her service weapon in the other. Looking slowly around the apartment, she finally holstered the sidearm. "Quite a setup you've got here," she said warmly. The complement was accompanied by a smile that was somehow less warm.

"It had to look real," Cyrus replied. He was dusting off his clothes. Wreckage from the heavy oak doors had been strewn across half the sitting room. "Your boys don't half ass it when it comes to breaching charges."

She nodded. The compliment finally brought warmth to her demeanor. "You said 'sick,' meaning there was a weapon, or weapons, trained on you. We came in loaded for bear, per *your* protocol."

"You won't hear me complaining," Cyrus said with grin. "I take it you picked up the other two at the listening post downstairs?"

"As soon as you got them to indicate they were down one floor, the building manager was able to tell us exactly where we would find em'. It was a slam dunk."

Cyrus saw that she was studying him. She looked as if she had something on her mind. "Ok, lets have it. Something's bothering you. Out with it."

Agent Shaw continued her long look into his eyes for a few additional moments and slowly walked nearer. "I've done my share of surveillance on informants wearing a wire. Every one of them had one thing in common. They all want to get in and out as quickly as possible. Every one of them was in a hurry to get it over with."

Cyrus waited for her to continue. It seemed that police detectives weren't the only fans of the uncomfortable silence bit. Once again, he wasn't falling for it. The silence was hers to fill.

"But not you," she finally continued. "You're the first civilian I've had who didn't seem in a rush to pull the ripcord. And you're absolutely the first civilian to suggest revisions to HRT commander's plan."

She let another silence fill the air again before continuing. "Why do you suppose that is?"

Cyrus chuckled, the question, a veiled compliment if he was correct, actually warmed his spirit. "No mystery there, Agent Shaw. I'm a reporter. I want the story. In order to get it, I have to get all the facts. Getting the facts takes time and a lot of patience. In this case it took more than a little bit of acting."

She laughed. A real laugh this time, he saw amusement reach her eyes. "No doubt there. You should get an Academy Award for this performance. You hoodwinked two experienced Chicago cops. Two cops who, apparently, are very good at lying themselves."

She thought for a moment before continuing in a much more serious tone. "What you did today was brave. Brave, but *very* dangerous. Those guys could've killed you. There was no guarantee we'd make it through the door in time. Is any story really worth your life?"

Cyrus took a moment to consider the question. "It's a fair point, but you forget I had leverage. Like you said, these guys weren't amateurs." His expression made it clear he wasn't taking any of this too seriously. "I had something they needed. They couldn't kill me until they had my notes or until they found out who knew I was working on the story. They wanted me gone but their first priority was containment. They needed me alive for that."

As Cyrus watched Shaw watching him, he knew she wasn't entirely buying it. "To be fair," he continued, "I was concerned about the short bald bastard. He wasn't as sharp as his friend and I was starting to think he might start shooting. It's why I pulled the plug when I did." He left out the fact that if everything went completely wrong or if the FBI had let him down he still had a contingency plan. It was her job to cover his back—but if she wasn't up to the task, he had that covered too.

He wasn't really concerned about Cue Ball but it was advantageous for her to think otherwise. She was sharp. She'd recognized he was cooler under pressure than he should have been. He didn't need her getting curious and digging into his past. She might find out that, in another life, the reporter gig wasn't his true calling.

"We know a lot," Shaw said, apparently moving on despite the suspicious look she was giving. "We know this is a five man crew. And, thanks to you, we have four of them in custody. Your work is done. Go write your story. It's my turn. I'll put them in separate rooms and make it clear the death penalty is on the table. Plus, they're cops. They know the score. The threat of being put in general population should get them talking."

She was referring to the prisons general population ward. Police officers are not normally remanded to Gen Pop. They tend not to live very long in circulation with the rank and file. A cop in general population might as well have a big red bull's-eye painted on his prison issue uniform.

"And if those threats don't work," she continued. "I make an offer to all four of them. The first one to give up the fifth man gets a reduced sentence." She stopped for a moment considering the thought. "I think I'll leave that off the table— maybe hold on to it as a last resort. I want to see everyone of these assholes prosecuted to the full extent of the law."

She was speaking through gnashed teeth now. "There's nothing worse than a bad cop."

Cyrus was pretty sure she was talking to herself with that last part. She looked pissed. It didn't matter. He was starting to like the lady. As much as he could like an FBI agent. Still, she had done good work here today. She kept her word and he had gotten his story. And, to her credit, she hadn't tried some bullshit excuse to talk him out of publishing. Her higher-ups would have expected her to. Hell, they'd likely ordered her to work him on the matter. But she hadn't toed the line. She really did hate bad cops and she knew his story would cause other cops to think twice before crossing the line.

"Well," Agent Shaw said as she pulled the walkie-talkie from her belt. "I've got some crooked cops to put in the box and you've got a story to write. You be safe out there."

Cyrus stepped forward and shook her hand. "You too, Agent Shaw. Give 'em hell."

Cyrus watched Shaw leave. He stood alone in the silent apartment for some time. Esmeralda would be gone by now. Her part had been played. It was her job to serve coffee before immediately leaving the penthouse via the service exit. It had been his job to stand there and look uncomfortable while she served coffee to his guests. In his experience, it was the nuances that made the act look real. The way the detectives saw it, they were just two more guests to walk through the front door so the maid was serving them coffee just as she had countless others before them. But it was a sham. They had known it was a sham and he at least suspected that they knew it was a sham. But that didn't let him off the hook when it came to making things look good. He had to sell it, if he wanted to get the story and walk away without a bullet in his ass.

Speaking of which...

Cyrus walked to the massive picture window overlooking the Chicago skyline. His eyes were fixed on a rooftop several city blocks distant. The details of the roofline were indistinct at this distance but it didn't matter. He already knew what was there.

He knelt down and pulled a small wad of C4 plastic explosive away from the base of the pane of glass. Then, rather casually, he pulled the silver "pencil" detonator from the wad of clay. Slipping the lump of C4 into one pocket of his Dockers and the detonator into another pocket, he looked out the window once more.

"I owe you one, Hondo." He was speaking very casually to the empty room while facing the window. "It's always good to know that someone I trust has my back. Next round of drinks is on me."

———

A man in a floppy jungle hat stood sighting down the barrel of a sniper rifle several blocks away. The rifle was mounted on a bipod that rested atop a large aluminum air-conditioning vent. Beside the rifle was a small black box atop a miniature tripod. The black box beamed a laser into the distance. A set of headphones attached to the box were worn by the sniper.

"I owe you one, Hondo," said the voice from the headphones. "It's always good to know that someone I trust has my back. Next round of drinks is on me."

The man chuckled and rose up from behind the rifle. He pulled off the headphones and snatched the cell phone from his hip pocket. He tapped out a quick message and hit send:

> No problem, mate. Least I can do for an old friend!

The man immediately pocketed the phone. Without a moment's hesitation, he set about breaking down the rifle and laser listening device. There was no one to shoot today. His job was done. It would be eighteen-hour flight back to Australia but it really was the least he could do for the man who has saved the life of his wife. One thing was certain. Cyrus hadn't lost his edge. That son-of-a-bitch would do anything for a story!

Chapter 3

Oak Park, Chicago Illinois
Sunday, 3:12 pm

Finishing the final revision of his new article, Cyrus sat back in his chair. He was alone in the office of his two-bedroom apartment. Over the last half hour he had put the finishing touches on the second in a three part series of stories that the *Chicago Tribune* was referring to as the Chicago PD's Murder-for-Hire Program. It was a tasteless title but that much was beyond his control. The title grabbed attention and sold papers, something that was becoming increasingly difficult as readers continued to migrate toward online news sources.

Scattered around Cyrus's massive antique desk were dozens of lose scraps of paper. They were notes he used while writing. The practice was largely organizational. One of the benefits of his eidetic memory was virtually perfect recall of the contents of every piece of paper. Retaining information was easy. Organizing it and putting it to paper in a clear, concise manner was the challenge. The notes helped him plan the story and immerse himself in the content. The solitary experience of writing was something he enjoyed, particularly after a harrowing operation such as the one against the rogue police detectives.

His desk faced the center of a largely empty office. Two small, sturdy wooden chairs faced the desk. They were also largely ceremonial. Few people knew he had a home office—let alone its location—so visitors were few and far between. The wall to Cyrus's back was entirely covered in corkboard. That board was blanketed from end to end with thumbtacked photos, notes, and photocopied documents. But whereas his desktop was a functioning morass of the story he was currently engrossed in, the corkboard contained a series of more neatly arranged sections. Each segment was devoted to a story he was developing or monitoring in some way.

Such was the life of a freelance writer.

Cyrus tapped out the last few words of his story and took a long hard look at the screen of his laptop. Finally, he hit print. He always preferred to proofread a hardcopy. It was another ritual. The wall opposite his desk was dominated by a large bay window that overlooked the city street several stories below. A laser printer sat by the corner of the window. After a few moments it began to buzz with signs of life, the beginning of its warm-up routine.

The door to his office was tucked in the far left corner. The remainder of the left wall and the entire right wall were dominated by floor to ceiling built-in bookshelves. The shelves were virtually packed end to end with hardcover volumes. He had collected them over the course of many years. He was a writer, but like most writers, he was first an avid reader. And every one of these books was one with which he had spent quality time. And again thanks to his photographic memory, virtually all of their imparted wisdom was squirreled away in some corner of his mind.

He glanced at the checklist written on a notepad beside his MacBook Pro and ran through it one more time. The *Los Angeles Times* had picked up his story for their web edition. That was covered. In fact he had already submitted it via their website. The same went for a pair of newspapers in New York. One of those papers was running the story on its site and in the print edition. It was convoluted these days, each paper trying one scheme or another to shuffle readers either to or from the print version or web site. The only thing they seemed to know for sure was that they didn't want their subscribers reading the other guy's paper. The print world certainly wasn't what it used to be. But that was why Cyrus was making a killing with investigative journalism. When he could break a big story, he could sell it all over the country. The papers were in chaos but they were still buying his work.

Looking back at his list, he considered the additional stories that were sure to follow. Once the case made it to court, headlines would be made all over again. Plus he had already heard from Agent Shaw. Two of the four members of the kill squad had flipped on their mysterious fifth associate within an hour of being hauled into interrogation. The remaining two corroborated the fifth member's identity before the day was out. Shaw hadn't been forced to make hard choices when it came to cutting a deal. The FBI would seek a change of venue as Illinois didn't currently support capital punishment. Cyrus wondered if it was the threat of the death penalty or just the promise of being placed in general population that had done the trick. Then again, for a Chicago cop going to prison, those options were likely one and the same.

All in all, this was going to be a good month's work. And Hondo was due compensation for his support on the roof a couple of days back. Cyrus knew the man would be offended if offered cash. Their relationship didn't work that way. Fair enough. Cyrus had set up a college fund for Hondo's four-year-old-daughter. He started it with a hefty deposit, and planned to contribute to it over time. Truth be told, freelance writing wasn't even Cyrus's bread and butter. It would be good to do something constructive with the extra money.

The chime of the front door bell pulled Cyrus from his contemplation. It took a moment for him to realize the buzzer was his. It was almost never used. No one visited his home.

Pressing the intercom button on the panel beside the front door, Cyrus answered simply, "Yes?"

"Mister Cooper? My name is Allan Underwood. I've come to speak with you regarding Mister Walter Meade."

Cyrus felt his jaw tighten at the mention of Meade. This was unexpected, and he'd never heard of Allan Underwood. "I'm sorry," Cyrus said after only a moment. "I don't know a Walter Freed." Why not mess with the last name? Maybe it would sell the lie.

"Ah, no. I was told to expect as much," the man chuckled. "Mister Cooper, I'm sorry for the intrusion. If I could have a moment of your time I'm sure I can explain everything."

Alright. He wasn't going away that easily. Cyrus was going to have to see it through. "Ok. Come on up." He hit the button to release the lock on the street level entrance out front.

Cyrus returned to his desk where he saved the document that was still up on the computer's screen. With a tap of the keyboard, he activated the software screen lock and secured the machine. Pulling out the top left desk drawer, he retrieved a 9mm Springfield. A quick check of the magazine and a press-check of the chamber confirmed it was locked and loaded. He stuck the gun down back of his jeans before grabbing a flannel shirt from the back of his office chair. Pulling it on, he headed back to the front door. The shirt would be enough to hide the gun but it wouldn't get in the way if he needed to use it.

A few minutes later there was a knock at the door. Cyrus opened it to find a weathered old man in an expensive dark suit. The man was about five foot six and must have weighed 190 pounds. He was very nearly as big around as he was tall. It must have made for an interesting challenge for his tailor. Still, the man had kind eyes. The patient sort that hinted he was here to deliver bad news. Cyrus judged the man to be in his early seventies but he might have been off a decade one way or another.

"Mister Cooper," the old man said with an outstretched hand. It was a statement, not a question. He seemed to know Cyrus on sight and felt no need to confirm his identity. "I'm sorry I didn't telephone first. My name is Allan Underwood. I'm the attorney for Professor Meade's estate."

Tentatively, Cyrus shook the old man's hand. "Estate? Ah…please, come in?"

Cyrus showed Underwood into the office and over to one of the chairs opposite his desk. He sat in the matching chair, choosing not to take his customary place behind the desk. If this man was whom he claimed, this was a matter of some delicacy.

"You said you're a lawyer for Meade's estate?" Cyrus asked cautiously, starting the conversation where they'd left off. "Am I to assume that Walter is…" He let the statement hang rather the finish it himself.

"Oh, my! I'm sorry. You didn't know! You haven't heard?" Underwood looked aghast, as if he had just made the most unforgivable mistake in the business. "I'm so sorry—I suppose you wouldn't have heard. Walter said you only spoke sporadically. I'm sorry, yes, he passed several weeks ago."

"Meade—err—Walter, he spoke of me?"

"Oh, yes! Frequently!" The old man chuckled. His smile was warm and Cyrus could see something more there. A deep regard for Meade, perhaps? "We spoke often about a great many things. Your name often came up in conversation. I hope you know, Walter held you in very high regard?"

This brought a grin from Cyrus. "Well, I don't know about that. We didn't know each other all that well. We've only spoken a few times. He was a very interesting old fellow. But I can't say I knew him all that well."

In part this was true, but to a larger extent Cyrus wanted to vet Underwood's knowledge of the old man and their relationship. Much of what he and Meade discussed was sensitive in nature and he wasn't comfortable discussing Meade's business with anyone. Walter Meade had told him things in confidence, some of it fairly outlandish and difficult to believe but private just the same. Cyrus had never been sure if the old man was on the level, off his rocker, or somewhere in between. But Walter Meade had been brilliant, there was never any question about that. And he certainly was a person of importance in Washington. Cyrus had witnessed a demonstration of that first hand. He'd never seen the wheels of bureaucracy move so swiftly as when Walter Meade had been in trouble. Still, he didn't know Underwood and this could be a snipe hunt. Early in their relationship Meade had asked for discretion pertaining to their discussions and Cyrus would honor that. Information here would flow in only one direction. But if Meade had indeed passed, arrangements would need to be made.

"Didn't know each other all that well?" Underwood asked. He gave Cyrus a sly and appraising glance. "I was Walter's friend first and his attorney second. He would dine at my home several times a month. He loved my wife's cooking. Anyway, the way he told it, you had a mind that was uniquely open to the mysteries of the universe."

"That does sound like something Meade—err, Walter would say."

"Walter had access to the greatest minds of our time and he had some very interesting opinions in regards to each and everyone of them. It would have made for an amazing memoir," he cast Cyrus a knowing glance. "Were such a thing not subject to treasonous consequences."

Ok, maybe this guy did know the old man as well as he claimed.

"But of all these so called 'great minds,' he was most impressed with you! He said you were the only person he ever met that would see him when he would show up out of the blue, day or night. You would let him throw absurd hypotheses about, and you would converse with him as frankly as you would discuss the day's weather. I can tell you one thing with absolute certainty. He was impressed that you never asked where he was getting his crazy ideas and never considered him mad for being serious about them."

Cyrus had to laugh. Ok, he was buying it. Underwood had him convinced, he surely must be a close friend to Meade if he knew about those conversations. His description was right on the money. It wasn't uncommon for Meade to show up unannounced. And they would have lengthy discussions about the strangest subjects. But each and every talk seemed of vital importance to the old man so Cyrus dug into the meat of each matter and they would kick the issue of the day around. More often than not, when all was said and done, the old man left with that excited glint in his eye. That urgent and anxious look, like a kid who just woke up on Christmas morning. A kid who couldn't wait to get downstairs and play with his new toys. Cyrus never really understood what it was all about, but the conversations were never dull and always proved to be an intellectual challenge.

"He was just a crazy old man who had a very active imagination," Cyrus concluded. He always suspected there was more to it, ever since the day they first met in Washington. Still, he had never broached the subject. He smiled thinking about DC. Had they really met that day? He was certain that Meade didn't remember ever seeing him in the coffee shop. But after all that had happened, it had been the events of that afternoon that brought Walter Meade to Cyrus's door. Fate was funny that way.

"Yes," the older man said. He rubbed his chin with a distracted, faraway look in his eyes. "He always suspected you might feel that way." His eyes snapped back to the moment and he smiled at Cyrus. "Anyway, to the business at hand!

"I'm seeing to Walter's last will and testament. He has left you his modest estate in the mountains of Colorado."

Cyrus was taken aback. He leaned on the arm of his chair and considered Underwood's statement. "That must be a mistake. Surely he had family or friends who—" He didn't know how to continue. "He once mentioned a vacation property he had out in Colorado. He said it was his sanctuary. I got the impressing he really loved it there."

"That he did, my boy! He always said that he did his best thinking out there. But it wasn't a vacation retreat. He lived there. It was his home. And certainly he had friends, but no surviving family. And he was very precise. He wanted you to have the property."

"His home? He lived there? The way he would pop up now and again, I assumed he lived here in the city. Colorado is quite a trek…and he wasn't a young man…" Cyrus's mind spun with the contradiction. Meade had a tendency to show up at his door randomly and unannounced. Cyrus could just as easily have been home as not. Would the man have traveled all the way from Colorado to make unannounced visits? Maybe he'd simply been in town on other business. But that often? And traveling so frequently at his advanced age? In truth, they had met more often than Cyrus has admitted to Underwood.

Underwood watched Cyrus carefully. He could see the wheels moving as he considered the dichotomy of the scenario. "Yes," he said simply, "Walter did love to travel."

"In any case, Walter has left you the property in Colorado as well as a trust that will see to the payment of the taxes, insurance, and utilities for the next 100 years."

"Wait—Excuse me?"

"Yes, Walter believed that his inheritance should not be a burden on those who accepted it. So, in your case he ensured that taking possession of the estate would place no financial burden upon you."

Wow... That did sound like the Walter Meade that Cyrus knew. Always thinking half a dozen steps ahead. Apparently, even in death.

Cyrus could find no reason to refuse the property. As much as accepting this gift troubled him, it seemed that Meade had gone to great lengths to make it a done deal. "Well, I guess Walter has made me an offer I can't refuse."

"Excellent! Walter hoped you would see it that way." Underwood pushed himself up from the chair with some effort. "I shall email you the details within the hour. Walter left me your contact information."

Cyrus was still taking it all in as he walked the old lawyer to the door. Just before reaching it Underwood stopped and turned to Cyrus with a questioning glance. "If it's not inappropriate of me," he asked, "I've always wondered...how was it you had so many conversations with Walter without ever asking where it was all coming from?"

"To be honest, I always suspected he was writing some sort of science-fiction. Some of the ideas would've made for great novels. I half expected a book to show up on my doorstep one day. He had that kind of flair. You know, a way with words—interesting mannerisms." Cyrus cocked his head as he drifted in contemplative through, "eccentric tendencies."

"Ahh, you saw a kindred spirit!"

"I'm sorry?"

"Your novels! Walter loved your novels! He even sent me a copy every time one came out. I must admit, I'm more of a fan of mysteries but your science fiction is great fun. And my grandchildren are huge fans!"

Cyrus was thunderstruck at the comment. "My novels? Walter knew about my books? What—How—I publish those under a pen name. No one knows I write those books. I've gone to considerable trouble to make sure no one knows I write those books!"

"Ahh, yes," Underwood laughed deep from his belly. "Well, again, that was Walter. He knew everything there was to know about the people he worked with. He needed to, in his line of work. I'm sure you can appreciate that. Truth be told, he was even a fan of your other series, the ones written under your *other* nom de plume. Though I think that had more to do with fatherly pride than actual appreciation for the genre." With that, Underwood had yet another, much deeper laugh.

"Oh no," Cyrus muttered hanging his head. *Crap. Crap! Crap! Crap!* This was mortifying. No one was ever to trace that line of books back to him. That series was a persistent best seller and it accounted for the lion's share of his income. He could retire off of that money today if he chose to. But it wasn't the kind of writing that he would ever be proud of. Certainly nothing he would share with friends.

Underwood tamped his laugh down to a chuckle and slapped Cyrus on the shoulder. He saw the ashen look on the young man's face. The lad was devastated. "Cheer up, my boy. My wife is your biggest fan! The best romance novels she's ever read, she swears to it!"

The old man turned and stepped out the door, before stopping to look back at Cyrus. He handed him a business card. "Not to worry. Your secret is safe with me," he said with a wink.

Oh god, Cyrus thought. He glanced at the business card. The phone number caught his attention due to the unusual format. He looked closer. The card showed Allan Underwood's office address as London, England.

Cyrus looked up to see Underwood already heading down the hall, halfway to the elevator. "Excuse me, Mister Underwood?"

The old man turned.

"This card has the address of your London office. Surely you have an address here in Chicago?"

"I'm sorry, my boy. Just the one office. It's just me. One tired old lawyer," he said with a smile. "Not to worry, I shall email you the details as soon as I return to my hotel. Thank you for your time."

Cyrus's mind was swimming as he stepped back into his apartment and closed the door. Again things were not making sense. First Meade was living in Colorado full time but dropping in on Cyrus in Chicago at random intervals. Now Meade's good friend, Underwood, was saying that he had dinner with the man several times a month but Underwood's office, and presumably his home, was in London, England? Meade was certainly eccentric but surely he was too old to be traveling so pervasively.

Chapter 4

Switzerland. It was too far out of the way as far as Dargo was concerned. An unusual place to meet especially since his employer, Nil Bayer, was a Russian like himself. This detour to Switzerland seemed pointless. The elegant chateau where they now stood also seemed an unnecessary distraction. Dargo knew that Bayer had rented the house for the week but didn't know why. Looking at the man, he was starting to draw his own conclusions.

An aged academic, Bayer's distinguishing feature was his somewhat egg shaped head. While well proportioned for his lanky body, it was quite wide at the top and very narrow at the jaw. Penetrating dark eyes that hinted at the malignant personality within. A short sprig of dark hair capped the very top of his head. He wore an expensive Italian suit and a delicately framed set of glasses. Bayer was the boss but Dargo had done his homework. Nil Bayer was an extremely wealthy man. Dargo had one of his tech geeks conducting a financial examination of the man. As of the last update, the operative still wasn't confident he had uncovered all of Bayer's holdings. After leaving the Russian Science Academy more than two decades earlier, it seemed that Bayer had developed some sort of filament, a component used in every light bulb manufactured within the last twenty years. Though seemingly inconsequential, apparently there was something unique about his design. The rights to the simple technology had made Bayer hundreds of millions of dollars over the last ten years alone. Unfortunately, all the money in the world couldn't buy the man a winning personality.

Bayer walked slowly back and forth before the large hearth which was located in the center of the back wall of the richly appointed study. He swirled the remains of his brandy in a snifter as he paced. Dargo stood station to one side of the fireplace and watched Bayer without comment. Bayer had been in the process of berating him, though Dargo refused to be drawn into an argument. Arguing with ones employer was unprofessional.

Dargo's full name was Ian Dargoslav. He was a large Russian with short gray hair, gray eyebrows, and a trim gray beard. He had a hard, weathered look about him, but he was in remarkable shape for his age. Though 58 years old, few would have guessed it to look at him. He was still tall and broad shouldered. Dargo had served several tours in the military, first in the Russian armed forces, and later taking his expertise to the private sector, after retiring with distinction. After serving many years as head of security for a wealthy European family, he had once again returned to 'consulting,' which was how he came into the employ of Nil Bayer.

"And you say the attorney, Underwood, has met with the heirs to the estate?" Bayer asked.

"Correct. He met with Comrade Meade's lab assistant, Miss Reese Knoland, in Santa Barbara, before flying to Chicago to meet another beneficiary. I handled the surveillance in California and sent a team to follow Underwood to Chicago. After, he flew back to the UK." Dargo made his report in crisp concise details. His Russian accent was mild but his English marked only with a clipped brevity. He was fluent in English but it was by no means his native tongue.

"But we still don't have the location of the schematics, or the transport access codes?" Bayer asked accusingly. Dargo knew the man's temper was growing short. The operation was taking longer than expected. What Bayer didn't understand was that these things could not be forced; there was no way to rush progress.

"I do not believe the lawyer possessed any intelligence. No overt or covert exchange was made," Dargo confirmed.

"So we've waited for nothing!" Bayer snapped. "I want you to pickup the attorney and Reese Knoland. Use any means necessary to extract the information I require!"

"With respect, *sir*," Dargo said. It was more of a growl than a statement. "That would be a mistake."

That brought a thick vein to the surface of Bayer's forehead. It was obvious he didn't care to be contradicted by a subordinate. How had the man survived working for the science directorate? Bayer was financing the operation, so by extension, he was ultimately in charge. It seemed something of a power trip for the aging ex-scientist.

"Walter Meade is dead," Dargo explained. "He was known to be secretive and circumspect with project details. It is probable that he did not share details of Meridian with his subordinate or his attorney. Bring any of them into custody and we will only draw the attention of the authorities." Dargo looked Bayer square in the eye. "At that point any hope of finding what you seek will be lost."

All of this was true, but there was more to it. Dargo sensed that Bayer had little concern for collateral damage. And though Dargo's job technically made him a mercenary, he had seen enough senseless death to last a lifetime. He didn't care to see any meaningless loss of life, no matter how entitled his employer believed himself to be. Dargo had lost a daughter to senseless tragedy and he had strong personal beliefs on the matter. But he knew his employer would view his opinions as weakness so he kept them to himself. He worked for Bayer but he didn't need to respect the man. Besides, what happened in the field was his purview. Bayer be damned.

"Very well," Bayer finally acquiesced. "What course of action do you suggest?"

Dargo replied without hesitation. "Continue surveillance on all project members. They are only now preparing to get back to work following the death of Comrade Meade. If anything is to be learned, now will be the time. Underwood is likely a dead end. I will leave wiretaps and bugs at his home and office. I do not expect him to be of further use. If he conducts any business pertaining to Comrade Meade, we will know. Keeping a team on him is waste of manpower.

"Also, my man in London located a burn safe in Underwood's office. We will not be able to open the safe without triggering the destruction of its contents. I have an alternate plan in mind. I will report back any tangible results."

"I thought you considered the man a dead end?" Bayer accused. Frustration burned in his eyes. "Plus, your plan fails to guarantee results…and we have no idea how long it might take for someone to lead us to the schematics or the hardware."

"With respect, there are no guarantees. We investigate what leads we have. We cannot force results." Dargo thought for a moment. He weighed his next words before he spoke. "All of this would be unnecessary if Comrade Meade had been handled with greater care."

The pulsing vein returned to Bayer's forehead just as Dargo knew it would. Bayer had not fully explained what had happened prior to bringing Dargo and his team on board, but Dargo had put things together on his own. At some point Bayer had tried to pick Professor Meade up and force the information from him. It hadn't gone well and Meade had died while in custody. All of this had happened under the command of Arnold Peck, Dargo's predecessor. Bayer never explained what happened, but Dargo was part of a small and exclusive community of operators. Word was that a newcomer, someone previously unknown to the community, had hired Peck. A short time later Peck had simply disappeared. Soon after taking the job, Dargo realized Peck had been working for Bayer. And the more he grew to understand Bayer, the more he suspected Bayer had had Peck killed after Meade died on his watch. All of this meant a great deal to Dargo. It indicated that Bayer was prone to rash judgment and thereby prone to mistakes. He could not be trusted and was deadly when crossed. Bayer was too comfortable employing mercenaries and he didn't have an issue leaving a trail of bodies in his wake.

Dargo did know a little about Professor Meade's death. Apparently the old man had been drugged in an abduction attempt several years prior. The team trying to snatch the old man had botched the dosage of a sedative that resulted permanent damage to Meade's heart. Had it not been for his bad heart, Meade would likely be locked in a hole somewhere with Bayer's interrogators working on him right now. Dargo found such an approach barbaric. The results of interrogation by torture were unreliable and dangerous. This had been proven when Professor Meade had expired.

The consummate professional, Dargo would get the information his employer required but he would limit the number of casualties at the same time. Unfortunately, the situation left him stuck running a series of surveillance operations across the globe, all the while watching his back since he didn't have any faith in Bayer.

Finally Bayer relented. "Arrange surveillance on the lawyer. Contact me as soon as you have new information. You are dismissed."

Feeling the phone in his breast pocket vibrating even on his way out of the room, Dargo didn't bother to retrieve the device until he reached the hallway. His employer had a penchant for micromanagement, and it was a situation that would prove unacceptable.

Dargo tapped the screen. "Da?"

"The hardware has been secured," the voice on the end explained, without elaboration.

"There were no complications?"

"No," the voice confirmed. "Yuri said that your Miami contact was most accommodating. But, sir—do you have any idea how much Yuri paid for this hardware?"

Dargo smiled and considered Bayer's condescending tone and the smug set of his shifty eyes. "Not to worry," he said with a genuine smile. "The client can afford it."

Tapping the phone's touch screen, Dargo terminated the call and continued down the hall. The fact that he had just spent a vast sum of Bayer's money on what would likely prove a fool's errand somehow struck him as satisfying. It was unprofessional, but amusing just the same. Besides, whether it was on this job or the next, Dargo knew that he would make good use of his new high tech toys.

Chapter 5

Berton Springs, Colorado
Tuesday, 2:12 pm

It was early afternoon when Cyrus pulled into Berton, Colorado. A small town nestled in the arms of the Colorado Mountains, it boasted a population of nearly three hundred, according to the sign he passed at the city limits. Berton offered absolutely no claim to fame as far as Cyrus could find. He had Googled his destination prior to leaving Chicago and was shocked to find virtually no information about the town or its history. The place was literally a tiny dot on a map, nothing more. There were no historic annotations, no population statistics, and no Street View images. So much for the information age. Berton appeared to be a virtual black hole in cyberspace.

This held tremendous appeal to Cyrus.

The full extent of the city spanned almost a dozen interconnected streets. He quickly understood what the town lacked in population it more than made up for in rustic appeal. A small but modern looking schoolhouse marked the border at one end of town. Main Street was lined with customary businesses such as a diner, a gas station, a general store, and the like. Dead center of town was home to an old but well maintained municipal building that must have been a hundred and fifty years old. According to the signs, the building functioned as the town government center as well as the post office and a very small police station.

All of this was taken in as Cyrus drove slowly in one end of town and out the other. It didn't take long. His phone's GPS app guided him east, up a winding road that stretched further up the mountain. Before long the road resorted to a series of switchbacks as it traversed a steep vertical climb, all the while surrounded on all sides by a dense pine wilderness.

Finally the GPS indicated a right turn. Cyrus left the wide, deserted blacktop in favor of a dirt and gravel driveway. The path was well maintained and free from potholes that were common to such unpaved surfaces. It was also about a car and a half in width, more than enough room for his four wheel drive Ford pickup.

The driveway wound deeper still into the wilderness until, after nearly a mile, he finally reached a clearing. The woodland had been driven back to accommodate a large single story house with a giant front yard and a wide circular drive. The driveway looped through the yard allowing vehicles to approach and depart the house without having to turn around. The loop joined with the house at a large portico wide enough for two large SUV's to park abreast.

The house itself was a sprawling single story ranch layout finished with a combination of beautiful rustic siding and indigenous rock. Large windows overlooked the front yard that was comprised mostly of flat river rock since grass was not common at the high elevation. The yard at the far right of the house ended at an eighty-foot cliff which yielded a breathtaking view of the untarnished valley beyond.

Cyrus took all of this in on the slow advance up the drive before parking under the overhang. He parked immediately in front of a pair of oversized french doors marking the home's entrance. After retrieving a large duffle bag from the bed of the truck, he glanced back the way he'd come. The yard pushed back the wilderness about 250 yards. From there, impossibly dense forest surrounded the property from the west as well as the south—the direction he had come. To the east was the sheer ledge overlooking the valley. To the north, behind the house, the mountain rose at a seemingly impossible grade. Somehow nature had found a way to laden the incline with yet more forest.

To call the scenery beautiful would be an understatement. Standing still he could hear nothing but the wind gently sweeping through the clearing and the occasional sound of something skittering through the brush beyond the tree line. This was a far cry from Chicago. He could see why Meade found the location so appealing.

For all of its charms, it was still the commute that Cyrus found puzzling. Berton was a very small town. It barely had a post office let alone an airport. There had to be an airstrip somewhere nearby. It was the only explanation for Meade's ability to live here while still visiting Chicago, London, and Washington D.C. so regularly. He would take a closer look at a map once he was settled and had a chance to get online.

Pulling a key from his jacket pocket, Cyrus released the deadbolt on the front door. He entered a 12-digit code into the security panel just to the right of the doors.

Inside he could hear the beeping of the home's alarm system. He tapped another 12-digit code into the touch panel on the wall inside. A pair of different 12-digit codes just to disarm the alarm system? He'd never seen anything like it—at least not on a residence. Not on anything short of a high value military installation. He idly wondered where one draws the line between security conscious and paranoid.

If the outside of the house was paradise, the inside was warm, tasteful and sparse. The entry way led into a large open floor plan with a substantial living room to the right and a short hallway on the left. A formal dining room was directly ahead with an expansive industrial grade kitchen off to the right. Beyond the living room was a hallway leading to the home's four bedrooms.

The floors of the entryway, kitchen and hallways were tiled in large pewter color ceramic while the living room was carpeted in a thick berber. The living room was wide and spacious with a pair of plush couches near the set of large front facing picture windows. Four oversized, cushy matching chairs were scattered throughout the room along with a series of end tables. The far wall of the living room was dominated by the mantle of fieldstone and etched concrete around the fireplace. To the left and right of the hearth were gigantic built-in bookcases that must have been ten feet tall. A great vaulted ceiling rose up over the entryway, living room, kitchen and dining room.

Cyrus walked around the open area taking it all in. The place was clean—immaculate actually. Everything was very precise. The furniture was arranged just so. The bookcases were free from dust, the fireplace must have been gas fueled because even the walls of the hearth were clean. The logs in the fireplace looked real. He had to touch one of them to be sure they were imitation. *Gas it is.*

Looking around, something seemed out of place. He was having trouble putting his finger on it. Then it clicked. There was no television in the living room. *Not bad*, he thought. *This could be paradise after all!*

A walk down the short hallway to the left lead him to a spacious laundry room complete with a washer and dryer that looked out-of-the-box new. There was a countertop and cabinets built in around the washer and dryer. Cabinets hung from the walls over the counters and the machines. No expense was spared. The cabinets in the laundry room matched the quality and design of the ones in the kitchen. Likewise, the countertops were the same marble as the kitchen. Meade clearly knew what he wanted when he built the place. He hadn't skimped on a single detail.

Across from the laundry room Cyrus found a large walk-in closet. The short hallway ended at a door leading to the four-stall garage.

Flipping the switch on the wall, Cyrus stepped into the garage. He was standing at the top of a platform five steps above the concrete floor of the wide-open garage bays. The concrete was polished and sealed. The walls were drywalled and painted with the same care and quality as the home's interior. The ceiling was at least fifteen feet high with row after row of lighting ballast hung to chase away every possible shadow.

A large Ford F250 pickup truck sat in the closest garage bay. It was jacked up on wide beefy tires. It had a heavy-duty cow catcher on the front and mounting linkage for a snow plow. There was an industrial grade winch attached to the front bumper. Cyrus took a long look at the jacked up 4x4 and tried to picture 80-year-old Walter Meade behind the wheel plowing snow. It was a hell of a thought. He wasn't sure he could see it. But then again, he wouldn't put anything past the old man.

The two center bays were empty, but parked in the far stall were a pair of four wheel drive ATV's. They were big red Hondas that looked brand new. They had thick rugged tires, and both machines sported rather heavy-duty looking winches on their front ends. He supposed that wasn't a bad idea living way up on the mountain the way Meade did. It wasn't like he would be able to get help quickly if he got stuck or ran into trouble. The winch was a good investment. One that, apparently, the old man had made on all his toys.

And that brought Cyrus to the tarp stashed behind the ATVs. Pulling it back he found a pair of snowmobiles. These also looked like new. So new, he wasn't sure they had ever been used. Again, up here all alone, the sleds could mean the difference between life and death in case of an emergency. It seems that Walter Meade had thought of everything.

Returning to the entryway, Cyrus grabbed the massive duffle and headed for the far hallway, beyond the living room where he knew the bedrooms would be located. Four bedrooms, according to the specs provided by Allan Underwood. More than Walter needed, he had said. But it was likely that Walter entertained guests from time to time. He had no family but he was a good man so, certainly he had friends. Maybe that would explain why he had two of everything; two ATVs and two snowmobiles. Still, it was odd. Meade had never mentioned family, though Cyrus had never asked. It wasn't that he didn't care; it was just a unique attribute of their relationship. They honored each others privacy. Well, at least Cyrus had. Apparently the old man knew all kinds of Cyrus's secrets.

What he wouldn't give to have one more conversation with the old guy. There were so many questions he would ask this time around. Questions he felt entitled to ask given all he now knew.

Walking slowly down the hallway, he looked into each of the bedrooms as he passed. Every one was spacious and as equally immaculate as the rest of the house. They were all furnished but devoid of any personal touches. The bedrooms had a feel more like upscale hotel rooms.

At last, he reached the master bedroom, the last door on the left. He set his bag on the floor and took a deep breath. *Wow. What have I done to deserve this?*

The room was large, easily 20x30 with a king size bed on one wall and a scaled down version of the living rooms fireplace on the opposite side. There were two large dressers matching the style of the massive bed. A large mirror hung over one of the dressers. Several different pieces of modern art hung on the walls. As in the living room, the two sides of this scaled down hearth were floor to ceiling bookcases packed end to end with hardcover novels.

The ceiling was vaulted with a large fan hung in the center. The left wall contained two doorways. One leading to an enormous walk-in closet, the other to a bathroom complete with multi-jet shower and a large Jacuzzi.

Cyrus sat on the side of the bed and considered the circumstances. Meade had clearly done alright for himself. And this was all paid for, free and clear? Plus taxes and utilities would be paid from an escrow account? It was insanity. Was this really

Meade's way of thanking him for saving his life? Or was there more to it? From what he knew of the man, things were never as simple as they first appeared.

He pulled back the zipper on the bag at his feet and removed a file folder. Dropping it on the bed, Cyrus took a deep breath. The folder contained Meade's autopsy report. It had been on his mind the entire drive west from Chicago. Cyrus had contacted an associate in Miami as soon as Allan Underwood left his apartment. His friend specialized in acquiring different forms of restricted material and information. In this case, Cyrus had requested Walter Meade's medical files and autopsy report. As always, his friend had come through.

Reviewing the file wasn't strictly necessary. The entire contents had already been committed to memory. Somehow it seemed more respectful to do it this way. He flipped open the folder and started leafing through the reports again.

The cause of death summary concluded that Meade had suffered myocardial infarction or, a heart attack, in layman's terms. The report referred to existing heart problems stemming from an issue some years prior. While vague, the report alluded to an earlier heart related trauma. Cyrus knew why the report was ambiguous. The details of the incident were considered a matter of national security. Some time back, a team of foreign nationals attempted to kidnap Meade from a coffee shop in Washington DC. The kidnapping was thwarted, but not before Meade was dosed with a powerful drug. Apparently the dosage was botched. That mistake resulted in permanent damage to the old man's heart.

According to the report, the medical examiner had concluded that Meade's heart had been seriously damaged some time in the recent past and the man had simply succumbed to the inevitable. It wasn't unreasonable. Meade was well into his eightieth year and he was running on a bum ticker. But there were two details in the report that had not been explained to Cyrus's satisfaction.

Two fingers on Meade's left hand were broken. The ME had concluded that the fingers were broken prior to the man's death, likely just before he expired. The ME posited the fingers were broken as the man fell to the ground while suffering his heart attack.

The second issue was the minor bruising at the base of Meade's skull. The ME had reported the injury as perimortem and also attributed it to the fall. An old man taking a spill that broke two fingers on his left hand and bruised the back of his head seemed something of a paradox…It didn't add up. It would have to be a complicated tumble.

The big problem was the photo of the broken fingers. Two fingers on the left hand appeared twisted together, side by side and broken at virtually the same place. There were no other broken bones. Not even bruising on the rest of the hand. The report even included an X-ray. In this case, a copy of an X-ray, but the break was clearly visible. Those broken fingers had been on Cyrus's mind for hundreds of miles. Shortly after crossing the Colorado border he realized what it was that troubled him.

Cyrus met Meade years earlier through an odd twist of fate. But they had grown to become friends. They spent endless long hours discussing many outlandish topics. Often plots from books or movies, even scientific theory. Cyrus found the old man to be an endless fount of knowledge and shockingly well read when it came to the most obscure science and science fiction.

For Cyrus the conversations were enjoyable because the old man could always take whatever crazy idea Cyrus had and he could add to it or expound on it in some way. As a writer, these conversations were rocket fuel for Cyrus's imagination.

Meade had often been a valued resource when Cyrus was working on a new book. It didn't matter the plot or subject, as soon as there was a draft worth sharing, Meade was the first person Cyrus queried for a critique. Cyrus still had half a dozen works not quite ready for publication. Every one of them had been shared with Meade prior to his passing.

And it was one of those drafts that clicked for Cyrus when he thought of Meade's two broken fingers. In a mystery novel Cyrus drafted, the victim of the story was attacked by an ex-coworker in the middle of the night. The villain had ambushed him while he slept, injecting him with an overdose of insulin. The victim awoke with a start, feeling the pain of the injection. By then the overdose had been administered and there was nothing he could do.

The antagonist simply sat back and waited for the overdose to take its toll. The victim sensed his faculties failing as he struggled to find a way to leave a clue, some way to let authorities know that his death was no accident. As the man crumpled to the floor in his last moments of life, he found himself in the fetal position. His killer was already paying him little attention, already searching the room for whatever it was he hoped to find. The unfortunate victim did the only thing his failing body would allow. There, on the floor with his knees raised to his chest, he took advantage of his killers lax attention. While the man wasn't looking, the victim reached up under his night shirt and, using the edge of his finger nail, carved four letters into flesh of his abdomen. He only hoped the two words would bring him the justice in death that he had not found in life. The man had hastily scraped into his own skin the letters N O and O D.

The draft of that book still sat on Cyrus's hard drive. It was the first novel he had ever written. Cyrus knew the book would never be published, but on a whim he shared the draft with Meade. The idea of leaving a dying note was cliche, Cyrus had said. Meade commented that perhaps the dying man could try something simpler. Perhaps if he intentionally broke a couple of his fingers, it would be enough to cause authorities to take a closer look at the incident. They would suspect the man had been tortured. No solution was discovered, but a decision followed regarding the worst books written by their favorite authors. But now, thinking about Meade's two broken fingers, Cyrus had the sick feeling his damn book was on the old man's mind as he lay dying on the floor. Those broken fingers weren't the result of a fall. The location of the breaks and the circumstances of the Meade's death brought Cyrus to a chilling conclusion. Meade had broken his own fingers in a desperate last-ditch effort to leave a message. Meade hadn't died of natural causes. He'd been helped along.

This also explained the bruising on the back of Meade's head. The ME didn't recognize the marks but Cyrus did. He'd seen those marks before. Someone had pressed the barrel of a gun against the base of Meade's head. That the bruising wasn't worse indicated it likely happened shortly before his heart failed.

Cyrus couldn't take the evidence to the police. It would be dismissed as circumstantial—if they took him seriously in the first place. Plus the police wouldn't be aware of Meade's attempted kidnapping years earlier. That would put it in the jurisdiction of the FBI. But the FBI would've been read in on the autopsy results already. There was no doubt that several government agencies had already reviewed the reports. Cyrus never knew what agency had employed Meade, only that he had clout. If no one was investigating Meade's death, it wasn't going to do any good to draw attention to it now.

That was ok. Cyrus had already decided to look into things personally. First he needed to get a better understanding of who Walter Meade really was. They had been friends for years but they had always been friends with great respect for each other's privacy. As a result, Cyrus knew surprisingly little about the man's professional life. He knew that Meade headed some kind of think tank or research group somewhere on the west coast but he had no idea what the group studied or specialized in. The entire time, Meade had shown an equal respect for Cyrus's past. He never asked questions regarding it, not even tangentially. Cyrus always harbored a suspicion that Meade was somehow already aware of his past and it was why he was so careful to avoid referencing it. But if that were the case, it meant that Meade had a rather impressive high-level intelligence clearance. Cyrus had wondered but never inquired. The past was a demilitarized zone in their friendship. Neither ventured there though they both likely knew more than they let on.

Cyrus decided to settle in at Meade's home before digging into the mystery that was Professor Walter Meade. He respected the man's privacy in life. But now the man was gone, and if Cyrus was right, the man's last mortal effort was to leave a message indicating that he had not died of natural causes. And he had left a message that only Cyrus could interpret.

Chapter 6

Berton Springs, Colorado
Wednesday, 1:00 am

The chirping of a distant alarm pulled Cyrus from a deep sleep. He sat up from where he lay sprawled across the bed in the master bedroom. Wiping the sleep from his eyes, it was several seconds before his eyes adjusted and he finally remembered why he wasn't in his own apartment. Pale moonlight spilled through the pair of bedroom windows making the already unfamiliar room more disorientating. The long cross-country drive had really done him in. Not only was he completely out of sorts, but he had fallen asleep fully dressed.

Blinking slowly once more, he realized an alarm had woken him. Was it the home's security system? No, that didn't seem right. The tone wasn't loud enough and it sounded too distant. Plus the sound didn't have the urgency he expected from a security system. Something different then, he thought.

Walking carefully across the dark room, he knelt beside his still-packed duffle bag, pulled back the zipper on the end compartment, and retrieved his Springfield. While he was fairly certain the alarm wasn't security related, it was better safe than sorry. Running a hand across the short stubble of hair on the top of his head, he shook off the last dregs of sleepiness and was ready to go.

Stepping into the pitch dark of the hallway, the alarm's tone become clearer, though still indistinct and muffled. As he tread carefully down the hall, he was able to better vector in the source of the sound. At the end of the hall, just before reaching the living room, he stopped at a closed door. He hadn't looked behind this one yet. Whatever was making the sound was somewhere beyond.

Silently, he turned the knob and pulled the door. As he did, he glanced beyond the threshold. He found only darkness. But now, with the door open, there was no question. The tone was coming from somewhere in the distance below. Reaching along the wall beyond the doorframe he found what he expected, a light switch. Flicking the switch with his gun up and at the ready, he kept his torso tucked beyond the jamb. Overreacting? Sure. But there'd been times when listening to that little voice in the back of his mind had saved his skin. So, when in doubt, he always listened to the voice.

In this case the voice was speaking out of turn. An empty stairway was all that greeted him.

Cyrus made his way down the stairs at slow and deliberate pace. He didn't know what to expect. He wasn't aware the house had a basement.

His mind was still clouded by exhaustion, and he was struggling to make sense of the unfamiliar surroundings, sights, and sounds. He had driven straight through, out from Chicago, stopping only for gas and a quick bite to eat. No wonder he'd crashed out so hard. He hated to admit it, but he was still drained from the fatigue.

At the bottom of the staircase he reached a platform. The path doglegged to the right before dropping the last four steps. He rounded the platform and finally reaching the bottom but saw little beyond what light spilled out of the stairwell. He found another switch and part of the basement became bathed in light. He realized there were several additional switches beside the first and flipped those as well.

Much like the garage, the basement was well lit by evenly distributed light ballasts that left virtually no corner in shadow. The ceiling was about ten feet high and ribbed with the bare joists from the floor above. Polished and sealed, the concrete floor had a smooth and industrial finish matching what he'd seen in the garage.

The basement was wide open and completely uncluttered. The house's furnace was situated in a corner along with a water softener and an oversize water heater. There was a large eight foot wide freezer along one wall, and very little else. The source of the chirping alarm was nearby. Still, even in the wide-open space it was difficult to pinpoint the source. The sound was reflecting off of the unadorned concrete walls.

He noticed a small half-height server cabinet suspended from the wall in the far corner. It had steel posts on its four corners but its walls were composed of smoked glass making the cabinet semi-transparent. He could see the dim flicker of lights behind the glass.

The cabinet was bolted to the concrete wall. It was about four feet tall, though suspended up off the floor so the cabinet's contents sat at eye level. He could see a thick conduit fastened to the wall behind the enclosure. The padded plastic channel ran up to the ceiling before branching off. This would be where the phone and television lines terminated. It would also be where the alarm system's central processor was housed, he reasoned.

Pulling open the cabinet door, he found a thin rack mounted 1U server. It was an ultra thin, high density server that was only 1 3/4" tall, but wide and deep like a pizza box and positioned on sturdy sliding rails. Mounted above it was a compact monitor in a 2U drawer enclosure. He grabbed the handle on the drawer that housed the computer screen and pulled. When the drawer reached full extension, the flat panel monitor that was folded down inside the drawer flipped up like the screen of a laptop revealing a keyboard and trackpad beneath. The entire assembly was very common in computer data centers where space was at a premium. Cleverly, the screen and keyboard automatically folded themselves away as the drawer slid closed. It was overkill, but absolutely first-class hardware.

After sliding the monitor away, Cyrus examined the rest of the cabinet's contents. There was a voice-over-IP conversion box wired for three phone lines. Overkill for a home, but certainly fitting given the old man's propensity for a first-class setup. There was also a wireless access-point. That was a welcomed site. The information Allan Underwood had provided along with the keys and the access code to the house included the password for the home's wi-fi network.

There was also a 24-port gigabit network switch with half of its ports used. Likely several of those 12 ports were actually used for phone lines—maybe even parts of the security system. He made a mental note to take a closer look at the security system in the morning. Then he leaned closer. There was something unusual here. He would need to figure it out before he accidentally locked himself out.

The last piece of hardware in the cabinet was the network router. He recognized that as an off the shelf Airport Extreme. They were good routers. He used one at home. It had proven more reliable than several of the Linksys routers that had blown out over the years. But there was one component he couldn't find, something that absolutely should have been there. The network switch was hardwired into the Airport network router. That was correct. But the Airport router needed to uplink to some sort of cable, DSL, or satellite modem. In a worst case, maybe even a cellular modem. So far up in the mountains, it was hard to guess what sort of infrastructure the house might have access to. But there was nothing. The router was the end of the line. There was no uplink of any kind. That would've been fine if there was no active internet access. But according to the lights on the front of the router, an uplink was established. The router clearly thought it had access to the Internet. But from what he was seeing in the wiring configuration, it simply wasn't possible.

At this point Cyrus realized that the alarm tone had stopped. Not just stopped, but stopped as soon as he'd opened the cabinet. He was so interested in the hardware, he hadn't even noticed. So what had caused the alarm? And why in the middle of the night? He looked through the cabinet again, searching for an error light on one of the components. He found nothing.

Contemplating the oddity of the situation, he slowly closed the cabinet. As the latch snapped shut, the low whirring sound of the servo motor drew his attention. A small panel extended from the side of the cabinet. The panel blinked to life with a message requesting that he place his right thumb against the display.

At a loss to explain this strange turn of events, Cyrus raised his hand and pressed a thumb against the screen's glass surface. The screen flashed green before displaying a message that read, "User identified. Please state your name…"

What the hell had Meade been up to? Despite himself, Cyrus couldn't wait to see where this went next. Apparently his thumbprint was recognized. Could his voice print work as well? "Cyrus Cooper."

As Cyrus said his name, a waveform spectrograph slid across the bottom third of the screen. Within moments the visual waveform was overlaid with dozens of tiny crosshatched icons and tinted various shades of green. Finally, the voiceprint image cleared and the entire image flashed green. The message at the top of the screen changed. "Voiceprint confirmed. Welcome, Cyrus."

A moment later, the wall to the left of the server cabinet drew his attention. It had developed a fine, perfectly straight, vertical line starting at the floor and reaching almost to the ceiling. A section of the wall four feet wide and eight feet high retracted into a recess behind the wall before sliding away to the side. Everything happened without more than a whisper of noise. Light ballasts on the ceiling beyond flashed to life revealing a large workspace.

Shocked and not knowing what to make of this, Cyrus stepped cautiously across the threshold of the secret room. There was a long deep marble countertop bolted to the wall on his right. The wall to the left was lined entirely with four-foot tall file cabinets. They were extremely old cabinets—maybe old enough to qualify as antique. Cyrus had seen a model very similar in historic video footage shot at Los Alamos Laboratories while the world's first atomic bombs were being developed. He had even read humorous antidotes about their locks in one of Richard Feynman's memoirs. Feynman, a Nobel Prize winner, had great fun defeating the cabinets built-in tumbler-based locks, back in his day. The cabinets had the same distinct, dated look, complete with the large combination lock dial built into the front bezel.

Stacked between the counter on the right wall and the cabinets on the left were piles of dusty cardboard filing boxes. Most appeared to contain neatly organized files but several had spools of ancient reel-to-reel film sticking out of them. An old film projector on a stand was under a sheet of plastic in the corner. But for as unusual as all of these things were, it was the device along the back wall that immediately commanded Cyrus's attention. It was large and round, raised, with a pair of steps leading to a platform perhaps four feet across. The base of the platform was made of a chrome like metal, but its surface was dull and lacked any kind of luster. The phrase *Beta II* was inscribed into the metal in large lettering beside the steps. A very thick black cable ran from the bottom of the platform and attached to what looked like a heavy, primitive control box. The box hung from a stout pole that was the only protrusion from the edge of the platform. Though he couldn't hazard a guess to its purpose, it looked like the control box had been placed just off the back edge of the platform so an operator could reach it while standing on the platform. Like everything in this room, the strange machine looked very old.

The only object in the room that looked at all modern was an Apple iMac that sat in the middle of the countertop along the right wall. It had started to boot as soon as the overhead lights powered up. There was no doubt in Cyrus's mind, he'd been led to this room. Called there by the alarm's tone. The biometric sensor had confirmed his identity, allowing access to the hidden vault. If there was an explanation for the theatrics, the computer seemed the best place to start.

Cyrus pulled out the short stool and took a seat at the computer. The desktop contained only a single file, a video that was titled simply 'Play Me.mov.' He launched the file and the video immediately filled the screen.

The face of 80-year-old Walter Meade looked back at him from the computer's display. He seemed to take a moment to collect his thoughts. "Hello, Cyrus," the old man said finally, along with a warm smile. "Thank you for accepting the gift of my home. There is no one more deserving. I recall a conversation some time back. You said that city life was not for you. One day you hoped to retired someplace out of the way—a place where the world could pass you by." The old man laughed. "I must say, I know exactly how you felt. I've had that same desire many times in my life. This place is—I should say, was, my sanctuary. It was my escape from the world. Unfortunately, if you are seeing this, certain unavoidable events have kept me from retiring to my personal corner of nowhere.

"This vault contains the bulk of the research pertaining to my life's work—a project most recently known as *Meridian*. I've left this information with you because, to be honest, there's a great burden that comes along with it. What you choose to do with the contents of this vault, once you understand the depths of this burden, is entirely up to you. What I'm asking of you is no small favor—but if you're up to the challenge, as I think you are, you might very well succeed in changing the world.

"But first, a small history lesson to put everything you're about to experience in proper perspective. In 1902 a series of small meteor showers pelted the Earth's atmosphere. As you might imagine, accounts from that point in time are sketchy at best. But we have assembled some fairly reliable information in the decades since, enough to generate very detailed computer models of the events. The majority of the interstellar material burned up entering the Earth's atmosphere. But in several very rare cases there were surface impacts. At this point I believe all of the meteorites have been recovered. Out of every sample collected across North America, all were fairly unremarkable. Chemical and ore compositions that were not quite in line with what is found on Earth, but nothing extraordinary. That is, with one glaring exception.

"One of the recovered ore samples exhibited properties unlike anything in recorded history. While the composition of the sample was largely unremarkable, cursory laboratory tests demonstrated unheard-of inconsistencies. Tests that should yield precisely the same results every time, instead displayed wild fluctuations that, initially, could not be explained. That ore sample remains unique to this day. A similar sample has never been located.

"So," Walter said, refocusing on the camera and pulling his mind back from his tale. "All of the data is gathered here. All of the records, the test results, and films of the experiments, have been archived in this vault. As you will see, we are on the verge of something very special. Something that will change the world. Sadly I wasn't able to bring the project to fruition before my time was up. A critical component remains beyond my reach. Until this point, my source of Halon-Seven has been limited, but there is now hope. Recent evidence suggests that additional reserves might yet exist—though I haven't a clue how to acquire them."

Meade stopped again, taking another several seconds to collect his thoughts.

"There is so much more that I wish I'd shared with you—so much more that you need to know about this mess I've left with you. Unfortunately, if you are seeing this, time was not on my side, and the clock ran out before I could share the secret of my life's work. So, I turn to you, my friend. As you have done for me so many times in the past, take a look at the project and its data. Help me complete my work. Everything you need to know is contained within this vault."

Walter took a deep breath and looked into the camera for several long seconds. Cyrus had the distinct impression that the man was looking right at him, here and now, not an image captured in time. It was eerie. Finally, Meade found his words. "The choice is yours, my friend. But this undertaking is a one-way trip. Not to be overly dramatic, but once you go down the rabbit hole, there is no turning back. Once something is learned, it cannot be unlearned.

"If you are willing to help me in my last request, the next step is simple. There is a raised platform at the back of the room. Simply step onto the device and turn on the main power key located on the control interface. The Mark II requires sixty seconds to come to full power. After sixty seconds, the light under the glass protective cap will glow green. Flip the cap, and toggle the switch.

"Now this last part is of paramount importance. The final step is to press the large red button on the left of the control interface. Once you press that button, you will have five seconds to place both of your hands directly to your sides and stand in the center of the platform. Please understand, *this is critical.* You must stand in the center of the platform.

"Good luck, Cyrus. Thank you for being a loyal friend to a weary old man."

Then, on the video screen, Walter Meade looked down at the keyboard of the computer he was using to record the video and tapped a button. The video ended. The screen went black and the computer's desktop returned.

Cyrus stared at the screen for several moments, not really seeing the screen but replaying in his head the expressions on Meade's face as the man told his tale and asked for help. The old man clearly knew he would not be able to complete his project. From the sound of it, this project had consumed a great deal of the man's life. Without a doubt, Cyrus suspected Meade had been one of the greatest minds of our time. *What sort of project would've captured such a man's attention for so long? What sort of science could keep a man like Meade interested for years and still leave him stumped?* And what possible solution could Cyrus find that a great mind like Walter Meade's could not?

Spinning around on the stool, he took in the contents of the vault with fresh eyes. Whatever all of this was, apparently it was everything to the old man. And he had left it to Cyrus.

What am I getting myself into?

In truth there was never any question. Backing out or refusing the undertaking wasn't a consideration. Cyrus walked slowly toward the platform. It was old. It had a high-tech look to it, but an old antiquated high-tech look. Like something built in the sixties when they thought the world would be full of flying cars come the year 2000.

Cyrus slowly climbed the platform. As he stepped into the middle, he looked down. It was the first time he realized that he was wearing only socks on his feet. He found it amusing, but it made no difference. What the hell did this thing do anyway? The old man conveniently left that out of the story. It was an obvious part of his sales pitch.

The control panel was hanging at waist level at the side of the platform. After taking a brief look at the simple controls, Cyrus turned the key thirty degrees. He heard a loud click as the industrial grade contacts inside the switch locked in place. A moment later he heard the sound of electricity, a hum buzzing below his feet. A static charge filled the air.

He waited for the toggle switch to turn green.

As predicted, roughly sixty seconds later the light beneath the protective glass cap went green. He flipped the protective cap and snapped the switch into position. Again, it was another solid click indicating the internal components were substantial and not modern low resistance, low grade, mass produced parts. "Why the hell not?" Cyrus muttered to himself and laid his palm on the large red button. It took more force than he expected, but he pressed it. He quickly returned his hands to his side and confirmed he was standing in the center of the four foot wide circular platform. He smiled at the sight of his socks on the platforms cold surface. It felt like a sheet of glass beneath his feet. There was obviously a great deal of electricity flowing beneath the platform. Even a thin layer of rubber afforded by a pair of shoes would've been welcome right about now…

There was a flash of light followed almost instantly by a second, brighter flash. He felt static electricity dance in the hair all over his body. He sensed it spreading across the surface of his t-shirt, up the hair on his arms and down the hair of his legs under his jeans. The static made the day old stubble on his jaw and the short bristle of his hair tingle. There was one final flash of light.

Then the entire room went pitch black.

Cyrus stood completely still in the darkness. The static dissipated completely at the same moment the lights had gone out. His ears popped and he felt a little off balance.

What the hell was that?

What was this machine supposed to do anyway? Somehow blowing every breaker in the house didn't seem very impressive.

Standing in the darkness, Cyrus tried to remember if there had been any emergency light fixtures in the vault. He didn't have a flashlight on him, and he was now stuck in the basement of a house he was barely familiar with. It wasn't the end of the world. He would blindly stumble his way in the direction of the staircase and feel his way up to the first floor. Once there, the ambient moonlight coming in through the windows should make it easier to find a flashlight or a candle.

Taking one tentative step forward followed by another, he was feeling for the edge of the platform with the toe of his sock. He felt the lip of the platform and stepped down onto the first stair.

As soon as he stepped onto the first stair, the room's ceiling lights flickered and started coming to life. With the first flicker of light, Cyrus froze. He was off balance midway to the second step and he lost his footing, tripping to the hard tile floor. With what remained of his dexterity, he recovered before falling on his face. But he was shocked. It was all he could do to pull himself fully upright as he looked around the room slack-jawed. Was he dreaming? Had this all been a dream? Was he still upstairs asleep in bed?

Cyrus was standing in the middle of a small room, maybe fifteen feet square. The walls were drywalled and painted an institutional off-white. The tile floor was some sort of utilitarian gray. The lights over head were fluorescent and recessed into a tile drop ceiling. They hummed and flickered as they continued to warm-up. He turned around to discover that the platform he had been standing on was different as well. It was no longer bulky and clunky like a piece of 1960's or 70's technology. This device had similar characteristics but was finished in tight rounded corners of chrome and brushed steel. The platform surface was made of some sort of highly polished glass like composite material.

What the hell is going on?

Walking cautiously across the room, he felt the cold tile beneath his socks. He reached the sliding glass door separating this room from the next. The door was tinted with a smoke color that made visibility into the next room impossible. Beside the door was a light switch with a motion sensor built in. At least that explained the lights turning on when he began moving around. Now if someone could just explain what the hell had just happened. Cyrus was starting to wonder if he had experienced a stroke or an embolism. One minute he was stumbling around Walter Meade's mountaintop home in the dark searching for the source of an alarm and the next he was standing...he didn't know where he was standing! He didn't know what was going on, and he was starting to get pissed. Why couldn't Meade just come out and say what he wanted to say? What the hell had he done?

Cyrus slid the glass door slowly to the side and stepped into the next room. The lights were out here, too. There was enough ambient light to see he was standing in an office of some kind. He was looking out over a twenty by thirty room separated by the low walls of several office cubicles. Each cubicle was setup as an active workstation, deserted now in the middle of the night. The far end of the room was lined with windows that stretched from floor to ceiling.

Crossing the room to look out the windows, Cyrus realized he was several floors up in some kind of office building. It must have been eight or ten stories down to the large empty parking lot scattered with a few lonely streetlights.

Where the hell am I?

Chapter 7

Cyrus slowly paced the darkened office, deep in thought. The entire experience was unprecedented and more than a little disconcerting, but he had to admit it wasn't entirely unexpected. More than a few of his conversations with Walter Meade hinted at the man's pursuit of some sort of teleportation technology. It wasn't like the concept was strictly the stuff of fiction anymore. A lab in Switzerland had managed to teleport a half-dozen photons a distance of several inches under strictly controlled conditions. Admittedly, that was a far cry from what he had just experienced.

Speaking of which…Cyrus pulled the cell phone from his pocket and walked to the front windows overlooking the parking lot below. He tapped an icon and brought up the phone's GPS app. Moments later his exact location was displayed. He was on the west coast of California, about a block and a half from the Pacific Ocean in Santa Barbara, California!

Oh, this just keeps getting better and better. What has that old bastard done? Couldn't he just ask for help like a normal person? This was awfully theatric.

A flash of light from the back of the office pulled his attention back to the moment. The lights had just turned back on in the teleportation room. He could see the muted glow filtering through the smoked finish of the sliding glass door. Reacting on instinct, Cyrus ducked into the hallway at the side of the room. It led to a pair of restrooms just off the main office. Peering around the corner, he watched the door to the teleportation room. His right hand found the grip of the Springfield still tucked into the back of his jeans. He decided to leave the gun where it was—glad it was there just the same.

A few moments later the door to the back room slid open and a young dark haired woman stepped through. Nervously, she looked around the dark office as if expecting to meet someone. Finding herself alone, she seemed increasingly on edge. She appeared to be contemplating a dash back into the teleportation room.

"Cyrus?" She had finally made up her mind and found her voice, unsteady as it was. "Cyrus Cooper?"

Cyrus watched and waited another moment. She was skittish—even a little afraid. But that was to be expected if she were going to meet a stranger in a dark room in the middle of the night. He wasn't any crazier about his present circumstances. She was likely even more uncomfortable than he. It was better not to let her twist in the wind any longer.

"Over here," Cyrus said as he stepped slowly around the corner. He was careful to keep his voice low. This late at night and in the darkness, even low conversational tones were enough to make someone jump.

"I'm Cyrus," he continued. "I'm afraid you have me at a disadvantage. You clearly know who I am. Unfortunately I've only just figured out *where* I am...It's rather disconcerting."

She laughed softly, relief registering in her eyes. "Yes, I'm sorry for that. I'm Reese Knoland. I was Walter Meade's research assistant. I'm sorry for all of this."

Her eyes still shifted nervously. "This was one of Walter's many protocols. He told me you would arrive one night. He setup a system to ping me when you did. I was supposed to meet with you."

While she was speaking, Cyrus approached to within only a few feet. It was the first time he got a clear view of her. The pale moonlight shone through the large windows and cloaked her in contrasts of highlight and shadow, but she was attractive. Mid to late twenties with raven dark hair pulled back in a ponytail and pale, almost porcelain white skin. The contrast was obvious even in the diffuse light. She was maybe five foot six with a slim athletic form.

"Walter knew you'd have questions, and—well," she looked more than a little uncomfortable having been put in this situation. "To be perfectly honest, he thought you might be a bit put off, being led here the way you were."

Cyrus sputtered a laugh at that. "You could say that! It strikes me as melodramatic. So he sends you here to meet me? I'm sure the old man thought a pretty face would temper my irritation. Why didn't—"

Oops. He caught himself, but it was too late.

Cyrus cringed as he considered what he had just said. He looked Reese square in the eye. She met his gaze. "I'm sorry," he said with sincerity. "That sounded much worse than I intended. I only meant the old man knew this little production was going to irritate me. I apologize.

"I knew Walter had an associate by the name of Miss Knoland. I guess I was just expecting a contemporary of his to be…someone a little closer to his age. Not a smoking hot—" He stopped himself.

Ahh! His second attempt was even more of a disaster than the first!

She wore a dark t-shirt than accentuated her form and jeans that didn't do her an injustice either. The ponytail and the late hour suggested to Cyrus that his arrival had caught her even more off guard than it had him. She had likely been home in bed. His arrival would've trigger an alert, likely sent to her cell phone. She'd rushed here to meet him. And she had used the teleporter to get here. That meant there were at least a few of these things in operation. One here at the office, one in the vault hidden in Meade's basement—now *his* basement—and at least one more at or near Reese's home.

While the logical part of his brain obviously still functioned, Cyrus was hard pressed for something to say that wouldn't end in further embarrassment. He was tongue-tied and he couldn't believe it. A woman hadn't had this effect on his since the eleventh grade. And now he was making a complete fool of himself. She was attractive, but come on! His verbal skills had de-evolved to those of a teenager. Meade held this young woman in very high regard. Cyrus had a sinking feeling that Meade was setting him up to take over work on the project—

what had he called it? Meridian! And while Cyrus was a long way from making that decision, he knew that the first impression he made with Reese would be crucial. He needed this to work. Ideally, he needed to salvage this introduction, but he was reticent to open his mouth and risk a third failed opportunity. He could only guess what sort of foolishness might pour out next.

Though she didn't appear offended by his clumsy slips of the tongue, Reese was quiet. Her eyes seemed to study him, perhaps waiting for him to place his foot in his mouth yet again. It was hard to tell given the poor lighting but Cyrus thought he saw a flush of color in her cheeks. Was she blushing? She'd maintained eye contact, amusement dancing in what he could see of her gaze.

Cyrus shrugged. There was no going back on that now. He looked her in the eye and searched for the right thing to say. She continued to meet his gaze. There was a kind of empathy in her stare. She seemed as off balance in this situation as he. At least from what he saw, she was not put off by his foolish comments.

Their eyes lingered for several long moments in silence.

Something changed in Reese's expression. A tiny sly smile touched the corners of her lips and she held up one finger signaling him to wait. She turned on her heel and retreated into the teleportation room.

———

Reese paced quickly back and forth across the teleportation room. She had suffered anxiety over this very moment. Walter had arranged this entire situation to impress upon Cyrus the true marvel of the teleportation technology. But she knew it for what it really was—a chance for Walter to finally show Cyrus the fruits of their quasi-collaboration. A great part of what had been achieved here was due in no small part to Cyrus's contributions. But the man had no idea! She knew Walter had thought of Cyrus as a son. But for all of his professional and personal respect, the old man had never shared the secrets of the project with Cyrus. This awkward display was nothing more than a posthumous plan to right that wrong. And she was a pawn in his design.

For the several years that Reese had worked side by side with Walter, she had heard him speak of Cyrus many, many times. So often, in fact that she had wanted to meet the man. She had even come close to asking Walter to introduce them on several occasions. But she never followed through. Walter had gone to great lengths to keep parts of his life compartmentalized. And for reasons she didn't know, the old man had felt the need to keep Cyrus away from the project. By extension, that meant they would never meet.

Soon, she found out that Walter's health was failing. It was terrible news, seeming to strike out of the blue. The old man had a great deal of preparations to make. He was explicit in his instructions to her. Arrangements were made for Cyrus to replace him on the project. Walter's share of the hard science was taken care of. They had the physics licked; another scientist wasn't what they needed. Cyrus and Reese would be the ones to see this project through. Walter would be leaving the project in their hands, and they would lead the development team together.

Walter had made a point of explaining that only a portion of Cyrus's talents were detailed in his personnel file. While Reese was aware of Cyrus's contributions to the project thus far, Walter had said he was afraid there would be issues that required Cyrus's less conventional talents.

What the old man had meant by that, she never knew. *What sort of talents could Cyrus have that were so unique?* Walter had said simply that it was not his place to speak for Cyrus. He had asked simply that she trust him and trust his judgment on the matter.

It had been a foreboding premonition, given Walter's rush to conclude his part of a project that had consumed the bulk of his career. She thought many of the problems with the old man's health had started after an issue several years ago, in Washington, D.C. It was a matter Walter had also refused to explain. She knew only that the old man had nearly died, and Cyrus had been somehow involved.

Putting all of that aside, and now reasonably certain that the blush had faded from her cheeks, Reese headed back through the sliding glass door.

Stepping into the main office, Reese stopped and looked around. Cyrus was standing right where she'd left him. Still, she looked around in an exaggerated manner as if trying to find something. Finally, she met his gaze and smiled. She walked up to him and extended her hand. "You must be Mister Cooper. My name is Reese Knoland. Walter has told me so much about you!"

Cyrus looked stunned for half a beat. She watched as he realized she was offering an opportunity to start over. He smiled broadly and accepted her proffered hand. "Cyrus, please—my friends call me Cyrus."

Chapter 8

Off the Coast of Santa Barbara, California
Wednesday, 1:10 am (2:10 am Colorado Time)

The gentle rocking of the boat would've made it easy to doze off. This was one of the many reasons Dargo had taken the night shift. As the team's commander, he made the shift assignments and had the freedom to do as he pleased. But after many long years in the field, Dargo was still a grunt at heart. He wouldn't task a man with an assignment he wasn't willing to do himself. A stalwart leader, he would settle for nothing less than absolute dedication from each and every man on the team.

It was the quiet monotony of the surveillance nightshift that troubled him at the moment. The confines of the yacht's aft salon were far more comfortable than he preferred. The plush accommodations left him concerned his men might let their guard down and become sloppy. The warm air circulating off the stacks of surveillance equipment more than kept the Pacific Ocean's chill at bay. The long slow hours could break the most disciplined of minds. Both men on shift with him certainly seemed comfortable. Perhaps too comfortable. Dargo considered cracking open the sliding glass door at the rear of the room. The icy ocean air would keep them alert. Creature comforts led to slow minds, and slow minds were a liability.

With a sour grimace, he pushed his harsh concerns aside. A surreptitious glance at each face confirmed that they were both sharp and still on task. Each man wore a headset, and both had their attention focused on the computer screens before them. There was no need to make them uncomfortable, so long as they remained sharp. Scratching absently at the two days worth of steely gray stubble on his jaw, Dargo swallowed the last dregs of his cold coffee.

"Sir," called one of the men over Dargo's shoulder. "We have movement. Someone is in the office!" The man spoke in Russian.

"Put it on screen," Dargo responded quietly and with little concern. It was the middle of the night and likely only the cleaning crew.

The fifty-inch LCD panel mounted on the forward bulkhead came to life, showing a video feed from a camera at the top of the yacht's communications array. The view was monochrome, but the image was remarkably crisp and detailed, considering its focal point was nearly a mile distant. Advanced optics and software in the camera corrected for the pitch and yaw of the rocking boat. The camera's cutting edge processor made the high-speed adjustments essential for keeping the night-vision lens in perfect focus.

"Is cleaning crew?" Dargo asked in his broken Russian-accented English.

"Negative," one of his men answered. "They clean twice a week, and they cleaned the facility last night."

"What happened?" Dargo continued. "I did not see a car enter the lot. Did someone arrive via the underground structure?"

"Negative," the second operative confirmed. "There have been no unaccounted for arrivals."

"Audio?" asked Dargo.

"Audio is up," responded the first operative. "We're getting the feed. Whoever is there, they are not making noise. I heard a door open right before I put the video on the main screen. Nothing since."

Dargo didn't care for this surprise. If he hadn't been here to witness this first hand, he would've assumed his men had missed something. But that didn't seem to be the case. He glanced at his wristwatch. He made a note of the time in his log and confirmed what he already knew: the last one to leave the office was Chad Brewster, at 18:22 hours. *So from where had this mystery guest come?*

"I've got a face," the second operative reported.

Dargo returned his attention to the wall-mounted screen. A man stepped from the gloomy darkness of the deserted office and approached the windows at the front of the building. He looked out over the parking lot and possibly at the bay beyond. A puzzled expression filled his face. He pulled what appeared to be a mobile phone from his pocket and held it up as if trying to get reception. Judging by the furrow of his brow, the man was not happy with the results. Dargo glanced at his own phone, sitting on the counter beside the computer keyboard. He had a full signal.

So what is the problem?

"Capture still photographs," Dargo ordered. "Run facial recognition."

Dargo leaned forward in his seat and studied the frozen frame of footage that was up on his computer's display. His forehead wrinkled as he studied the monochrome image. It didn't seem possible. He didn't need the database to identify this man after all. What were the chances of Cyrus Cooper showing up here, after all this time?

Leaning back, Dargo scratched absently at the stubble on his jaw. His employer wanted Meridian. But nowhere in the mission brief had Cyrus Cooper been mentioned. Could his appearance be a coincidence? Dargo knew better. In intelligence circles, there was no such thing as coincidence. This would complicate things.

The second operative waved a hand in the air and set about flipping a series of switches on the control panel beside his computer screen. "I've got another noise," he said as he flipped the last switch and routed the audio to the room's surround-sound speakers. "There may be another target in the office."

The three men listened intently, waiting for the slightest sound to come through the speakers. "Cyrus? Cyrus Cooper?" Dargo recognized the voice instantly. It was Reese Knoland. He'd been surveilling her and the rest of her team for some time.

"Over here," a male voice sounded from the distant office. "I'm Cyrus."

The first operative looked at Dargo and chuckled. "So much for facial recognition, sir."

Dargo just shot the man a cold glare. Under normal circumstances, he might've appreciated the irony of the target literally identifying himself in such a way. But just then he was more troubled by the unexpected presence of Cyrus Cooper and what it would mean for this operation. Unfortunately, it meant he would need to contact Bayer.

Chapter 9

It was an awkward start, but Reese had let him off the hook. Cyrus thought that said a great deal about her. The fact that Walter Meade had orchestrated the uneasy meeting said a great deal as well. He could've simply asked Cyrus to drop by the Santa Barbara office and meet with Reese and discuss her team. Instead he had chosen a more dramatic path. A midnight signal had drawn him to the basement of the house on his first night there. He had been led, step by step into finding the secret vault, its archive, and the message from Meade. But it was the shocking teleportation from the basement vault in Colorado to the tenth floor offices in California that had been the old man's true intention. That was the hook. The rest would be bait, intended to galvanize his interest. He was being toyed with, like a fish on a line. Meade had coaxed him onto the teleportation platform, and he had been sent to a midnight meeting with Reese Knoland with a dramatic flourish.

He realized the old man knew him far too well. If asked, he would've been reluctant to accept a part in the project. Hell, based on what little he knew of the project, he could already anticipate any number of political, economic, maybe even theological challenges to the technology. But the dramatic reveal was well played. The hook so neatly set that Cyrus couldn't turn back without knowing more.

"So," Reese said, pulling him from his revelry. "I'd like to sit you down with the team and make introductions. Walter told me to expect you. We can get you up to speed and explain the project."

"That sounds like a good plan." He looked at his watch. It was going on 3:00 am—well, 2:00 am in California. The timing was awful. They couldn't gather the research team until a more respectable hour. He could go back home, but he didn't have a chance in hell of sleeping again before morning. Not after all that had happened. He was wired, and he had endless questions. Getting up to speed was the only way to satisfy his need to understand his circumstances. But right then, with everything swirling in his mind, thanks to Meade's shock and awe campaign, he didn't even know where to begin.

"I don't suppose you're interested in grabbing a drink, maybe a bite to eat?" Again the thought shot from his brain to his mouth before his mental filter had engaged. The comment sounded like a threadbare pickup line. He looked down at the floor, rubbed the corners of his eyes at the bridge of his nose and took a deep breath. What was it about this woman?

Rather than be held back by his own embarrassment, he shook his head at his own foolishness and looked her squarely in the eye. "I've got a million questions. I don't even know where to start. If I go home now, there's zero chance I'll get any sleep before morning."

Her demure smile made it seem she had never considered the ambiguity of his suggestion. Maybe he was getting the wrong vibe from her. If she hadn't considered the possibility that he found her attractive, she would never consider the potential impropriety of the statement. But that didn't match the glint he was seeing in her eyes. The thought had occurred to her. She was just classy enough not to embarrass him.

Nice!

Reese struggled not to laugh at his latest gaffe. At least she wasn't the only one feeling off balance at their awkward meeting. She concentrated on selecting a place where they could find dinner at the late hour. "I'm in. I know just the place. But we need to make a stop first." She glanced down at his shoeless feet and up again, giving him a shy smile.

Cyrus followed her eye and shrugged. "What can I say? One minute I'm walking around the house in the mountains, and the next—poof! I'm lucky I have pants on!"

Now she couldn't help but laugh. And she was pretty sure she was blushing again. The mental image was both comical…and interesting.

Dammit. She was almost certain he knew she was blushing this time.

"Alright," Reese said struggling with her composure. "First step, back to your place. We have to get you presentable!"

She led him back into the teleportation room. The lights once again engaged as they entered. She pulled a smartphone from her pocket and tapped a few times on the screen before stepping onto the platform.

Cyrus waited at the base of the platform.

"Well?" she asked. "Are you coming with, or are you waiting for the next car?" She always found the allusion to elevators amusing when referring to the transport platforms, given the disparity in technology.

"Ah, you mean we can go together?" he looked a little unsettled. "We won't end up as conjoined twins or something? I remember what happened in that movie, *The Fly*. It didn't work out too well for Jeff Goldblum!"

Her eyebrows arched at the thought. She'd worked on the project for years and had never made that connection. "Very funny. That was an entirely different technology—*and it was fiction!*" She stepped back only a few inches and waved a hand, directing him onto the platform. It would be tight, but she was good with that.

God! she thought. This wasn't like her. She was acting like a schoolgirl. Fine, as long as she could keep from blushing again, she would count it as a win.

Cyrus ascended the steps of the platform and stepped close in front of her. They were virtually toe-to-toe. The platform was four feet wide. They could have stood comfortably shoulder-to-shoulder. She supposed he wasn't familiar with how the platform functioned and was reluctant to be near the edge when they teleported. He wouldn't know that there were safeguards to prevent transport, should something on the platform break the plane of the transport barrier. She bit gently at the corner of her lip and looked up into his face. She could tell him.

Nahh!

Without looking down at the phone in her hand, she tapped the button to initiate transport. The ten-second delay started counting down.

Wait a minute. The perimeter safety mechanism that prevented transport was one of the ideas that Walter had come back with after one of his trips to visit Cyrus. Walter said he got the idea from Cyrus. But that would mean—

She looked up into his eyes. He smiled and gave her a wink just as the lights flashed and the trip was over.

Cyrus gave Reese a coy wink, which was followed immediately by a mild flash of light. His ears popped. The trip was over. He looked around, expecting to be back in the basement vault of the house in Colorado. He was still having trouble thinking of it as his house. But he wasn't in the basement. They were standing in an empty walk-in closet. The teleportation platform was an identical match to the one in California. Had she taken them somewhere different? No, he recognized the carpet on the floor. They were standing in the closet of one of the spare bedrooms. The closet's light turned on when they teleported in. He saw the motion sensor over the light switch beside the door.

Stepping back to the edge of the platform, he motioned for Reese to exit first. She still looked up at him with a suspicious pinch to her eyes. He smiled, confident he was finally past his embarrassingly awkward stage with her. It seemed they had moved on to flirting. She suspected he knew of the platform's safety protocols. It was true, he had unconfirmed suspicions. Meade had once started a discussion about strange safety procedures involving laser-based sensors. The teleportation platform seemed like a practical application for everything they had discussed. He suspected those sensors and protocols were now used to prevent a transport from initiating, while part of the payload was not entirely within the confines of the pad. Still, he wasn't willing to bet his life—or an appendage—on those assumptions. So he had played it safe. Better for Reese to think him flirting than to have an accident. Besides, he could flirt and play it safe at the same time.

Out in the bedroom, Reese had turned on the overhead light. Cyrus walked out and smiled. "Make yourself at home. I'll find my shoes and throw on a fresh shirt. I wasn't expecting company." He headed for the master bedroom across the hall, while she turned left toward the living room.

Cyrus walked through the doorway of the master bedroom and pulled his t-shirt off over his head. He tossed it on the floor beside his duffle bag. He would need to get the rest of his clothes moved over. It might be time to make a list. He would need groceries, too. Arriving with no idea what to expect from the property, it could've been a shack or a rustic cabin. He certainly hadn't expected a spread like this. He could see this being home, settling in here and being comfortable, even happy. At least he had solved the mystery of Meade's uninhibited travel. The old man must've been using the teleportation platforms to move between Colorado and Chicago. And between Colorado and Santa Barbara. Likely between D.C. and London as well, he reasoned.

How many of these platforms are out there?

Pulling the gun from the back of his jeans, he was going to leave it on the nightstand. After a moment, he thought better of it. He still didn't know what he was getting into here. It wouldn't hurt to be carrying. But he would do it right this time.

Digging into the outer pocket of his duffle, he found the holster for the Springfield. He slipped the weapon into the holster and the holster into the back of his jeans. The holster had a clip that snapped over his belt and kept the rig in place. Pulling a dark, button-down shirt from his bag, he slipped it over his shoulders. Buttoning it up, he left it untucked. It would work well in hiding the handgun. After grabbing a battered pair of hiking boots, he switched off the light and headed for the living room.

He found Reese standing stock still in the center of the living room. She seemed lost in thought. He didn't say anything. Instead, he sat down on the couch and began lacing up his boots, all the while wondering what she was thinking.

After a few moments, she snapped out of her funk and looked around. "I'm sorry," she said quietly. "It's different being here, since he's gone."

Ahh, that's understandable. He had no idea how close Reese had been with Meade. He was only aware of the broad strokes. For example, he knew they had worked together for several years. And that the old man referred to her as his associate. But when Reese introduced herself earlier, she claimed she was Meade's research assistant. He assumed she was being modest. He knew for a fact that Meade considered her a peer, not a subordinate. But beyond that, Cyrus had no idea what their relationship really might have been. "Were you close?"

She looked at him for a moment and thought, then shrugged her shoulders. "It was hard to tell with Walter. I would say I was as close to him as anyone he knew. But he was a very private person. It's no exaggeration to say this project was his life. He'd been working on it since he left college. He never married. In the time I knew him, I don't think he ever even dated.

"This place was more than a home to him. It was his sanctuary. The number of people who have been in this house could be counted on one hand." She thought for a moment. "I guess you could say we were close. We spent Thanksgiving and Christmas Eve here together the last two years. But I always thought he did that out of pity. My parents died a couple of years back. I think Walter realized the holidays were hard for me. He invited me up here so I wouldn't be alone."

Cyrus wasn't sure how to respond. Certainly it made his heart ache to think of someone like Reese losing her family. Seeing the far off look in her eyes when she spoke of them made it clear that it was still a fresh wound. But that wasn't what she was really getting at, so he stayed on point. "I think you're selling yourself short. The Walter Meade I knew didn't do anything unless it was what *he* wanted. He was a kind and generous man, but, like you said, he was a private man, too. If he didn't want you here, he wouldn't have asked you to share the holidays with him."

It was a tricky subject. She was clearly missing the old man. He wanted to make her feel better, but he meant every word. Meade had had his share of secrets. Cyrus got the sense that he was just now scratching the surface of those secrets. Meade had spoken highly of Reese, had referred to her as his contemporary, rather than as his assistant. The old man had made her a part of his meager private life. Clearly Walter Meade had thought very much of this woman.

With a small sniff, Reese wiped a tear from the corner of each eye. "Thank you. I suppose you're right. I guess it just struck me as strange, seeing the place without his personal effects."

"I wondered about that. What happened to his stuff after he passed? You said he didn't have a lot of friends and even fewer knew where he lived? Who cleaned the place out?"

"That was me. You're right. He didn't trust many. But he did leave an extremely detailed will. You must have met Mister Underwood?"

Cyrus nodded.

"Everything was detailed in the will. He asked that I take all of his clothes and donate them to charity. He wanted all of his financial records scanned to disc and the originals destroyed. He even stipulated that I dispose of all his personal toiletries. He wanted the place spotless and ready for you to move in, when the time came. You taking over this house was very important to him."

"And you were the one who had to do the cleanup and take care of all that? I'm sorry. I would've been happy to clean up. It's the least I could do."

"Oh, no. You don't understand. My instructions were just to take care of the clothes, the bills, and dispose of a few things. There was no mess. Walter was the most fastidious person I've ever met. The house was immaculate. I think the most I had to do was pick up a couple of books that were lying around. Even the bathrooms were spotless. That's just the way Walter was."

Cyrus considered all of that. It was shocking how little he really knew of the old man. He knew some of Meade's most closely guarded secrets, but that was entirely thanks to a chance encounter some years back. It bothered him that he would never have the chance to know the man better. He had enjoyed their discussions immensely, and it saddened him knowing there would be no further conversations. And it troubled him that Walter had passed some weeks ago, yet Cyrus had known nothing about it. He hadn't even been able to attend the service.

"Anyway," Reese said, this time she pulled Cyrus from his funk. "I'm starving. How about that bite to eat?"

"Absolutely. You pick the place, and I'm buying."

That settled, they were ready to go. Before heading to the transport platform, Cyrus ran down to the basement. He wanted to lock up the vault before leaving, but it turned out not to be a concern. Once again, Meade had thought of everything. Activating the teleportation platform must have closed the vault door automatically.

That brought a question to mind. It was curious. Why two transport platforms in the house? One locked in the vault and one upstairs in the closet? The one in the closet seemed much more modern. The one in the vault almost looked like an early prototype. Given the archived records and the reels of film stored in the vault, it seemed the likely case. There must have been a reason Meade hadn't used the old platform as his 'daily driver.' That seemed to be the function of the platform upstairs. It was just one of the many questions he intended for Reese.

He headed back upstairs. Reese was waiting in the spare bedroom. They entered the walk-in closet. This time, the large control panel Cyrus saw inside the door of the closet made more sense. It was a security panel just like the one beside the front door. Meade had installed it there so he could control the security system as he came and went, via the platform.

They stepped onto the platform together, toe-to-toe again. Reese's close proximity caused his pulse to quicken, and he felt his skin warm. Actually, it was more than that. He could feel the heat from her body. The thought made his pulse quicken further. She could've stepped away if she wanted to, he was sure of it. There was enough room for the two of them on the platform, and she knew that he knew. Still, she didn't move away. That decision wasn't lost on him.

As before, Reese tapped a series of commands into her smartphone. This was another subject he wanted to discuss. The device in the vault had a simplistic but heavy-duty control panel. But it seemed she could control the modern platforms directly from her phone.

She looked up at him. The corners of her lips curled into a pert little smile. Yes, she could've moved away if she wanted.

Moments later there was a flash of light, a pop of his ears, and they were standing in the dark. This time the popping of his ears made sense. The house in Colorado was high up in the mountains, while just about everything in Santa Barbara was close to sea level. Although the teleportation was instantaneous and painless, the human body was still subject to the change in barometric pressure.

Reese stepped from the transport platform first and made her way to the light switch in the dark. They were standing in the spare bedroom of her two-bedroom apartment. There was a small daybed against one wall and a small desk against the other. The transport platform took up a good portion of the remaining floor space.

"My turn to change," she said. She pointed down the hall to the left. "The living room and kitchen are that way. Make yourself at home. I'll only be a minute."

She left Cyrus and turned the corner into her bedroom, shutting the door behind her. Walking across the room, she looked at herself in the mirror. *Wonderful!* No one looks their best at three o'clock in the morning. She changed out of her t-shirt, selecting a more presentable and form-fitting button-up top. She liked the way it accented her trim waist and full breasts. The top was a little low cut, but she liked that too. *God, am I really doing this?* She felt like a teenager again, which was silly. Then again, she was twenty-seven years old and hadn't found time for dating in *far too long.* This infatuation was giving her a charge. What was the point in denying herself that harmless fun?

Turning back to the mirror, she pulled her hair from the ponytail and quickly brushed through it. Her raven black hair fell just past her shoulders. She'd been in a rush to get to the office after receiving the automated page on her phone earlier in the night. She'd thrown her hair up in her hurry to get out the door. But now they were going out. And, if she were honest with herself, she wanted to look her best. She was pretty sure she was getting a vibe from Cyrus and wanted to make the most of it.

Just as she was about to turn and head for the door, movement from behind caught her eye in the mirror. She turned with a start as a dark skinned man bolted from the darkness of the closet. He wore baggy clothes and a baseball cap, and he had something in his hand. She drew a breath to scream, but what he had in his hand prevented it.

The man lunged with a stun gun. It was a heavy duty, industrial weapon in the shape of a short baton. Before she could exhale a scream, he touched the end of the stun rod to her side jolting her instantly into unconsciousness.

Chapter 10

Cyrus stood on the balcony overlooking the empty beach ten stories below. Beyond the sand, a stunning full moon reflected back in the gently breaking waves of the wide open bay. What Reese's apartment lacked in space was made up for with an impressive view. It must've been amazing to wake each morning to the sound of waves lapping at the shore. He could picture her sitting there drinking coffee and taking in the distant horizon.

The balcony was about fifteen feet wide and close to ten feet deep. Enough room for the small bistro table and chair set off to the side. A thick, wrought-iron handrail ran the perimeter of the balcony. Each apartment along that side of the fifteen-story building had a matching terrace. A privacy panel extended from the side of the building, secluding each balcony from the ones on either side. It offered some semblance of privacy in a building packed with hundreds of people. The apartment certainly had its selling points, mainly the beach and the view, but Cyrus would take the mountains of Colorado any day.

The sound of movement inside the apartment drew him to glance over his shoulder. He expected Reese to be ready any moment.

"All set—" he started to ask as he did a double-take. It wasn't Reese standing in the apartment, but two burly Latino men in dark baggy clothes, brandishing automatic rifles.

He had only a fraction of a second to take action before the two men opened fire. The balcony offered no protection at all. The tiny table and chair set would do nothing to stop an onslaught of automatic weapons fire, and advancing into the apartment was out of the question. He'd be running into a hail of bullets. His options severely limited, he turned his back on the gunmen, dropped his shoulder and ducked head first over the edge of the balcony. The sound of fully automatic gunfire filled the air even as his feet cleared the railing.

The two men stopped firing a few seconds later and just looked at each other, obviously shocked their target would choose a ten story swan dive over a bullet. One of the men nodded to the other and pointed to the balcony. He wanted his partner to check on the target.

"Really, Holmes?" The second shooter hissed. "Vato just took a header into the parking lot! He's history!"

The first shooter responded by baring his teeth at the smaller man and pointing again to the ledge. He held his finger to his lips. Keep quiet, the obvious signal.

"Really? You're worried about the noise? We just opened up on the whiteboy with ten pounds of lead! The deaf old lady next door just had a heart attack, and you want me to be quiet?"

But the look in the eye of the larger man left no room for debate. With a shake of his head, the smaller man headed for the balcony. He tromped through the broken glass—the remains of the sliding glass door—making no attempt at stealth.

Cyrus was hanging on to the outside of the railing that surrounded the balcony. As he'd thrown himself over the rail, he'd grabbed at the heavy iron balusters, the evenly spaced vertical iron slats between the handrail and the floor of the balcony. His fall had finally been arrested when his slipping grip reached the base of the baluster in each hand. The side of his face, and then his chest, had smashed into the end of the concrete slab that comprised the balcony. It hurt like hell, but it was better than a ten-story fall onto the sandy beach below.

Still, this wasn't a good long-term plan. It had saved him from the initial hail of gunfire, but—

Oh crap!

He looked up to see that one of the wrought iron balusters had broken lose under his weight. It was bending outward as it gave way. If he was lucky, he had a few seconds before it snapped off entirely.

He heard the sound of crunching glass and knew one of the gunmen was coming to confirm his demise. Two men had fired on him, and Reese was nowhere to be seen. That could indicate there was at least one more assailant in the apartment. He would need to make quick work of these two if he was going to get to Reese in time. The failing iron bar in his right hand had given him an idea. He adjusted the grip of his left hand. It would need to support all of his weight. He quickly worked the loose iron bar with his right hand. It snapped free of its corroded old weld.

He freed the bar just in time. As he looked up, one of the gunmen leaned over the railing and glanced down. The man hadn't expected to see Cyrus hanging from the base of the railing. His eyes went wide in surprise. He opened his mouth to say something, but never got the chance. Cyrus swung the iron bar at the man's head with everything he had. The impact sounded like someone had kicked a ripe melon. The man's body instantly sagged as he lost consciousness. Cyrus dropped the iron bar and used the opportunity to reach up and grab him by the collar. With a solid pull, the body came over the rail and plummeted to the sand ten stories below.

One down, one to go. Only Cyrus realized that he had lost the iron bar in the process.

Crap!

So much for stealth. Now he could only hope that the other gunman would come to investigate what had happened to his friend. Cyrus reached into the small of his back and pulled the Springfield from its holster. There, hanging one-handed from a balcony ledge, he contemplated the good practice of keeping a round in the chamber. If he had needed to chamber the first round, he would've been hard pressed to do it with just one hand.

Gnashing his teeth, he couldn't hold on much longer. His left hand was starting to strain. He steadied the 9mm and waited. Sure enough, the second gunman neared the ledge. There was no sneaking up when the floor of the ledge was covered in shattered glass—Cyrus could hear it grinding under the man's shoes as he approached.

Not willing to waste time or give up any small element of surprise, Cyrus used the little strength remaining in his left arm to pull himself up to eye level with the balcony. The gunman was only a step away with his rifle at the ready. It took Cyrus only a fraction of a second to aim and squeeze the trigger. The single shot from his Springfield might as well have been a cannon in the stillness of the night. His ears rang from the discharge. He lowered himself back behind the protection of the ledge just as the gunman collapsed to the floor of the balcony.

Cyrus slipped the gun into the holster behind his back and slapped his right hand around the nearest baluster. He tested this one carefully, ensuring it would carry his weight. The added support of his right hand eased a portion of weight from his aching left arm and shoulder. It felt like heaven. There was no time to waste. Moments later, he had scaled the railing. With relief, his feet once again touched the relative safety of the balcony.

Drawing his gun once again, he ducked to the side of the shattered sliding glass door. He looked over at the body of the second gunman. The man was flat on his back with his head and shoulders inside the apartment, right where he'd landed after being shot. The bullet hole just below the thug's left eye was unmistakable.

Cyrus's mind spun with the implications of what had just happened. He'd left this life behind years ago. He had walked away and made a fresh start. Was this really happening? What had Meade gotten him involved in? But it wasn't entirely unexpected, was it? On some level he'd sensed something was off. He hadn't carried a gun in years. Not until today. And he had already used it.

Dammit!

He heard a loud bang inside the apartment and he peeked around the corner of the shattered door frame. A man had just exited the front door with something over his shoulder. He had only caught a glimpse, but he was pretty sure he'd seen Reese thrown over the man's shoulder. The sound Cyrus heard was the front door opening, slamming back against the wall. He started to round the corner of the door frame when a series of gunshots peppered the wall beside him. He ducked back and heard running footsteps. There was no choice, he had to hazard another look. A second man, armed with an automatic rifle, had just crossed the apartment and was ducking out the front door. He fired several additional shots at Cyrus before slipping out of sight.

Cyrus stepped into the apartment with his gun up and ready. He had to be sure there were no more attackers lying in wait. A quick sweep assured him he was alone. There were two gunmen left, and they had taken Reese. *What the hell is going on?* He'd sort that out after he got her back.

Not entirely sure it was his best plan—but lacking a better one—Cyrus took a deep breath and stepped out into the hallway. His gun was raised and searching for a target but he was alone. The pounding of footsteps echoed up the stairwell as the two gunmen took it downward. They would be heading for the main parking lot. *An open air staircase*, Cyrus thought. Stepping to the outer edge, he could see the parking area, ten floors below. A black van was idling at the nearest edge of the lot, about forty yards out from the base of the building. If the kidnappers got to the van, Reese would disappear.

Cyrus realized he didn't have to beat them to the van, he just needed to close the distance and maintain the element of surprise. Without a moment's hesitation, he kicked off both hiking boots and went charging down the stairs.

While the kidnapers made no end of noise tromping downward at full speed, one of them with an unconscious woman over his shoulder. Cyrus made good time, and silently, reduced to stocking-covered feet for the second time that same night.

Round and round he circled, following the staircase down one story after the next. He was closing the gap, but they had a hell of a head start. His intent was to keep them from reaching the van, and he didn't need to catch them for that.

Reaching the fourth floor, Cyrus abandoned his pursuit. His heart was pounding, and his head was throbbing after bashing it against the concrete balcony. But his hands were steady—that was what mattered. That, and the full moon.

He reached the railing of the open-air staircase and took a steadying breath. The two kidnapers emerged from the base of the stairwell and began their sprint for the waiting van, some forty yards out. One man had his rifle cradled in his hands while the other man, larger in build, had Reese over his shoulder and a handgun in his meaty grip. Both were running with a loping, winded gait.

Cyrus took another steadying breath and bided his time. The big guy was the greater danger. He would start there—take him before the sight picture grew smaller and the distance grew. The further the man got, the greater the chance of hitting Reese. Cyrus raised his weapon and sighted for only a brief second. Then a gentle squeeze of the trigger and an instant response. The large man dropped to the ground like a marionette with its strings cut. Reese spilled to the sandy grass in an unconscious heap.

The second kidnapper spun around at the sound of the gunshot and raised his rifle. He wasn't sure where the shot had come from, but he knew he was in mortal danger. Jinking left and right, he searched for the shooter that had taken his partner. Even in the muted light of the full moon, he couldn't see anything. He looked back at Reese before raising his weapon, obviously understanding she was his only defense against the invisible shooter.

Cyrus couldn't let the kidnaper use her as leverage. Would the man shoot Reese? Did he intend to use her as a human shield? It didn't matter. The man never got the chance to attempt either one. Another round from Cyrus's handgun dropped him where he stood.

A voice called from the idling van and another man stuck his head out the window. He saw the pair of his compatriots lying on the crabgrass, halfway to the van. He grabbed a rifle and stepped from the van to investigate. Cyrus convinced him this was a foolish idea by placing three rounds in the pavement at his feet. The man didn't need any further instruction. He jumped back behind the wheel and tore off into the night.

Cyrus took a few minutes to watch the scene from his perch at the rail of the fourth-floor. No more activity. Approaching sirens could be heard in the distance. Certainly, neighbors had already dialed 911. This would be a hell of a mess to explain. Especially since Cyrus wasn't sure what had happened.

Confident no more dangers were lying in wait, he dashed down the remaining stairs to retrieve Reese. She had taken a minor scrape to the forehead when the kidnapper dropped her. She was fine, though still unconscious. The man who had carried her was another matter. Cyrus's shot had entered the top of his skull and blown out his jaw. It was a grisly mess. Cyrus had aimed high in an effort to keep the shot as far away from Reese as possible.

The second shooter was less gruesome, though the single shot had killed him just as instantly. He'd caught the bullet at the base of the skull, right where SWAT team snipers were taught to target armed hostage takers. Of course, SWAT snipers did it with the benefit of a rifle, a scope, and often a spotter helping to range the target. Making the shot with a handgun was tricky business, and it was why Cyrus hadn't been willing to let either man get closer to the van. The further away they were, the more dangerous the shot would have become.

In less than two minutes Cyrus had inventoried the contents of both men's pockets. They both carried wallets and cell phones. He memorized the details from their driver's licenses and put their wallets back in place. He pulled the batteries from both cell phones and removed their SIM cards. Without wasting a moment, he pulled off both of his socks and proceeded to stuff the disassembled phones into each. Using bare hands, he dug a hole in the sand under the nearby bench. Tucking both socks into the hole, he covered them over. The socks would keep sand out of the phones until he could retrieve them. He didn't need the police recovering their potential treasure-trove of information. Once the phones became evidence, accessing their data would become significantly more complicated.

Finally, Cyrus hefted Reese and carried her to the bench. He laid her down on the wooden surface with her head resting on his leg. He brushed the dark hair away from her face and tried to make her comfortable. She'd be hurting when she woke.

He typed out a short message on his cell phone. Satisfied, he set it aside. All he could do was wait for the police to arrive. It was the fastest way to get medical attention for Reese. Besides, there was no hiding from this mess.

Chapter 11

Santa Barbara, California
Wednesday, 5:33 am (6:33 am Colorado time)

Reese opened her eyes to find an EMT leaning over her. She was laying on a wheeled gurney on the path to the parking lot outside her apartment building. Everything was blurry. A man beside the EMT was talking to her, but she couldn't make out his words. She squinted against the pain in her head and tried to concentrate. After a moment, things came into focus, and the man became coherent.

"Ma'am, I said, are you alright? Can you hear me?"

She nodded and struggled to sit up. Speech was still beyond her grasp. She looked around. The sun had yet to peek over the horizon to the east. She could hear the sounds of the ocean to the west. There were squad cars and rescue vehicles, with lights flashing, scattered across the parking lot. And there were cops. There were cops everywhere.

That's when she saw Cyrus. Two dozen yards up the path, he sat on a park bench with his hands cuffed behind his back. A dour police officer stood on either side of him. What was going on? Why did her head hurt so badly? The last thing she remembered—*Oh no!* The man hiding in her closet! *How had that turned into this?*

A commotion in the direction of the apartment building drew her attention. It was a pair of men in white lab coats wheeling a gurney from the bottom of the stairwell. A black body bag was strapped to the cart. She looked around, scanning the faces in the crowd, as if something she saw might explain what had happened. Her eyes met Cyrus's. He looked exhausted but smiled when he saw her sitting upright. He looked relieved. Deeply relieved, she was sure of it. What the hell had happened?

"Miss Knoland?" a voice from the other direction caught her off guard and gave her a start. She turned to find a tall black man in plain clothes. A detective, she would bet on it. He had that look. The cheap suit, the calming voice. "Miss Knoland, I'm Detective Franklin. Are you up to answering a few questions?"

She only nodded, still unsure of her voice.

"The EMT tells me that you've only just regained consciousness. I don't want to rush you. You've clearly been through a lot. I just need your statement. I'm trying to put together what happened here tonight."

"I—" she cleared her throat. "Excuse me. I'm not sure I'll be much help. The last thing I remember, I was in my apartment. I was changing clothes. We were going out for something to eat."

———

Detective Franklin was a twenty-two year veteran of the Santa Barbara Police Department. A homicide detective for fourteen of those years, he had a no-nonsense approach to the job and was proud of his work.

Flipping a page in his notepad, he prepared to take her statement. This crime scene was a mess. But the way the evidence was shaping up, it might not be a homicide after all. It was starting to look like an attempted kidnapping. He didn't like that. There were four dead bodies, and someone would be called to pay. It didn't matter that those gang-bangers were street trash or that the city was better off without them. There were bodies, and it was his job to get to the bottom of it.

"Were you meeting someone tonight?" he asked in a calm, professional voice. He did his best to start the interview with a clinical detachment. This woman had suffered a trauma. But as of yet, he didn't know if she was a victim or part of the crime.

"Yes—well, no. I'm sorry. I'm still a little scrambled. Cyrus and I had just come back to my apartment. I was changing in the bedroom when something happened." She got a far away look in her eyes as she struggled with a memory that seemed lost in fog. "Someone was hiding in the closet. As soon as I saw him, he jumped out and hit me with something. I—I don't know what it was…"

"Yes, we think he used a stun baton. The EMT found a wound on your side consistent with a high voltage shock. It would've incapacitated you. We found the device among one of the dead men's possessions."

"Dead men?" She looked sincerely stunned. After a moment, she started to speak but stopped short. Rubbing her forehead, she took a moment. She shook her head in frustration, clearly no more able to make any more sense of things than he. "I don't understand. What happened here?"

"That's what I'm trying to determine, ma'am." He looked around the crime scene trying to decide on his next line of questioning. "Ma'am, could you tell me about Cyrus Cooper?"

She nodded. "Cyrus is a friend. We met up earlier tonight. We were just making a quick stop here before going out for a bite. The man in my closet—did he hurt Cyrus?"

"Hurt him?" Franklin lowered his notebook and nearly laughed. "No, he didn't hurt Cyrus. But I think a couple of his friends gave it a shot. The good news is that Cyrus is fine. The bad news is that I have four dead gang-bangers and *a whole lot* of questions."

Reese looked confused by the explanation, but she didn't ask for clarification. She shook her head as if the confusion hurt physically. Based on the EMT's report, he was sure that it did.

"Look, Detective?" she said finally. "I think there's a good chance that even the medic knows more than me about what happened here tonight. Could you stop skirting around the issue, and tell me what's going on?"

Franklin ground his teeth. He looked around. What had happened? As much as it galled him, everything about Mister Cooper's story had checked out. The deadbolt on the front door showed signs of tampering. The perp who picked it must've had just enough skills to pop the lock but not enough to do it without making a mess of the lock's finish. Crime scene techs had found a mess inside the apartment, indicating several assailants had laid in wait for an indeterminate amount of time— at least several hours. They had either raided the victim's junk food stash or brought a copious supply of their own.

Franklin had interviewed the two neighbors who called 911 following the outbreak of gunfire. One of them reported seeing two of the deceased wandering the halls of the tenth floor around noon the previous day. Brawny Hispanics were not common to the neighborhood, so they had stood out.

Then there was the evidence that bothered him most of all. Crime scene tech and medical examiner's preliminary findings corroborated Cooper's story. A body found on the beach beneath the balcony had its head smashed in, and the corpse in the apartment had suffered a single gunshot at close range. The ME concluded that the shot had been fired from an extreme low angle, consistent with the shooter hanging from the balcony edge. Gunshot residue was swabbed from the edge of the concrete near the broken rung of the railing. Unless the crime scene techs came up with something inconsistent with Cooper's story, these two deaths were a clear case of self-defense.

The other two shootings were even more troubling. Cooper's statement indicated he had pursued the remaining two gunmen in an effort to retrieve Miss Knoland. Who did something like that? He had just narrowly escaped his own death when two men opened fire on him with automatic weapons. To avoid being shot, Cooper had jumped over the railing of a tenth floor balcony. And he still managed to take out the two men attempting to kill him without falling to his death? And after all that—after climbing back to safety—he didn't stop to dial 911. He'd gone after the pair of remaining armed kidnappers instead.

No. There was no question. Mister Cooper was not who he claimed. An investigative journalist from Chicago wouldn't react to a situation like this. But a professional operator would. That would make him military? Maybe NSA? Hell, he could be a private contractor. If that was the case, Franklin would grind him under his boot like a bug. He didn't like the idea of anyone running around his city and shooting it up.

Franklin set that line of thought aside. What did he know? Cooper had the presence of mind to lose his shoes before pursuing the kidnapers down the stairwell. They'd found his shoes outside the apartment on the tenth floor. That meant he was sharp. He could chase down the kidnappers without giving up the element of surprise. But if Cooper's story was to be believed, the two fleeing men had a head start, and he'd had little hope of catching up. To that end, Cooper had given up his chase when he reached the fourth floor. He'd fired two shots, killing both men as they ran the forty yard stretch between the apartment building and the getaway van parked in the lot.

Really?

It was hard to believe. Two men running away, and at a distance—with a handgun! That only worked in the movies. Normal people simply didn't make a shot like that. Franklin thought he might be able to, if he dumped the entire contents of his magazine down on the men. But the evidence confirmed that Cooper's gun was missing a total of six rounds. *Six rounds?* Three of those slugs were lodged in the asphalt of the parking lot, further confirming Cyrus's claim that he fired on the van's driver to scare him off. That meant the two previous shots were kill shots, and they likely indicated the young man could've taken out the driver of the van had he wanted. The SWAT team boys could shoot like that. But they had rifles. And scopes! And spotters to help range targets! He would have to talk with some of them when he got back to the precinct. He wanted to know what kind of skill was required to make a shot like that. And Cooper had taken the shot at one of the men while he ran with the girl slung over his shoulder.

Was Cooper that good, or that reckless?

Franklin ground his teeth once more and thought about the pair of shoes lying at the top of the stairs. It galled him to admit it, but he was going with skill rather than luck. The man was intelligent and skilled.

The question remained, was this a homicide or an attempted kidnapping? And as much as he wanted to know who the hell Cooper was, the more pertinent question was, what was Miss Knoland's role in this? The evidence indicated that she'd been the intended kidnapping victim. But why?

Still, he could understand her need for answers. The entire series of events was a blank spot in her memory. He went on to explain to her, in general terms, how they had concluded that the four armed men had lain in wait for her to return to the apartment. Their apparent objective had been to abduct her. He provided the broad strokes of what Cyrus had gone through in being attacked on her balcony, killing the two men, and then pursuing her kidnappers. He explained that Cyrus had shot the two men dead not far from where she now sat.

With each addition to the story, Miss Knoland's face grew more ashen. As much as Franklin hated to admit it, the idea that someone wanted to abduct her seemed genuinely shocking. If there were answers to be found, they would come from digging into her past, her financial records, and her known associates.

––––––––––

Franklin told Reese he had all he needed from her for the moment. He warned that he would be in touch. More questions were sure to follow. She nodded and thanked him. She thanked the EMT and slid cautiously off the gurney. Then she walked over to Cyrus on rubbery legs. The officers on either side of Cyrus watched her with apprehension but said nothing. A glance was exchanged between the two men before they widened their cordon and allowed her a seat on the bench.

"It's looking like dinner and a drink is turning into breakfast," she said, giving Cyrus a weary smile. She put her hand on his knee. "Are you okay?"

He returned her smile. "I say we skip breakfast and just go for a drink."

Something had changed between them. The awkward 'just having met' or 'getting to know you' stage was subverted by the shared experience. She still wasn't sure what had happened, but she did know one thing. If it weren't for Cyrus, she would be in a world of trouble right now.

Cyrus felt Reese lean against him. Even sitting on the bench with his hands cuffed behind his back, her touch sent a warm rush through his body. It was just what he needed. He was tired. He was banged up. And most of all, he was about to get crabby about the handcuffs. He wasn't sure what Detective Franklin's issue was, but the man seemed to be in a foul mood.

"Can I ask you a personal question?" Reese was whispering from where she leaned closely beside him. She didn't look at him. Her tone was serious.

He was afraid it was going to be the question that he'd been asked before. She would want to know how he felt about killing those men. It was a horrible question. The question ate at him. Not because he felt guilt over what he'd done. Just the opposite. If he was justified in his actions, there was no guilt. He had a clear conscience. No remorse. That was the part that actually bothered him. Somehow it seemed wrong to be ambivalent. Plus, dammit, this was supposed to be behind him. That's what hurt. How could he explain these things to her when he couldn't understand them himself?

He needn't have bothered. "You lost your shoes again?" she asked finally. "Is this going to be an ongoing issue with you?"

He couldn't help it. He laughed. He laughed out loud. It was unusual for him, and it felt good. Wiggling his toes down in the cold sand, he shook his head. There was something special about this woman.

Cyrus saw a black town car slalom slowly through the parking lot and approach the perimeter defined by police cars. It was a nondescript sedan that had no special markings or plates, but something about it called out to him. When the driver and the passenger stepped from the vehicle at the same time, he knew what it was that had drawn his attention. These people tried so hard to be nondescript that they were actually rather overt. They'd never learn. Even the way they dressed screamed federal. Both men wore crisp dark suits. The passenger scanned the gathered personnel and quickly identified Franklin without hesitation. That stood to reason. They were briefed on things like this before reaching a crime scene. The chip on Franklin's shoulder was about to grow by two sizes.

The two suited, government men approached Franklin. While Cyrus couldn't hear what was said, he knew what was being expressed. He could tell by the indignation on Franklin's face. The three men conversed for several minutes, Franklin doing all the listening. Every word his spoke seemed to come through clamped teeth. Finally, one of the suited men nodded to

Franklin. The conversation was over. The two suits turned and headed back to their car.

When Franklin stepped in front of Cyrus, it was clear he was trying to be intimidating. Cyrus wasn't startled. He didn't care. He knew Franklin had his marching orders. This was confirmed when Franklin dismissed the two officers standing sentry. The shifting personnel stirred Reese. She had fallen asleep against Cyrus's shoulder.

"I don't know who you are," Franklin growled as he released Cyrus from the handcuffs. "And I don't know who you know—but this isn't over. This is my case. And if I find evidence that this didn't go *exactly* the way you claim, I'll have you back here so fast it'll make your head spin!"

"Fair enough, Detective." Cyrus said quietly. He gave the man a tip of his imaginary hat before he and Reese headed back up to her apartment. It was a crime scene now. She would gather a few things and clear out until the police were done and the landlord had a chance to patch the place back together.

It had been a hell of a long night, and Reese couldn't remember an important part of it. That didn't sit well with her. Nor did the fact that someone had tried to kidnap her. She could only assume that someone was targeting the project, through her. But it was hard to believe that the secret had gotten out. And, if the detective was right, gang members had tried to kidnap her. That didn't track at all.

Cyrus hit the call button on the elevator. "You have a car, right?" he asked.

"Of course, why?"

"Because we can't use your platform to go back to the office now. We'll have to do it the old fashioned way." He grinned. "You still remember how to drive there, don't you?"

She laughed. Was it really that easy for him to make jokes after all that had happened? Had he really just fought for his life against four armed men and survived? Is this what Walter was referring to when he'd talked about Cyrus Cooper's unique skills?

"We need to call your team in for a conference as soon as possible," Cyrus explained as they stepped into the elevator. "Someone was targeting you. They could be targeting the rest of the Meridian team as well."

"You just read my mind." She was already tapping on her cell phone. It took only a moment to send a message to the entire team. It was an emergency code, another one of Walter Meade's protocols. This one would immediately direct everyone to a fallback location for an emergency meeting.

Suddenly Walter's paranoid plans weren't so paranoid after all.

Chapter 12

Payton Street, Santa Barbara, California
Wednesday, 8:12 am (9:12 am Colorado Time)

Reese had sent a coded message to every member of the project. According to the protocol, they were to drop everything and meet at a pre-determined location, some distance down the coast. Per the procedure, each member of the team had texted back an acknowledgment. But there was one exception. Alfie Ahmed, a lab technician, hadn't responded and he couldn't be reached on his mobile. After Reese was attacked at her apartment, Cyrus admitted concern. They needed to get the entire team into protective custody as quickly as possible. He suggested they visit Ahmed's home to investigate.

Cyrus turned Reese's black VW Jetta onto Payton Street, located on the outskirts of Santa Barbara. The car rolled slowly past the evenly spaced, single-family homes. Reese pointed out Ahmed's residence when she located the correct house number. She explained that she'd never been there, but was pretty sure Ahmed lived alone. A small blue Toyota pickup was parked in the driveway. Rather than pull in behind it, Cyrus continued to drive past. He didn't say anything, but she could tell his eyes were probing the neighborhood for anything out of the ordinary. Nothing must've stood out, because he seemed satisfied.

Cyrus turned the corner and circled the block. When they made it back to Ahmed's street, he pulled the car to the curb a half dozen houses before reaching Ahmed's driveway. He turned the engine off and dropped the keys into his jacket pocket.

Before their trip to check on Ahmed, they'd driven back to the office and used the platform to return to his house in Colorado. Cyrus had reloaded his gun and grabbed a couple of additional magazines. He had explained that meeting with Walter's team was turning out to be much more complicated than anticipated. It was pure chance that he was even armed the night before. He wouldn't rely on luck again. He'd also taken a lightweight jacket, explaining that, while it would be uncomfortably warm in the California sun come mid-day, the jacket would hide his gun. It wasn't lost on her that such thinking seemed second nature.

She walked silently up the street at his side. They had no idea what they might be walking into, but it didn't seem to slow him down.

As they approached Ahmed's home, Cyrus's eyes scanned the surrounding area for signs of observation or ambush. They passed a few cars parked along the street. Each of the cars had dew on its roof and windows, a clear sign that they'd been stationary throughout the night. The morning sun was not yet in a position to burn away the moisture. She could tell Cyrus was eyeing the passenger compartments of each car as they went, but if she weren't watching his mannerisms closely, she would've missed his attention. It was striking how he could appear so at ease while remaining so on edge.

He stopped. She realized he was looking at three cigarette butts lying spent and extinguished in the street. He only gave them a moment's consideration before moving on. She wanted to ask what he was thinking, but they were approaching Ahmed's yard and the opportunity was lost.

Without pause, Cyrus stepped off the sidewalk and into Ahmed's front lawn. As he went, he snatched up the morning newspaper from where it lay, having been delivered before dawn. He pulled the paper from its plastic bag, wadded the bag up, and stuffed it in his back pocket. Without missing a stride, they mounted the short set of stairs leading to the front door.

Very briefly, Cyrus showed Reese where to stand, just off to the side of the door's frame. Casual and unassuming, but out of the line of fire in the event someone started shooting from the other side of the door. He quickly pulled his gun and slid it under the folded morning paper.

It was staggering how matter-of-factly he'd facilitated all of this. It hadn't required any planning on his part. He just knew what to do.

———

Cyrus pressed the doorbell button and double checked Reese's position. She was at the corner of the door. It was the best possible position, should someone opened fire from the other side. It seemed unlikely, but he'd seen it happen. They heard the bell ring on the opposite side of the door, but they couldn't hear anything more. Just when he was about to ring the bell for a second time, approaching footsteps became audible.

The door opened, and a small, dark skinned man stood before them. He was dressed in pajama pants, a wrinkled white t-shirt, and a pair of crooked glasses. "Alfie!" Reese exclaimed, putting Cyrus at easy. "Are you alright?"

Glancing over his shoulder, Cyrus double-checked the street. They were still clear.

"Of course, I'm alright. Why wouldn't I be?" Alfie Ahmed spoke with a mild British accent. He was a slight man, no more than 5' 9" at most, and maybe 130 pounds, if Cyrus was generous. The man had tangled, dark, curly hair and olive skin.

"You haven't answered your mobile," Reese explained. "I sent an emergency message this morning. You're the only one who didn't respond."

Ahmed looked at Cyrus as if noticing him for the first time. He patted the pockets of his robe as he searched for his phone. "Let me find it. Please, come in."

Cyrus cast a weary eye into the dimly lit interior of the single story house. All the shades must've been drawn. It was dark, given the time of day. He stepped through the door first with his gun leveled beneath the fold of the newspaper. Reese cast him an apprising glance, but said nothing. She followed him through the door.

Cyrus had been correct. Throughout the house, blinds were drawn. The house consisted of an open floor plan, so the entryway, kitchen, living room, and small dining room were all visible from where he stood. He could hear Ahmed muttering to himself as he moved from room to room in the back of the house, presumably looking for his phone.

Other than the shades being drawn, there was nothing unusual or off-putting. The furnishings were sparse. The living room had only a large ratty couch and a threadbare La-Z-Boy recliner. Both were parked before a massive flat-screen television. The television had no receiver or DVD player. Only an Xbox One game console. Judging by the array of snack food wrappers spread between the couch and the TV, Ahmed had recently been on a gaming binge. It would explain the drawn shades and his somewhat nonplused manner. He had likely been up all night.

Ahmed returned from the back bedroom holding up his smartphone. "Battery's dead. I'm sorry to put you through the trouble of coming out here." He thought for a moment, as if hearing what Reese said for the first time. "You said there is an emergency?"

"Yes! Please get dressed," she said with some impatience. "Something's happened. I'll fill you in when we meet with the rest of the group."

"I don't understand." He looked at Cyrus suspiciously. "Who is this?"

"Later! Get dressed! We have to go. The others will be waiting, and we don't have time to waste."

"Please, calm down. I'll just change my clothes. Why are you acting like this? We can be back in the office in seconds!"

Reese took a deep breath and tried to calm herself. Cyrus could tell that the thought of her team being in danger had started to erode her patience. "I'm sorry, Alfie. You didn't get my text. I sent a code 1412. We won't be using the platforms. We're meeting at a fallback location, and we must get there quickly."

Judging by the mention of the code 1412 and the wrinkles it produced on Ahmed's forehead, the man finally had a glimpse of the situation's gravity.

"What's happened? *And who is this man?*"

Reese only responded by glaring at the young man. The wrinkles returned to his forehead. Finally, he turned and hurried down the hall. Clearly Reese was accustomed to dealing with such idiosyncrasies.

"He's a good lab tech," she said to Cyrus, as if reading his mind. "He's just young. And now I think he's more than a little frightened."

"What exactly does a code 1412 entail?" He tossed the newspaper on the kitchen counter and holstered his gun.

"Professor Meade had an entire binder full of these codes. He required the team to memorize them. Some of the information was rather verbose. But the gist of 1412 was to drop what you're doing and get your ass to a specific, secure location. In this case, it's a building to the south, along the coast. We can't tell anyone where we're going, and we don't bring anyone or anything with us. We just drop everything and go. Until now, I had no idea why he'd devised such severe contingencies."

Cyrus understood why. He also knew that the fallback location would be someplace safe that had no ties to the project or any of its members. It would be a safe house that Meade set up long ago. Such procedures were not uncommon in espionage circles. And from what Cyrus was learning about this project, Meade had more than a little cause to be paranoid.

Ahmed returned wearing a fresh set of clothes. His hair was still disheveled. At least he finally understood the urgency of the situation. They all filed out the front door, Ahmed locking it behind them.

Reese told Ahmed they were parked further up the street and instructed him to meet them at the fallback location. Cyrus and Reese crossed the yard and started up the street, while Ahmed headed for his truck.

When Cyrus reached the spot at the curb with the three extinguished cigarette butts, he stopped cold. He turned around and watched Ahmed step up to the side of his truck. The man tapped the button on his key fob and the car alarm chirped as it disarmed.

"Whoa!" Cyrus bellowed and started running toward Alfie Ahmed. "Alfie! Don't touch the truck!"

Though Ahmed looked up at Cyrus with a slack-jawed expression, at least he stopped short of grabbing the door handle. As Cyrus came around the truck, Ahmed seemed to realize something was wrong. He stepped away from the vehicle with a confused expression on his face.

Reese rounded the truck as Cyrus started making a circuit of the vehicle, looking carefully through each of the windows. "What do you see?" she asked.

"Nothing yet. It's just a bad feeling." He had completed a trip around the truck but found nothing out of the ordinary. Ahmed was standing about ten feet away, watching the exercise with an expression one might have after finding a dead bug in their salad.

Cyrus slid out of his jacket and pulled his gun, holster and all, from the back of his waistband. He wrapped the gun in the jacket and handed it to Reese. At the sight of the gun, Ahmed's expression became more extreme. Cyrus ignored him. He didn't have time to coddle the kid. Alfie did seem a rather dramatic lilting flower. *Thank God, Reese has more fortitude.* She was holding up remarkably well, given the strain of the circumstances.

Dropping to the ground and rolling onto his back, Cyrus slid under the front of the Toyota. It was dark. He pulled out his phone and launched the flashlight app. It wasn't as good as a real flashlight, but it brought the vehicle's undercarriage into crisp detail. Moving slowly around the underbody, he found the leads snaking up to the battery. While the underbody was filthy with dirt and grime, two clean wires were spliced into the truck's electrical system. It was not a good sign.

He followed the new wires back toward the passenger compartment, where he found what he feared. A rather sizable wad of plastic explosive was jammed up between the firewall and the engine block. The wires led right to the bomb's ignition cap.

Shit.

This meant Reese wasn't the only target. The rest of the team was in danger as well.

Cyrus reached up and carefully removed the pencil-like, short, metal stub that was stuck into the plastic explosive. That was the detonator. He took care not to touch the metal with his fingers. Not because it could cause detonation, but because there was a chance of pulling fingerprints from it. Once the detonator was out, he jerked the wires free of the splice that linked them to the electrical system. The bomb now disarmed, he reached up and pulled the wad of explosive free from the frame of the vehicle and crawled out from under the truck.

Cyrus held up the explosive in one hand and the wire and detonator in the other. Reese's eyes went wide. The little bit of pink to her normally pale complexion drained away. Ahmed faired less gracefully. He looked like he was going to be sick. It took only seconds for his face to transition to a horrible gray pallor. His eyes were wide, and he'd lost the ability to blink. He dropped to his knees and wretched into the grass.

Reese finally found her voice. "Is that what I think it is?"

Cyrus only nodded. He was holding the wad of plastic explosive up in the sunshine. It was a malformed wad. Once in the shape of a block, someone had squished it into a misshapen mound to better stick to the truck's undercarriage. And, as he'd hoped, there were fingerprints evident in the surface of the pliable clay material. It was odd that they were dealing with someone with the skills to set a bomb but not intelligent enough to avoid leaving trace evidence behind. It wasn't very professional. That was the part that confused him most. Maybe it would make more sense once the fingerprints were run.

But first things first. They needed to meet with the rest of the team and get everyone into protective custody. Cyrus looked at Ahmed who was still horking in the grass. The guy was on his hands and knees, trembling.

"Maybe you better ride with us, Alfie," Cyrus suggested. "Come on. We'll get you something to drink on the way. Maybe some breath mints, too." After the words came out, he realized they were his first to the kid since they met. Until now Reese had done the talking. He decided that the words could be construed as insensitive. It was not what he'd intended. "It's okay, Alfie. The first time someone tries to blow you up is the hardest." He waited a beat. "It gets easier."

Alfie stopped where he was, on his hands and knees in the grass. He sat back on his haunches and looked at Cyrus. His expression read as if he were trying to decide whether Cyrus was from another planet or not. Then, after several long beats, Alfie's face turned into a small smile for the first time. The small smile spread into a broad grin, as the absurdity of the situation and Cyrus's comment sank in. "Maybe some gum would be good," was all he managed to say. But he climbed wearily to his feet and followed Cyrus and Reese back to their car.

Chapter 13

Payton Street, Santa Barbara, California
Wednesday, 8:08 am (9:08 am Colorado Time)

One of the operatives walked across the kitchen and poured a cup of coffee. He looked at Dargo and raised the pot, in question. Dargo simply shook his head and glanced down at his half-empty styrofoam cup. Surveillance locations changed, it was the shitty coffee that remained constant. It didn't matter what continent or what country, the coffee was always terrible. He wondered how many cups of the swill he'd swallowed over the decades. As the younger operative walked back across the room and sat down at the surveillance station, Dargo wondered how many similar young soldiers he'd worked with in that same time. It was not lost on him that there were few he encountered on follow-up missions. This was not a profession that allowed many to grow to old age.

At the age of fifty-eight, in this game, Dargo was considered an old man. These days he felt it, too. Though, to be fair, it wasn't the years so much as the mileage. But for his part, Dargo had suffered the mileage far better than most. He was still strong and healthy. He still towered over many of the younger men he commanded. Six foot six, he still tipped the scales at two-twenty. And while youth was a valued resource when recruiting foot soldiers, his services had only come into greater demand as of late. Soldiers were in ready supply. Experienced operators—men who knew the right and wrong times to pull the trigger—were in increasingly short supply.

All the same, Dargo sensed his time in the game was running short. His enthusiasm for the profession was not what it had once been. But, if he were honest with himself, that was only part of his malaise. Sure, these thoughts had been on his mind for some time. But last night's revelation that Cyrus Cooper was part of his current mission had put things into a new perspective. He wasn't sure how he felt about the kid's involvement. He still couldn't decide whether he wanted to crush the kid's windpipe or warn him of the impending danger. Complex feelings had never been a part of the job, and Dargo felt equally compelled toward both options.

"Sir," a voice called in Russian from across the room. "I have something. A black Volkswagen Jetta initially made a slow pass of the target. It has since circled back and parked forty meters west of our location."

Dargo tapped a series of keys on his laptop and brought up one of the external cameras mounted on their house's exterior. His team had secured a home across the street and two homes east of Alfie Ahmed. Ahmed was the only remaining member of the Meridian team. The rest had fallen off the face of the planet. Surely they had gone to ground. But why not Ahmed?

Dargo's technical team had wired up the exterior of their house with a number of hidden high-resolution cameras. They had an unimpeded view of the front of Ahmed's home as well as the street and sidewalks leading to it from both directions.

Last night, the team surveilling Reese Knoland's apartment had contacted Dargo to report an abrupt outbreak of gunfire on the same floor as her apartment. Soon after, the team had piped over a live video feed displaying the events as they unfolded. Cameras hidden in the hallway and stairwell outside the apartment had told much of the story. But Dargo had opted not to place surveillance gear inside the apartment, due to the increased risk of discovery. He had watched in fascination as two Hispanic men tried to abduct Miss Knoland from her home. It came as no surprise when Cyrus gave chase and shot both of the fleeing men dead before recovering Miss Knoland. What had surprised him was the follow-up report from his team. It turned out that prior to recovering Miss Knoland, Cyrus had apparently been attacked by two more men with automatic rifles. Somehow the young man had managed to throw one of the men from the tenth floor balcony and shoot the other in the head.

If Dargo's information was to be believed, Cyrus had been out of the game for a number of years. The young man had walked away from the Coalition following Dargo's last encounter with him. That resignation was a crucial deciding factor for Dargo. The resignation was proof that Cyrus found the collateral damage of that mission unacceptable, and it was the only reason Dargo had chosen not to hunt Cyrus down and kill him for all that had happened.

But if Cyrus Cooper was back in the game, it meant one of two things. Either Dargo had been fooled by his supposed resignation, or Cyrus was sincere in his disillusionment and had somehow been forced back into the fold. And if Cyrus was sincere, it meant there was something more going on than Dargo had been led to believe.

Putting his personal concerns aside, Dargo knew he faced a still greater paradox. The live video feed his men had sent of Cyrus's fight with the Hispanic gunman had followed his own sighting of Cyrus in Meade's office building by only minutes. That Cyrus had managed to exit the office unobserved was troubling. But that he'd managed to cross the city in a matter of minutes was simply unexplainable.

"Sir, I have confirmation," the technical operative reported, pulling Dargo from his dilemma. "Cyrus Cooper and Reese Knoland have just arrived on scene."

Dargo tapped a series of commands into his computer and adjusted the camera view while he watched Cyrus and Reese approach the front of Alfie Ahmed's home. Dargo had considered further surveillance on Ahmed to be his last chance to leverage a situation that was slipping from his grasp. The rest of Professor Meade's research team had suddenly gone to ground, following the attack on Reese Knoland. Impressively, there had been no hint of an alarm being raised. Ahmed was the only member of the team who failed to go into hiding. So Dargo had gone to the surveillance post to monitor the situation personally.

The circumstances had escalated even before he arrived on site. Dargo had still been in transit when the head of the field team contacted him reporting that a pair of Hispanic men had arrived and conducted a sloppy recon of the street. Shortly after, one of the men had crawled under the Toyota pickup truck parked in Ahmed's driveway and secured some sort of device to the undercarriage. They then departed minutes later.

When Dargo arrived on station, he took a look under the Toyota. It was a gamble, but a calculated one. He risked exposing his operation by approaching the pickup truck, but he needed to understand what the Hispanic men were doing. Had they attached surveillance gear to the truck? If so, why weren't Dargo's techs able to piggy-back the signal coming from the device? It turned out not to be a tracking device but a plug of plastic explosive that was left behind. All in all, a rather sloppy job, at that.

All said, Dargo had been observing the research team for several weeks. In that time he had come to the conclusion that Ahmed was not a key member of the team. As such, he decided to leave the explosives in play and see how events transpired. First, the attempted abduction of Miss Knoland, and then a car bomb targeting Alfie Ahmed? Something could be learned no matter how things unfolded.

And now Cyrus was here.

By way of the concealed surveillance cameras, Dargo and his tech watched as Cyrus and Reese entered the home of Alfie Ahmed. As soon as they passed through the door, the tech switched to a laser microphone that, when pointed at a window, would pick up the vibrations of the glass surface and convert them into sound. It made for the perfect long-range wireless bug.

Dargo listened to the conversation inside the house, across the street, in such crystal clear fidelity that he might have been sitting in the room with the participants. He listened as Miss Knoland chastised Ahmed for not responding to the scramble code she had sent. That explained why everyone had disappeared so abruptly. Professor Meade had prepared for such a situation. The old man was craftier than Dargo had been led to believe. Radioing the rest of surveillance team, Dargo made sure they were ready to deploy. He had put them on standby prior to his arrival the night before. If Ahmed left, he wanted the man followed. He initially hoped the young lab tech would lead him to the rest of the Meridian team. That was, until Dargo discovered the bomb rigged under the truck. It would've negated his ability to track Ahmed, but he had still hoped to come up with a lead. Waiting to see who arrived to investigate the explosion would prove useful. It might still lead him to the research team. All the same, now he was fortunate enough to have a full compliment of surveillance personnel and vehicles standing by. If Cyrus was on site, Dargo knew his team could track him. Cyrus would personally lead him to the rest of the team.

As Dargo watched, Cyrus, Reese, and Ahmed left the house. Dargo was concerned to see Cyrus head for his own car up the street while Ahmed made his way to the Toyota in the driveway. Now Dargo wished he'd removed the explosive. Ahmed's death would only complicate matters.

But at the last moment, Dargo watched as Cyrus stopped and turned back to the truck. He called out to Ahmed before sprinting toward the man. Cyrus suspected something was wrong with the truck! But why? What had he seen? Dargo watched in fascination, as Cyrus circled the vehicle before finally crawling underneath. Moments later he emerged holding the disassembled explosive device.

Dargo was speechless. He had no idea how Cyrus had concluded that the truck was rigged, but he watched in amusement as Ahmed spilled the contents of his stomach in the grass. The realization that someone wanted you dead could be jarring. Finally the three targets made their way up the street to Cyrus's car. Dargo radioed the first follow car to ensure it was in position. It was overkill, but he had nearly a dozen backup vehicles ready to swap in and pick up the trail. He would have to move them around more aggressively now. Cyrus would most certainly be on alert after finding the explosives.

Chapter 14

Santa Barbara, California
Wednesday, 8:33 am (9:33 am Colorado Time)

The rendezvous with the research team was delayed.

Shortly after leaving Alfie Ahmed's home, Cyrus noticed a white Toyota Corolla in the rearview mirror. The car had done nothing suspicious other than follow them through several random turns. Then, as quickly as it appeared, the Toyota was gone. To an untrained eye, it would've meant nothing. Such was the nature of the nondescript car and its brief time in pursuit. But Cyrus knew differently. Shortly after it disappeared, he picked up a black Caprice. The Caprice followed them for several miles and a number of inconspicuous but indiscriminate turns. Identifying a tail was the goal of Cyrus's haphazard course. The trick was to drive normal while plotting an unpredictable course; at the worst, his driving pattern would indicate he was a bit lost. If a vehicle stood out in the rear view, it meant there was a tail.

In tradecraft, this was known as a surveillance detection route (SDR). A good tail was hard to spot. The tail he'd picked up was proving to be exceptional. He knew they were there,

158

because as soon as he'd picked out a follow car, it quickly fell away and was replaced by an alternate vehicle. New and constantly changing follow cars were very difficult to identify. The efficiency and dexterity of the constant rotation provided him a number of key pieces of information. First, he wasn't being tracked by an individual—he was being stalked by a team. Second, the team was extremely professional. The follow cars had drivers proficient at blending in. Lastly, it meant that the team had resources. Normal follow teams would drive a considerable distance before trading one tail for the next because the number of vehicles was finite. This team had a rich roster of experienced drivers. The cars kept changing, and they were always unique.

But the team conducting surveillance was also at a disadvantage. Every change of the follow car required the carefully orchestrated handoff of the target. It was crucial to prevent drawing undo attention during the handoff, but it was also essential not to lose it in the process. With all of this in mind, handoffs were never conducted more frequently than absolutely required.

The tail on Cyrus was passing him off like a hot potato. They were aware of his skills in counter surveillance. The observation raised more questions and provided no answers. Logic dictated that Cyrus had picked up the tail upon leaving Ahmed's house. Even though he had detected no surveillance of the house, it was entirely possible that something had gone unnoticed. Especially if these guys were as skilled as they now appeared. But why have all of these resources tied up watching Ahmed's home after they had already planted a bomb in his truck? Fine, leave one observer behind to ensure that the bomb went off, but the tail that he had now indicated that an entire team had been lying in wait. He could've picked up the tail prior to his arrival at Ahmed's home, but he felt certain it would've caught his eye earlier in the morning. He was confident in ruling that out. All of this led to a growing suspicion that two parties were interested in Alfie Ahmed—one that planted the bomb and a second that was content to sit back and surveil the events as they transpired. But as much as the evidence pointed toward this new conclusion, why would someone go through the trouble of surveilling Ahmed while still doing nothing to prevent his murder? The contingent of follow cars might be a clue. Either the surveillance team was there to watch Ahmed, or they were there to track whoever showed up to visit the man.

With questions stacking up and no answers to be had, Cyrus decided to continue as planned. It seemed more critical than ever to get the research team off the streets and stashed some place safe. It took longer than expected, but he eventually eluded the tail. In the end it had been victory through attrition. He kept driving until they either ran out of cars or suffered a breakdown in organization. Whichever it was, he finally evaded his pursuers, and he did it without providing any overt signs that he knew he was being followed. It wasn't nearly as dramatic as it was in the movies, but it was effective.

Chapter 15

Faria Road, Ventura, California
Wednesday, 11:55 am (12:55 pm Colorado Time)

It should've been a straight shot south down the 101. Given the skill of the team tailing them, it was well over an hour before they saw the last signs of the surveillance team. Sooner or later even the most skillful tail would succumb to the rigors of city driving. All the same, Cyrus ran another full hour of SDRs before finally feeling confident they were finally alone. Only then did he point the car south to complete the original 30-minute drive.

Most of the drive was along the western coast of California. They were almost always within sight of the ocean to the south and west while it was mountainous terrain to the north and east. The fallback location was a second-story set of small offices over a large woodworking shop, just off the craggy coastline.

As he had done before, Cyrus had driven the Jetta past the address once to get a lay of the land. As they passed, Reese identified several team vehicles parked in a lot beside the woodworking shop. The street had almost no traffic and nothing appeared out of place. Cyrus turned the car around a mile down the road and doubled back.

Reese was nervous. Her apprehension had grown since the discovery of the explosive in Alfie's truck. The lengthy drive only served to intensify her anxiety. The realization that they were being stalked hadn't helped either. For some reason, the threat to her team resonated with her in a way that the threat to her own safety had not. That was curious, she decided. Was that a healthy reaction to the situation? The logical side of her mind struggled for control, suggesting there was no such thing as a healthy reaction to these circumstances.

As Cyrus swung the car into the parking lot, Reese considered how best to address the team. Walter was gone. He'd been a natural lead, quick to earn the respect of everyone on the team. She had kept things operational since his passing, but had never been assertive when it came to taking a leadership role. That would have to change. Walter had intended for her and Cyrus to continue the project after his passing. The problem was, she didn't have a clue where to begin. They were under attack and she was out of her depth.

Cyrus stopped her at the door to the stairwell leading to the upstairs offices. "Could you go up and get everyone settled? I need to make a call." He thought for a moment. "They'll be spooked by your emergency transmission. Try to get everyone pacified. I'm afraid my being here will only further raise their hackles."

"You think you know how they're going to react?" She didn't think he was wrong, but she wanted to understand the logic that brought him to this conclusion.

Cyrus nodded. There was a sparkle in his eyes, something tangle hinting at what she suspected to be a guarded level of intelligence. He was still thinking, contemplating the situation. For whatever reason, he seemed to downplay his own talents— and not for the first time. "I figure the team is a bunch of civilians, and a group of academics at that. Likely accustomed to a certain routine, a certain way of doing things. Each one of them agreed to Professor Meade's protocols when they signed on, but I'd bet none of them expected a situation like this. Right now, they're probably up there climbing the walls and wanting to know what's happened—what's really going on. They'll be scared."

He stopped a moment. She could tell he wasn't through with the thought, but he was trying to decide whether it was better to leave it at that. "Scared people have a tendency to do very foolish things," he continued. "That's why Meade had this isolation protocol ready. It's a good plan. If worse comes to worst, you put everyone in one spot and deal with them as a group. There's less of a danger to the project if they're contained. Maybe more importantly, they're less of a danger to themselves."

Taking all of that in, Reese wasn't sure how to respond. Maybe she should've just let him keep his thoughts to himself. He had a pessimistic way of looking at the situation, and at a group of people he didn't know personally. There would certainly be people prone to reacting poorly in a situation like this, but her team was a group of well-educated, extremely intelligent individuals. Walter had chosen each because they were the best in their fields.

For lack of a better response, she chose no response. But for the first time since their meeting, she found herself reluctant to look Cyrus in the eye. Instead, she simply turned and started slowly up the staircase.

Cyrus watched Reese walk away. The was no question that his analysis had not met with her approval. She thought he was being close-minded and dismissive. He took a deep breath and pulled out his cell phone. While he was sure that Meade's well-designed protocol included a plan for sequestering the development team while the threat was investigated, he couldn't be sure that the plan itself had not already been subverted. With Meade gone, there was no way to be sure. The only way to ensure safety and secrecy was to break with the current protocol. He would come up with a plan of his own.

For that he would need help.

By the time Reese reached the doorway at the top of the staircase, she could already hear raised voices beyond. It was the sound of chaos, half a dozen people bickering—most speaking at once. She steeled herself before pushing through the door.

The office beyond was a large, mostly empty space. There were eight utilitarian steel desks evenly spaced throughout the twenty-by-thirty-foot space. Each desk had its own chair and telephone. Aside from that, the space was spartan. There was absolutely no additional furniture, no plants, and no decoration of any kind. Her team sat scattered around the center of the room in a rough circle. Some sitting on empty desktops, others were perched on the edges of uncomfortable World War II era office chairs. As soon as she entered the room, all voices stopped and all eyes fixed on her. Her stomach churned as she focused on appearing strong and confident, even though she felt anything but.

"What has happened? Why have we been called here?" The question had come from Sanjay Patel, one of two mathematicians on the project. Sanjay was about five foot six and 140 pounds. His coarse black hair was already thinning dramatically at the crown of his head, despite the fact that he was only 27. Today, like every other, he wore his trademark button-down shirt with a sweater vest. It was his custom, no matter the weather conditions.

"We have been waiting for hours!" he continued. His voice was already growing in outrage. Reese expected him to be the prominent dissenting voice of the group and he hadn't disappointed her. She'd made it all of three steps through the door and he was already starting to read her the riot act.

"Stop it, Sanjay!" the tall blonde woman standing at the edge of the room chastised. "Give her a minute to breathe!" This was Tracy Clark, the group's computer systems and network specialist. At five foot eleven, she virtually towered over Sanjay. And since she was a woman, Sanjay cowed to her admonishment. Tracy was tall and thin with a runner's physique. With blonde hair and blue eyes, she had a stunning beauty that would've opened doors for her no matter what career path she chose. But it was her intelligence that set her apart and found her a home on this team.

Sanjay lacked the confidence to bully women the way he tried to dominate men. Reese knew she was now the exception to his unspoken rule. For her the dynamic was now different. Sanjay wanted to be the alpha male; he liked to challenge authority above all else. What he lacked in physical acumen, he believed was counterbalanced by his intellect. Since the team was now her responsibility, he would bully her in an attempt to secure a dominant position atop the new hierarchy.

"I only want to know what the hell is going on!" Sanjay hissed back.

Reese cleared her throat. "I'm sorry we're late. We ran into a complication at Alfie's place after he didn't respond to the 1412."

All eyes turned expectantly to Alfie Ahmed. He virtually withered under their stares. Reese was afraid he was going to be sick again.

"Did you say *we?*" This was from Chad Brewster. He was a broad-shouldered, burly young man, only couple of years out of college. He had the look of the all-pro lineman which he'd nearly been. But, as is so many times the case, an unfortunate injury had prematurely ended his football career. Chad had fallen back on his education and gotten a degree in mechanical engineering. His build and many of his mannerisms were holdovers from his football days. He had the look of a big dumb jock, but the appearance was deceptive. He was sharp. "You're not here alone?"

"No, I'm not here alone," she said with a sigh. She wasn't going to get anywhere until everyone calmed down. "That's one of the things we need to talk about. If everyone could please gather round and take a seat, we have some urgent issues to discuss."

This sparked an entirely new chorus of outbursts with nearly everyone speaking over one another. Only two of those in attendance abstained from the bickering. The first was Alfie Ahmed, who stared blankly at the floor. He still looked like he might be sick. The second was Dennis Driscoll, the oldest member of the team at 30 years of age. Dennis was about 225 pounds, with a pronounced gut, thick curly black hair, and bushy pork-chop sideburns. It was no surprise that Dennis was silently taking everything in. He was the quiet member of the group. He was also the second mathematician on the team, which meant he was partnered with Sanjay. Reese always thought of Dennis and Sanjay as the *meek* and the *monger*. But they produced results, as much as she could do without Sanjay at times.

"Hey!" Reese finally yelled. "I said get over here and sit down!"

The loud bark and sharp orders were a never-before-seen occurrence that stunned the group into submission. They finally quieted. It took only moments for the group to arrange office chairs and take their places. In the span of seconds, they looked less like an angry mob and more like a class awaiting a lecture.

Reese was fuming. She'd blown her cool and that was bad enough. But what had really gotten under her skin was how perfectly Cyrus had predicted this. These people were primed to come unglued. But there was an even more unpleasant realization that brought a twisting pain to the pit of her stomach. He was right. They really were a danger to themselves.

Dammit!

On top of that, she felt guilty for thinking poorly of his take on the situation. Cyrus had only spoken his mind. He wasn't judging or criticizing, simply giving an objective assessment. But rather than take it under advisement, she had dismissed his opinion. What rattled her more was that she sincerely felt bad about it. Tensions were high. She was entitled to make mistakes as much as anyone. So why did she feel so guilty for such a minor misstep? Was she developing feelings for him? It wasn't really a question. She knew that she was. But they had known each other less than 24 hours. She knew almost nothing about him.

She pushed the thoughts aside. It would be enough to pay more attention to his assessments in the future. It was a mistake she could learn from. Now they needed to move on.

Oddly, she realized, her brief mental side trip on Cyrus had calmed the burning pain deep in her stomach. That was interesting...

"You've all heard Professor Meade refer to his associate, Mister Cooper, over the last couple of years. He was the consultant who suggested the platform's laser array. The quantum data link was another of their collaborative brainstorms." She scanned the faces and concluded that everyone was paying attention. Even Alfie seemed to welcome the chance to focus his attention on something less grim.

"Well," she continued. "As of late last night, Mister Cooper has joined the team."

"Excuse me, Reese," Sanjay butted in. "I hardly think this news is worthy of every one of us dropping what we were doing and racing down the coast, to some second-rate office."

Reese's eyes lit with flames. She had never felt like throttling another living person like she did right now. He had no tact, no patience—he was just an ass! If he only knew what she'd been through in the last 24 hours!

Cyrus was standing just beyond the door and listening to the exchange. All in all, Reese was handling the group well. Cyrus was already developing a strong dislike for Sanjay. Maybe that was something they could work on. All the same, it seemed like a good time to join the conversation. He was pretty sure Reese was about to blow a gasket.

Cyrus pushed the door open with his foot and walked into the room. All eyes vectored to meet him. He smiled and held up the two travel flats containing to-go cups of coffee. A bag of donuts dangled from his clenched fist. "Morning folks!" he smiled. "The new guy springs for breakfast, right?"

Looks from across the room were a mix of everything imaginable. They were completely off balance. All the better, as far as he was concerned. They would need the mental reset in order to process the current situation.

Reese's eyes met his. He saw the tension melt from them as he stepped closer. It was a relief. He wasn't sure how she would react to him walking in on her dressing down of the troops. The corners of her lips threatened a small smile.

Okay then, it's a welcomed interruption after all.

Cyrus set the coffee and donuts down on the desk in the center of the group. Everyone was silent, but their eyes followed him. They looked at him as if he had come from another planet. He didn't react, just took a seat beside Reese on top of a desk in front of the group.

"Please, eat up folks," Cyrus said with a smile. "Once you hear what we have to say, you might not have much of an appetite."

To Cyrus's satisfaction, not a single question was asked. Not so much as a word was whispered. Collectively they seemed lost, unsure what to do, given the circumstances. They slowly started passing around the styrofoam coffee cups, and a few even helped themselves to donuts.

Once everyone was situated, Cyrus began recounting the events of the past eighteen hours. He started by explaining the attempted kidnapping of Reese, the attempt to kill him, and the bomb that was found in Alfie's truck. He went on to explain how someone had attempted to follow them to this meeting. An unknown force was targeting the group. Apparently some team members were targeted for abduction, while others were targeted for outright assassination. Until they could figure out who was behind the attacks, no one was safe.

To that end, Cyrus had arranged a safe house. The team would be relocated until the threat was neutralized. They all knew a project like theirs would be of paramount interest to any number of foreign governments, as well as the dozens of multi-billion-dollar-a-year businesses that the technology threatened to disrupt or even make entirely obsolete. There had been a breach in security. Until they identified that breach and any complications related to it were neutralized, the team would be safe only if moved to an undisclosed, off-the-grid location.

Cyrus anticipated pushback from the team when it came to going into hiding. He wasn't disappointed.

"You must be joking!" Sanjay sneered.

It didn't surprise Cyrus that Sanjay was the first to fight the plan. In fact, he would've put money on it. He had't even looked at the team dossiers, though that would be a high priority with the work that was to come. Sanjay had a cantankerous way about him. It was as if he *tried* to rub people the wrong way.

Sanjay stood and looked around the room. "I, for one, have no intention of hiding from this threat. If we run now, when do we stop? We must act decisively. We must respond. To run and hide is the act of a coward!"

The rest of the eyes in the room watched Sanjay carefully, but Cyrus also saw those same eyes looking to Reese and himself for a response. It was critical to deal with Sanjay now. He was making a power grab. He was campaigning and giving a pep talk, but he had no idea what he was saying. It bordered on gibberish. He would blindly put himself and others in danger, if only to gain a leadership position—even if it was suicide.

Cyrus looked to Reese. He didn't want to overstep. He'd already done as much outside by predicting the response of those in this room. She thought he'd been judging them harshly. It hadn't been his intention. He was only putting himself in their shoes. But fair enough, she didn't know him that well. They would work on that, he hoped.

Reese met his eyes. What he read there was steadfast support. There was no question or concern in her eyes. She looked to him as if she already knew he had a response locked and loaded. A slight nod of her head was his go signal.

"Okay, Mister Patel, tell me," Cyrus let the statement hang in the air for a moment while Sanjay's eyes met his. "We're open to any and all ideas. What plan of action do you suggest?"

To his credit, Sanjay didn't waste a moment thinking before he responded. "We contact the FBI. They will certainly offer protection!"

"The FBI? That's a good call. But are you willing to turn Meridian over to the federal government?"

His face contorted. "Certainly not!"

"What would you tell the authorities?"

Sanjay paused for a moment to consider but the look he gave Cyrus indicated that he knew better than to be indecisive now. It would only hinder his power play. "Simple. We are the targets of a terrorist group. We already have the attack on Reese and yourself, as well as the bomb from Alfie's car. That is all the evidence we need!"

Cyrus scratched his chin in a display of consideration, but it was an act. He knew the possible directions Sanjay could take his argument, and had opposing points for every one of them. He had already considered and dismissed each possible course of action before coming to the course of action he'd suggested.

This conversation was about clipping Sanjay's wings.

"We do have evidence, I'll give you that. But the funny thing about the feds? They won't just take you at your word, assign round-the-clock protection, and leave it at that. They *insist* on an investigation. That evidence will get the feds to pay attention but you need to be prepared for the questions they'll ask once you open that door. Questions like, why are you being targeted? Who is targeting you? What are they after?" Cyrus looked out across the room. All of the eyes that seemed invigorated by Sanjay's simple solution now started to see it for what it was. "And those are the simple questions. You can't invite the feds into your life and not expect them to pick it apart. Once they're onboard, they'll find out about Meridian. Once that genie is out of the bottle, there's no turning back."

Sanjay raised his hand and opened his mouth to counter the point, but he stopped before saying a word. Cyrus suspected the man's long-term vision for the future of the project included securing a very important place in the history books. This technology would change the world. The scientists who developed the technology would be forever remembered as pioneers. In the end, Sanjay's vanity wouldn't allow him to risk his place in history. It was either that, or something more personal that shut the man down. Maybe he didn't care to have the feds digging around in his personal life. Either way, Sanjay finally shut his mouth and sat down. He made no reply.

Everyone sat in silence. There simply were no easy answers. There was no easy fix.

Chad was the first to speak up. "So where do we go from here?"

"As much as we don't like it, we go to ground. The team will be sequestered so far off the grid that even you won't be able find yourselves." Cyrus saw the questioning looks from the group. He knew he had their attention now. "You'll have all of the amenities of civilization, but it'll be 1970s civilization. Hot and cold running water, heat and air conditioning, television and whatnot. But there will be no telephone and no Internet access. One hundred percent off the grid. It's the only way to ensure your safety right now."

That was the bombshell he was dreading. He could tell by the looks on several of their faces, the lack of cell phones and Internet access was a virtual deal breaker. He cut that off before another fit could ensue. "Let me remind you, there is a very real threat out there. Four men tried to kidnap Miss Knoland, and she was the lucky one. They tried to kill me, and they put a bomb in the engine compartment of Mister Ahmed's truck. Make no mistake, the people behind this mean you harm. And they won't stop until they get what they want."

That did the trick. The silence of the room became malignant. Cyrus had attended funerals with cheerier faces.

Tracy Clark raised a hand somewhat timidly. "So while everyone is in lockdown, who's going to solve our problem? If not the FBI, who can help?"

This was a good sign. The group was coming to terms with the situation, and someone was finally asking the right questions. "That's my job," he said with what he hoped was a confident smile. He hadn't signed up for this, but here he was. And while this was taking him somewhere he'd sworn to never return, this was work he was good at. Or, at least he had been good at it, once upon a time. It was time to dust off those old skills and see how badly they had atrophied. A number of things were already not making sense, and he had a growing list of questions. It was time to put these people into hiding, and it was time to start digging deeper into the mess Walter Meade had left him.

Step one was to take a closer look at Meade's files.

Chapter 16

Wenzler Laboratories, Paulson, New Jersey
Monday, May 18, 1903

Over the course of 1902, a series of unprecedented meteor showers were witnessed throughout the world. The display made headlines across the planet. Though a visual spectacle, virtually all of the celestial material was vaporized while entering Earth's atmosphere. Only a handful of meteors ever made landfall. Those located in the United States were quickly retrieved for study. Of those collected, a single meteorite exhibited unusual properties and warranted more than a cursory examination.

Unlike most of the specimens that survived atmospheric entry, the meteorite designated as J-189D was large. It was, at most, half the size of a loaf of bread but it dwarfed all siblings from the era. But its size was only the first unique property J-189D had to share. Its secrets began to unfold when it displayed unusual magnetic characteristics. The magnetic abnormalities prompted further examination, and a number of intensive tests were scheduled as a result.

Initial testing of J-189D was conducted at Wenzler Laboratories in Paulson, New Jersey. It was a small government-funded facility with less than two-dozen scientists on staff. Though lacking in manpower, the lab was staffed by some of the greatest scientific minds of the time. Despite this, J-189D's greatest secret was discovered entirely by mistake. It was an accident that, with time, would send untold ripples through the scientific community.

Initial examinations of J-189D yielded unexpected results. The unusual magnetic properties were enough to capture the attention of Wenzler researchers, but the real mysteries of the meteorite soon followed. Sometimes even the most brilliant minds require a nudge from the hand of fate.

At one point, sample J-189D was being transported from the primary laboratory to a neighboring room, only a few doors down. Due to circumstances that were never determined, the sample was dropped. The impact with the lab's tile floor broke J-189D into a pair relatively equal-sized fragments.

The accident was soon thought to be advantageous, since it allowed the research team to split into a pair of groups, each studying a portion of J-189D in seclusion. While the teams worked in adjoining labs, their experiments were conducted independently. The objective was a series of blind A-B examinations that were compared at the end of each day.

Unfortunately, these tests exhibited inconsistent results from the very beginning. Even initial baseline examinations returned wildly varied results. The inconsistencies made it clear that there was something very unique about J-189D. In many scenarios, the meteorite simply didn't conform to conventional laws of nature. In test after test, results continued to baffle both teams of scientists.

Until finally there was a breakthrough.

It had been another frustrating morning. The sample had displayed more aberrant results. The unpredictable behavior of the ore was stressing both research teams to their limits. Team Two had finally taken a break for lunch. Everyone needed to walk away and decompress. While the rest of the team retired to the commissary, the project head and leader of Team Two, Rumsfeld Pellagrin, surrendered to his emotional funk. He sat at the laboratory counter, staring at his team's portion of J-189D. Pellagrin did his best thinking before and after normal work hours. It was at those times when the lab was silent that his mind felt completely free. So he sat at the counter and rolled the shard of ore around in the palm of his hand. He stared at it, eyes unfocused and mind drifting as he contemplated its mysteries.

He spent nearly twenty minutes either absently bobbling the chunk of ore in one hand or passing it back and forth from one hand to other, all the while lost in thought. His mind drifted as he considered the most recent test results. They made no sense. Suddenly he snapped out of his daze and glared at the sample. He held it up to the magnification lamp bolted to the surface of the nearby counter. Before he could take a closer look, he yelped and dropped the chunk of stone. It smacked the counter with a thunk as he jumped away like a scalded child.

Pellagrin glared at the sample on the counter. Then his eyes moved down and to the right for a closer look at the palm of his hand. Blisters were beginning to form. Looking back to the sample sitting askew on the table, something seemed off. He leaned closer, trying to identify what had caught his eye. It looked as if the color of the ore had changed slightly. Moments later, the loose sheets of paper beneath the chunk of J-189D began to smolder and then smoke.

At a loss to explain what was happening and already feeling blisters on his hand, Pellagrin grabbed a pair of tongs from the tool tray a few feet away. Grasping the sample between the tongs, he pulled it from the smoking papers just before they burst into flames. He searched for a safe place to stow the meteorite, even as it was increasing in temperature. Quickening his pace, he carried J-189D with outstretched arms. His subconscious desire was to keep the strange material as far away from his body as possible.

He quickly located what was needed and deposited the sample in a large porcelain bowl on the far side of the lab. Stepping away from the bowl, he struggled to understand what had just happened. It was about that time he smelled smoke. Spinning on a heel, he found that the loose-leaf papers on his counter had indeed spouted fully into flames.

Dashing to the hallway door, he grabbed the fire extinguisher from its wall mount. Even as he crossed the room, Pellagrin was pulling free the short metal rod that activated the chemical reaction inside the device. By the time he reached the open flames of the countertop, he was already pressing the release valve.

Unfortunately, the extinguisher was a dud. The metal rod he'd pulled from the top of the canister was supposed to dislodge the lead plug beneath a glass vial located deep within the device. When the plug was freed, a small, concentrated dose of sulfuric acid was supposed to mix with a sodium bicarbonate solution and produce carbon dioxide, pressurizing the contents of the tank and expelling water from the tank's main reservoir. Frustratingly, the mechanical portion of the device had failed.

Cursing aloud, Pellagrin threw the useless red canister aside and bolted into the hallway. One door down, he ducked into the next lab and snatched the fire extinguisher from its wall mount. In doing so, he drew the attention of nearly every member of Research Team One. They were in the process of examining their portion of J-189D.

Pellagrin quickly returned to his lab and promptly extinguished the growing flames. By that time, the fire had spread to cover the majority of the countertop and had started to climb the corkboard on the wall behind it.

Attracted by the drama, several members of the team from the next lab arrived to investigate. Shocked to see the smoldering wreckage of the once pristine lab, the lead scientist from Team One, "Big Al" Jones, looked to Pellagrin for an explanation. Winded and already at a loss for understanding, Pellagrin only pointed across the room to the ore fragment sitting in the large porcelain bowl. By now the sample was glowing orange and yellow. It had grown to a temperature so great that thermal waves could be seen radiating from its surface.

Everyone was awestruck, gaping at the sample. It was spontaneously generating high levels of heat. Everyone realized this, but no one knew why. Jones asked what sort of experiment Pellagrin was conducting without the rest of his team. But when Pellagrin explained that there was no test, his counterpart from Team One looked truly thunderstruck.

Jones started to ask a question but stopped, only stuttering the start of an incomprehensible phrase. He stammered, lost in thought. Trying again, once more he failed to put together a coherent sentence. Finally, his eyes pulled back from where he was looking, far off in the distance, as if seeing the answer to his own question on the horizon. He looked Pellagrin square in the eye and waved for him to follow.

The two team leads left the lab, passed down the hall, and walked quickly through the next doorway to the facilities dedicated to the examinations conducted by Team One. Not understanding what was happening, Pellagrin followed, as confused and lost for explanation as he had been when the fragment began to burn the palm of his hand.

Jones led Pellagrin across his lab and over to a counter where a small metal cage was suspended over the open flame of a Bunsen burner. Jones stopped suddenly, and with a dramatic flourish, he pointed to the second sample of J-189D glowing orange and yellow with flames from the torch lapping up around its sides. Team One had been conducting an experiment— exposing the sample to extreme heat and observing the material's reactions.

As unbelievable as the circumstances were, the two teams conclusively proved their unlikely hypothesis over the subsequent three days. When one of the fragments was exposed to extreme temperature, the second fragment radiated that temperature to exactly the same degree. It didn't matter if one fragment was in the lab and the other was down the hall in a chest of ice. It didn't matter if the second fragment was ten miles away, locked in a lead-lined safe. If the first sample was heated to three hundred degrees, the second sample spontaneously heated to exactly three hundred degrees without fluctuation and without fail.

They conducted test after test. And what worked with temperature also proved true with electrical current. They put current through sample A and attached a voltage meter to sample B. Sure enough, the opposite sample tested at exactly the same voltage as its twin. They finally had an explanation for the inconsistency of their early tests. When one team ran tests on its sample, it was interfering with tests run by the reciprocal team.

Defying explanation, the two chunks of J-189D were linked at some unknown level. As illogical and unlikely as the strange link between the two fragments was, they were able to prove the connection, if not immediately explain it.

The discovery of the meteorite had proven to be truly extraordinary. But the experience was the start of a long and close collaboration between the head of Team Two, Rumsfeld Pellagrin, and the head of Team One, Albert Einstein—sometimes known by his unlikely nickname, Big Al Jones. Pellagrin would go on to develop his life's work, *Silent River*, based on what he learned from J-189D. Einstein applied his observations of J-189D and became the father of theoretical physics.

Chapter 17

Using the teleporter, Cyrus and Reese made several trips from the house in Colorado. The first was to collect some of Reese's electrical engineering hardware from the group's office in Santa Barbara. Cyrus was adamant that they take anything they might need from the office because they wouldn't be returning. That facility was public facing and listed on the web and in the phone book. It was therefore their most vulnerable location.

The second trip was to gather groceries and provisions. They would be using the Colorado house as a base of operations and needed to stock up accordingly. Walter Meade had been meticulous when it came to keeping his home's location private, so it had remained a secure location. And, given their easy access to the platforms and the resulting ability to teleport to locations all over the country, they were afforded a unique disregard for geography. They would leverage that. The Colorado house would be their safe haven.

The third trip was back to Reese's apartment. Since it was an active crime scene, they needed to take precautions. Not wanting to teleport into the middle of a room full of forensic technicians, Cyrus opted to first phone Detective Franklin. He said that he and Reese would be stopping by the apartment to pick up a few things and asked if it would be alright. Franklin said this was fine, but he wanted to arrange for an officer to meet them. Since it was still a crime scene, the officer would log everything they removed. Cyrus explained that he and Reese were only a few blocks from the apartment and asked if it would be possible to meet someone there now. Franklin told him that no one was at the apartment at the moment. His people had cleared out several hours prior. Cyrus arranged to meet a police officer at the apartment door at 5:00 pm. He had no intention of attending the meeting. He knew Franklin would find the call suspicious if he didn't schedule an appointment after asking questions, so he had to go through the motions.

The trip to Reese's was quick. They were careful to touch only what they needed, and they were in and out in less than ten minutes. Cyrus watched the front door while Reese made short work of packing what essentials she required. Taking too much would draw suspicion from the investigating officers. Plus, items such as toiletries, soaps, and shampoos had already been covered by the grocery run earlier.

That left them with one trip remaining. And Cyrus wasn't excited about going home. Still, he had gear back at his Chicago apartment that he couldn't do without. When he'd packed the truck and driven out to Colorado, he'd done so on a whim and to satisfy his curiosity. Cyrus had understood the property was his, free and clear. Allan Underwood was very clear on that point.

But he'd had no idea what to expect. With the long drive west to consider the many questions he had regarding Walter Meade, Cyrus had never seriously considered moving to Nowhere, Colorado. He had only stuffed the essentials into a single duffle and hit the road.

Now he was planning a trip back home to collect more of his belongings. It wasn't the journey that fueled his reluctance. Reese had checked the database and confirmed his suspicion. Meade did, in fact, have a teleportation site in Chicago. Meade was using the platforms to make short work of the trip between Colorado and Chicago. And while the trip back home would be easy, Cyrus had concern for what he might find there.

"One more trip and we can call it a day?" Reese asked as they walked single file into the spare bedroom of the Colorado house.

"It's been a long twenty-four hours," he agreed.

She pulled out her phone and tapped a few buttons on the display. "When we get back, I need to make a couple of changes to your phone. That way you can operate the platforms yourself." She showed him what she was doing. Launching an app, she entered a PIN to gain access. From there she could select a teleport destination from the list, or search a database of locations. The options were displayed in various formats, allowing her to sort by state, country, or search by keyword. All in all, it was extremely user-friendly.

"That's odd," she said squinting at the screen of her phone. "The destination in Chicago is listed only as *Chicago*. Normally there's an exact address and additional info about the site so we know where we'll be landing. This doesn't have any info at all. It just says Chicago."

Cyrus smiled, mostly to himself. "Yeah. I have a theory about that. Give it a shot. Let's find out if I'm right."

She looked at him with curiosity, but stepped aside allowing him up on the platform first this time. He stepped aboard and noticed her looking at him in surprise. She'd just realized that he had a gun in his hand. He did a quick press-check, ensuring there was a round in the chamber before lowering the gun to his side.

"Sorry," he smiled. "Just playing it safe. I have a guess about where we're landing, but I'm still not comfortable teleporting in blind. Not when there are people after us."

"Fair enough." She stepped up onto the pad, toe to toe with him and tapped the last few keystrokes on her phone, initiating the five-second countdown.

It's funny, Cyrus realized. They had teleported together several times in the last 24 hours. At first the experience seemed alien, but it was already becoming routine. Standing this close to Reese, though, was another matter. He felt the same tingling flutter every time she stepped near. In fact, the feeling had grown stronger with time. Then again, it could've had something to do with the way she now stood even closer than she had before. He could feel the heat coming off her body... He could feel the faintest touch of her breasts against his chest as she swayed slightly on her feet. And he could feel her breath on his chin.

There was a flash of light, and the journey was complete. And before Cyrus knew what had happened, he had pulled Reese up into his arms, drawing closer still as she kissed him deeply. He wasn't sure who had initiated it. Maybe it was better that way. She'd invoked so many feelings since their first meeting. He'd been sure she had feelings for him as well. In many ways, the kiss confirmed things he already knew. It made them tangible and real. There was something here, something they both wanted to explore.

"Wow," was all he could say when their lips finally parted.

Reese pale skin was pink. Her eyes fluttered, and she took a deep breath. "Wow, is right," she smiled shyly.

They both stood still for long moments, still holding each other close. Cyrus had the sense that he was supposed to be doing something, but it was several seconds before he finally snapped out of the trace like state and looked around. He still had the gun in hand. They were standing in an unfurnished apartment. In the living room. He laughed and slid the gun into the holster at the small of his back.

"Where are we?" Reese asked. She had finally recovered as well.

Cyrus led her by the hand along a short hallway to the front door of the apartment. As they walked through the place, his suspicions were confirmed. The apartment was completely empty. Meade must've used the apartment strictly to house the platform. When he reached the front door, he pulled it open and looked at the number stenciled on it. Number 9-12. He could only shake his head.

Reese didn't understand. "What is it?"

"That sneaky son-of-a-bitch! My apartment is one floor up, directly above this unit. I'm in 10-12!"

There was a pregnant pause, then they both burst out laughing. It was just like Walter Meade to do something cagey and divisive. It was simple, practical, and efficient. And at that moment they found it downright hysterical.

———

After walking the halls and checking the stairwells as well as both elevators, Cyrus was relieved to find no surveillance set up on his apartment. Still, as they reached the front door he pulled his sidearm. Slowly and quietly, he unlocked the door. He pushed through the doorway with the gun held high. The interior of the home was well lit, with ambient light shining through the windows of his office to the left and the windows of the living room at the end of the hallway, directly ahead. Sticking his head into the office, he found it clear. Likewise he checked the kitchen as they passed it on the right and his bedroom on the left. The living room was last, but everything was just as he'd left it. He turned back to Reese, who was waiting anxiously at the door, and waved her in. It felt overly dramatic, but the way things were he couldn't be too careful.

Cyrus pulled an empty backpack from the hall closet and handed it to Reese. "See if there's anything worth taking in the kitchen. I don't plan on coming back anytime soon." He thought for a moment. "Same goes for the rest of the place. If you see something we might need, grab it. I'll gather my clothes. Aside from that, most of what I need is in my office."

She headed for the kitchen while he ducked into the bedroom. He pulled another large duffle from the closet and started emptying the contents of the dresser drawers and stuffing the hanging contents of the closet into the bag. Finally, he looked around. The rest could wait. They had a lot to do, and needed to get moving. He pulled his last oversized duffle from the top shelf of the closet and took it and the overstuffed bag down the hall.

When he walked into his office, Reese was already there. She was looking at the patchwork of notes and photos tacked across the back wall. She heard him enter but didn't turn and didn't say anything. She was clearly intrigued by what she saw. The information stuck to the wall was a mishmash of seemingly random bits of information with little in common. But even the haphazard scraps and clippings had the ability to capture one's attention. Images of burned out cars, surveillance photos shot through restaurant windows, bank statements, and photocopies of receipts. Each one a disparate piece of information relating to a story he was developing.

"This is research?" she finally asked.

"Yes."

"All for one story?"

"No. What you're looking at covers three different pieces. Nothing researched well enough to write yet. Getting the facts takes time. It's slow going. So rather than twist in the wind on one story, I try to keep a couple going at the same time."

She looked over her shoulder, concern etched in features. "I've read some of your stories. You're telling me you work a couple of those at a time?"

He nodded. "When I can. I bore easily, and I have a hard time sitting still."

"It must take incredible concentration."

He shook his head. "Not really. I live a simple life. There isn't anything to distract me."

She looked like she had something she wanted to say but was considering keeping it to herself. Rather than pry, Cyrus left her to think for a few minutes. He went over to the desk and pulled several empty file folders out of a drawer. Pulling the research material down from the corkboard, he placed each case's information into a separate folder. Next, he started pulling additional files out of the desk and packing those as well.

Reese walked slowly around the perimeter of the room. She was still agonizing over something. "What's wrong?" he finally asked.

She faced him from across the room, but didn't make eye contact. It was unusual for her. He liked how she seemed to prefer looking him in the eye. In his experience, it was a surprisingly rare quality in people.

"I guess I wanted to ask…" she trailed off. She wanted to ask something but he didn't know what it was. He wasn't going to push.

"I wanted to ask you if you are seeing anyone." She pushed out with some effort. "At first, I didn't think that would be an issue, but after…you know… I guess it just has me rethinking things a little."

"No," he smiled. He was relieved that it was something so simple. "Not seeing anyone. Haven't had anyone special for some time, actually." Wow. Had he just said that? It wasn't something he was comfortable talking about. But somehow admitting it to her just seemed right. The words just popped out.

But she still seemed uncomfortable. His answer should have alleviated her concern. Did that mean that she *was* seeing someone? Was that what she was trying to say? Then it clicked. He understood. He followed her eyes to where she was looking at a photo on the end of the bookshelf across the room.

"Ah, yeah. That…" He left his packing behind the desk and walked slowly across the room to stand beside Reese. He took her by the hand and walked her over to the bookshelf. "Her name was Natasha," he said quietly, almost to himself. "She's been gone…" he had to stop and think. "Going on six years now."

Her eyes rose to meet his. She still held his hand. "You were close." It was a statement, not a question. That wasn't obvious by the photo. He just wasn't doing a good job of hiding it. Talking about Natasha was still difficult and it felt clumsy.

"Very close," he admitted. "And it was complicated." He laughed thinking about it. That was a first. He had never laughed at the idea before. Complicated was an understatement. "We were young. I was working a job in Europe at the time. We met under…unusual circumstances, I suppose you could say. I guess I knew all along it wasn't meant to be. I just wasn't willing to believe it."

"What happened?"

He watched her eyes. She was sincere. She really wanted to know. There was genuine concern there. "She died," Cyrus said quietly. There was a long silence. He shrugged. "Some things really aren't meant to be."

She wanted to ask more. She wanted to understand; he could see it in her eyes. But she seemed to understand he wasn't ready to talk about it. That impressed him. Maybe even scared him a little. She could see into his being. This was a painful subject. And for the first time in his life, he actually found himself wanting to share the story. He wanted to tell someone what happened that day six years ago, working undercover for the Coalition. The day that Natasha lost her life. The day Natasha was taken from him.

Reese gently wiped away the single tear that had fallen from his eye. He hadn't even felt it form. But she gently pushed it away. She rose up onto her toes and kissed him very softly on the cheek.

A single tear had formed at the corner of Cyrus's eye. It teetered there for long moments before finally breaking free and rolling down his cheek. This was clearly a very difficult conversation for him. Reese felt bad for bringing it up. But somehow the faraway look in his eyes made her think it was something he had avoided for too long already.

She wanted to know more. She didn't understand. *Natasha had died?* How horrible. Reese raised a hand and gently wiped away the tear. When she did, his eyes pulled back to the present, back from some faraway place. Her heart broke seeing that hurt in his eyes. Laying a soft kiss upon his cheek, she whispered the only thing she could say under the circumstances. "I'm so sorry."

But his eyes cleared and he looked down at her. He looked into her eyes, and his face brightened again. "Yeah, well," he said quietly. "To be honest, I haven't had a serious relationship since."

He smiled again and pulled her close. "Thank you," he whispered in her ear. "I've never talked about that before."

She pulled back and looked up at him. "Never?"

He shook his head.

"With anyone?"

He shook his head again.

Good lord, she thought. The woman he loved died six years ago. And this conversation was the first time he had shared his feelings about it with another person? Who could do that? How could he live like that? She was sure people had gone insane keeping lesser emotions bottled up.

"So," he said, clearing the air. "Let me grab a few more things, and we're out of here."

Cyrus went back to the desk and started going through the drawers again. While he did that, Reese turned back to the bookshelves. He had a massive collection of hardcover books. Some were very rare, antique leather-bound tomes. Many were newer. But all of them had their spines bent and cracked. That impressed her. He wasn't one to buy books for show. But could he have actually read them all?

Perplexed and impressed, she moved on across the shelves. She found timeless classics as well as modern thrillers and mysteries. There were technical and scientific journals, as well as biographies by historic figures and Nobel Prize winners. With curiosity, the contents of the bottom shelf caught her eye.

"Wow!" she said with some admiration. "It looks like you've got every novel Alastair Rose ever wrote!" She went down the shelf. There were twelve hardcovers lined up. But none of these had cracked spines. She pulled the first book from the shelf and flipped open the front cover. The binding popped as she paged through the first few sheets in search of something. Her eyes went wide. She looked up at Cyrus, her mouth agape. "Are they all first editions?"

Cyrus pulled the last of the important files from his desk and shoved them into the end of the duffle bag with his clothes. He shot her a glance and nodded. "Every one of them. *Autographed* first editions."

She looked back to the book and flipped the pages once more. Sure enough, she found the inscription! She looked back to Cyrus. It was curious. He didn't appear very interested in talking about the books. "I don't get it," she said. It was almost an accusation. "You must be a collector. But you don't seem very interested in them. It couldn't have been easy to get a set of first editions. The first printing of each book was a limited run. Rose intentionally kept the first printing short. Each book was in extremely high demand when it first shipped, but most fans had to wait for the second printing before they could actually get a copy."

"Yeah," Cyrus said with a knowing smile. "Most people don't know it, but Alastair Rose reserves the entire first printing for fans who signed up to his mailing list prior to the release of his first novel. It was 256 people. Every book that followed, those same 256 people were shipped a first edition as soon as it was available. Each book autographed and free of charge. It was his way of supporting the people who supported him."

"That's ridiculous! I'm just about the biggest Alastair Rose fan there is, and I've never heard any of that!" Her eyes narrowed. "How do you know that? Are you one of the 256?"

He didn't respond. He just watched her carefully, enjoying himself.

The knowing look he was giving suggested he knew more than he was saying. But that could mean—

"Do you *know* Alastair Rose?" There was a long silence. "No one knows Alastair Rose!"

Cyrus laughed. He moved to the front of the desk and sat on the edge.

Dammit! He's enjoying this.

"You seem to know a lot about the man. Why would I know Alastair Rose?" Cyrus asked.

She wasn't sure. It was something about the look in his eyes. She couldn't put her finger on it, but there was recognition there. He knew something he wasn't saying. He found this far too amusing for it to be—

No way…

"You?" her voice cracked, as if her mouth had betrayed the word passing through her mind at that very moment. But the second the word left her lips, she somehow sensed it was correct. She didn't know why, but she had confidence. "It's you. I don't believe it… You're Alastair Rose!"

"What?" Cyrus seemed genuinely shocked by the accusation. "Why would you say that?"

She laughed and slapped closed the book still held in her hands. "I've read every one of these books. And, I don't know, you read that much by one person and you just have a sense of them. A familiarity with their humor—their way of looking at the world. It's you! I'm sure of it! Everyone assumes Alastair Rose is some kind of hermit or recluse, because he's never been identified. People have even tried to track him—you—through the publisher's financial records. There have been two break-ins at the publisher's office, for god's sake! Everyone who has tried to identify Alastair has failed. The man's a ghost!"

Cyrus shrugged, and finally nodded. "Fair enough. He's a ghost. It's just a pen name. But there's no conspiracy to it. I'll tell you one thing. It turned out to be one hell of a viral marketing campaign."

She laughed, a really heart-felt laugh. "Wow! You're full of surprises. Alastair Rose is Cyrus Cooper! Why didn't you ever come forward? Don't you know how hard people have worked to find the man behind these books?"

"Hell yes, I know! But it sort of snowballed with time. At first I did it on a lark. Then people started posting questions online. 'Who is Alastair Rose?' That sort of thing. There was a lot of conversation. By the time the third book came out, it had become a big deal. Everyone was talking about it. People who would never have known about the books knew the name. But since people couldn't talk about the name without talking about the books, pretty soon the books were everywhere. The damn things even hit the bestseller list...Repeatedly!"

His smile lessened, and he just looked at her. "Can you imagine how crushed people would be if they put a face to the name now? After twelve books and all the build up? All the conversation? All the hype? If people found out it was someone boring like me, they'd be crushed."

Now she laughed. "I don't know if they'd be crushed, but I can see your point. It has grown into its own kind of monster." It was true. Things had reached the point where reality couldn't possibly meet with expectations. "Still, these are some of my all-time favorite books. I can't believe you wrote them!"

"Thanks. Tell you what, when we get this Meridian thing sorted out, I'll hook you up with a set of your own first editions." He grinned mischievously. "I know a guy."

He hopped down from the desk and returned to the empty corkboard. At the far right corner of it, he slid his fingertips between the edge of the board and the wall. That must've triggered a switch because a four-foot-wide section of the board popped forward. He grabbed the section and swung it to the side on a hinge.

Behind the floor-to-ceiling corkboard was a hidden compartment. A slightly reclined rack held a selection of rifles and shotguns. A tall section of pegboard held a dozen or so handguns of various makes, models, and calibers. And shelves recessed into the compartment were stacked high with ammunition.

Reese's eyes bugged at the sight of the arsenal. This was unprecedented. Every time she turned around, she was seeing a new side of Cyrus. "Well," she said, finally finding her voice. "You had a hell of a story for the books. The one behind these guns must put that one to shame. Care to share?"

Cyrus's eyes met hers. It was clear this needed some sort of explanation. "Yeah. There's a reason for all of it. I'm not a nut job. Let's just grab what we need and get out of here. We've been too long already. I promise I'll explain this, once we get everything secured."

Alright. That was fair. He went about selecting the weapons he wanted to take and loading them into the last remaining duffle bag along with all the ammo he could carry.

Reese turned back to the bookshelves. She shook her head thinking about the Alastair Rose conspiracy. There were endless theories that Alastair was someone in witness protection hiding from the mob, or some kind of reclusive eccentric who never left his home. All sorts of crazy theories were thrown about. But the truth was something far more mundane. That struck her as very amusing.

When she reached the end of the shelf, something different caught her eye. She was just about to ask Cyrus about it, but thought that now might not be the best time. Glancing over her shoulder, she saw him zipping the last duffle bag and closing the wall's hidden panel. They were about to leave. She thought for a second, then took advantage of his distraction. Grabbing three of the sixteen paperback books from the end of the bottom shelf, she stuffed them into the backpack at her feet.

"Ready to go?" Cyrus asked.

"All set," she confirmed.

They headed for the door. She had the backpack slung over one shoulder and Cyrus had a massive duffle bag in each hand.

————————

As they reached the front door, Cyrus got a funny feeling. A strange sensation tickled at the based of his skull and sent his eyes in the direction of the doorknob. He'd heard a floor board squeak in the hallway outside the apartment. He'd always liked that particular floorboard because it gave him a heads up when someone was standing at his doorstep. The squeak was always followed a second or two later by a knock or the electronic chime of the bell. But this time there was no knock.

Cyrus stopped dead in his tracks. Reese, caught off guard, walked right into him. He lowered both bags to the floor, turned quickly, and signaled Reese for silence. He was relieved to see that she was already on alert.

In one smooth motion, he pulled the gun from the holster behind his back. He could see a shadow move across the small gap at the bottom of the door. Someone was standing directly outside. He stepped to the side of the doorframe. Should the person in the hall start shooting through the wooden door, the thick wooden frame would dramatically reduce his chances of taking a round. He signaled Reese into the office a few feet away.

He was deciding how to best deal with the person at the door when the floorboard squeaked again and the shadow was gone. He was confused. A nosey neighbor? Someone trying to find the right apartment? Or, it could be—

Oh shit!

Chapter 18

Oak Park, Chicago Illinois
Wednesday, 4:42 pm (3:52 pm Colorado Time)

Cyrus turned and bolted down the hall. He made it six strides before the front door detonated in an shower of splinters. The concussive force of the blast smashed him to the floor and jolted the gun from his hand.

His ears ringing and eyes blurry, Cyrus rolled over in time to see a large figure dressed in black lunging at him with a large hypodermic needle in hand. At the last moment, he squared his body to the man and raised his feet, catching the man in the abdomen and arresting his approach. With a flex of his back and knees, Cyrus launched his assailant over his head, in the direction of the living room at the far end of the hall.

Climbing to his feet before the next attacker could reach him, Cyrus's hand slid up under his jacket and pulled free the short handle of a telescoping baton. With a snap of his wrist, the baton extended to its full two-and-a-half-foot length. It would be difficult to swing within the confines of a hallway, but not impossible. With a snap of his wrist, Cyrus flicked the tip of the baton down on the extended hand of the oncoming second attacker. He was instantly rewarded by the sound of snapping bone. The man shrieked in pain. Cyrus followed up with a devastating right cross, square to the man's nose. This time he heard the sound of splintering cartilage. A solid front kick to the man's chest sent him hurtling backward down the hall, where he collided with a third oncoming attacker. The two men landed in a tangled pile that blocked the hallway.

Spinning a hundred and eighty degrees, Cyrus turned in time to find that the first attacker had recovered and was advancing on him. The man had the large hypodermic needle at the ready and was looking to drive it home. Cyrus had no idea what was in the syringe and no desire to sample it first hand. The fact that no one had pulled a trigger yet made it a safe bet they wanted to bring him—or Reese, or both of them—back alive. That gave him the advantage, because the way this week was going, his reluctance to take another person's life was proving a luxury he couldn't afford.

The attacker feigned a lunge with the needle only to backpedal a half step before attacking with full force. Cyrus grabbed the wrist supporting the oncoming needle with his left and put all his power and weight into another right cross. He dropped forward to one knee as he followed through with all available momentum. The punch caught the oncoming man in the abdomen, right above the belt buckle. Between the attacker's oncoming inertia and the force of the punch, Cyrus had certainly knocked the wind out of him. Hell, there was a good chance the man had just involuntarily pissed himself from the force of the blow. Cyrus ducked and more or less threw the man over his shoulder. Flailing, he landed on top of his two unconscious comrades.

No sooner had the man impacted on the other two, than Reese stepped up and placed a Taser to the back of his neck. She clicked the trigger and a blast of light flashed in the dim hallway. The crackle of electricity was unmistakable. Cyrus suddenly realized why the other two men hadn't gotten up after he dropped them. Reese had zapped them into unconsciousness with a blast to the brainstem.

"Outstanding!" Cyrus said, flashing her a wide smile. She never failed to impress him. Grabbing the Taser out his duffle, she'd disabled each man as soon as he had put them on the floor.

Cyrus grabbed the hypodermic from the carpet and looked at it more closely.

"What is it?" Reese asked.

The needle was enormous. The sort of freakishly long thing doctors used on patients not because it was necessary, but because they could. Cyrus shook his head. "I truly have no idea."

He knelt beside the man on the top of the pile in the hallway and plunged the needle fully into his neck. He depressed the plunger. "Lets see if he likes his own medicine." Stopping the injection short, he left a small sample of the fluid in the chamber of the syringe.

Holding the needle up to the light, he confirmed that a small amount remained in the chamber. It would be enough to analyze. Next he broke the thick needle off at the base of the device, making it easier to transport. Finally, he took the big metal body of the syringe and one by one, pressed each of the three men's right thumbs against a different section of its chrome finish. That done, he dropped the syringe into a plastic sandwich bag and tucked it into his jacket pocket.

"We better get the hell out of here," he said to Reese. "The Chicago cops aren't high on my list of admirers right now, and that breaching charge is going to have a lot of people dialing 911." Cyrus grabbed the two largest duffle bags and led her into the hallway.

They took the staircase down one flight and ducked into Meade's spare apartment. This time they had a lot of gear to transport back to Colorado. Reese went first, taking the backpack and one of the duffles. Twenty seconds after she teleported out, Cyrus stepped onto the platform and tapped the activation code on Reese's phone. A five second delay, a flash of light, a popping in his ears, and he was standing in the closet of the spare bedroom in Colorado.

Chapter 19

Berton Springs, Colorado
Wednesday, 9:05 pm

Cyrus and Reese sat on the floor of the basement vault. Each had stacks of files and folders scattered around them. It was slow going, but they were piecing together a more complete history of Meridian. What they had learned was nothing short of shocking. Even for Reese, who'd been a member of Walter Meade's team since the project started, almost seven years prior. To her surprise, that was only the start of the project's most recent iteration, only recently codenamed Meridian. Other projects directly related to it, had come before. In fact, Walter Meade had worked on the technology behind the teleportation platforms since 1955.

Cyrus attempted a sip from his beer bottle and found it empty. "I'm grabbing another," he said. "You want one?"

She looked up from the sheet of paper she was reading. The distracted look on her face indicated that she hadn't heard him. A moment later his words sank in and she smiled. "Please! But a couple more folders and I think I'll switch to the hard stuff. This is incredible. How could Walter keep this to himself all these years?"

Cyrus couldn't argue the point. What they had read so far was mind-blowing. But keeping it secret did seem the best course of action. They had already uncovered documents proving that several accepted facts of American history were at best half-truths, while others were complete fabrications. And they all tied back to Meridian, a project of the upmost secrecy that had spawned some of the most revolutionary scientific advances in recorded history.

"You know what," she said, as she climbed up from the floor. "I'll get the refills. I need to stretch my legs anyway." She collected Cyrus's empty bottle on her way to the staircase.

Cyrus pulled himself to his feet and stretched. They'd been at this for hours. He'd been jotting notes on a pad of paper as they went, in an effort to assemble an accurate timeline. It was hard to believe, but the technology behind Meridian had been in the works since the very turn of the century.

Reese returned carrying four bottles of beer. She passed one to Cyrus, kept one for herself, and set the other two aside. "Miss Knoland, I get the distinct impression you are trying to get me drunk!" Cyrus said with an exaggerated slurring of his speech.

The corner of her mouth turned up in a mischievous smile and she raised one eyebrow suggestively. She tipped her bottle to him. He clicked his against it. "To taking advantage, and being taken advantage of!" Her grin only increased.

She was something, Cyrus had to admit. This week had been a roller coaster ride, and not only had she maintained her wits but she had managed to keep a sense of humor as well. And with what they had learned tonight, that was no easy task.

Cyrus took a long pull from the beer bottle and tried to clear the impure thoughts from his mind. It wasn't his fault. She was causing them… And she was clearly enjoying it.

Reese looked at him for several long moments. There was a slight flushing of her cheeks he was growing to enjoy. The pink color appeared when she flirted. Finally, Reese took a sip from her bottle and returned to her pile of papers on the floor. Cyrus stretched again, invoking several audible pops throughout his back and neck. He reclaimed his position on the hard concrete floor.

"Should we go over the updated timeline one more time?" Cyrus asked, holding up the notepad.

"Good idea. I'm still having trouble with it. I thought I knew everything there was about Meridian—but I didn't know any of this!"

"Okay," Cyrus said, flipping back several pages. "As far as I can tell, everything started in 1902. It began with a series of meteor showers that drew a lot of attention from the scientific community. By that time in history, scientists were already aware of several fairly large meteor impact sites dating back thousands of years. Somewhat disappointingly, most of the new meteors burned up entering the atmosphere. But there were several surface impacts, a couple even within U.S. borders. Those samples were tracked down and collected, but other than some unusual ratios of elements, there was nothing terribly special about them.

"But in the spring of 1902, a single anomalous sample was discovered. It had unusual magnetic properties. There was some kind of lab accident and the sample—J-189D, they called it—was damaged. The sample was pretty much broken in half. Skipping through the geek-speak, the meteorite turned out to be a virtual study guide for early physics. Scientists didn't know it yet, but they had just discovered quantum entanglement. The two pieces of ore were linked on a quantum level."

"Right," she said, picking up the story where he left off. "So they did some crude tests, at least by today's standards. And since the two parts of the meteorite were linked at an atomic level, the scientists found that they could do some extraordinary things. There are dozens of reports detailing the experiments, but there's one I like more than the rest. It was so simple that it was elegant.

"They took a common power cord and plugged it into a wall outlet. The wires on the other end had been stripped bare and were attached directly to J-189D, Sample A. Some 400 miles away in another lab, a second cord was attached to the reciprocal portion of J-189D, Sample B. Rather than attach the second cord to the wall, it was attached to a lamp. When current was applied to Sample A, it instantly lit the bulb of the lamp attached to Sample B—400 miles away! There was no dissipation of power due to distance, and there was no measurable delay in the lighting of the lamp. In fact, they concluded that the distance between the two portions of J-189D was completely irrelevant.

"It wouldn't be until 1921 that Albert Einstein actually developed a scientific principle to explain the phenomenon. Until then, they must've thought it was damn close to magic," Reese concluded with a satisfied smile.

Cyrus nodded in agreement. "It seems that Einstein's theoretical work in physics may not've been so *theoretical* after all. He was working with J-189D in the early 1900s. At the same time, he was divining his now famous theories, it stands to reason. According to these reports, that meteorite was the foundation on which modern science built our current understanding of physics. It actually makes me wonder where we'd be without it."

"I'm confused," Reese said with some trepidation. "What was it about the J-189D that was so special? I mean, what caused the entanglement?"

"That's the kicker," Cyrus said rather quietly. "There wasn't anything special about J-189D. Nothing to explain its entanglement, at least. It originally drew scientific attention because it had an unusual magnetic signature. But that was later explained by the disproportional concentration of iron that comprised the meteorite's outer structure. But those magnetic properties had nothing to do with the entanglement. In fact, it was almost as if the ore had just enough of a unique magnetic signature to ensure additional attention. But in and of itself, the magnetic properties were insignificant."

Cyrus went back to his notes. This part was a little sketchy as far as the extract timeframe. "So sometime in 1903, while working with the ore samples, Albert Einstein and Rumsfeld Pellagrin met for the first time. Pellagrin was the scientist who originally discovered the unique properties of the meteorite. Sometime between 1903 and 1907, Pellagrin had the remarkable idea that, if energy can be transferred between the two stones, it might be possible to transfer matter as well. He enlisted the support of then President of the United States, Theodore Roosevelt. Roosevelt must've virtually salivated over the idea of such a technology, because he pretty much gave Pellagrin a blank check and carte blanche to do research. And to his credit, Pellagrin built the original two platforms."

"But he couldn't make them work," Reese said picking up the story. This was the part where she felt she had a solid grasp. She had tread some of this very same ground, only a hundred years later. "It seemed Pellagrin's theories concerning matter transport were sound. But no one anticipated the monumental levels of energy required to cause the mass entanglement necessary to teleport complex matter. At one point, Pellagrin blacked out the whole of New York and Washington, D.C. in an attempt to power the platforms for a single test. Even then, he couldn't generate enough power to engage the platforms."

Cyrus picked up the story again. So far they were on the same page, which was an indication that they were interpreting the information correctly. "But Pellagrin had kept in touch with Roosevelt. So when intelligence crossed Roosevelt's desk indicating the Russians had some sort of secret new power generating device, Roosevelt passed the information on to Pellagrin. U.S. intelligence quickly discovered that the Russians were out collecting samples of their own during the meteor showers from 1902. Something in the samples they gathered was being used to generate previously unimagined levels of electricity.

"But international relations being what they were, and assuming that the teleportation platforms actually worked, the US had no intentions of sharing technology with Russia. Pellagrin had no diplomatic means with which to utilize their power source. So the crafty bastard did the next best thing. He tricked them into letting him use their power source!"

Reese took another drink and then shook her head. "Ok, I have to admit, I read that report three times, and I'm still not sure I understand what happened there."

Cyrus had a glint in his eye. He was jazzed over this part of the story. "Pellagrin must've been a genius. Certainly a genius for building the two test platforms with the technology of the day. But to pull off what he did, it was a masterful work of espionage."

Taking a small sip from his bottle, Cyrus considered how best to explain this part of the story. It fascinated him. It was a shame that history would never know what Rumsfeld Pellagrin had accomplished. "Pellagrin knew he couldn't ask the Russians for help. At the time, Tsar Nicholas II was ruling Russia. By all accounts, not their best ruler. He was cutthroat and devious. So Pellagrin used that. He had word leaked to Russian intelligence that the U.S. had just completed work on a powerful new super weapon. The weapon was being packed up in preparation for field trials and a demonstration for the Washington brass. He disassembled one of the transport platforms and mixed in enough extraneous parts to thoroughly confuse any would-be Russian scientists. The genius of the plan was leaking the hardware's transport schedule—which included an overnight stay in a warehouse—while it waited for a connecting train bound for Washington. Sure enough, the Russians put a plan together, infiltrated American soil, and stole the so-called super weapon hardware!

"The point being, if Pellagrin couldn't get the Russians to let him bring the power source to the U.S. for testing, he would trick them into stealing one of the platforms and taking it to the power source."

"That was the part that I didn't understand. How could Pellagrin be assured the Russians would take the platform to the same facility they were using to develop the power source?"

"I think that was deductive reasoning on his part. The Russians had set up a secret military research facility way out in the middle of nowhere. No one was even supposed to know the place existed. The area was largely uninhabited for hundreds of years. Even to this day, it's mostly unexplored. Only the occasional trapper ventured that far into the wilderness. It was also the most logical place for the Russian military to take the stolen hardware. They wanted their best scientists to examine the new American weapon. And the best minds were already located at that facility."

"I guess," she said, clearly unconvinced.

"Believe me, to this day, American intelligence makes bigger gambles for much smaller rewards." He knew from bitter, first-hand experience.

"So Pellagrin tricked the Russians into stealing one of the platforms and taking it to the same base in the Russian wilderness," she said coaxing him to continue.

"Right! Pellagrin must've been a hell of a guy. Not just an egghead in a lab coat. He actually went into the field for that operation. He crossed the Russian border entirely on his own and actually infiltrated the secret military installation. And he must've had confidence in the mission because he was already working undercover at the base by the time the stolen American hardware arrived. For that to happen, he would've left for Russia even before the information was leaked about the location of the platform. In those days, travel was a very slow process."

She laughed. "You sound like you really admire the guy!"

"Yeah, I guess I do. Pellagrin made one gutsy move after another and he pulled it off. Plus, keep in mind that Pellagrin was a life-long man of science. He did a tour in the Marine Corps, but he was first and foremost a scientist. He learned to speak Russian fluently, just for that mission. The man must've been brilliant on many levels. But to have the guts to breach a high security Russian base like that, all on his own? That's astounding."

"There's still one part of the plan that I don't understand," Reese admitted. "If Pellagrin's test of the platform was successful, he'd be teleported to his lab in the states. That would effectively leave the Russian's with a functional platform as well as the only fuel source that could power it. If the chain reaction hadn't destroyed the Russian lab, wouldn't he have left them with everything they needed to claim the technology for themselves?"

Even as Cyrus shuffled through a series of the folders he'd brought up from the basement vault, a smile was spreading across his face. "There was never any real danger of that," he said.

Finding the photograph he was looking for, Cyrus slid it across the table. It showed a burned out heap of melted electronic hardware. With no reference to scale and no note on the old black and white photograph, there was no way to be sure what they were looking at. "This is what happened to Pellagrin's alpha platform," Cyrus explained. "This is the device his team constructed and tested prior to the pair of platforms used in the Russian experiment.

"In that final alpha test, Pellagrin learned two things. The first was that the power required to drive the platform was beyond anything at his disposal. The second was that, if Fire Star could power the platform, the device would be destroyed in the process. Whether the Russian power source was powerful enough to fuel the platform or not, he knew he had one shot at it."

Reese looked distinctly uncomfortable at the idea. She stared at the photograph before finally looking back at Cyrus. "So, if the test worked, Pellagrin would be teleported to his lab in the U.S. But if it didn't, he—"

"If it didn't work, he and his platform would've been toast," Cyrus grinned. "See what I mean? The man was hardcore. He didn't know how to lose!"

─────────

Reese couldn't help but laugh. Cyrus's energy was contagious. Maybe now was the time to ask a question that had been on her mind since the gunfight at her apartment. She searched for a tactful way to bring it up. "You were a spy, weren't you?"

So much for tact. She had opened her mouth and the question just dumped right out. The humor in his eyes iced over between blinks.

He looked her in the eye for several long seconds, finally nodding his head slightly. He was clearly reluctant to talk about it. Should she just let it go? She was tempted—no need to reopen old wounds. Something about the subject was clearly painful for him. But then, given their current circumstances, wasn't it better for her to know who he really was?

She squirmed. "I'm sorry. I didn't mean to pry." It was a useless attempt to make herself more comfortable on the hard concrete floor. It wasn't going to happen. "It's just that so many of the things that happened today…" she struggled to find the words. "They should've thrown you for a loop. They would have caught most people unprepared. But you didn't falter. Over and over today, you just reacted. God only knows where we'd be right now if you…if you weren't…*you.*"

Cyrus was silent for a while. He nodded again, seemingly to himself. "No, it's a fair question. And you've got a right to know. To be honest, I don't like thinking about it. Talking about it is just that much harder."

He climbed up off the concrete floor and stretched. Several pops from his back and neck sounded twice as loud in the concrete-lined room. He pulled over a stool from the nearby counter and sat down. Taking a long pull from his beer bottle and finishing it, he set it aside.

"I was recruited by an intelligence agency while in college. That, actually isn't terribly unusual. The CIA likes to scoop up recruits right after graduation. I was different. I'd taken my self-imposed role as an investigative journalist for the school paper a little too seriously, and it got me into some serious trouble. It also put me on the radar of a small national security group called the Coalition. I fell for that whole *'serve your country'* song and dance, left school, and went to work for them. I was young and naïve. It seemed like the right thing to do at the time.

"Anyway…the next thing I know, I'm working some fairly routine missions all over Europe. Nothing too special. But that changed pretty quickly. It turned out I had what they referred to as a *'unique disposition.'* After that, I was moved into deep-cover infiltration operations and was dealing with some real cutthroat bastards. It was really treacherous shit. But when it came down to it, we were doing good work, and it was something I could be proud of. Plus, I was good at it." He shook his head. *"Really good at it."*

"All of that changed on my last op. Things went sideways on a monumental scale—stuff I still find hard to believe. Anyway, the entire mission was compromised, and in the end people died... Natasha died.

"Almost as bad as what happened in the field, the Coalition brass just wanted to sweep the entire situation under the rug and pretend it never happened."

Cyrus looked her in the eye. His pain was impossible to hide. She could see that this heartache was rooted to his very soul.

"Some things can't be swept under the rug... Some things shouldn't be. Someone had to be held accountable." The last part was mostly mumbled to himself.

With what she'd just heard, Reese felt her skin go cold. She was completely shocked by this moment of candor. Vague, though it might have been, she could tell it was difficult for him to share this experience. Finally she found her voice. "*Was* anyone ever held accountable?"

He nodded again, a faraway look in his eyes.

"And?"

"When I returned to Command, I turned in my report, along with my resignation. I walked out the door and never looked back. We can't change who we were or what we've done. But we do have control over who we are and what we do next."

She was speechless, and slowly pacing the small room. Feeling horrible, she regretted asking the question that had started the discussion. It must've been terrible. And she had brought it to the surface with her questions. There was more to the story—that was clear by the pained look that had settled over him. The experience was haunting him.

"I'm sorry," she said meekly. She was on the verge of tears. "I would've understood if you said you didn't want to talk about it. You don't owe me anything. You certainly don't owe me any explanations."

He smiled. The smile was on his lips, but it was having trouble reaching his eyes. At least he was trying. "Yeah, that's the thing. I think you're going to need to know some of that once you read this file."

He was holding up a folder she hadn't seen yet. She could feel the nervous curiosity in the pit of her stomach as she hefted the lengthy report.

"Oh, God. Do I even want to know?"

"You know that Meade was abducted a few years back while on a business trip in Washington, D.C.?"

"I know that there was an *attempted* abduction."

"Ah, I see," Cyrus said, as if this filled in a blank in his own understanding. "Well, this report explains what really happened that day. It's the day Meade and I met."

Reese took the folder and started flipping through the first few pages. It was a meticulous FBI report detailing the abduction and recovery of Professor Walter Meade. She flipped back to double-check the summary at the top of the first page. It clearly stated the abduction of Walter Meade, not the *attempted abduction*. Why had Walter lied to her? She looked more closely at the report. It was dated almost six years earlier and written by FBI Special Agent Shaw.

Chapter 20

Starbucks, the Corner of 7th and H Street
Washington DC
Approximately Five Years Ago

The coffee shop was busy. Coffee shops in Washington, D.C. were always busy. It didn't seem to matter what time of day. That was alright, Cyrus Cooper enjoyed people-watching. It was a welcome distraction from his latest article for 'The Post.' These days he preferred to watch people rather than interact with them. Most people were far more interesting from afar anyway. He could see a face and guess at their life story, supposing at their problems of the day. If he kept his distance, he didn't have to deal with the real-world complications of others. He'd had enough complications to last a lifetime.

Cyrus took another sip of coffee. It wasn't the best he'd ever had, but it was certainly among the most expensive. Why were people willing to pay top dollar for a mediocre caffeine fix? He looked back to the screen of his laptop. He was there for the free Wi-Fi. That and to watch people. But he supposed that everyone had their own justification for their visit. He continued typing, entering notes from an interview the previous afternoon with FBI Special Agent Mindy Shaw. He had contacted the FBI looking for an official comment regarding a story he was writing.

As expected, the FBI's official version of events differed greatly from the other independent interviews he'd conducted. At the conclusion of his interview with Agent Shaw, he had walked away with two key insights. First, the FBI would have another black eye once his story went to press. The official FBI report was so watered down by 'the company line' that at the end of a two-hour interview he was hard pressed to find any facts relevant to the actual story. That meant his entire trip to D.C. had been a waste of time.

The second insight was specific to Agent Shaw. Though she'd been hamstrung with the company line, Agent Shaw was a competent young agent whose talents were being wasted in the press department. She was sharp enough to know the official story was tripe, but professional enough to deliver it with a straight face, no matter how much it galled her. He couldn't help wondering where she would be in a few years time. Still stuck in the same meaningless post? Or would she make her mark at the FBI and move up the ladder? If there was any justice, she would find a promotion. Whichever boss had sent her to feed him their bullshit version of events certainly didn't deserve his position.

An awkward exchange at the service counter caught Cyrus's attention. One of the baristas was not as smooth and practiced as the others. While two of the three behind the counter moved with a efficient grace that was borne of experience, the third was literally tripping over the others every time he moved.

Must be a new employee.

But that didn't seem right. Cyrus looked closer. The other two were much younger, a college guy of nineteen or twenty, and the girl was perhaps right out of high school. They had their routines down. But the third barista was older, maybe late twenties or early thirties. He had serious eyes and chiseled features.

The third barista finished his order, carefully marking a cup with a black sharpie before placing it just short of the pickup counter. Without a moment's hesitation, he turned and ducked through the curtain in the back wall, behind the counter.

From his position at the back of the sitting area, Cyrus could see part of the service area behind the wall blocking the back room. The third barista quickly pulled off his apron and handed it to a pimply-faced kid along with a small wad of cash. Without a word, the man rounded the wall, strode across the shop, and headed for the front door. Cyrus watched the kid pocket the money and don the apron. The kid quickly returned to the counter and went to work.

What the hell is going on?

Cyrus's eyes went to the hard-looking man who was now moving quickly. Reaching the front door, he shot a look over his shoulder in time to see the pimply-faced kid place several drinks on the pickup counter. The hard-looking man slowed his pace and watched. Cyrus looked back and saw an old man take a tall, insulated cup from the counter. The hard looking man smiled as he pushed out through the door. Then he was gone.

Cyrus now watched with fascination. He was sure he'd just witnessed something of consequence, but he wasn't sure what it was. The entire maneuver was smooth. If the man behind the counter had looked more the part and was a bit more graceful, Cyrus would never have noticed the exchange. But for the life of him, he couldn't figure out what he'd just seen. He was tempted to stop the old man and have him get a fresh cup of coffee. Something about this situation wasn't right. But they were sitting in a coffee shop only blocks from the White House and the nation's capital. If some kind of operation was underway, odds were good that law enforcement was somehow involved.

Still, he wasn't seeing any hint of law enforcement. A sense deep inside of Cyrus encouraged him to take action. Something was wrong. He should do something. But he took a deep breath. He'd been fighting that inner voice for the last year. The voice had served him well in a past life, but that was a life he was determined to keep in the rearview mirror. That life had cost him dearly, and he would keep it locked away. The problem was the voice. There was a part of his brain he couldn't turn off. He was constantly seeing things others didn't. Like the bartender last night who was pocketing the cash from every third beer he served. Or the night manager at his hotel. The man had a glassy look in his eyes and capillary damage around the corners of his nose; he clearly made a habit of drinking on the job. Hell, even the cab driver that drove him to Starbucks had caught his eye. Cyrus had taken a quick look at the driver before getting in the cab. The end of an old revolver's handle was sticking from between the front seats. It had only been the very edge of the pistol grip; a professional hitter would never have been careless enough to leave the gun even partially visible…clearly the cabbie was skittish about being robbed.

There was always something going on, no matter where he looked. It was why he'd taken to people watching. He was trying to tame the voice that shouted at tiny aberrations. For his own sake, he needed to mollify the sixth sense that showed him what normal people missed. And now it was an old man with coffee. He had to remind himself that it was broad daylight and he was only blocks from the White House. It was far more likely he'd witnessed some sort of law enforcement operation. But if that were the case, why was the voice telling him that an innocent old man was in danger?

Goddamn voice!

Cyrus watched as the old man found a seat just two tables away. The man sat with his back to Cyrus. He set his coffee aside and placed an old leather satchel at his feet. He pulled a laptop from the bag, placed it on the table, and flipped it open. As the machine booted, the old man took his first sip of coffee. Clearly it was hot. Even from behind, Cyrus could see the old man scowl before he set the drink aside.

When the laptop completed booting, an odd login screen appeared. Cyrus was familiar with all the normal desktop operating systems. This computer was running something unusual. The computer was a normal looking MacBook Air, but the login screen was customized. Before logging in, the old man glanced around to ensure no one was eavesdropping. But before he entered a keystroke, he passed his thumb quickly over the camera lens built into the bezel at the top of the laptop's screen. After he did this, the login screen changed color. The old man entered his lengthy login credentials.

All of this added to Cyrus's already growing concern. The old man had some sort of hardcore security on the machine. People don't go to that sort of trouble unless they have something worth protecting.

The little voice was practically screaming.

Cyrus was about to call out to the old man, when he saw him reach over and pick up the coffee. Before he could act, the old man was taking a long drink from the to-go cup.

Shit!

The time to act had passed. Cyrus settled back in his chair. This was going to play out. There was nothing he could do. He wasn't used to such indecision. He was sure he was witnessing some sort of covert operation. The problem was that he didn't know who was on what side. But he was sitting in the heart of Washington. Surely that meant the authorities were behind what he was witnessing. His interference would destroy what was obviously a delicate operation. But as logical as the argument seemed, with every passing moment his doubts grew stronger. Something about all of this seemed increasingly wrong.

The old man went through normal routines on his laptop, while Cyrus watched surreptitiously from the corner of his eye. The old man opened his email client and started a new message. He entered the recipient's name and the subject. He took another sip of his coffee and began the body of the message.

From a distance, Cyrus could just make out some of what was on the screen. What he really wanted to see was the recipient's name. He didn't expect it to be useful information, but at this point, he was looking for any clue to help him sort out who was who in this little drama. Giving up any pretense of subtlety, Cyrus squinted his eyes and leaned across his table. He could just make out the name of the addressee, Hamilton Wayneright. The name was familiar.

Wracking his brain, Cyrus recognized the name, but he just couldn't place it. So much for his eidetic memory. He was coming up short this time. No problem. He had Google. A few keystrokes on his own laptop brought up the web browser, and he did a search.

Shit!

Hamilton Wayneright was the President's Chief of Staff!

There was a loud bang, and Cyrus's eyes darted up from the screen. The old man was standing in front of his table, his chair toppled over behind him. He was stooping forward and clutching his left shoulder, struggling to stay upright. He struggled fiercely against the pain—oddly making an effort to reach for his computer—but his body failed him before he could do anything. The brittle old man toppled to the floor with a crash of scattering chairs.

Screams came from around the shop.

Cyrus was already on his feet. He called out, directing a nearby man in a suit to dial 911, even as he dropped to his knees at the old man's side. He checked for a pulse. It was erratic but still strong. Cyrus looked up to see at least two people were already on their phones. He could already hear them chattering excitedly with emergency operators.

Rolling the old man onto his back, Cyrus loosed his tie and made sure his airway was clear. The old man was unconscious. He was clutching at his left shoulder when he went down. Symptoms of a heart attack. Cyrus's glance darted to the coffee cup on the table.

Maybe not a heart attack…

The rise and fall of the man's chest meant he was still breathing. For the moment, there was little Cyrus could do. The screech of tires drew his attention to the shop's front windows. With some effort, he could see the street through the crowd of gathered onlookers. An ambulance had just pulled to the curb.

But a quick glance at the two people who had called 911 told him they were still relaying the situation.

The timing was wrong.

The gathered crowd parted as the EMTs made their way through the front door, pulling a wheeled gurney. Cyrus did a double-take when his eyes fell upon the two EMTs. It was the second technician—

Take away his hat and uniform...it was the same suspicious barista from a few minutes earlier!

The pair of EMTs finally cleared the crowd and pushed aside the nearby tables. Cyrus made way. As the two men bent over the old man, Cyrus pulled out his cell phone and quietly snapped of a series of photos of each of the rescue squad members before casually slipping the phone back into his pocket. Getting caught snapping the photos would only complicate the situation, possibly endangering innocent bystanders.

The EMTs immediately set about strapping the old man to the gurney. No examination or triage was performed. That made sense. There was no need. They already knew exactly what was wrong with the old man.

There wasn't much Cyrus could do to stop them from taking him, not without risking collateral damage. So he went with plan B. He stepped around the busy EMTs and grabbed the old man's laptop. Closing the lid, he returned to his table. He slid his computer into his bag along with the old man's computer. Without wasting a moment, he headed for the front door.

Just before reaching the door, Cyrus passed one of the many tables abandoned as everyone flocked to the drama on the other side of the room. This table, however, held a smartphone virtually identical to his own.

Perfect!

He grabbed the phone as he passed, moving out the door without missing a step.

As soon as he hit the street, he noticed a third EMT sitting in the idling ambulance. It was a three-man team working like a well oiled machine. That meant there wouldn't be much time to recover the old man, once the ambulance pulled away. These people would disappear. He knew first hand; he'd once had similar training.

Tapping a few buttons on the screen of the stolen phone, Cyrus put the ringer on silent. He also made sure to disable the vibration alert. Even that could give him away. Last, he made note of the cellphone's number. As he rounded the back of the ambulance, he found the back doors wide open.

Perfect!

He stepped up and slid the cell phone into the narrow gap behind the cabinets used to store medical supplies. Without pause, he continued across the street.

Cyrus never looked back—he needed to keep moving. It was crucial to avoid any action that might draw attention from the operative behind the wheel of the rescue squad. He needed to get off the street. There was a good chance the EMTs would be looking for the old man's laptop. Once they finished securing the old man, they would find it missing.

Cyrus rounded the street corner and went down half a block before ducking into a Radio Shack. Once inside, he stepped behind one of the window displays. Like every other Radio Shack he'd ever visited, the store was deserted. The kid behind the counter couldn't be bothered to check on him. It was just what he needed. He set his bag down and pulled out his own phone.

Calling 911 in a situation like this was pointless. He would never convince the operator he had witnessed an elaborate abduction. He needed someone who would act fast. Someone with the authority to cut through the red tape. He still had contacts at the Coalition, but that was a door he'd vowed never to reopen. Plus, it was a slippery slope. There would be repercussions. Ideally he needed the FBI. But that would take even longer—

No, that's it!

Cyrus dialed the number from memory.

This would require a delicate but decisive approach. He knew there was a chance he could get the FBI involved, but only if he played his cards right. It took only two rings before the line was answered.

"Agent Shaw," the voice on the other end answered.

"Agent Shaw, this is Cyrus Cooper. We met yesterday. I'm working on the story about—"

"Yes, Mister Cooper. I remember you. What can I do for you?"

"Umm... Look, there's no delicate way to put this, so I'm just going to be blunt. Please hear me out. I just witnessed the abduction of an old man from a coffee shop on 7th and H Street, here in DC."

There was a long silence from the other end of the line.

"Agent Shaw? Are you there?"

"Ah, yes... I'm here. I'm just trying to decide if I heard you correctly."

"You heard me fine. We really don't have time to waste, you need to get someone on this."

"Okay," she said somewhat patiently. "You think you witnessed an abduction. Have you called 911? Why are you calling me?"

"I'm calling you because the 911 operator will just jerk me around. We're talking about a three-man team. They spiked the old man's coffee. A few minutes after drinking it, he collapsed in a crowded Starbucks. Sixty seconds after the man hit the floor, an ambulance arrived to wheel him away. Two men dressed as paramedics walked in, strapped him to a gurney, and then they were gone. Just like that. Right in front of everyone."

The silence on the other end of the line stretched on again. Finally Agent Shaw spoke. "Look, Mister Cooper, I'm sure there is a very logical explanation for everything you've seen. In times of stress, the mind plays tricks on us. The ambulance couldn't possibly arrive as quickly as you claim. You just lost track of time. It's actually very common in stressful situations."

"Look, Shaw! We don't have time for this. I know exactly what I saw. I know the timeframe involved. When was the last time you saw an EMT crew walk into a place, toss someone on a stretcher and head for the door? No triage, no examination? This was an abduction. It was a three-man crew. Look into it. The ambulance was real. The inside of it was fully stocked. One must've been reported stolen."

"Mister Cooper—"

"Don't talk—listen!" Cyrus didn't have time to be patient. "You think I'm crazy. Fair enough. I'd think the same thing in your place. But we don't have time for you to be skeptical. Worry about that later. *Now is the time for you to do your job.* A man has been taken, right here on American soil."

"*My job*," she said through clenched teeth, "Is to wipe the noses of whiny reporters and answer stupid questions all day!"

"That's your job today," Cyrus countered. A cool calmness had entered his tone. "But if you get on this and make the save, you can bet your ass it's a one-way ticket out of that dead-end position. You're field qualified, are you not?"

"Of course I am!"

"Then get off your ass. This is your chance to get in the field!"

She was quiet for a moment. He was sure she was considering the possibilities. "Let's say for the sake of argument that I believe you. I don't have the resources to go after these guys any more than you do. It would take me almost as long to convince my bosses to move on this as it would take you to convince the 911 operator."

"By resources, you mean manpower?"

"Correct."

"Then you already have everything you need. How many agents are moldering on press detail right now, just like you? How many of them are field-rated and just itching for a chance to do something with it?"

She was silent again.

"Shaw, this has to be done now. Time's wasting. If they're the pros I think they are, they'll just disappear. I'm going to text you photos of the perps, the tags from the ambulance, and a photo of the man who was taken. But your best bet is to put a track on this cell phone number..." he gave her the phone number of the stolen mobile phone from memory.

"Wait," Shaw said in confusion. "You have the cell number of one of the perps?"

"Of course not. I planted a stolen mobile phone in the back of the ambulance, before it left. It was the only tracking device I could improvise on short notice. But you have to hurry. They're likely to dump the ambulance before too long. Once they do, you won't be able to track them."

Cyrus intentionally failed to mention that he had taken possession of the old man's laptop.

"Alright, Mister Cooper," Shaw finally relented. "I sincerely hope I'm not going to regret this. But either way, you and I are going to have a serious talk when this is over."

Chapter 21

Berton Springs, Colorado
Thursday, 1:12 am

The house was dark except for the chandelier over the dining room table. Cyrus and Reese sat across from each other. Several file folders were scattered about the table. They had locked up the vault and retreated to the dining room shortly before midnight, both exhausted from the frantic pace of the last twenty-four hours. They'd made great progress piecing together a more complete understanding of Meridian's history, and they hoped to sort out some of the remaining details before calling it a night.

"The report I read didn't cover it," Reese said. She wiped the sleep from the corner of her eyes and took a sip from a wine glass. They had exhausted the remainder of the meager six pack of beer, purchased along with the provisions earlier that afternoon. As luck would have it, Reese discovered an extensive selection of wine tucked in a cubby beneath the staircase in the basement. "So you're saying the FBI was responsible for recovering Walter after the kidnapping?"

Cyrus nodded. "Agent Shaw came through. She rallied a contingent of agents from her press detail and tracked the signal of the phone I planted in the ambulance. They arrived just as the grab-team was switching vehicles. If she'd arrived five minutes later, who knows how things might've turned out."

Reese shook her head. It was an amazing turn of events. A shocking confluence of the right people being in the right places at the right times. For Cyrus to think so quickly in such a situation—for him to make contact with an FBI agent he'd met only the day before? And for him to convince the agent to go out on a limb and try to recover Walter like that? Who was this man? It was no wonder Walter sought Cyrus out after it was all over. They seemed destined to be friends. Cyrus had such a practical intelligence, he was not unlike Walter himself.

She wondered if Cyrus actually understood the contributions he'd already made to Meridian. He didn't seem to comprehend why Walter wanted him on the project. In light of the last twenty-four hours, Reese found the logic pragmatic and obvious. Neither she nor her team were prepared to deal with the practical realities of Meridian in the real world. Most of their work, to date, dealt with theoretical practicality. In theory, they were going to change the world. In theory, they would improve the quality of life for the whole of mankind. But Walter was right, they were academics. They weren't equipped to face those who would try to take Meridian from them or corrupt it for their own benefit. The team was in far greater danger than she had ever thought possible. They'd been blinded by idealistic shortsightedness. It was that naïvety which now threatened their very lives.

They could probably go to the FBI or even the State Department for help. But, as Cyrus's discussion with Sanjay had proven, those options were not as simple as they first appeared. At this point she agreed, they were better off putting their safety in Cyrus's hands. For reasons she didn't understand, he clearly had experience in these...*situations*.

Walter had spoken of Cyrus often. Reese frequently felt he was stretching the bounds of some unspoken confidence with some of what he shared. On several occasions he'd mentioned a desire to introduce the two of them. She suspected Walter hoped to play matchmaker. It was flattering because she knew he considered Cyrus the son he never had. There was a clear sense of paternal pride. Although she was interested in meeting the man he held in such high regard, she'd always discouraged Walter's suggestions. But since Cyrus had come into her life less than twenty-four hours prior, there'd been an undeniable attraction.

Walter had been right again.

She tried to get her mind back to the task at hand. This line of thinking wasn't productive. Intriguing, but not productive. "What happened to Agent Shaw? How did the FBI react to her going off on her own like that?"

Cyrus chuckled and started sorting through the stacks of manila folders. "There's a report somewhere detailing that." He stopped looking and opted to summarize it from memory. "Her immediate supervisor was outraged and wanted her censured. But since it turned out that Walter was a VIP in the eyes of the Defense Department and he rubbed elbows with some bigwigs in Washington, the Director of the FBI intervened. Shaw received a commendation for taking extraordinary initiative in the face of uncertain circumstances, or some such jargon. They found it exceptional that she'd improvised a field team and organized an entire operation on the fly. They didn't just promote her out of the press department, they promoted her entire field team to a new detail under her command."

"And she had you to thank for it."

Cyrus shook his head. "She made her own decisions. She put that team together, and she lead them. Based on the report I read, she was very aware of the strengths and weaknesses of everyone in her department. She was overdue for that promotion. She just needed an opportunity to prove herself."

Cyrus took a drink from his wine glass. "After I gave Agent Shaw a way to track the ambulance, I took Meade's laptop and headed back to my hotel. I figured it'd be only a matter of time before someone came to collect it. There was no doubt in my mind that the machine contained valuable information. I'm pretty sure Meade was making an effort to secure it when he collapsed in the cafe.

"It was weird though. No one ever came to collect the computer—I kept it in the hotel vault until I was finished in DC. I took it with me when I flew back to Chicago. Still, I figured it was just a matter of time until someone came to collect it. Even after several weeks, there was still no contact.

"Finally I pulled the laptop from my safe and booted it up. Or, I should say that I tried to boot it. That's when I realized why no one cared about the machine. It had been erased. There must've been some sort of remote wipe protocol built in. The machine had purged all of its information at some point, likely shortly after Meade was taken. That sort of security says a lot about the people controlling it. A man only bothers with that level of security because he's toting some seriously sensitive information."

Cyrus ran a hand through his short stubble of hair and yawned. "About twenty-four hours after I tried to boot the laptop, Walter Meade showed up at my door for the first time. He introduced himself and we talked for some time. He had a security detail with him. But even that was interesting. He didn't know me at that point, but he left his three-man detail out in the hall. Normally in situations like that, a member of the security team will enter a residence to sweep it prior to the VIP entering. But Meade told his guys it wasn't necessary. He left them in the hall and we sat down and talked for hours. It was all very strange because it was so comfortable and informal. We just sort of hit it off."

Cyrus scratched at the stubble on his chin. She knew he was pondering something. He either didn't know how to bring it up or he wasn't sure how to say whatever it was.

"What's on your mind?" she asked.

His eyes met hers, and he smiled. "I've been thinking about the current security concerns. Meade obviously thought I could be useful in a situation like this. But I don't understand how he knew there'd be a situation like this. How could he have anticipated attacks on the team? I'm missing a piece of the puzzle."

First she smiled. Then she laughed outright—she couldn't help it. "I'm sorry," she said self-consciously. "While I suspect Walter knew very well what you were capable of, his abduction not withstanding, his desire to have you involved with Meridian had nothing to do with your field experience."

She could read the confusion in his eyes. "Walter never spoke about the platforms? About the technology?"

That made Cyrus chuckle. "We talked about a lot of things. But always in the abstract. *Always.* Never specific details. He would stop by without so much as a phone call. We'd kick around whatever problem was on his mind, and then he would go."

"But you never asked what he was working on? You never wondered where his ideas were coming from?"

Cyrus shook his head. "This might be hard for you to understand..." He paused while he searched for the right words. "I'm used to dealing with people with secrets. When I was with the Coalition, I was trained to keep those secrets. As an investigative reporter, I need to do the opposite. I need to know what questions to ask—know where to look when something seems off. When it came to Walter, I just knew what questions not to ask.

"There's a problem that's somewhat unique to people in my former line of work. The job requires people who are very good at reading between the lines...at seeing what other people don't see. The trouble starts when those people retire. That sense that was once so important suddenly becomes a slippery slope, and it can do a lot of damage. You start to see things in the people you deal with in day-to-day life. You notice when they're lying or when they're telling a partial truth. It's fine when you're on the job or in the field. Then it can save your life. But when you see those things in your personal life, it can make normal friendships tough and relationships impossible.

"The reason being that people—friends—constantly tell half-truths. Often to spare another's feelings. They do it for any number of reasons, really. But when you pick up on all those tells, and it's second nature to dissect their motivation for what they just did or what they just said, it can be terribly destructive."

"You make it sound like a mental condition."

Cyrus responded with a slow knowing nod. "Some field operatives get wound pretty tightly. It's a hazard of the job. They have to be tuned in to everyone and everything around them, 24/7. When they leave the field, many have trouble adjusting to normal life. It can manifest as any number of mental conditions. Some guys become paranoid. Some just burn out. Far too many end up eating their own bullet. It's common—it happens to more of us than not. It's one of the reasons I left that life. I choose to take people at face value. That's how normal people live. They don't dissect the actions of everyone around them, always watching for anomalies.

"The point being, I just took every conversation with Meade as the talk that it was. Always interesting, always thought provoking. That voice in the back of my mind that speaks up when something is off or out of place? I locked it away. I used the conversations with Meade to help me hone that discipline."

Reese gave some thought to all Cyrus had said. Certainly being a human lie detector was harmful to relationships great and small. No one should be one hundred percent honest with the people around them. It defied the natural order. There were times when it was necessary to omit information, however trivial, to spare the feelings of another. She couldn't imagine how difficult it might be for someone trained so thoroughly in detecting these tells that they saw deception everywhere they turned. She could see it eventually becoming detrimental.

"Those ideas that Walter brought to you?" she started. "They were key issues relating to Meridian. Many of them were roadblocks we, the team, hit. When that happened, Walter would visit you and discuss the problem. He would return the next day, more often than not, with a great new idea or a different approach that would lead to a workaround or an outright breakthrough. A number of the innovations currently employed on the platforms were yours!"

Cyrus laughed. "I think Meade was exaggerating my contributions. I don't know anything about teleportation. I've read a little about quantum physics, even quantum entanglement, but I'm no physicist. I don't even know enough to be dangerous."

Reese finished her wine and poured them each another glass. "Then you're going to love this," she said with a coy smile.

"Early in the project, we were trying to encase the entire contents of the transport platform in a magnetic field. The next step was to entangle every atom within that field with the atoms encased in a duplicate field, located on the paired platform. Prior to our experiments, quantum teleportation had been successful but only on a single photon at a time. Our approach intended to entangle the entire contents of both platforms, resulting in a quantum bridge between the two devices. The bridge would last only a fraction of a second, long enough for the contents of the platforms to instantly swap positions. But while this approach was theoretically possible, it required astronomical levels of energy to entangle any matter of consequential mass."

She made penetrating eye contact with Cyrus again. "The energy requirements were entirely prohibitive. Each platform would require its own dedicated high output nuclear reactor.

Essentially, it was the same problem Pellagrin faced in 1908 with his test platform. The difference being, we didn't have Fire Star."

Cyrus whistled and sat back in his chair. He ran his hands through his hair again. His eyes drifted into the distance as he considered the ramifications.

"The goal of this project is," she said in a very serious tone, "and always has been, to create a network of teleportation platforms putting every location on the planet within easy reach. Professor Meade's sole intent for this project is—was," she corrected herself, "to create an extensive network of inexpensive teleportation platforms that would be safe to operate, and available to everyone in the world. He wanted to revolutionize travel, solve a significant portion of our pollution problems, and unite our people in a way never before imagined.

"The platforms will have the power to do all of that. But if each device requires its own nuclear reactor, that's simply never going to happen. They must be inexpensive to produce as well as operate. And safe! Nuclear-powered platforms are neither cheap nor safe. We need to produce millions of them, or none at all. If they're ubiquitous, then everyone on the planet has equal opportunity. Imagine the entire world using safe, instantaneous travel.

"Walter believed it was absolutely critical that the platforms be available to everyone to use free of charge. He wouldn't allow them to be a tool strictly for the affluent and powerful."

Cyrus leaned forward. He understood. "So the power requirements are a problem?"

"No," she said with a smile. "Power requirements *were the problem*. But you and Walter solved it!"

Cyrus sat back in this chair and rubbed his eyes. Exhaustion was setting in, but they were finally getting to the meat of the matter. Understanding the project would be the key to understanding the threat they faced. He waited for Reese to continue.

"Two things made a difference when it came to the platform power requirements. The first part of the solution was your idea." She had a smile that made Cyrus suspect that she wanted him to guess what his contribution might have been. He had no idea, and he lacked the energy to speculate.

She nodded in understanding and continued. "Your suggestion did away with magnetic field as a means of controlling the mass entanglement onboard the platform." She let the statement hang in the air for a moment.

"Lasers?" he said with a nod of understanding.

"Your idea was so simple and practical that it bordered on genius! Rather than entangle the entire contents of the platform, we would generate a laser containment field around the contents of the platform. The concept went right back to the original work of Einstein and Rosen in the 1930s! And it was poetic since the very first groundbreaking work in quantum teleportation was done with photons. After all, what is a laser if not an array of photons?"

She laughed and rolled her eyes. "It seems a little funny, explaining your idea *to you.*"

He had to admit it was amusing, but necessary. "Please, keep going. Keep in mind that when I discussed these things with Walter, we were speaking in the abstract. I was never aware of the project. I knew nothing about Meridian. So while you might credit me a solution, you're being generous. All I ever did was brainstorm on matters I didn't fully understand."

She laughed. "Rather than entangle the entire contents of the platform at a sub-atomic level, the platform's perimeter is wrapped in a laser field. Then photons that compose the field are entangled, and when the right signal is passed to the particles, the quantum bridge is engaged. The contents of the two platforms are instantly swapped!"

"Right!" Cyrus slapped a hand on the table and grinned. He now remembered the full extent of the conversation. "It would be like placing the contents of the platform in a box made of entangled photons. Rather than entangling every single atom on the platform, you just entangle the surface of a three dimensional box. Whatever's inside the box just goes along for the ride. So you're saying the power needed to entangle the perimeter field was less than that needed for the entire contents of the platform?"

Her jaw dropped at the thought. "By several orders of magnitude! I don't recall the exact equation off hand, but the power requirement was a tiny fraction of the original implementation."

Cyrus absently scratched the rough stubble of his jaw again. *Damn, that is something.* "So a nuclear reactor is no longer required?"

She waggled her hand. *Kind of yes, kind of no.* "That got us part of the way there. But the breakthrough solved a lot of safety concerns. Prior to that modification, the platforms channeled so much energy that there was no way to adequately prevent overload or safeguard against tampering. More simply put, there was just so much juice running through the hardware that any sort of malfunction could cause the device to go critical. The resulting damage could range anywhere from a massive EM discharge, to an explosion that could destroy a city block. No… Until we were able to limit the power requirements using your suggestion, the platform had no chance of leaving the research and development stage."

She took another sip of wine and pursed her lips in thought for a moment. "We got the first prototype platforms online a couple of years ago, before the implementation of the laser field. As I explained, they had massive power requirements, so the two prototype platforms were drawing power directly from nuclear power stations. One on the East Coast, one on the West."

"A couple of years ago?" Cyrus was confused. "You didn't have your first operable prototype until a couple of years ago?" This didn't match with what he read in the files from the vault.

She shook her head. These facts clearly troubled her as well. "No," she said. "Prior to what we read tonight, I had no idea prototype platforms were built before the start of Meridian. We—the team, that is—were led to believe we were breaking entirely new ground."

He nodded. "And now we know this project has been in the works, in one form or another, since the start of the twentieth century."

"That part still blows my mind! I can't imagine what sort of work they could've been doing with quantum teleportation as far back as the early nineteen hundreds." She absently rubbed the corner of her eyes at the bridge of her nose with her thumb and forefinger. "The technology of that era? It would've been like cavemen trying to build a jet airliner!"

Cyrus laughed. He couldn't argue that point. But according to Professor Meade's documentation, scientists had been enamored with the prospect of this technology for more than a hundred years. And why not? The technology really would change the world. But what were the motivations of project leaders prior to Professor Meade? Certainly the tech would yield untold strategic value for the military. Even in the private sector, there were hundreds, maybe thousands of uses.

The number of ways to abuse the technology was also nearly limitless. It was becoming clear why Walter Meade considered the technology as disruptive as it was beneficial. While the advantages were great, so were the potential negative consequences. Flooding the market with the new technology could destroy financial markets virtually overnight. There were unavoidable consequences. Big oil concerns would collapse. Shipping companies would fail. There was potential for global economic disruption that would ultimately lead to the failure of banks, which in turn, would take entire markets along with them.

With this in mind, Meade had devised what he referred to as a progressive deployment strategy. He intended to put the technology in the hands of international shipping companies first. This would give those companies a chance to revise their business models and transition away from the ocean-going freighters and airliners used for international transport of goods. At the same time, this initial stage of deployment would allow the public to grow slowly comfortable with the idea of teleportation and the technology behind it. Meade anticipated a certain amount of pushback from the less progressive members of society. There would be those who questioned the safety of the technology, no matter how much testing was conducted or how many safety protocols were involved. By allowing shipping companies first access to the platforms, the technology would gain traction and support, as it was slowly rolled out for wider use.

In turn, the platforms would gradually be expanded into additional markets. They would be made available to governments around the world. This would yield tremendous economic advantages and further support and acceptance of the technology. For that to work, Meade believed it was critical for the technology to be made available to all United Nations members, not just favored nations. This provided everyone equal footing in the global arena and prevented any sort of arms race for technological superiority.

The next, and most important stage called for the deployment of Meridian technology more widely as a means of public transportation. The slow rollout and deployment was to take years. This would garner public acceptance of the technology, but it would also allow auto manufacturers, airlines, shipping companies, and the like to alter, revise, and update their compromised business models. The ultimate goal was the deployment of the Meridian platforms with a minimum of economic and social disruption.

From very early on, Walter Meade understood that Meridian was a veritable Pandora's Box. It could be a boon to the world or it could cause untold harm. With a proper deployment plan, he believed he could bring the life-changing tool to the world, while minimizing negative consequences.

This was the crux of the problem for Cyrus. Corporations, militaries, nations—many, if not all, would be willing to kill everyone on the team if it allowed them solitary access to the technology. The first to possess it would have a decisive advantage over any and all competition. This meant the list of suspects interested in Meridian was virtually endless. Literally anyone could have been behind Meade's death.

Reese continued her line of thought without realizing the rabbit hole into which Cyrus's thinking had descended. "After our first successful test, one amazing unforeseen consequence became shockingly apparent—"

She had Cyrus's full attention once again.

"Once the transport was complete, the platform discharged a staggering amount of power!"

"How staggering?"

Her eyes were absolutely glowing as she considered how best to phrase her reply. "The power discharged was 1 to 2 orders of magnitude greater than the power needed to initiate the transport."

Cyrus was at a loss for words. All he could do was stare. It was the holy grail of modern science to develop a process of generating power, one that released more energy than was required to initiate the generating reaction. She was saying that such an energy release was a byproduct of the teleportation process? The implications of this were almost as earth-shattering as the teleportation technology itself. But by 1–2 orders of magnitude? That meant the power generated by the teleportation was 10–100 times greater than the power required to initiate transport.

He opened his mouth to speak but found no words. 10–100 times? He tried again but once again failed. This was truly unexpected.

"Okay," he said, finally finding his voice. "What about negative side effects from the teleportation or the excess energy? Radiation? Volatility?"

Slowly, she shook her head. An enormous smile spreading across her face. "No radiation. Nothing unusual. It's completely safe, so long as the excess energy is channeled into a capacitor of some kind, or grounded out. As I said, it was a completely unexpected result. Luckily, Walter was excessive when it came to grounding the test platforms. Following the first successful test, the excess energy was simply bled off into the earth."

She laughed and rolled her eyes theatrically. "I make it sound like the first transport was a resounding success. That wasn't exactly the case. The teleport completed without issue but the resulting power dump blew every fuse and relay in both platforms. It blacked out the grid for twenty square miles around the receiving device, too. But the results were worth the headache—the monitoring equipment failed, but the readings we got before that point were off the charts!"

"What'd you do to prevent the issue on subsequent tests?" Cyrus had a good idea when he asked the question, but he wanted to be sure.

"We worked on lots of ways to buffer the power. But they all fell short. There was just too much power coming out of the platform after transport. In the end, Walter came up with a better idea. He suggested we pipe the excess power back into the power grid. The amount of energy generated by a single transport was significant.

"We did some models and an exhaustive analysis. Once we have an array of platforms in regular use throughout the country, we'll be able to do away with our reliance on nuclear power entirely. Actually, we'll have a surplus of energy like we never imagined."

Cyrus didn't waste cycles contemplating further benefits from the new technology. The threats to the team were substantial. Everyone and their brother would kill for the cutting edge science whether it was ready for production or not. Secrecy was their only defense, and that secrecy was already compromised. There was one saving grace. Whoever knew about the project would want exclusive access to the technology. That meant the threat was contained. If he could eliminate the threat, the secret and the team would be safe again. But for how long?

"So every time we use a platform, a massive amount of power is fed back into the local power grid?" Cyrus wanted to make sure he understood the technology correctly.

"No," she said simply. "It will be when the system goes online publicly. Walter decided not to feed the excess juice into the grid while we're still in the testing stage. He was worried that someone might be able to locate the platforms by doing an assay of the nation's power grid. He thought it would be only a matter of time before it caught someone's attention. We're talking about a lot of power…even with our limited number of platforms."

This was Cyrus's concern when Reese first mentioned pushing power back into the grid. It threatened their anonymity. He wasn't entirely surprised that Meade had considered the issue before him.

"What about the need for a nuclear reactor? Did the laser field reduce the power requirements enough to power the device from a conventional source?"

She shook her head. "No, unfortunately. But Walter came up with a workaround. There is a component in each platform that functions as a buffer and a battery, essentially a capacitor. When the power is released immediately following a transport, it flows into the capacitor. It essentially acts as a battery, retaining a charge long enough to initiate subsequent transports without a need for a nuclear power source. And since it's the receiving platform that has the power spike, each platform simply needs one initiating transport from a platform that is attached to a nuclear reactor, or has a stored charge of its own. After that, the network becomes self sustaining.

"But no power will be pushed back into the grid until we're ready to take the system public."

Cyrus considered all of this. It was remarkable. It was truly the stuff of science fiction made real. They were on the cusp of a very interesting time in human history. He couldn't help but wonder how history might remember Professor Meade and his team. He wondered what part of history had yet to be written. Meade was already dead. Could he keep the rest of the team safe and protect Meridian until it could be released to the world?

Chapter 22

Cyrus was sitting at the kitchen counter when Reese wandered in for her first coffee of the morning. She had on a gray tank top and a pair of gray sweat shorts. Both accentuated her trim figure. Her hair was pulled up into a ponytail. He wondered how she could look so attractive having rolled straight out of bed.

When she noticed him looking, Reese smiled warmly. Was she thinking about the kiss they shared just before heading to their rooms the night before? He hoped she was. The thought had crossed his mind more than once in the hour he'd been up and at work on his laptop.

"Good morning," Reese said quietly and gave him a peck on the cheek. "I thought you might be in bed. Yesterday was a long day. Been up long?"

"Not long," he said with a shake of his head. He nodded to his MacBook Pro. "I wanted to ask you about this. I took a look at the server cabinet downstairs. There's a router and a modem but the modem isn't uplinked to anything. I logged on to

246

the Wi-Fi to see what would happen, and I'm actually getting access to the Web. Not only that, but it's fast. Really fast!"

She had rounded the counter and was pouring herself a cup of coffee. Her smile brightened. "That's something, isn't it! It's the same technology we use to connect the computers embedded in the platforms. We call it QDL—short for Quantum Data Link."

"You're saying it's a wireless connection to the Internet?"

"Not in the conventional sense." She took a sip of coffee, followed by a slow deep breath. She looked refreshed. "The modem you saw would normally be attached to a cable or DSL line that connected the house to the outside world. We removed the hardwired uplink and replaced it with a QDL interface. It's a microcircuit with an optical data link attached to a photonic-node. That node is paired with a twin at a data center in California.

"It was another one of Walter's ideas." Her eyes tightened with a concerted focus. She looked almost like she was accusing him. "I think it was another idea you discussed with Walter."

Cyrus nodded. He couldn't hide a knowing grin. "It was. But I had no idea he'd built a prototype."

She smile proudly. "We did more than prototype it. It's a key technology linking the platforms. Almost all of the safety protocols utilize QDL. The instantaneous two-way communication allows a pair of platforms to do all kinds of preflight checks before engaging the quantum bridge."

Cyrus could offer only a questioning look in response.

"Say you're about to teleport to a platform located at the Santa Barbara office. It's not really a concern now, but one day these platforms will be in constant use by people all over the world. So, when you step on the platform here and select your destination, your platform utilizes the Quantum Data Link, confirming the status of the destination platform. If the destination platform is clear, you can teleport immediately. But if the destination platform is occupied or out of order, the data connection will prevent your platform from engaging at an inopportune or possibly dangerous time.

"And since the QDL is an instantaneous data communication that isn't hindered by distance or *any* form of interference, that communication is one hundred percent reliable. That's a far cry better than any communication technology used today."

Cyrus nodded as he considered the potential. This certainly answered a number of his questions pertaining to the safety of the platforms. "So Meade used QDL to link the house to the Internet. Does that mean that our Web access can't be traced back to us?"

Reese set down the cup. Her head tipped slightly as she considered the question. "I don't see how. Assuming someone was tracing the data, they'd only be able to follow it back as far as the datacenter in Santa Barbara. The data would be routed through the collocation facility's infrastructure until it reached our router. Once it hits our router at the colo, every packet instantly hits the router here via the permanently entangled photons of the QDL interface. Assuming someone back-traced the Internet traffic as far as our router at the colo, they'd have no way of knowing where the data went from there. Once it hits the QDL, it could go anywhere in the world.

"Heck," she continued. "In theory, it could go anywhere in the entire galaxy!"

The thought made Cyrus smile. The QDL technology was a breakthrough all on its own. The ability to link distant sites with no limit on bandwidth? No latency? It would revolutionize networking. Which raised another question.

"Could the same thing be done with a cellular phone?" he asked with more than a little hopeful enthusiasm.

"Absolutely! We've tested it. The world's first mobile phone that will literally work anywhere on the planet with no possibility of a dropped call or loss of signal."

Cyrus was shocked. This was groundbreaking. "You've actually done it? You married a cell phone with the QDL and it worked?"

"Sure," she said with a modest shrug. "Give me your mobile and a half hour, and I'll have you up and running. Your phone will still work with your existing carrier. What I'll do is crack open your phone and disconnect the internal antenna and attach a QDL interface. Your QDL will be linked to a node here, or somewhere else, that will connect to the cellular network just like normal. It's sort of a retrofit."

Cyrus could barely contain his enthusiasm. "That's brilliant! Does it work for data too?"

"Your phone's data connection will send the traffic over the QDL just like it does the voice information. Voice and data, anywhere in the world with no dead spots! Can you hear me now?"

He smirked at her poking fun at Verizon Wireless's abused marketing slogan. It brought another question to mind. "What stops this from being a free standing product? This seems like a technology that any mobile service provider would pay a mint for."

Some of the enthusiasm drained from Reese at the suggestion. "To be honest, I'm not sure."

The question made her more than a little uncomfortable. "What's wrong?"

"Well," she said quietly. "It was a topic of great debate within the group. Several of us wanted to pursue licensing the technology to some of the existing mobile phone carriers. It seemed like the natural evolution of mobile technology. But Walter was dead set against it."

"The technology could potentially be worth hundreds of millions of dollars. Maybe even billions. Is there any technical requirement that would limit deployment? You know, like there is with the platforms?"

"No, none. But Walter wouldn't hear of it. It caused a lot of tension for the team. I don't think it helped that Walter wasn't willing to explain his reasons for keeping quiet about this aspect of the technology."

"I'm willing to bet it was a question of exposure. He was worried about drawing attention from the wrong people. I don't think your team realizes that anonymity is their number one defense right now. People would do *anything* for Meridian. Walter knew the best security money could buy wasn't worth nearly as much as anonymity.

"If QDL goes public, the team behind it will get attention. Walter knew that attention was a danger to everyone as well as the future of Meridian. He wouldn't risk the exposure."

"Some of the team saw the QDL as a chance to get the recognition that was denied when Meridian couldn't go public. In truth, I'm sure some of them also wanted to cash in. Walter always intended for Meridian to be a not-for-profit endeavor. It was going to change the world, but it wasn't going to make anyone rich. You may have noticed—some of us have overly inflated egos. Recognition and wealth were constant concerns for Walter. He was worried that either one might cause one of us to do something stupid."

This was the thought that pulled Cyrus from his bed at sunrise. He wanted to take a closer look at the members of the Meridian team. The more he thought about it, the more he was convinced a team member had leaked project details to an outsider. Taking a careful look at the team was the logical place to begin his investigation.

He had already e-mailed Special Agent Shaw, asking her to pull the records of everyone on the team. Doing so meant she would be going out on a limb for him. Since this was not an FBI investigation, accessing those files would constitute a violation of protocol. To that end, he had contacted her via a private e-mail address, making every effort to keep their interactions off the radar. And, of course, she could always refuse his request. All he could do was ask. After that, the ball was in her court. Such was the nature of their relationship, professional but with rather blurry boundaries. Plan B was a freelance information broker out of Miami, with whom he had worked in the past. That plan had its own disadvantages. Plan C would mean going to one of his contacts at the Coalition, and he wasn't nearly as confident of their discretion. The Coalition traded in lies, misinformation, and subterfuge. It was their currency. He really didn't want to take Meridian anywhere near his old outfit. Shaw was his best bet, if she was willing to bend the rules.

"So, my plan for the morning is to pick up the team and move them to the secure location. I heard back from my friend.

He's got everything ready. We can have them buttoned up by lunch."

That was the second topic of his early morning e-mail exchange. Preparations were complete. The team would be on lockdown until the threat was eliminated. After he and Reese met with the group the prior morning, Cyrus had put them up in an out of the way motel that was far off the beaten path. It didn't have Internet access or cable television. Even the maid service was questionable. The place barely had running water. It was a stopgap while a trusted friend prepared the safe house. The safe house was a location better suited for the team to hide out for the long term, should it come to that. At this point, Cyrus had little idea who was after Meridian, and he had no idea how long it might take to sort things out. But such preparations took time, so despite protests, the team was sequestered in a fleabag motel beyond the outskirts of Bakersfield.

"Great," Reese said and set her coffee cup aside. "Let me take a quick shower, and I'll be ready to go."

"Actually, I was hoping you would sit this one out."

She offered a puzzled look in response.

"It might be a little paranoid, but I'd like to keep you and the team separate. Whoever is behind this tried to kill Alfie and kidnap you. Alfie was a lot further down the totem pole. I have no idea what plans they might have for the rest of the team. Kill them? Grab them? All the same, I want to keep you in a separate location. That way, if everything falls apart, they can't get the entire team." Cyrus had to admit that it was a shitty last resort, but it was, after all, a last resort.

She nodded absently as she considered the logic. "It's your call," she concluded. "Is there anything constructive I can do while you take care of the kids?"

He smiled and closed the laptop. He slid his stool away from the breakfast counter. "There are more files to slog through in the vault. Could you take a look at them? See if you can put some more pieces of our puzzle together? We still don't know who is after us or why."

"You got it."

Her smile. It never failed to send a rush of warmth through him. If he were honest with himself, he would question his motivations for keeping Reese separate from the rest of the team. Certainly it made tactical sense for all of the reasons he had stated. But there was a more selfish reason that he hadn't voiced. Having her near stirred feelings in him that he hadn't experienced in a long time. Even more surprising was his desire to tell her these things. That wasn't at all like him. Internalizing his emotions had always come naturally. Sometimes to a fault. Maybe she was good for him. Where would things go from here? Part of him was excited to find out. Part of him was troubled. Tomorrow was promised to no one. He knew that from bitter experience.

"I need to shower and change," he said, pulling his thoughts back to the moment, before they reached a much darker place. "Could you set my phone up to run the platforms?"

Cyrus thought the day was off to a good start. He had a plan of action, and it felt good. Hondo was already on a private international charter, lugging one of Meade's platforms to some hidden, far off corner of the world that was to be their safehouse. Once the team was on lockdown, it would ease his mind a great deal. And, with Reese searching Meade's files, there was a chance she might find something that would point him in the right direction and offer a hint at resolving the greater threat to the team. That left him with just one stop to make before he met the team in Bakersfield. It was a side trip that was virtually guaranteed to yield valuable intelligence.

Chapter 23

Miami, Florida
Thursday, 1:15 pm (11:15 am Colorado Time)

The humidity was stifling. It was the first thing that came to mind every time Cyrus considered visiting Florida. Such a beautiful state, but one to be avoided during the summer months, if at all possible. In this case, the stop was unavoidable. He needed information, and for that, there was just one man he could trust.

With a cautious eye, he drove the rental car slowly down the crowded upscale urban street. It was lined with high-end boutique shops of every persuasion. Finally locating a parking spot, he swung the vehicle up parallel to the curb and climbed out. Traveling around the country using Professor Meade's platforms was proving to be extremely efficient. The man had devices stashed in key locations across the country, even internationally, according to the database. Why the platforms could only be produced in a limited quantity remained a mystery. What was it about the ore that was being used as a super-capacitor that made it so unique and so hard to come by?

He'd rented the car using a fake ID and credit card. Now he stuffed extra change into the parking meter. His thinking was simple; it was the little things that could draw attention and give you away. Something foolish like a parking ticket or getting pulled over for speeding were prime examples. They were simple mistakes that resulted in information being entered into databases. Those databases were routinely mined by automated systems that were getting increasingly efficient when it came to discovering anomalies. Even small anomalies were cause for concern when it was necessary to stay off the proverbial radar.

All the same, his trip to Miami was unavoidable. Cyrus no longer had direct access to the lab and fingerprint analysis facilities he required. When he walked away from the Coalition, he walked away from their support. Luckily he still had resourceful friends in low places.

A bell chimed as he pushed through the door of the upscale electronics shop near the middle of the block. The store was fairly small, but the entire front wall was floor-to-ceiling windows, polished to perfection and glowing with natural light. All manner of electronic equipment was scattered throughout the shop, arranged neatly on fashionable, real-wood display tables and counters. Everything was bright, shiny, and high tech.

But Cyrus wasn't here to shop. He headed directly for the service counter at the back of the store. A short young lady, barely out of her teens, waited behind the counter. She had short dark hair and glasses with thick black frames. She looked a great deal like her father.

"Is Nathan in?" Cyrus asked with a smile.

She returned his smile and held open the waist high gate that separated the counter from the showroom floor. "He's expecting you."

Cyrus nodded as he passed and continued through a doorway beyond the counter. There he found a short hallway. A head popped from a doorway along the wall at the far end. A man with short, bushy gray hair and a short, gray, stubbly beard beamed with excitement.

"Cyrus! There you are, come on back!"

The head ducked back into the room and Cyrus followed.

Nathan sat on an expensive Aeron office chair in front of a counter packed with complicated electronics. There was an elaborate computer system attached to several different high-end scanning and printing devices. The counter had a wing that extended into a peninsula. That section of the work surface was dedicated entirely to manual cutting, printing, gluing, and binding tools. Nathan was a jack-of-all-trades. One of his most profitable talents was document forging. He could do the high tech computer-aided work, but he was also a master of the old school art that required the trained eye and skilled hands of a seasoned pro.

"I'm glad you have time to see me," Cyrus said as he stepped into the room.

The man's face lit up at the sight of his old friend. "I always have time for you, my boy!"

Nathan made sure he had eye contact with Cyrus before tapping his index finger to his right ear. He archived his eyebrows twice, theatrically. "I didn't know you were in town. I'm so glad you looked me up."

The message was clear. The place had been bugged. But it appeared the bug was audio only. This wasn't entirely surprising. Nathan worked almost exclusively for the CIA, strictly off the books. But the spooks made a point of keeping their eyes, or in this case their ears, on their contractors. In theory, Nathan wouldn't have known about the bug. But if he had let the CIA get the drop on him, Nathan wouldn't have been the skilled resource Cyrus needed at the moment.

"Well," Cyrus said with a chuckle. "You always said to drop by if I was in town. I was just passing through. I thought I'd pop in and say hello."

"Fantastic! I was just thinking of you the other day. I was reading your latest piece on the corruption in the Chicago Police Department. You really turned some heads with that one! It's the talk of the town, even way down here."

"Tell me about it. I'm not terribly popular in Chicago right now."

Nathan chuckled and scratched at the stubble of his beard. "I should think not."

Grabbing a tablet computer from the counter beside him, Nathan passed it to Cyrus, who looked at the screen. There was a blank notepad app on screen. Cyrus nodded to the older man and pulled out the stylus and began writing on the device.

"So what're you doing in Florida?" Nathan asked.

Cyrus knew the man would normally not ask such a question. It was bad form in the trade. People in his line of work didn't discuss such things. But since they weren't supposed to be communicating in a functional capacity, and since someone was listening in, certain topics were requisite.

"I'm researching a new story. Part of it led me down to the 'Glades. I'm still not sure if anything will come of it, though. It's kind of the nature of this type of reporting. For every story I break, there are a lot more that fizzle."

"Not like the old days."

"No," Cyrus said, his voice growing momentarily more serious. "Not like the old days. Had enough of that to last a lifetime."

"Understandable. It can be messy business." Nathan thought for a moment. "That's why I'm happy here with my printers and scanners. No one looking to stick a knife in my back while I work, or put a bullet in my head while I sleep."

Cyrus continued to scribble notes on the screen of the tablet.

"Do you have time for a drink?" Nathan asked expectantly. "There's this great little place just down the block."

Cyrus passed the tablet back to Nathan. "I wish I did, Nate. But I really need to hit the road. How about next time?"

Nathan finished reading the tablet. He looked up and nodded. "Count on it," he said.

Cyrus pulled three plastic bags from the pockets of his cargo pants. One bag contained two cell phones with their batteries removed. These were the phones he'd taken off the street thugs the night they tried to abduct Reese. Nathan would be running them for prints and pulling their call logs. A second bag contained a wad of plastic explosives. The detonator pencil was also in the bag, though rolled in cotton and taped up to prevent contact with the explosive. Bag three contained the chrome cylinder and the plunger of the hypodermic Cyrus took from the men who attacked his apartment. Visible thumbprints lined the body of the aluminum cylinder. Nathan would run them as well. The cylinder also contained a sample of the substance with which he was to be injected. Once Nathan had a chance to analyze everything, Cyrus would have a much better idea of what he was up against.

Nathan took the three plastic bags and placed them in a heavy steel cabinet drawer. He slid it silently closed and locked the drawer with a key he kept in his hip pocket. He flipped through a stack of file folders on the corner of his desk. A moment later he located the one he wanted and handed it to Cyrus.

"No worries," Nathan continued. "I'll walk you out. I want to introduce you to my youngest daughter anyway."

Neither man made mention of the folder as they left the room.

Chapter 24

Cyrus slipped behind the wheel of his rental car and started the engine. He flicked the air conditioner on high and took a deep breath while silently coaxing the cooling unit into action. He flipped open the file folder Nathan provided. When Cyrus had sent an encrypted email to Nathan to arrange the meet, he had asked a favor. The folder contained the results of that request, the complete autopsy results for Professor Walter Meade.

He read the extremely detailed report, but at first glance it held no surprises. It seemed to conclude what Reese had explained. Meade had suffered a severe heart attack and had not survived. There was some bruising near the base of his skull, and he had broken two fingers on his left hand. Both had occurred shortly before death, likely the result of a spill he took as he fell victim to his failing heart. Mild trauma to the chest and ribs was obvious and consistent with CPR procedures.

Liver temperature and lividity indicated Meade's time of death to be between 5:00 pm and 7:00 pm.

Next Cyrus flipped to the police report. It was surprisingly lacking in detailed information. It concluded that Meade was alone in his hotel room when he suffered a heart attack. He'd been unable to reach the telephone in time to call for help. He wasn't discovered until the cleaning lady came to work on the room, late the following morning. Meade had still been dressed from the night before, and the bed had not been slept in.

Next, Cyrus flipped to the photos shot by crime scene technicians. There wasn't much to see. Meade was found flat on his back, not far from the sofa, in the sitting room of his hotel suite. The telephone was on a table across the room. Presumably, the man was on his way to the phone when he collapsed and expired. The police hadn't bothered with much in the way of crime-scene documentation or photographs, likely because they didn't believe it was a crime scene.

Next were the photos from the morgue. The shots were more complete and professional. Close-up images of the back of Meade's skull showed the bruising. Cyrus carefully studied the purplish marks along the hairline. It was difficult to tell what was bruising and what was discoloration due to the pooling of the body's blood following death, but the irregular pattern that was visible into Meade's hairline above the base of the skull made the difference noticeable. What concerned Cyrus was the cause of this bruising. If the old man had fallen on the way to the phone, as the medical report suggested, there was nothing on which to bang his head. Furthermore, it was a very unusual part of the skull to strike in a fall.

Moving on through the photos, Cyrus found shots documenting mild bruising of the chest, consistent with the application of CPR. Flipping to a set of x-rays included in the folder, he examined the high-resolution color copies. It was a shot that presumably documented mild fracturing of the ribs attributed to CPR. It didn't matter how closely Cyrus looked at the films, he couldn't make out the difference between the ribs and the supposed fractures. He would take the medical examiner's word on the matter.

But looking at the films, something occurred to him. He flipped back through the stack of papers and returned to the police report for review. Though he could recall the details of the document with perfect clarity, he wanted to see the original again. He had to be sure.

There it was, just as he knew it would be. The police report indicated Meade had expired alone in his room and was not discovered until the following morning. But if he was alone, why were there indications that CPR was performed? The police report's conclusion clearly contradicted the evidence.

His mind racing, Cyrus flipped through the stack of photos almost mechanically. His eyes weren't really seeing the images before him anymore. He was working through the conflicting information within the reports. How could the authorities miss something like that? Was this conclusive? Were there alternate events that could result in the same evidence?

The flipping of photos stopped cold. He was looking at a close-up of two broken fingers on Meade's left hand. This photo was shot at the crime scene before the body was carted away to the morgue. It was a photo shot some time prior to the photograph included in the pathology report he had reviewed, back in Colorado. Although the first photo led him to suspect the fingers of Meade's hand were broken intentionally, the photo from the crime scene left no doubt. The angle of the fingers was grotesque and more pronounced. It was not the sort of injury one suffered when they stumbled and fell.

Now the pieces were starting to line up, and things were starting to make more sense. One more question stood out as a possible glaring mistake in the staging of the scene. Tapping quickly on his cell phone, Cyrus dialed a number from memory. Several rings later, Underwood answered.

"Mister Underwood, it's Cyrus Cooper. I hope I haven't caught you at a bad time." Even as Cyrus said the words, he was doing the time conversion in his head. It would be nearly 7:00 pm in the UK.

"Not at all, not at all! But please, call me Allan." Underwood said warmly. "Just sitting by the fire, enjoying a good book and a bottle of wine. What can I do for you?"

"When we first met, you explained that Professor Meade was a personal friend."

"That's right. We were friends for a great many years, in fact."

"And, as I recall, you mentioned he would visit you, when he was in Europe."

"That's correct. He visited often."

"Can you tell me, where did he stay when he was in London?"

The silence of the phone line first made Cyrus wonder if the call had dropped. Only he knew better. Underwood wasn't sure how to answer the question.

"He never *stayed* in London, did he?" Cyrus finally asked.

There was another brief silence on the other end. Cyrus knew Underwood was trying to divine his understanding of

Meade's work. "No, he never stayed overnight in London," the old man said cautiously.

Because he didn't have to, Cyrus considered silently. *Why stay in a hotel when he could be back in his own bed every night?*

Confidence returned to the old man's voice. "It seems you've been a busy man."

They were skirting the subject, talking about it without using the words, but there was clearly a teleportation platform in London. Meade would not stay in a hotel when he could just as easily return to his home in Colorado. Cyrus suspected Underwood knew about the technology, but he needed to vet the man. Underwood had needed to do the same. No doubt Underwood knew something of the secrets that awaited Cyrus when he had taken his first trip to Meade's home in Colorado. It had all been part of a plan laid out by Meade and left for Underwood to execute.

"Allan, what would you say if I told you that I suspected Meade's death was not entirely due to natural causes?"

Silence filled the other end of the line. Finally Underwood returned. "Walter always suspected something like this might happen. What have you found?"

"Nothing conclusive…but I've got a stack of anomalies that make for pretty damning evidence. First, the police report indicates Meade was alone in his London hotel room when he expired. Based on what you and I know, there was really no reason he would have a hotel room in London. Second, there are signs that someone performed CPR. But that's not possible if you believe the assertion that he was alone in the hotel room when he died. Lastly, there was bruising on the back of his skull, the likes of which I've seen before. The bruising is left after the barrel of a gun has been pressed against the back of a man's head."

"I see." The old lawyer's voice sounded very far away. "Then it wasn't a heart attack?"

"No, I think it was," Cyrus concluded. "He had an attack a few years back. He was drugged in an attack—"

"You're referring to Washington, D.C.?"

"Yes. The perps messed up the dosage when they drugged him, and it resulted in permanent damage to his heart. His health was never the same after that. I think someone grabbed him while he was in London. They worked him for information. I think the people who grabbed him didn't know about his bad heart, and it failed on him. I think they performed CPR, and when they couldn't bring him back, they needed to cover it up. They put him in that hotel room and staged it to look like he died alone."

"The authorities didn't catch any of these details?"

Cyrus was asking himself the same question. "I don't know. I think they found an 80-year-old man on the floor of his hotel room, with obvious signs of a heart attack. Maybe they just didn't look too hard. But that scenario bothers me. He was an important man. He knew a lot of people in Washington. It's one thing for the bobbies in London to overlook this sort of thing. I expected a lot more scrutiny from his friends on-high. I'm surprised no one looked closer after the fact."

"Yes, well—" Underwood was searching for the right words. "It might not be all that surprising. Walter burned many bridges in Washington over these last few years. His project was considered a matter of national security for many decades. But in recent years, he was feeding the powers-that-be information, supporting a conclusion that the project was no longer viable."

Now it was Cyrus's turn for silence. He was at a loss for words. "I don't understand. *We know it works.*"

"You've no doubt given some consideration to the economic and political fallout that would ensue, should such a technology be controlled by any singular power?"

"Oh…" Cyrus now understood. "He knew that his government wouldn't be any more altruistic with the technology than any other?"

"Precisely."

"So he kept the work to himself and took it underground?"

"More or less. He didn't need to hide the work, once he turned in enough reports showing how and why the project goals were wholly unattainable. He didn't want the technology brought to market by any single player. No matter who controlled it, not only *could* it be perverted, it most certainly *would.*"

"He was going to open source the technology?" Cyrus finally understood. "Free to everyone… Something no one person or nation could control?"

"Precisely!"

Cyrus considered this information. "And it got him killed," he concluded.

"I fear you may be right," the old man agreed. "And when Walter passed, he left the project in your hands. He believed you were the only one who could see the project through to completion."

"But I'm not a scientist."

"Walter knew that. The team doesn't need another scientist. It has those in spades. Walter did the heavy lifting. As I understand it, the hard science is complete. He *wanted* someone who could protect the team. He *needed* someone trustworthy and altruistic. Someone to see this through. What he needed, is exactly what you have to offer. It was his life's work in every sense of the phrase."

Cyrus considered the magnitude of the undertaking. It wasn't really that much more responsibility than he had already assumed. A wise man would walk away from all of this. But that sort of wisdom wasn't a part of his DNA. As much as he hated where this responsibility might take him, this was the right thing to do. He had no choice in the matter. He would see Meade's work through to the end. There was a good chance it would land him back on the Coalition's radar, and that would have consequences. But right now it was a triage situation. He would worry about the here and now, and he would sort through the rest as it came.

Thanking Underwood for his help, Cyrus disconnected. He slid the phone back into his pocket and pulled into traffic. He had his work cut out for him.

Chapter 25

Bakersfield, California
Thursday, 1:22 pm (2:22 pm Colorado Time)

Cyrus used the Colorado platform to teleport to a self-storage unit near the western side of Santa Barbara. It was one of those lockers the size of a garage stall, with an overhead retractable door. Only the day before, he and Reese had relocated a transport platform from the office, setting it up in the storage unit prior to declaring the office off limits for the time being. The storage space provided them anonymity and the ability to come and go unnoticed day or night. The locker also made it easy to hide the ten-year-old Jeep Cherokee Cyrus had bought just for the move.

Driving the Jeep to the nearby airstrip, Cyrus rented a helicopter with seating for six and made the short flight to Bakersfield. The trip took less than twenty minutes, where the journey by car would've taken closer to three hours. Landing in Bakersfield, Cyrus rented a Chevy Suburban, using a credit card under a false identity. He drove to the motel on the outskirts of the city limits.

The No Tell Motel was every bit the classless dive the name suggested. The sign along the street was ancient plastic, cracked and broken by a rock or gunshot. Maybe both. The motel looked ten years overdue for being condemned. As Cyrus pulled into the parking lot, he was struck by the same sense of despair he'd felt when depositing the team the prior afternoon. Heartache and dread permeated the place.

The motel was a single story, a long plaza, rooms one next to the other, stretching maybe three hundred feet from end to end. A dilapidated manager's office was located at the left end with a large plate glass window overlooking the parking lot. That window looked like it hadn't been cleaned in two presidencies. The front door was propped open with a crumbling cinderblock.

There were perhaps a dozen doors spanning the front face of the structure. Each was covered in cracked, peeling paint and was labeled with a brass room number that had oxidized with decades of neglect.

Cyrus had phoned upon landing in Bakersfield. He wanted the team packed and ready to roll when he arrived. After he parked the large SUV in the middle of the parking lot, he climbed out and took in the area. There wasn't a car to be seen. His was the only vehicle in the entire lot, just as it had been the day before. When he spoke with the clerk the previous day, he learned that his people were the only customers registered. Evidently nothing had changed.

He had taken the rooms furthest from the office, located on the far right of the building. He'd parked the SUV at the center of the lot as a precaution. Parking directly in front of the unit you were using was considered bad tradecraft. It was like a virtual arrow pointing to your exact location and was the next closest thing to wearing a t-shirt with a target stenciled across it. These basic precautions were still second nature and too deeply ingrained in his personality to be forgotten. His head swiveled as he crossed the parking lot and approached room twelve. He was on alert for something out of the ordinary, signs of observation, or anything out of place. Old habits died hard.

When he reached the door of room twelve, nothing had raised his suspicion. As soon as he knocked, the curtain of the window beside the door pulled back slightly. He heard the click of the deadbolt and the slide of the door's security chain. Dennis Driscoll opened the door. Unfortunately, the man's normally pudgy neck-bearded face and ruffled appearance hadn't improved after a night in the dingiest of cheap motels.

At least his smile was sincere. "Mister Cooper! Come to rescue us from this squalor, I hope?" Driscoll said with a chuckle.

"Call me Cyrus. And yes. Not a moment too soon, I take it?"

Cyrus was glad it was Driscoll who answered the door. Sanjay had taken his call from the airport, and as usual, the man was insufferable. Before Cyrus could deliver his brief message asking the team to gather their things, he was made to sit through Sanjay's long-winded bemoaning of the accommodations. For the second time in two days! It wouldn't happen again.

A change of the expression in Driscoll's eyes caught Cyrus's attention and instantly brought him to alert. Cyrus saw Driscoll's eyes shift to a position over his shoulder and flash with concern. Cyrus reacted by spinning around while raising a bent elbow to eye level. As he did, he heard the crackle of electricity and felt his elbow impact with the side of a man's head.

As his eyes caught up to the sudden burst of motion, Cyrus saw a large Hispanic man drop a Taser and collapse to the sidewalk. The fallen man was instantly replaced by a second, this one more stout. He looked as a fireplug would if someone disguised it in a sweat-stained wife-beater and gold chains. The man instantly swung a fist, catching Cyrus in the solar plexus. With the wind driven from his lungs, he struggled to stay on his feet. Cyrus saw the shorter man draw back his fist in preparation for another swing. The man's fist was wrapped in a set of brass knuckles.

No wonder a single gut-shot had nearly leveled him!

As the shorter man threw what Cyrus knew would be a knockout-reinforced fist to the head, he reacted on pure instinct. With no oxygen in his lungs and his vision darkening, he parried the street brawler's devastating swing. The fireplug put so much power into the right hook that he was thrown off balance when it failed to connect. Cyrus took advantage and gave the man a shove with his left hand while drawing his gun with the right. Without a moment's hesitation, he fired a single shot into the shorter man's upper leg. It took him right out of the fight. The bastard would live, but only because Cyrus was careful to avoid his femoral artery.

As Cyrus turned to ensure the first attacker was still down, he felt cold metal pressed against the base of his skull. Then everything went black.

Cyrus collapsed to the concrete, just beyond the open door to room twelve. A third Hispanic man had made a sprint across the parking lot in the time it took him to drop the other two. The third man was also armed with a Taser baton. He placed it against the base of Cyrus's skull and sent 50,000 volts into his body before Cyrus could react.

"Back inside. Now!" the man yelled, as he shoved his chrome 9mm in Driscoll's face and shouldered him through the door.

Olivas quickly surveyed the gathered group of scientists. After spending the last ten hours watching the hotel from the bushes across the street, he was ready for some action. Twenty minutes ago, the two neighboring rooms were vacated. All of the occupants had congregated in room twelve. That event prompted a phone call to the boss who had agreed with his assessment of the situation. The geek squad was preparing to move out. When the black Suburban pulled into the lot and the lone man approached the room, the Hispanic thought they had lucked out. He figured they would make short work of the newcomer, grab the hostages, and be on their way. But looking at his friends still lying on the concrete, he decided they'd been overconfident.

He herded the five hostages to the back of the motel room before returning to the door. Pulling his two friends inside, he needed to get them out of sight before they attracted attention. Ancho Menza, the larger of his two friends, was just starting to show signs of life after taking that elbow to the head. But Poco had taken a bullet to the leg, and he was bleeding all over the place.

Olivas, the only one left standing, held his gun high for everyone to see. "Everyone stays quiet, and nobody gets dead! Stay in the back and don't move, less I tell you different. Come near me and I'll shoot you dead!"

They seemed to get the point. He knelt beside Menza. The big guy was still dazed. Olivas slapped the side of his pudgy face, trying to draw his attention. When he saw Menza's eyes focus again, he knew the big man was back with him. "Go get some towels. Poco's shot. You gotta stop the bleeding." He pointed to the bathroom in the back corner of the room.

Poco was holding his leg, trying to stem the flow of blood. It did little to reduce the flow of thick plasma that continued seeping between his fingers. If they could stop the blood loss the man would live, but there was no question the wound hurt like hell. Olivas wished he could just shoot the white guy and leave with the hostages. But the boss wanted them all brought back alive, especially the guy who had just arrived.

Olivas rolled Cyrus face down on the concrete, still just beyond the threshold of the door. He bound his hands behind his back using a large plastic zip-tie. "You and you!" He pointed to Dennis and Chad. "Put him in the back!"

Finally having the front of the motel clear, Olivas closed the door, blocking out the only natural light. Two small lamps on either side of the bed lit the room's dreary interior. Menza tied off Poco's wound using a belt as a tourniquet.

Pulling a cell phone from his pocket, Olivas glared at the hostages. It was a silent dare to any of them to make a noise. Satisfied his malicious sneer was sufficient, he turned his attention to the phone. He tapped a series of buttons on the screen and raised the phone to his ear. "Si. We have them... No. We're missing the girl. The gringo turned out to be a handful. Two of my boys are down... Si, that's the man... Si." He taped a button on the phone, ending the call.

Cyrus listened to the one-sided conversation from his position on the floor. His eyes were closed. Judging by the sounds of the room, he was along the back wall. The team was standing between him and the bastard who tased him, and from the sound of it, two of the attackers were in bad shape following their scuffle. Bolts of pain continued to surge through his head. He could still see strange shifts of light on the inside of his eyelids. A Taser. He'd been hit before, but this time was more intense. The burning feeling on the back of his neck confirmed a suspicion that the device had been applied to the base of his skull. No wonder it felt like his brain was being poked with flaming needles.

Cracking his eyes open, he found his situational assessment to be correct. He was face down on the stained carpet near the sink outside the bathroom. He took it as a good sign; it didn't appear he had been unconscious for long. Not long enough for his attackers to stick them all in a van and cart them off—or kill them. He still didn't know what they wanted, though the one-sided phone conversation he'd just overheard suggested they'd be taken into custody. Preventing that would be the first order of business.

Glancing over his head, Cyrus saw the legs of the research team. Everyone was standing with their backs to him. They were focused on what was happening at the front of the room. Tipping his head further brought a staggering rush of pain. Once his vision cleared, he saw one of the thugs tending to the wounded leg of the other.

The man in charge put his phone away. He looked over the group and waved his gun threateningly in their direction. It caused the group to take a collective step backward. Satisfied with the group's submissive behavior, the man grinned. He turned his attention to his two friends working on the gunshot wound at the front of the room.

When the group took a collective step back, someone's foot hit Cyrus's shoulder. He looked up in time to see Tracy Clark glance down at him. She'd almost stepped on him. She nearly said something aloud, but he quickly shook his head and squinted his eyes—a silent shush before she made a sound.

She looked around quickly before squatting down beside Cyrus. "Are you alright?" she whispered.

"Do me a favor?" he nodded his head upward at her. "Slip one of those hair pins into the back of my cuffs."

She looked confused. "I don't understand." Her voice was so quiet he could barely hear her.

"Pull one of your hair pins. When I roll over you'll see what they used to bind my hands. Just stick the pin up along the strap and into the binding block. Trust me." He gave her a wink and a grin to buoy her confidence. Slowly, he rolled onto his side so she could see his hands.

A moment later he felt her hand brush against his. The tension on one of the restraints instantly sagged. He pulled his hand free and rolled onto his back. To Tracy's credit, she had instantly resumed a standing position and returned her attention to the front of the room as if nothing had happened.

Two seconds later and Cyrus had freed his remaining hand. He knew he was out numbered, out gunned, and thanks to the stabbing pain behind his eyes, he would likely have trouble getting to his feet quickly. But if he acted fast, he would have the element of surprise, and he could capitalize on the fact that two of the three thugs were focused entirely on the wounded man's leg. Glancing slowly around the room, he looked for anything he could use as a weapon. The nearest he could find was the clothes iron sitting on the edge of the bathroom counter, only feet from where he lay.

Close enough.

Quietly, and making slow movements, he pulled himself to his feet. It was critical not to draw the attention of anyone in the room. Certainly not their attackers, but he didn't want his fellow hostages seeing him either. Their shift in attention would draw the scrutiny of the thugs, and the odds would shift against him.

His vision swam for a few moments after he reached his feet. But there was no time to waste. Even through the stabbing pain and vertigo, he reached out for the iron. He took it in his right hand and picked up the slack of the hanging power cord in his left. The moment his vision cleared, he was in motion. It was nothing complicated or dramatic. He simply shouldered through the group of hostages as they watched the drama at the front of the room. Two steps later he was within reach of the man in charge—the man with the gun. Cyrus had already wound up for the swing so he let a powerful right cross fly. The swing, reinforced with the mass of the fifteen-year-old iron clenched in his fist, connected with the man just as his head turned. The force of the blow lifted him off his feet and sent him flying. He hit the curtains drawn against the windows behind him. The hundred and eighty pound Hispanic man smashed through the glass and went crashing to the concrete sidewalk outside.

The entire assault took place in less than two seconds and left the two men on the floor no time to react. By the time either man looked up to see what had caused the crashing sound, they were both looking down the barrel of a chrome finished Colt .45 that Cyrus had retrieved from the floor.

"Holy shit!" It was Chad. Evidently, he was the first to break free from his shock. "Way to go!"

Better than brass knuckles, Cyrus thought as he looked back at Chad. While the rest of the group either looked like they were going to be sick or might be in shock, Chad seemed to be dealing with the events better than the rest.

"Here, take this," Cyrus said, as he passed the Colt to Chad. "Keep it pointed at them. Never get closer than two arms lengths. And if either of them so much as moves, just pull the trigger."

"Right on!" Chad accepted the gun. His eyes were bright and filled with adrenaline. He looked like a kid on Christmas morning.

Right on? It was true that different people dealt with extreme circumstances in different ways. But Chad was an odd one. Still, Cyrus took a look at the guy and he seemed solid and relatively unfazed by all that just happened.

Good enough.

Passing by the two men still sitting on the floor, Cyrus exited the room and knelt over the unconscious body of the first man who know lay on the sidewalk fronting the motel. A quick search of his pockets revealed everything Cyrus needed. He found the man's wallet, several sets of industrial zip-ties, and the cell phone that the man had used to call his boss.

————————

Twenty minutes later Cyrus was ready to vacate the No Tell Motel. As he suspected, the motel clerk was found stabbed to death behind the counter of the front office. The thugs eliminated the man preemptively, leaving no one to call for help when they moved in on their quarry.

Cyrus kept the death of the clerk to himself. The team was holding up well given the circumstances. That dose of reality might put some of them over the edge. Other than some mental trauma, most were in surprisingly good spirits. They were just happy to be alive and glad to be leaving the fleabag accommodations. One positive thing had come from the drama. No one was questioning the necessity of going into hiding anymore.

Cyrus loaded the team into the Suburban and headed out. A few blocks down the road, he stopped at a pay phone and called 911. He reported hearing gunshots near the motel. The police would arrive soon and find the three would-be kidnappers trussed up in the office of the hotel, along with the knife used to kill the clerk. He knew that wouldn't be the end of the police investigation. The damage to room twelve would leave many unanswered questions. The rooms were registered under a false name, though, and everything had been thoroughly wiped down before they had left. The authorities would be hard pressed to make any connection to him or his people. It was the best he could do given the circumstances.

Once back at the Bakersfield airport, Cyrus loaded everyone onto the helicopter and made the quick flight back to Santa Barbara. From there, they piled into the over-crowded Cherokee. Ten minutes after leaving the airfield, they arrived at the storage unit where the teleportation platform was hidden.

Cyrus pulled the overhead garage door down, sealing them all inside the storage stall. He locked the garage door from the inside using a simple sliding bolt that went from the back of the door and slipped into a hole cut into the door's track. Not even someone with a key could open the door from the outside after that.

He slid along the side of the SUV to where the group was waiting for him at the back of the narrow garage. The only light came from two bare overhead bulbs.

Everyone was looking at him expectantly. The group was quiet after the events of the day. The bitching and whining, once a constant from certain members, had dried up as the reality of the situation had set in.

Cyrus pulled the phone from his pocket and entered the unlock code. He dialed a number from memory. The call was answered after one ring. "All set?" was all he asked. He listened to the voice on the other end of the line and smiled. "They're on their way." He clicked off.

"Okay, folks," Cyrus said addressing the team. "As we discussed, you're going off the grid. No outside contact until this is sorted out. I trust today has shown the kind of danger we currently face. But don't worry, the safehouse will look like club med after that motel."

"Where are you sending us?" Sanjay asked, as he looked at the raised platform.

"For your protection, even you won't know the location of the safehouse. Not to worry, though, everything you need will be provided. Step right up."

Two at a time, the team boarded the platform and were literally gone in a flash. In the span of five minutes, the team was transferred, and Cyrus stood alone in the storage unit.

He looked around the silent, empty space. It was only the platform, the SUV, and himself. The quiet and the dim light was soothing. The stabbing pain behind his eyes remained, a lingering reminder of the Taser and the men from the motel. Finally, he stepped onto the platform and tapped a series of buttons on the screen of his phone. The platform's five-second countdown began.

It would be good to get back home.

Chapter 26

Berton Springs, Colorado
Thursday, 5:20 pm

Cyrus made a quick stop in Miami before heading home. He needed information, but showing up at Nathan's shop twice in one day would surely draw suspicion from Nathan's watchers. He needed to be discreet.

He stopped at a nearby messenger service and arranged for a delivery to Nathan at his shop. The package contained the cell phone and IDs taken off the three men who had attacked the motel in Bakersfield. Nathan would pull the call history from the phone and run the backgrounds of the three thugs.

Writing a note, Cyrus asked him to put a rush on the background checks. Since Nathan already had a solid lead on the Latino crew that attacked Reese's apartment, it wouldn't take long to confirm these three were part of the same crew, if that was the case.

After the brief side trip, it was home to Colorado. Cyrus considered his circumstances with amusement as he stepped from the platform. It was funny that the house already had the feel of home. More so than his apartment in Chicago ever had. The apartment always had a temporary sense to it. But something about the house, particularly out in the middle of nowhere, just seemed *comfortable*. It was quiet, safe, and secure. The feeling was starkly unfamiliar, but one he was growing to enjoy. Still, he had to wonder how much of that contentment was thanks to the seclusion and how much was the result of his time with Reese. She had had an even more profound impact on him than the house.

Cyrus found Reese sitting on the floor of the basement vault. When her eyes met his, he saw them light up. The smile on her face was twice as obvious in her brown eyes. She pulled herself up from the hard concrete floor and crossed the room with the gracefulness of a dancer, virtually throwing herself into his arms. He pulled her close and breathed her in. He had been away only a few hours, but he had missed her. He wasn't prone to developing feelings so quickly.

As if proving their bond, Reese pulled away only far enough for her mouth to find his. Her kiss was deep and consuming. Time stood still as he held her, their kisses growing more and more impassioned, their bodies pressed more and more tightly together.

Finally they both broke for air. Cyrus looked down at the pale skin of her face. Her cheeks were a deep pink, and she was out of breath. He was too, for that matter. "I missed you," she said quietly.

"Keep it up, and I'll leave over and over, just so I can come back to this." His words were quiet but his smile was wide. He still held her locked in his arms.

She laughed. Her eyes remained locked on his. He knew this was one of those moments, an important point in their relationship. He wanted to take her up to his bed right then. For that matter, he was certain she wanted the same thing. But as much as the timing felt right, it really wasn't. Not if she was who he believed her to be. The decisions they made now would have repercussions, and it was important that they start this relationship off right. For the first time in a very long time, he felt the desire to truly connect with another person. This…this would be great. But he knew they could do better. But how could he explain as much without her misunderstanding?

Her eyes searched his for a moment before her smile shifted. He could read something different in her expression, but it wasn't clear what she was thinking. She wasn't disappointed… It was as if she understood. It was as if she was thinking exactly the same thing and had come to precisely the same conclusion.

"So chivalry isn't dead?" she said with a coy, sexy smile. She kissed him gently once more before pulling herself free. "Just don't make me wait too long," she said in a barely perceptible whisper before stepping away.

Looking back over her shoulder, she motioned for him to follow. "Come on. It isn't much but I made some sandwiches. We can eat while you tell me how it went."

Cyrus stood there for a few moments and watched her prance away. She was something, there was no doubt about that.

He touched the screen of the security pad beside the wiring cabinet, and watched as the vault door slide silently shut. Then he followed Reese upstairs. She wanted to know how things had gone. That would be a story.

———————

They sat at the kitchen breakfast counter, a plate of sandwiches between them. Until he'd taken the first bite, Cyrus hadn't realized how hungry he was. He devoured two turkey and swiss on wheats and downed a bottle Modelo before he finished the story of his run in with the thugs at the motel. He downplayed the drama of the situation, but Reese was getting good at reading between the lines.

For her part, she listened with rapt attention, stopping him only to clarify the occasional detail. By the time he'd finished recounting the events of the morning, it was clear they did in fact have a leak.

"Do you have any suspects?" Reese asked, referring to their leak.

He waggled his hand. *Maybe, maybe not.* "I'm working on it. I want to pick your brain. I need to know more about the project, if I'm going to put the pieces together."

"You think the leak is on the team?"

Cyrus thought for a moment, choosing his words carefully. "You tell me. Other than the six members of the team, who knows else about Meridian?"

Reese sat back on her stool. Her eyes went distant as she gave the question deliberate consideration. "The question isn't as easy to answer as it would've been two days ago. Two days ago, I would have said it was contained to the seven members of the team."

Her eyes dropped and her expression deflated as something occurred to her. "*Six* members of the team," she corrected. "I still can't get used to Walter being gone."

With a slight nod of understanding, Cyrus gave her a moment to sort her thoughts. As far as he was able to determine, she was the closest thing to family Meade had had. "What changed?"

"Those files!" she sputtered nodding her head in the direction of the floor and the basement beyond. "All the documentation Walter left you in the vault—I didn't know anything about it. As far as I knew, Meridian started seven years ago, when I joined the project and Walter set up the lab. *The current lab.*"

She thought for a few moments. Cyrus could almost see the gears moving in her mind. "I should've known better," she concluded.

He only gave her a questioning look.

"I thought we started the project from scratch. But if that were the case, we made some really radical leaps very early on. I guess I didn't understand that in the beginning. My background is in electrical engineering and software design. Walter was the physicist. He assembled the team based on their specialties and pointed us in the direction we needed to go.

"Thinking about it now, it seems so obvious! We literally hit the ground running. Something we could only have done if our work was based on earlier research."

Cyrus nodded. "And, as it turned out, that earlier research has been a work in progress since the early 1900s."

Reese took a sip of her Mexican beer and looked Cyrus squarely in the eye. "If those records are accurate, American scientists have been chasing this white whale for more than a hundred years. And some of the greatest scientific discoveries of our time were found in pursuit of Meridian."

Cyrus only nodded.

There had been a long-standing search for an energy source powerful enough to fuel the Meridian platforms. In 1939, scientists believed a fission reaction could be achieved by splitting a single atom of uranium-235. If anything could power Meridian, surely it was nuclear fission.

According to the records before them, the famed World War II Manhattan Project wasn't an attempt to build the world's first atomic bomb. The goal was safe, inexpensive, limitless energy. Energy enough to power Meridian. But splitting the atom turned out to be both outrageously powerful and devastatingly destructive. It was a complete failure as far as Meridian was concerned. But in the eyes of the American military, it was the ultimate weapon. So the military took that science and made it a tool of war. And thanks to revisionist history, no one would ever know the altruistic intentions of brilliant minds had been perverted into something sinister.

Somewhat ironically, the crude atomic research of that day was eventually refined to become, in some small way, the type of power source that the original Meridian team had sought. Nuclear power was used extensively in the first rounds of successful testing, decades later. At the time, a nuclear reactor was the only energy source powerful enough to entangle the contents of a platform and engage the quantum bridge. That was, until Meade and his team made a series of breakthroughs of their own.

Meade's team managed to drastically reduce the platform's power requirements. At the same time, they learned that a tremendous amount of energy was released from the receiving platform following the completion of a transport event. It was a revelation. At first they worked to simply dissipate the excess energy in an effort to prevent catastrophic overload. But it wasn't long before Meade realized that the platforms were able to provide an energy surplus as a byproduct. The only hurdle that remained was to develop some sort of battery or capacitor to store the energy expelled from recipient platforms. If they could store that energy surplus, it could be used to power subsequent uses of each platform making the system self-sustaining.

"If I understand things correctly," Cyrus began. "One technical obstacle is keeping Meridian from deployment?"

"Basically, yes. Right now we're using Halon-Seven as a super-capacitor on the functional platforms. But the element is exceedingly rare, and we have a finite supply. Basically the platforms that are currently in operation are the extent of our capability. Our supply is depleted."

"Halon-Seven is the ore I read about? It had some sort of unique properties allowing it to act as a battery?"

She laughed. "That's one way to put it. If Halon-Seven is a battery, it's the battery to end all batteries. The material has the properties of a superconductor but it functions at room temperature—something no known superconductors can do. And, unlike any conventional battery, it can charge and discharge massive levels of energy at rates so fast that we can't properly measure them. It's most accurately described as a super-capacitor."

"So where does Halon-Seven come from?"

Reese's face grew serious. "We don't know," she said quietly.

"What? What do you mean, you don't know?"

How could they not know?

"Walter said that what we were using constituted the entire known supply of the material. He never told us—he never told me—where that supply came from."

"I don't understand," Cyrus was absently scratching at the stubble on the side of his jaw. "How is it possible no one knows where it came from?"

"How could we not know that the origins of Meridian dated back to 1900?" she countered. "There's a hundred plus years of skeletons in this particular closet. Halon-Seven might've only come into the story recently, but with the levels of secrecy we're dealing with, nothing should surprise either of us."

That was true.

"So far everything we needed to know has been in the vault," Cyrus said finally.

"I was thinking the same thing. We haven't been through all of the files. I was about to check the last file cabinet when you got back. But I still haven't found anything, and to be honest, I don't think what we're looking for is there.

"In truth, Halon-Seven is a massive scientific breakthrough all by itself. A superconductor that operates at room temperature? All current superconductors must be cooled to near absolute zero in order to function. Halon-Seven represents a breakthrough that would revolutionize dozens of cutting edge manufacturing processes. But it's pretty much meaningless if we only have a finite supply."

Cyrus saw where she was going with this. If there was no documentation explaining the origin of Halon-Seven or why there was a limited supply, it was because Meade considered the information extremely sensitive. If Meade considered the secrets of Meridian of paramount importance and chose to leave the documents in a hidden vault, what did that say about his concern for Halon-Seven? Whatever its origin, Meade must've considered it far more sensitive.

"Do you know why it's called Halon-Seven?" Cyrus asked.

Reese shook her head. "Walter provided the name along with the substance. To be honest, I don't think I ever asked."

"What about the material itself? Why is it so hard to come by?"

She shrugged. "Another mystery, I'm afraid. Walter never said—and I never asked. All I know is that the element is exceedingly rare, and he was scouring the planet for more of it."

Cyrus thought for a few moments. He was trying to get a bird's eye view of the project, and the gaps in details concerned him. He decided to move on to facts with which he felt more confident. There were a few questions he suspected might be considered sensitive. He wasn't sure how Reese would react to them.

"Tell me about Meridian," he said. "When this technology goes public, there'll be an amazing amount of money to be made." He considered his words carefully. "Every home will eventually have its own platform. Many businesses will likely be equipped with several of the devices. Distribution companies will have large-scale versions to move bulk materials, and so on. There's a lot of money to be made building and selling the platforms. Then I suppose there's ancillary income such as patents and contracts for maintenance and a dozen other things I haven't yet considered.

"What I'm asking is, who benefits from all of that? Where does all the money go?"

It was the basic principle for any criminal investigation. It didn't matter if it was theft, murder, or industrial espionage—you followed the money. It might not provide all the answers, but it would get the investigation moving in the right direction.

Surprisingly, Reese's smile only became broader. "The platforms will be built and sold at cost. Walter intended this project to better mankind, not to make him or the team wealthy. If—no, *when*—we solve the technical hurdles, the entire system will be run as a multi-national not-for-profit-organization. Essentially we'll open source the technology."

Ouch.

It was what Cyrus was afraid of. She was proud of the endeavor, and good for her. It was an admirable goal. It was altruistic. But it was unrealistic, too, because it ran counter to human nature.

"What's wrong?" she asked. She could see the answer to his question had soured his disposition.

It was time to lay it all out for her.

"A substantial problem comes to mind," he started. "Those goals are amazing, and the world would be a better place if more people felt the same way. But there are a lot of people with a vested interest in keeping Meridian off the streets. The world wide, low cost deployment of Meridian? There's a lot of people out there that wouldn't want to see this reach the market."

"I don't understand."

He had two ideas, but he'd considered only one well enough that he felt comfortable giving it voice.

"All of those people, companies, and organizations that have something to lose if Meridian goes public—what do you think they would be willing to do to keep it from seeing the light of day?"

She looked stricken. "You think one of them is behind the attacks?"

"I think that any or all of them might be willing to kill, just to maintain the status quo. It's the military that really troubles me. There isn't a military group on the planet that wouldn't bury every one of us just to keep Meridian for themselves. We're talking about the ultimate tactical advantage. I think the list of suspects needs to include any person or company with an interest in keeping things running the way they are, as well as every government, military, or intelligence service in the world. Hell, even terrorist organizations would see this as a potential weapon."

Reese's eyes were glazing over as the true weight of his words struck home.

"What I'm trying to say," he said confidently as he took her hand, "is that the safety of the project and the safety of the team lies in anonymity. That anonymity is in danger right now. But there's good news. I think I've got a bead on who's after the team. And, if I'm right, that person won't have shared Meridian with anyone. If I can ensure that, I can close the loop, and everyone will be safe."

She looked him in the eye. Her eyes hinted at the question she didn't want to ask. "When you say 'close the loop?'"

"I mean to do whatever is necessary to ensure Meridian and this team are safe again. This is bigger than the seven of us. If it falls into the wrong hands, I can't even imagine the potential damage."

She nodded. While the calm words and the conviction of his tone were reassuring, he could see she knew he was talking about killing whoever was after them, if it meant eliminating the threat.

Cyrus noticed his own change in attitude for the first time. He had counted their group as numbering seven. The subconscious indication being that he now considered himself one of them. When he saw the troubled look in Reese's eyes replaced by something stronger and more confident, he wondered if she had come to that same conclusion.

"So," she said in a voice that was at first shaky but growing in confidence. "We eliminate the threat, secure Meridian, and then we work on a way to prepare the world for the technology?"

Cyrus smiled. "That's the plan!"

"I can live with that."

Cyrus raised his bottle, and Reese clinked hers against his in a salute. "Why don't we take this to the living room and get more comfortable? I want you to tell me more about Walter," he said with a smile. "And I'd like to talk about our safehouse. It's a little unconventional, but rather ideal given all that's happening."

Chapter 27

Undisclosed Location, Australia
Friday, 11:50 am (Thursday 6:50 pm Colorado Time)

Cyrus looked around the small room as he stepped off the transport platform. Reese held his hand. The room was chilly and poorly lit. The walls, floor, and ceiling were all bare, unadorned concrete. Two small light bulbs hung from unprotected metal boxes attached to the face of the ceiling.

"Great place you've got here," Cyrus said with a grin, and shook the hand of the only other occupant of the room.

Harvey 'Hondo' Roberts was a tall, wide-shouldered man ten years older than Cyrus. The man had a short scruff of a beard, piercing blue eyes, and skin darkened from many long hours in the Australian sun. He wore his customary short-sleeved, khaki-colored button up shirt, similar colored cargo pants, and work boots. A tattered and worn floppy-brimmed bush hat sat atop his head.

"Great to see you, mate!" Hondo said and pulled Cyrus in for a bone-wrenching hug. "You're looking fit. Glad to see civilian life hasn't made you soft!"

Cyrus laughed at the irony. "I'm not feeling much like a civilian these days," he said. The comment was amusing because the man was well aware of the more prickly details of the preceding days. "Hondo, I'd like you to meet Reese Knoland. She took over as team lead after Meade passed."

Hondo's eyes gleamed and he flashed Reese a proud grin. "Very glad to meet you, miss. Clearly you're the brains *and the beauty* of this little group," he said, and flashed her an exaggerated wink. He tipped his head back toward Cyrus. "So, tell me... What is it you need him for again?"

This brought an unexpected laugh from Reese, while Cyrus could only shake his head. "I'm in charge of breaking stuff. I've got a list and everything. Keep it up, and you'll be next on the list."

Cyrus motioned to Reese. She lowered a backpack from her shoulder and placed it on the cold floor. Then she removed a pair of smartphones from one of its zippered compartments and handed them to Cyrus.

"These should come in handy," Cyrus said, and he handed both phones to Hondo. "One for you and one for the missus. Think satellite phone, but on steroids. You'll get reception anywhere on the planet—even down here. Unlimited calling, unlimited data."

Hondo took the phones but cast suspicious glances at Cyrus and Reese. "What's the catch?"

"Just one," Cyrus admitted. "This technology isn't for public consumption, so keep it on the down-low."

"That's it?"

"That's it."

Hondo burst out laughing. He slapped Cyrus on the shoulder. "Come on, I'll show you to your team's plush accommodations!"

Hondo stepped into the frigid concrete corridor and glanced back over his shoulder as he walked. "It can be a bit on the chilly side, but it's solid and safe. This bunker was built back in the early days of the cold war. It was engineered to withstand nuclear detonation on the surface. You won't find a safer place above or below ground."

"How far below the surface are we?" Reese asked.

"It varies, but we're always in the 100 meter range. The facility was built courtesy of the Australian taxpayers and later abandoned and forgotten. I'd say no one's been down here in at least twenty years. I had a devil of a time airing the place out in preparation for your crew."

"Did you have any trouble reassembling the platform?" Cyrus asked as they continued on.

"None at all," Hondo offered with a single shake of his head. "She bolted together with ease. It's really an impressive design."

Hondo had only experienced a part of the platform's ingenious design, Cyrus knew. As Reese had explained to him the night before, once a platform had been taken apart and reassembled, its internal computer was sophisticated enough to engage a diagnostic routine that realigned the infrared laser array that encircled the contents of the platform a fraction of a second before teleportation took place. The platforms were a marvel of modern engineering in so many ways.

They came to an intersection in the hallway and Hondo quickly turned right. Cyrus stopped for a moment and looked down the opposite hall. Just like the hall they'd just left, light ballasts were attached to the ceiling every twenty yards. The hall to the left stretched off almost endlessly into the distance.

The underground complex was enormous.

"The facility is entirely self contained," Hondo explained as they walked on. "It has several diesel generators and enough fuel reserves to power the place well beyond the zombie apocalypse. Water comes from a natural spring, but there are redundant filtration systems as well. Come judgment day? This is where I'll be, I'll tell you that for nothin'!"

"How about comms?" Cyrus asked.

"We're too deep for radio communication. The blokes who built this place hardwired antenna lines that run all the way to the surface. But I disabled 'em, per your instructions. There's no cell reception. But I set up a jammer anyway. Better safe than sorry. So no radio of any kind, no phone, no TV. You know what your guys are most upset about? They can't get on the bloody Internet!"

Reese laughed. "Sounds about right."

"Has anyone made more of a stink than the rest, as far as making contact with the outside?" Cyrus asked. He couldn't keep the hopeful anticipation from his voice.

Hondo led them around another corner and kept walking. This place was amazing. They'd passed dozens of doors already. Almost all were unmarked. The shelter could have offered safe haven for hundreds, if not thousands of people.

"No," Hondo said without much thought. "Sorry to disappoint. If I had to guess, I'd say that little scare they had before coming here put things in perspective."

Yeah, Cyrus thought. *Getting taken hostage by a group of Mexican drug runners does tend to make an impression.* That was actually why he was here. He hadn't planned on visiting the team so soon, but after receiving the results of the background checks from Agent Shaw, he suddenly had a large piece of their puzzle. He was here to double-check the way those pieces fit.

Stopping before a pair of massive double doors, Hondo punched a six-digit code into the panel on the wall. A buzzer sounded, and he pulled one of the doors open. With a flourish of his hand, he gestured Cyrus and Reese inside.

They stepped into a large room with a high ceiling and a number of wide wooden tables. It looked like a commissary. The floors were tile and the concrete walls were painted some sort of neutral institutional color.

As Cyrus, Reese, and Hondo entered the room, all eyes turned to them. The research team was gathered there. They were scattered about various tables with their laptops open and documents spread out around them.

Tracy Clark was the first on her feet. She rushed over to Reese, as if anxious for news. "Has something happened? Can we come home?"

Cyrus shook his head. "No, I'm sorry. We're here to check in and make sure everyone is settled."

The disappointment was evident on Tracy's face. Actually, it was obvious on most faces, though no one spoke up.

"I need to get everyone's home address and house key. We were lucky to find the bomb on Alfie's truck. I've got a feeling the rest of you were lucky you left home when you did. I'll go by each of your places and check them out. I'll look for anything that might be rigged, signs of surveillance, that sort of thing. If I can get some more evidence, maybe there'll be something that'll lead to whoever is behind this."

Cyrus and Reese went around collecting address information and keys from everyone in the group. It was all for show. Not only did Cyrus know where each of them lived, but he had already sent Hondo to each of their homes. None of them were rigged. The only one targeted with explosives was Alfie Ahmed. At first it made no sense, until the paperwork arrived from Nathan. When Cyrus combined it with the background reports provided by Agent Shaw, a glaring commonality surfaced. Pieces of his puzzle were lining up, and part of the overall picture was beginning to take shape. Unfortunately, the details specific to the team that attacked him in Chicago were still not fitting.

After collecting all of the personal information, Cyrus doubled back and stopped at the table in front of Chad Brewster. "Hey, can I talk with you for a minute?" he asked quietly, making an effort not to draw undue attention.

Chad didn't say anything. He simply followed Cyrus out of the room. Once in the hall, they both followed Hondo down an adjacent hallway, until he stopped in front of a door and pushed it open. Hondo flipped a switch on the wall and stepped back into the corridor. "It's all yours," he said to Cyrus.

The room was small, about fifteen feet to a side. Other than the light switch on the wall and two light housings on the ceiling, the walls were unadorned, bare concrete. A large steel table occupied the center of the room. There were only three chairs arranged around it. Cyrus motioned for Chad to take the single chair on the far side of the table while he waited by the door. Reese arrived a moment later and took one of the chairs on

Cyrus's side of the room. Finally, Cyrus closed the door and took the last remaining seat beside Reese.

Chad was beginning to look uneasy. "What's going on?" There was a defensive tone to his voice. "What do you have to say to me that you couldn't say in front of everyone else?"

Cyrus set down a thick manila folder he'd been carrying since they arrived at the bunker. "I want to speak with you about Walter Meade," Cyrus said calmly.

Chad looked at Cyrus, clearly confused. He looked at Reese, as if seeking further understanding, perhaps hoping she would offer some elaboration. But Reese said nothing. Prior to the meeting, Cyrus asked her to sit in on the interview, but he was very specific in requesting that she not react to anything that might be directed toward her. He knew it was asking a lot. It was a normal reaction to respond when spoken to. He needed her to suppress that instinct if Chad tried redirecting, or deflecting questions.

"I don't understand," Chad said finally. "What about Walter?"

"I never had a chance to work with him in the lab or see him on a day to day basis," Cyrus explained. "If I have a better understanding of the lab, the work environment, the way that things were, I'll have more information to work with. Somewhere in all of that will be the key to finding whoever is attacking this team."

"And you think that whoever is after the team has something to do with Walter?"

Cyrus ran his fingertips over the unlabeled surface of the closed folder before him. It was a tactful way to draw Chad's attention back to it. If Chad had a reason to lie, he would wonder whether anything in that folder would undermine his subterfuge.

"The Meridian team has been attacked on several occasions," Cyrus said simply. "And no one knew more about Meridian than Meade."

Cyrus was being calm and non-threatening. He touched the surface of the folder once more and saw Chad's eyes twitch to the folder a few seconds later.

"What was it like working for Meade?"

Chad shrugged his shoulders and sat back in his chair. "I dunno. He was the boss, but he wasn't a bad boss," he said after giving it a little thought. "I guess he was kinda the perfect boss. He was patient and even-tempered. I worked for a guy while I was in high school. He was a hothead. The guy yelled about everything. It wasn't that way with Walter. Walter was very good at expressing what he needed. And when something wasn't just how he wanted it, he would explain what had to be changed. He never got upset. Come to think of it, I don't think I ever saw the man lose his temper—not once."

Nodding, Cyrus absently tapped the side of his thumb on the surface of the folder and pretended to consider this information. In truth, it was all exactly what he expected to hear about the old man. He had already spoken with Reese extensively about Meade.

"What did you think of the project?" Cyrus asked after a few moments of contemplation.

Chads eyes lit up just thinking about Meridian. "What can I say? It was the opportunity of a lifetime! It's something straight out of science fiction. I mean, I'm just a draftsman. I do mechanical drawings. Walter could've picked anyone to fill that spot. But I get to be a part of a project that's going to change the world. What's not to love?"

Cyrus couldn't help but smile. The guy was right. It was the opportunity of a lifetime. At least he knew it. So why had he thrown the team under the bus? That was the part that wasn't making sense.

"Do you really believe that?" Cyrus asked.

"Believe what?"

"That Meridian would change the world?"

"Without a doubt!"

Cyrus nodded. Chad seemed sincere. It wasn't just the words he used but the way he spoke them. Cyrus could literally see the excitement in Chad's eyes. The project was important to him. "What did you think would happen to the team after Meridian went public?"

Chad was silent.

Cyrus let the silence stretch.

"I don't understand the question," Chad finally countered.

"Did you think you'd become famous?" Cyrus asked bluntly.

"Absolutely!" Chad was smiling proudly. "Don't get me wrong. I know the eggheads will be the ones to become household names. They're the ones who did the science. They're the ones who made the impossible possible. I'm just the guy who turned their specs into blueprints and fabricated the hardware for the platforms.

"I'm nothing special, but I'd like to think I'll be remembered after I'm gone—remembered as part of the team that changed the world forever. Even if it's just my name next to theirs in the history books."

And there it was, one piece of the puzzle that hadn't been present before just slipped into place for Cyrus. Chad wasn't just the one who did the drafting for the plans, he also fabricated the platforms. It was a distinction Cyrus hadn't made before.

Chad seemed sincere in his pride at being a part of the project. He even seemed accepting of his limited contribution to the endeavor. It was a shame that Cyrus was going to have to take him apart for what he had done.

"Did you think that being a part of the development team would make you rich?" Cyrus asked finally. This was the crux of his line of questioning.

"I'm sorry?"

"Once Meridian went public, did you think you were going to become wealthy?"

"I don't know," Chad admitted. "I guess I hoped there'd be some sort of compensation once the use of the device took off. But it was a long shot. The professor was going to open source the technology. He didn't want to make money with it. For him, it was all about improving the world."

"Right," Cyrus admitted. "But you didn't know that early on. Early on, you had your heart set on a big payday. It didn't matter that Walter was paying you well while you were on the project. You expected to be cut in on the project, once it went public."

"No," Chad said shaking his head. "Professor Meade was clear on that point. It was very important to him. He wanted everyone in the world to have access to the technology, not just the rich and powerful. There was no money to be made."

"Which is why you found a way to make money from it on your own," Cyrus said, and laid the palm of his hand flat across the folder before him. "You decided to cash in and make some money before the project went public. But in the process, you made promises you couldn't keep!"

"I don't know what you're talking about!"

Cyrus placing one finger down on the folder and glared at Chad. "Tell me what you did!"

Chad only stared back.

"The more questions I have to ask, the worse this is going to get for you." Cyrus's voice had grown calm again. He knew the contrast would be unsettling. "I'm giving you one last chance. Tell me what you did. Until I understand, I can't fix this."

Chad slammed his fist on the table and stood. His chair slid across the floor and tipped over. The crashing sound was intensified by the echoing effect of the bare concrete walls.

"This is bullshit! I don't have to take this from you!" Chad said and headed for the door.

"You better take a deep breath," Cyrus warned as Chad crossed the room. "We're having a friendly talk right now. Once you step foot outside that door things become a lot less friendly. But either way, we're still gonna have this talk."

Cyrus's voice was calm and measured—a stark contrast to the palpable tension that filled the room. Chad was a big guy, physically imposing. He had at least a fifty-pound advantage over Cyrus. Still, sometimes words carried more effect than the most dramatic action.

Cyrus remained in his seat. He hadn't moved in the slightest, despite Chad's outburst or the crashing of the chair. Reese had nearly fallen over but caught herself at the last moment. She was half sitting and half standing over the chair, looking back and forth between Cyrus and Chad. Chad had stopped with his hand on the steel door knob, the knob half turned. He didn't look back, but he seemed to be considering Cyrus's words.

Reese continued to hover over her chair for what seemed like an eternity. No one spoke. With a slight exhale, Chad looked back over his shoulder and studied Cyrus. He still hadn't moved. He wasn't even looking at Chad, who was now standing behind him. Cyrus's hand was still planted firmly on the file folder.

At last, the door latch clicked as Chad released the knob. Slowly, and without a word, he circled back to his side of the table. He righted the toppled chair and retook his place. His face was red. Was it anger? Humiliation?

Cyrus immediately made eye contact and continued as if nothing had happened. "Tell me about Bola Alvares," he said simply.

Chad shook his head and started to speak. Cyrus raised a hand, holding up a single finger. He looked Chad squarely in the eye. "Look, you know that I know. So don't skate around this. Own up to what you've done, answer my questions, and give me what I need to fix this."

The look in Cyrus's eyes showed very clearly that he would accept no more excuses. He was done wasting time.

"Bola Alvares," Cyrus started. "Mexican drug lord. Tell me what you know."

Closing his eyes, Chad took a deep breath. He exhaled and looked back at Cyrus. "I don't know where to start."

He appeared sincere. It was a good sign. They were done playing games. "Why don't we start with your brother, Brian. He's currently serving eighteen years at Folsom State Prison for working for Alvares."

This was a ploy on Cyrus's part. He had raw data. From it he could infer conclusions. But a proper interrogation could turn these guesses into facts. Raw data could also be used to convince a suspect that the interrogator knew more than he really did. That was Cyrus's goal, to use the intel he had to draw out additional information, and with a little luck, finally get a leg up in the investigation.

"My brother was convicted of laundering money for Alvares," Chad said quietly. "He went to prison, and Alvares is still living large with his sports cars, his mansions, and his private jet."

"So you don't think much of the man. It didn't stop you from taking his money."

Chad sat silently. He seemed to be chewing over something in his mind.

"Time's running out, Chad," Cyrus warned. He tapped his index finger on the folder in front of him. "Talk to me now, or I'm taking all of this to the FBI and the DEA."

Chad's look turned questioning. "You can't do that without exposing Meridian!"

Pushing out his chair, Cyrus picked up the folder. He rose and looked down at Chad. "Then you don't know me very well. With what I have here, you'll be put away for so long—your brother'll be the one coming to see you in prison! No one's going to be asking about Meridian."

Cyrus only made it half a step toward the door before Chad stopped him. He wanted Chad to sweat, so it was with a show of reluctance that Cyrus finally returned to the table.

"This is your last chance," Cyrus said sternly. "The next time I stand, I'm leaving this room, and the conversation will be over. If you can't see that I'm throwing you a lifeline, then you deserve everything you have coming."

Reese hadn't moved since maters had escalated. Cyrus could almost feel the anxiety radiating from her, and he knew she wanted out of the room. Still, to her credit, she'd managed to maintain a level of composure that both surprised and impressed him. Her resilience under pressure would only help to weaken Chad's resolve.

"I know what you're getting at, and you're right," Chad said after a long silence. "I was upset when I realized the Professor intended to take Meridian public without making a profit. What was I supposed to think? We were working on a project that was bigger than anything in history. Forget Google! Forget Apple and Microsoft! This could've been the biggest payday ever!

"The Professor could've charged anything for the technology, and people would pay it. What choice did they have? There were any number of revenue models that would've been endless money-making machines. But he wanted to run it all as a not-for-profit? That was crazy! He wasn't thinking straight!"

Reese broke her silence for the first time. She leaned forward on the table, her eyes drilling into Chad's. "This wasn't about getting rich. All Walter wanted was to make the world a better place!"

Chad leaned back in his seat. The aggression drained from him as if he were a deflating balloon. "He didn't have the right to make that choice for all of us," he said quietly.

"Yes he did!" Reese snapped. "He had every right! This was his project! His technology! His idea! He brought every one of us onboard. He made us a part of something special. He made us a part of history! It was his call! He could've done it without us if he wanted!" She sat back in her chair, looking exhausted from the emotional outpour. "He had every right," she said, almost to herself.

"Tell me what you did," Cyrus urged. "Tell me about the $500,000 dollars."

After staring at the tabletop for several long moments, Chad finally raised his eyes to look at Reese. After a few long moments, he shifted his glance to Cyrus. "I contacted my brother. I asked him to put me in touch with Bola Alvares. And when I made contact, we made a deal."

Chad looked expectantly at Cyrus. He anticipated a question. Cyrus didn't bother, the question was obvious. He let the silence drag on, and Chad finally continued.

"I told Alvares about the technology. I explained that it was still years away from production but that we had working prototypes. I offered to sell him two platforms."

Cyrus thought Reese was going to climb across the table and throttle Chad. While he expected this turn of events, from her perspective this was shocking. "You sold Meridian? You sold Meridian to a drug dealer, of all people? Are you crazy? That would make it impossible for the authorities to stop him! You not only sold out the project—you sold it to the devil?"

It's a fair point, Cyrus thought. There were a lot of things Chad could've done with the technology. But as far as Cyrus was concerned, it was actually a good thing Chad had taken it to a smuggler. It was in a smuggler's best interest to be the sole purveyor of such a tool. Sharing Meridian, even sharing knowledge of Meridian, could undermine its usefulness. A drug smuggler would keep such a secret all to himself. That was ideal from where Cyrus sat. It would make it easier for him to close the loop.

"And the $500,000?" Cyrus asked.

"That was the down payment." Chad ran his hands through his hair. He looked haggard and tired. The interview was wearing on him. "Another nine point five million would be paid upon delivery."

Cyrus saw Reese's jaw drop.

"What?" Chad said with a tired smile. "I told you the Professor was leaving a lot of money on the table."

Again, Reese looked like she would jump from her seat. Cyrus laid a comforting hand on her arm. Her eyes were burning with rage when she turned them on him. But as soon as they met his, the flames fizzled and her blood quickly cooled. She took a deep breath, but the rosy color never left her cheeks.

The corners of her mouth pulled into a barely perceptible smile, and with an almost indistinguishable nod she thanked him for his calming presence.

Reese's gaze fell back on Chad. "Ten million dollars? That was your price? That's all it cost to sell out the project—sell out your team—your friends? This isn't about leaving money on the table. It's about doing what's right. For God's sake, Walter took care of all of us. He left us each something in his will. He paid off every one of your student loans. Doesn't that mean anything to you?"

Chad's eyes dropped back to the top of the table. Cyrus could see Reese had struck a nerve. "Of course that meant something to me. It meant a great deal, actually. But I didn't know about that until after! I'd already made the deal with Alvares by the time the Professor died."

"So," Cyrus said, trying to pull the interview back into productive territory. Emotional areas were to be avoided. They were a quagmire. The productive pace of questioning could be easily lost. "You sold two of the platforms to Bola Alvares for $500,000 up front and the remainder due upon delivery. But you hit a problem, didn't you?"

Chad nodded. "Yeah. I was largely responsible for fabricating and assembling the platforms. I thought I could build an extra pair in my spare time without anyone noticing. Those would be the two I sold to Alvares."

"What about the Halon-Seven?" Reese asked.

"That was the problem," Chad admitted. "What I didn't know—what the Professor apparently never explained to some of us, was that we had depleted our reserve of Halon-Seven. At first I thought it was just a temporary issue, and we would find a new supply. It wasn't until I overheard Sanjay say something about Halon-Seven that I learned there wasn't any more. That's when I knew I was sunk."

Cyrus nodded. "You couldn't make good on the delivery to Alvares. You'd built the platforms, but you didn't have the Halon-Seven needed to make them work."

Chad nodded.

"But that wasn't your only problem," Cyrus pushed. "Even if you had the Halon-Seven, you needed to reprogram the QDL interface. If you didn't reprogram it, Alvares's platforms would be a part of the network. You needed the QDL adjusted so the smuggler's platforms would be on their own private network, where they would never be discovered."

At that realization, Chad looked like he was going to be sick. As Cyrus suspected, Chad hoped he hadn't made that connection.

"Wait a minute," Reese said. "That doesn't make any sense. *I'm the only one who can recalibrate the QDL.*"

Cyrus waited for Chad to explain, but Chad chose to remain silent.

"He knew that," Cyrus said with disappointment. "That's why the thugs were waiting in your apartment the night we met. Chad was trying to cover his own ass. He told Alvares that the platforms would never work without your help. That's why they were kidnapping you and trying to kill me."

Reese's eyes snapped back to Chad. Cyrus knew that she was waiting for him to dispute the allegation, but no words came from Chad's mouth. Nothing could be said. He'd gotten himself in deep, and when he was in over his head, he'd been willing to pull Reese right down with him.

Cyrus watched as tears filled Reese's eyes. After a few moments, she rose and left the room, never saying a word. Cyrus felt for her. He was no stranger to betrayal.

"Something happened between you and Bola Alvares. You did something to piss him off. What was it?"

Chad raised his head only slightly. He couldn't look Cyrus in the eye. The man had been broken. There was no fight left in him. "I was screwed," he said. "There was no way out. At first I thought it was only a matter of time before we had a new supply of Halon-Seven. Then I found out there wasn't any more. And I realized I would need Reese's help. There was no way she would help me. She believed in the project as fully as the Professor."

Chad took a deep breath and thought for a moment. "I was stuck, and I was stalling for time. I was trying to find a way to fix what I'd done. That's what got Alvares pissed off. He wanted me to make good on my part of the deal."

"That's when Alvares had his guys put the bomb in Alfie Ahmed's truck."

Chad looked at Cyrus. He didn't understand. What Cyrus was saying confused him.

"Alvares wanted you to know he was serious. He figured blowing up a member of your team would make the point clear. It would get you back on track and convince you to make good on the deal. He picked Alfie because he's the most expendable member of the team. Taking him out wouldn't cost him the delivery of his platforms."

"Oh God!" Chad doubled over red in the face and suddenly choking on his own breath. He was truly floored by the realization. He was the reason the bomb was planted in his friend's car.

For Cyrus, this explained why Alfie was targeted when none of the other team members were attacked. He had walked into the room with everything else sorted out, but the truth of the car bomb had just clicked for him while he was sitting there. Sure, the gang made an attempt to kidnap Reese, but the lone attempt on Alfie finally made sense as well. Things were falling into place.

There was only one question left on Cyrus's mental checklist. He wanted to know what Chad planned to do about being short the missing Halon-Seven. But the more he thought about it, there was just one way around that. Chad would've stolen that from a pair of the active platforms and done his best to cover his tracks. And if the investigation was leading to him, he still had ten million dollars to fall back on. He would've run.

Two things were certain. First, nothing had gone according to plan for Chad Brewster. Second, things were about to get a lot worse for Bola Alvares. It was time to close the loop.

Chapter 28

Berton Springs, Colorado
Thursday, 7:30 pm

Time zones around the world would be one of the more unique challenges of instant global travel. It was the first thing Cyrus considered as he and Reese stepped off the transport platform in the spare bedroom of the Colorado house. As he tapped the transport authorization codes into his phone in preparation for the return trip, he realized it was 1:30 Friday afternoon in Australia. But after arriving in Colorado, his phone read the time as 7:30 in the evening, and it was only Thursday. Instant travel was going to present a fundamental series of scheduling issues. Though, in fairness, those were only the tip of the iceberg. New protocols in vaccination and other medical procedures would surely need to be established as well. When a person could cross the planet as easily as they crossed a room, the world quickly became a much smaller place.

Society would change in so many ways. But first, he had to eliminate the threat posed by the Alvares Cartel. That was the order of the day. Well, maybe that could wait until tomorrow.

Cyrus was tired. Looking at Reese, he could see she was feeling it too. A good night's sleep would do them good. His plan was simple. He was going to hit Alvares head on. But not tonight.

He went about starting a fire in the living room hearth. Within minutes he had a blaze that radiated a warmth not found in the subterranean tunnels of Australia.

"I'm famished. Are you hungry?" Reese asked, as she sank into the sofa before the fireplace. She pulled a blanket over herself. Her eyes looked heavy.

"Absolutely," he answered without hesitation. "Have a taste for anything special?"

She thought for a moment before she smiled. "Yeah, actually. How do you feel about Chinese?"

"That works for me."

"I'm thinking takeout. Pick something up and bring it back here?"

He nodded.

In a matter of minutes they decided on their order. Reese pulled out her cell and phoned in the order. Cyrus would run out and pick it up.

"Give me your phone," Reese said. "I'll pin the location of the restaurant on the map so you don't get lost."

"Get lost? Where did you order from?"

Her coy smile hinted at an unlikely answer. "This little place I haven't had in years. But it's the best Chinese food I've ever had."

Cyrus waited for the other shoe to drop.

"It's in Manhattan."

He couldn't help it. He burst out laughing. The absurdity of sitting in front of a roaring fire in Colorado ordering takeout from a place in New York struck him as comical. This would take some getting use to.

Reese laughed, more at his response than anything. "It's not as bad as it sounds. The restaurant's only a few blocks from the transport site!"

"No problem," he smiled and handed over his phone. With a few taps on the screen she tagged his destination on the map.

"If you don't mind, I'm going to take a bath while you're gone. I'm wrecked. If I stay on the couch I'll be asleep by the time you get back."

He crawled away from the fire and leaned over her on the couch. A mischievous grin crept across his face. "I'll make you a deal. You think of me while you're scrubbing all your naughty bits, and I won't mind at all."

She pulled him closer and kissed him deeply. "On second thought, why don't you stay? You can take that bath with me?"

Her kiss and hungry eyes were making his heart beat faster. The temptation was exhilarating. "Why Miss Knoland, I like the way you think," he said quietly and kissed her again. "Unfortunately, you've already placed the order. But hold that thought. I'll be back before you know it. Then it's you, me, and a roaring fire."

That brought a girlish giggle from Reese that surprised them both. Her hand covered her mouth in embarrassment. They both roared with laughter.

"It's a date," she said in a low whisper in his ear. "Maybe I can find a nice bottle of wine?"

"You're on!" He gave her another quick kiss and headed for the spare bedroom. Manhattan was only a few steps away.

Chapter 29

Cyrus stepped off the teleportation platform. His movement activated the motion-sensing trigger for the lights of the room. He was standing in the small living room of a studio apartment. There were no furnishings, except for the pair of small tables that held lamps. They were the only source of light in the small open space. A thick set of old drapes were drawn against the windows.

Checking the display of his phone, Cyrus confirmed he was actually in New York before heading for the front door. As he stepped into the hallway, he took note of the number on the door. It was apartment 812. He pulled the door shut, ensuring the lock latched firmly behind him, and headed down the hall following the sign toward the elevator.

The elevator ride to the lobby was brief. The elevator car was old but well maintained. When he reached the lobby, his suspicion regarding his location was confirmed. The building was neither high-class nor low-rent. Strictly middle of the road—nothing attention grabbing. He found it interesting that

317

Professor Meade chose to keep the platforms in apartments around the country. It made a certain amount of sense. People frequently coming and going wouldn't draw attention the way they would at a location like the storage locker. The negative side was the paper trail. Payments would be made on these properties. There were utility and tax records. Cyrus made a mental note to contact Allan Underwood. He needed to know how the properties were sheltered. Public records were a potential loose thread that could be used to identify the locations of the platforms.

Passing through the double doors of the lobby, Cyrus stepped onto a busy Manhattan street. Traffic was heavy and moving slowly in both directions. The sidewalk buzzed with the constant bustle of pedestrians, even at nearly ten o'clock at night. *The city that never sleeps, was that New York?* It seemed appropriate. The townspeople of Berton Springs, Colorado were likely safely ensconced in their beds come ten o'clock.

Double-checking his location on his phone's map, he turned right and started down the street. He was only a few blocks from The Happy Taste of China.

When he turned right at the next corner, he experienced a curious sensation. There, in the bustle of at least a hundred people, he felt he was being watched. Surreptitiously, he glanced around. There were any number of possible prying eyes, but no observer stood out. He kept walking. Foot traffic was heavy. Maybe that was all he was experiencing. It was unlikely anyone knew he was here. His trip to New York had literally been a spur of the moment decision.

But by the end of the next block, the tingling sense in the back of his skull had become a force he couldn't ignore. As he reached the next intersection, the crosswalk to his left received a walk indication light, allowing pedestrian traffic to move across the busy boulevard. Without hesitation, he turned and crossed the street.

A glance to his left made him nothing more than a New Yorker ensuring he wasn't about to be run down while crossing a busy street, but Cyrus capitalized on the look and picked out two men in his peripheral vision. They broke cover, sprinting to make the crossing before traffic routed them. A two-man tail. And where there were two, there could be more. Who were they? How had they found him so quickly?

Cyrus had already given a great deal of thought to the Bola Alvares issue. The more he considered it, the more confident he was that these men where not a part of Alvares's crew. Based on the prints he'd lifted from the team at his apartment and the information Nathan had run down for him, Cyrus knew those men were Europeans, not Mexican. Two of the three in his apartment hailed from the Baltic Rim, and one was from Russia. If he were to wager, he was betting the men following him now were a part of a second force interested in Meridian. But who they were and why they were interested was still unclear. It seemed unlikely that Chad Brewster would've sold Meridian to a drug lord and the Europeans as well.

On a whim, Cyrus turned down a dark deserted alley. He maintained a consistent pace. He wanted to appear as though he knew exactly where he was going. He also wanted to draw his tail to a secluded location where he could find out what they knew.

Thirty yards down the murky alley, he could hear the sounds of footsteps keeping pace with him. Two men. They were going for his ploy. He continued on.

About a hundred and fifty yards in, a figure stepped from the shadows and blocked his way. The man was maybe six foot two with wide shoulders and dressed in dark clothes. *Crap,* Cyrus thought. He should've expected this. The team at his apartment had three men. With two men behind him, he should've expected the appearance of a third. The goons behind him must've been in radio contact with the third, for him to route Cyrus like this. It spoke to their organization. They were professionals, not street thugs, like the drug runners.

"That's far enough," the man in front of Cyrus said, holding up a gloved hand. In his grip was a semi-automatic with a suppressor attached. The gun was not unexpected, but the silencer increased the odds that he intended to use it.

"Marco," the man ordered. "Take his weapon!"

The man's voice was deep and accented. Slavic…*Russian,* Cyrus was fairly certain. One of the men behind Cyrus approached. A quick pat down and the man found and confiscated Cyrus's Springfield. The man who searched him took the gun and quickly stepped out of reach. *Yep, they're pros.* They knew the importance of staying out of arm's reach, even when a man was unarmed.

"You've caused a great deal of embarrassment for my team," said the man with the gun.

Cyrus was watching the man's weapon hand. It was steady. There was no waver in his aim. It was difficult to keep a gun leveled on a target for an extended period of time. Far more trying than people realized. This man was doing it without any drift of the barrel.

"I assume you're referring to my apartment in Chicago?" Cyrus didn't know where this was headed, but he wanted answers. If the guy with the gun—Boris, he named him for the moment—was feeling chatty, he would gather as much information as possible.

Cyrus looked over his shoulder. Behind him, the two men had spread out. He was now standing in the center of a triangle. All three men now had guns pointed in his direction. But it seemed to be the man in front of him who was calling the shots. Boris had his gun leveled and he was ready to use it. The two men in the rear held their guns more casually. They didn't expect to need them.

"Da," the man in front said. Yeah, Russian was a solid bet. "We were warned that you were skilled. But our men did not take this information to heart. You made quite a mess."

Cyrus shrugged. His eyes were now fully adjusted to the low light of the alley. He could make out vague details of the man before him as well as the surrounding alley. Nothing within reach could be used as a weapon. "I had no choice," Cyrus said calmly. "One of them wanted to stick me with a needle! I don't like needles. They scare me to death."

This brought a chuckle from Boris. The laugh sounded familiar. Cyrus's eyes strained in the darkness. He tried to pull more details from the man's face but it was no use. He was cloaked in shadow.

"Do I know you?" Cyrus asked.

"Nyet," the man said with confidence. "We have never met. But I know *of* you. I know a great deal about you. Cyrus Cooper, formerly Coalition. Supposedly retired. But I no longer believe this." The man was silent for a few moments, as if contemplating something. "You and I must have a conversation, Cyrus Cooper."

"I'm a lot more conformable talking when I don't have a gun pointed at me."

Again the man chuckled. "I am sure that is true. But the information I require is not the type you are likely to give willingly. So, you see, the gun is necessary."

"Alright. Tell me what you want to know. Let's get this over with."

"Just like that?" the man asked with surprise. "Let us be realistic. You have no intention of being forthcoming."

Cyrus put on his most winning smile. "You won't know until you try. Ask away. What have you got to lose?"

The man was silent. He seemed off balance by Cyrus's willingness to have a conversation. He was trying to decipher the ploy Cyrus was playing at. For his part, Cyrus was working something out. It was a fairly solid bet these men were here for Meridian, but it was also possible, though less likely, they were here on another matter entirely. While Cyrus had a plan to close the loop on the Alvares Cartel, he needed to know for certain whether Meridian had suffered another exposure.

"Very well," the man concluded. "I want you to tell me everything you know about Project Meridian. We know you have hidden the research team. You will give us access to these people and all of their research."

Damn. The Russian *was* after Meridian. Taking care of Alvares would plug one leak, but there was another exposure. He'd have to sort that out, too.

Something more nagged at Cyrus. The man before him sounded oddly familiar. But the few features he could make out in the darkness didn't match with the voice he was hearing.

An easy glance over his shoulder told him what he needed to know. The two armed men behind him were still out of arm's reach, but they had settled into easy stances holding their guns in relaxed positions.

Cyrus directed his attention to the man before him. "Look man, I know you, don't I? Your voice is very—" Cyrus stopped mid-sentence and shifted his gaze past the gunman and into the distance slightly to the left.

The gunman, being on alert, noticed Cyrus's shifting eye movement and instantly reacted. The man shifted to his right as he shot a glance over his left shoulder. But the dark alley was empty.

As soon as the man's attention began to shift, Cyrus was in motion. With a minimum of body movement, he dropped a telescoping baton from the sleeve of his jacket and into his right hand. A barely perceptible snap of his wrist and the device extended to its full two-and-a-half-foot length. His movements were so minor that they did little to draw the lax attention of the two armed men behind him.

Just as Boris was returning his attention to his quarry, Cyrus swung his arm and brought the end of the baton down across the man's gun hand with devastating force. The sound of shattering bone was unmistakable. With a flick of his wrist, he brought the baton back across the side of the man's head on the return swing. Boris dropped to the pavement and remained there.

Cyrus turned with a swing that knocked the gun from the hand of one of the men at his rear. He knew he didn't have time to take a swing at the remaining man before he got a shot off. Changing his tactic, Cyrus simply dove at the third man, catching him with a shoulder to the chest. Together they crashed to the alley floor. Cyrus rolled and came up just as the second gunman tackled him, driving him back to the ground. As Cyrus's head bounced off the pavement, he reasoned that the man on top of him had lost his gun in the darkness and was now simply attacking hand-to-hand. Although his vision swirled from the impact with the pavement, he was happy with hand-to-hand.

The second attacker pummeled Cyrus with a right and left hook to the head. Cyrus's vision was a mess. He couldn't tell which way was up. He finally managed to raise his arms to deflect the blows. Grabbing the man by the wrist, he twisted with everything he had. The man would have to give up his position on top or suffer a broken wrist. As Cyrus hoped, the man gave in to the pressure and rolled away.

Before Cyrus could get to his feet, the third gunman was upright and heading his way. As the man lunged, Cyrus pulled his knees tight against his chest. His attacker's flying tackle landed squarely on the soles of Cyrus's boots, and with a thrust that used every bit of energy he had, Cyrus pistoned his legs outward. The aggressor was launched through the air in an awkward flight that resulted in him crashing against the brick wall of the alley with a sickening snap. The man would not be getting up again.

Cyrus pulled himself to his feet in time to come toe-to-toe with the second attacker. The man looked a little worse for wear, but he was back for another round. He lunged at Cyrus before he had proper footing. For Cyrus, the world was still spinning. Smacking his head on the pavement had rung his bell. What he wouldn't have given to have the baton back in hand.

The man grabbed Cyrus and slammed him against the brick wall. Without pause, he started throwing body shots left and right. Cyrus clinched his abs in an effort to take the beating without having the wind knocked from his lungs, but it was only a matter of time. The man before him was only a dark blur. Through muddled thoughts, Cyrus realized he needed to end this now or risk losing the fight.

Another blow to the body and Cyrus countered with a devastating head-butt to the man's face. The world around him was topsy turvy, but he still recognized the sound of shattering cartilage. *That would be the bastard's nose. Good!* As his attacker dropped back a step, both hands going to his face, Cyrus hit him with an uppercut containing all of the energy he had left.

The snapping of the man's jaw was unmistakable, and Cyrus heard more than saw the man topple to the pavement, like a marionette with its strings cut.

Cyrus stumbled and shook his head. His vision was swimming, but he was beginning to steady. Something was nagging at him—a thought at the corner of his mind. Three. Three. Three? *Three!* There were three attackers. He looked around the alley. One of the men was in a heap at his feet. The other was in a pile at the base of the alley wall, his neck at an oblique angle. He wouldn't be getting up ever again. Where was the third guy? Boris…the one who had done all of the talking.

There was a clicking sound behind him. Cyrus recognized it immediately. It was the sound of the hammer being drawn back on a handgun.

Cyrus froze.

"You broke my hand, you bastard," the Russian sputtered through clinched teeth.

This wasn't good. Cyrus still couldn't see straight. He was just barely standing under his own power, and now the Russian had the drop on him. His addled mind searched for a play, some kind of move that would get him out of this before his brains were vented into the night air.

He heard the Russian start to laugh. It began as a chuckle. "Father said you were not to be underestimated," he said. His laughter grew. "I did not believe him! But you? You're like that damned Energizer Bunny!"

The man's laughter gained intensity. Cyrus couldn't help it, he started to laugh too. He didn't want to, but now he could feel the barrel of the gun pressed against the back of his head. Somehow this struck him as funny…ridiculously funny.

Through his laughter, Cyrus decided that both he and the Russian were likely suffering concussions. The situation was rather amusing after all that had happened, but it wasn't that funny. Still, for the life of him, he couldn't help laughing.

Something finally clicked for Cyrus. The man's voice. It was so familiar. And now that laugh? He knew it too…but he didn't know the face. "Dargoslav!" Cyrus said, as the name finally popped into his head. "Yuri Dargoslav! You're Dargo's kid?"

The man's laughter died down to a chuckle. "Da," he said finally.

"I know your father," Cyrus said calmly.

"Da! He warned me of you. I should have taken him more seriously. Now I think maybe we both have concussion, no?"

"Why are you doing this?" It was a direct question. It was all Cyrus could manage given the circumstances.

"You really need to ask this?" Yuri slurred. "Father said to bring you in alive. He has questions for you. But you make this difficult. Would be easier to kill you!"

Yuri chucked again. *Yeah,* Cyrus thought. They were in bad shape. Another blow to the head would be bad for either of them. But then again, Cyrus figured since Yuri was pressing a gun against his head, he probably had it coming.

In a flash, Cyrus spun, pushing the gun away with one hand and delivering a brutal right cross with the other. Yuri hit the ground in a heap.

Cyrus took a deep breath and looked up and down the alley. He was alone—the last man standing. But it hadn't been an easy fight. His vision was finally returning to normal. Well, close to something that might pass for normal. And he wasn't feeling nausea. That was a good sign. In fact, he was rather hungry.

Hungry? Oh, crap!

He was late picking up dinner!

It took a moment for the sheer absurdity of the idea to make its way through his semi-muddled mind. He had just been in a fight for his life, but somehow he was more concerned with his impromptu date with Reese. Even after what had just transpired, he couldn't fight back the small grin that crossed his face.

He was feeling like himself for the first time in years.

He searched the three men for anything useful but found nothing. They carried cash and short-range walkie-talkies attached to headsets, but nothing more. No identification. Not even a mobile phone between them. He found his Springfield and the baton on the floor of the alley. It took only a moment to reclaim his weapons and to strip the men of theirs. He tossed their guns into a dumpster before reaching the street. As he started walking up the block he dropped the magazines for their guns down the nearest storm drain.

Walking on, he pulled out his phone. He launched a special app simply called Burner. The app let him make a call from a single use number that was independent of his normal phone's identification. It was the software equivalent of having a pre-paid burner phone. The same anonymity of a burner phone but without going through the trouble of carrying the disposable device. Using the Burner app, he dialed 911 and reported that an ambulance was needed. He gave the address of the nearest street corner and told the operator that the EMTs would need to check the alley. When the operator asked his name, he simply hung up. His last encounter with Yuri Dargoslav's father, Dargo, had been tense. They had a complicated history that went back many years. Cyrus had no idea whether Dargo wished him ill. All the same, killing the man's son wouldn't improve the situation. Better to get the young man help now and see what a roll of the dice got him.

A quick check of the map on his phone, and Cyrus confirmed his location. He turned and disappeared into the crowd.

Chapter 30

Berton Springs, Colorado
Thursday, 8:02 pm

Tucked under a blanket at the corner of the couch, Reese was reading a paperback by the firelight. Candles were spread intermittently along the perimeter of the room.

She saw Cyrus's dark silhouette move in the corner of her eye. "How was the bath?" he asked as he headed directly for the kitchen.

"Amazing!" she said with such enthusiasm that it was almost a purr. Lounging in a hot soapy tub had invigorated her. Though the whole time she was soaking, she couldn't help letting her mind wander. She had joked about Cyrus joining her in the Jacuzzi, actually surprising herself with the brazen remark. Not because of the offhanded quip but because she realized it was Freudianly sincere. She had known him only two days. Such a response was decidedly unlike her.

Had it been only two days? *My God... So much has happened.*

Still, she'd never experienced such consuming feelings before. She wasn't the type to give in to infatuation. Was it the thrill and horror of all that had happened? The rational part of her mind would make it easy to write it off as such, but in truth, there was more to it. She couldn't deny she felt something special for Cyrus. She was usually a very rational person, pragmatic and deliberate in her decisions. He had an effect on her, and she liked it.

This was not a rational time. Her world was being turned upside down. The only one who seemed to have any bearing at the moment was Cyrus. It seemed logical for her to be drawn to him at such a time. He was good under pressure, and he made her feel safe. Was that all she was feeling? Was she really attracted to him, or was it that he buoyed her in a time of extreme turbulence? She still wasn't sure how he'd saved her at her apartment, or how he had identified Chad as their leak. There were so many things she didn't know about him—so many things she wanted to know.

Were her feelings a mistake?

She thought of their first kiss and the rush it had brought. And the tingle she felt being close in his arms. Never wanting it to end. No... There was no doubt that things were out of control, but there was one thing she knew with absolute certainty. The feelings she had, the comfort he brought, it was all real. And her feelings were growing stronger with time. She didn't know where the future would take them, but it was the only thing about the last week that felt solid and real.

"Did you get lost? You were gone a long time." She needed to clear her mind. There was time enough to worry about these things later. She closed her book and set it aside. It was one of the three bodice rippers she had swiped from the shelf in

Cyrus's apartment. Of course her choice in reading material hadn't done anything to help her cool her jets while she waited.

Reese threw her fluffy down comforter aside and followed Cyrus to the kitchen. After her bath, she'd dressed in a comfortable pair of black yoga pants and a form-fitting, dark gray tank top. It was casual attire, the most casual she'd worn in front of him so far. But she was planning on a comfortable night in, and besides, she liked the way she looked in the outfit. The way they fit her body left little to the imagination. It was low key, but admittedly, she had aspirations for where the evening might lead.

When she reached the kitchen, Cyrus had his back to her. He was taking plates and glasses down from the cabinet. Reese noticed his discarded jacket lying on the end of the counter. It was dirty and torn. She was going to ask about it when he turned.

Her jaw dropped when his face met the light. The entire left side of it was purple and swollen. His hairline was caked with dried blood. More blood had coagulated along his left ear. The right side of his face had fared better. It was swollen but wasn't as discolored, and it wasn't bleeding.

"My God!" she gasped. "What happened!"

Cyrus smiled, but he kept arranging the place settings, as if his appearance were the most natural thing in the world. He tore into the two paper takeout bags and started setting out food containers.

"I'm sure it looks worse than it is," he said mildly.

When there was no response, he finally stopped and looked her in the eye. She realized her hand was covering her mouth. All she could do was stare in shock.

"No, really," he assured her. "You should see the other guy."

"Jesus, Cyrus," she muttered, finally found her voice. "No joking—what the hell happened? You went to New York—Manhattan. Were you mugged?"

Cyrus laughed. "No, not mugged. But I think we have another security issue. Someone has at least some of the transport sites under surveillance. As soon as I arrived, I picked up a tail. I lured them into an alley so I could get as much information out of them as possible."

"I'm sorry, did you say them? *As in more than one?*"

Cyrus grinned sheepishly. It was that coy smirk that she was growing to both enjoy and lament. "It was a three-man team, just like Chicago. All three Eastern European, *just like Chicago.*"

Reese closed her eyes and took a deep breath. How did he do this? She was feeling queasy just thinking about what little she knew. He had lived through it. But it seemed of little concern to him. "You intentionally drew three men into a dark alley, so *you* could interrogate *them*? How did that work out for you?"

The look Cyrus gave her was quizzical, but so matter of fact that she couldn't help it. She cracked a smile. A moment later they were both laughing.

"Come on, lets get you cleaned up," she said.

"That can wait," he urged. "The food's getting cold."

Just shaking her head in reply, Reese took his hand and led him from the kitchen and into the bathroom adjacent to the master bedroom. She pointed to the whirlpool tub. "Have a seat," she ordered. "I'll grab the first aid kit."

She went to the closet and pulled out a large, blue, plastic box with a bold red cross emblazoned on the lid. Laying it out on the counter for easy access, she looked back to where Cyrus sat on the edge of the large tub. "We only picked this thing up the other day. I never expected we'd be using it—certainly not before the week was out."

"Stick with me, Reese. I'll show you things you never dreamt of!"

She rolled her eyes and shook her head. Stepping back, she was concerned about the amount of blood on his shirt. "Better take it off," she said pointing at his shirt.

"It's okay," he grinned. "It's not my blood."

She arched a brow and didn't know what to make of the statement. Was that a good thing? It must be, right? Yes, she decided. She didn't want it to be his blood…but what had he done to the other guy? Other *guys*? Blowing out an exasperated breath, she waved a hand. The shirt had to go. It was trashed.

It took a little effort but Cyrus pulled the shirt free. The blood had matted to his skin. Reese could see that his movements were awkward and clumsy. He was no doubt becoming stiff and sore as the effects of his injuries settled in. Finally getting the shirt over his head, Cyrus tossed it into the corner of the room. It hit the tile floor with a wet splat.

Struggling not to gasp out loud, Reese felt a sense of vertigo seeing his bare chest and ribs. They were dark with red and purple abrasions. There would soon be extensive bruising. His face and head had taken a beating, but apparently, that paled in comparison to the rest of his torso.

What the hell had happened in New York? *He only went to pick up takeout!*

She wet a washcloth in the sink and went about gently cleaning the abrasions on his face and hairline. She chose not to say anything more about the bruising on his torso. "You can always be counted on to do the unexpected. For example, who in their right mind would take three dangerous men into a dark alley with the intention of interrogating them? Is it safe to assume that they were armed?"

"They were."

"Is it safe to assume they resisted your attempts to extract information?"

"They did."

Reluctantly, she smiled. "You learned something anyway, didn't you?"

Cyrus smiled. "See, you do know me!" There was a bemused playfulness to his manner the belayed his devastated physical condition.

Reese rinsed the rag in the sink and knelt before him once more. She began cleaning the abrasions on the other side of his face. All things considered, they were rather minor. There was a small cut to the scalp that bled down the side of his face but it didn't even need stitches. Just a thorough cleaning and it would likely heal in a day or two. The purple swelling on the side of his head was actually the worst of it. Except for the back of his head, where a significant bump had formed. Calling it a goose egg wouldn't do it justice.

She couldn't bring herself to ask about it. He'd obviously taken a serious blow. It was enough to make her start paying more attention to the responsiveness of his eyes. It was one bit of good news. His pupil response seemed normal. She decided to watch that for the next few hours. Still, he had to have one hell of a headache. She felt queasy just running her fingers over the knot.

She couldn't help thinking that he looked as if someone had used him as a punching bag. His witticisms aside, it made her wonder what the other guys really did look like. Truth be told, she was still achy and sore from being knocked around during the abduction attempt at her apartment. By comparison, Cyrus looked as if he'd played Wile E. Coyote in an episode of the *Looney Tunes* Road Runner cartoon.

She worked diligently at cleaning the abrasions, at one point pulling what appeared to be small chunks of asphalt out of his hair. She tried hard to keep focused on the task at hand. She was very aware of his close proximity and his musky scent while she worked. She could feel his breath on her skin, even feel the heat radiating from his body. She felt the curious flutter in her chest and an unexpected weakness in her knees.

This was terrible. She felt like a schoolgirl with a crush.

It was wonderful. *Ahh!*

As soon as she set to wiping the dried blood from the side of his ribs, she found something unexpected. It turned out that some of the blood on his shirt was his own. Somewhere in the scuffle he'd taken a blow to the ribs that had broken skin. Apparently it didn't hurt, but it had bled. The gash was wide and fairly deep. It needed stitches.

It wasn't something Reese had experience with, but she knew Cyrus wasn't willing to go to the emergency room. So she dug into the medical kit, screwed up her courage and set about suturing the wound. Fourteen stitches later she tied off a somewhat clumsy knot and was finished.

Cyrus studied her handy work and gave her a proud nod. "I think you missed your calling. You sure you've never done that before?"

Reese felt her cheeks flush. She was pretty sure he was humoring her. The entire experience had been without grace, and she'd torn his skin on at least two occasions. She feared she might have done just as much harm as good. At least she finished without vomiting!

Somehow he gave her a sense of confidence she hadn't had before. If someone had told her a week earlier that she would be stitching up a bloody flesh wound, she would've sworn they were crazy. Now, as much as the idea didn't appeal to her, she was pretty sure she could do a better job, if she had to do it again.

It was interesting that Cyrus had sat through the entire procedure offering a supportive tip here or there when she needed it, but never once had he so much as winced in pain or made a comment regarding her clumsiness with a needle. She hadn't even used a local anesthetic. Still, even for the experience that it was, she was proud to make it through. Maybe some emergency medical training would be a useful skill somewhere down the line.

"What's this?" Reese asked.

She was pointing at a nasty scar on his abdomen, just above the belt of his jeans. It had once been a ragged wound that had not been stitched professionally. What remained was a prominent scar. She ran her finger slowly along the two-inch-long, pale line that was long since healed.

"A keepsake from the old days," Cyrus said dryly. "A reminder that things don't always go according to plan. And when that happens, people get hurt."

"It looks like you *really* got hurt," she said quietly. "Do you want to talk about it?"

Cyrus looked her in the eye and studied her gaze for a few moments. He shook his head only slightly. "I wasn't the one who got hurt. There was a lot of collateral damage.

"I'd be happy to talk about it…someday. Just not right now. And it's never a good idea to dump all your personal crap on someone you're really interested in. We've got a good thing going. I don't want to mess it up with old baggage."

A sadness had settled into his eyes and she sensed a deep seated pain behind whatever had happened. He offered a weak, forced smile. She would leave it alone. They would talk about it when he was ready. In any case, she suspected he had a great many interesting things he might one day share. She hoped they would have the time together to find out.

"Okay," Reese said. She wanted to change the subject. She had plenty of other questions to ask. "You think someone is watching the platforms?"

"It's the only thing that makes sense," he said. "They may not know about the platforms themselves, but they seem to know about the locations where they're kept. There's no logical reason for these guys being all over me as soon as I arrived in Manhattan. They did the same thing in Chicago. I don't believe in coincidences."

"That would mean that someone on the team sold us out. Is this part of what Chad did?"

Cyrus thought for a moment. "It seems unlikely. The crews in Chicago and New York were more professional than the Mexicans at your apartment. The same with the bomb on Alfie's car. That was really clumsy. Right now, as unlikely as it seems, I'm thinking we've got two parties trying to get their hands on Meridian."

"You think there might be a second leak?" She didn't want to believe it, but that seemed like the only explanation.

"It's possible," Cyrus admitted. "But it could be more complicated than that. The good news is that I recognized one of the guys from tonight. I know where to start looking for a second leak.

"You know, now that I think about it, there's something I've been wanting to ask you."

She glanced at him expectantly for a moment before returning to work cleaning a wound. "What's that?"

"When we were talking with Chad, you mentioned that Meade had paid off the student loans of everyone on the research team. Tell me about that."

"Oh, yeah! That was unexpected. We found out about it after he passed. His lawyer, a guy named Underhill—"

"Underwood?"

She looked at him in confusion for a second. "That's it, Underwood. Anyway he came by the office. Said he was settling Walter's estate. Walter had made arrangements for each of us as part of his will. I guess he knew each of us had student loans we would be paying on for the rest of our lives. He had a provision in his will that paid them off. That's how the lawyer, Underwood, explained it."

"Was Meade wealthy?"

Reese stopped working to consider the question. "You could say that," she said. She looked up into Cyrus's eyes. "Obviously, he had this place. But I don't think he ever brought anyone here. I've been here before, but that was only because he knew I didn't have family. I would sometimes spend Thanksgiving or Christmas here with him. But he made a point of keeping this place to himself." She thought for a moment. "But, yeah. I'd say he was wealthy. He had a number of patents that brought in a steady income. He could've lived comfortably off those, if he chose to."

She thought again, looking at Cyrus suspiciously. "Walter left you this house and the land it sits on, but you didn't know he was wealthy?"

She saw confusion in his eyes.

"I guessed as much," she admitted. "But I would've expected Underwood to explain that when you took possession of the property."

She watched his eyes carefully. "In addition to this house, Walter owned most of this mountain. That became yours along with the house."

Judging by the look Cyrus gave, this was all news to him. He actually looked a little dizzy at the realization. "Underwood must've left that part out," he admitted.

"If he did, it was at Walter's request. If I had to guess, knowing what I do about you, he might've thought you wouldn't accept the gift if it were too lofty."

The shy look on Cyrus's face told her she wasn't far from the mark.

"He told you about his patents?" he asked.

She laughed. "Well, no, actually. I only found out about them when Underwood visited."

She was reluctant to continue with the next part of the story. To his credit, Cyrus didn't push. He waited patiently until she was ready to continue.

"He informed me that Walter left the patents to me in his will," she said finally.

The surprise was clear on Cyrus's face.

"I know!" she said. "That was my reaction! I guess it was for lack of a better option. He didn't have any family either. He could have set something up and left them to charity... I'm really not sure why he left them to me," her voice trailed off, as she contemplated the question.

"It's not that hard to imagine," Cyrus said with confidence. "He always spoke very highly of you. He had profound respect for you. I'm actually not surprised he left them to you. I shouldn't be surprised he had some patents tucked away making good money, either. He was a brilliant man who had a very long career."

"Well, anyway," she said. "It's my understanding that the proceeds from those patents spent a lot of time accruing interest in a bank somewhere. And that was used to pay off the loans. That much was classic Walter. He would've wanted to make sure everyone was taken care of."

Cyrus nodded. "Yeah, that I can see. But something occurred to me when we were talking with Chad. The team was working on a project they knew would change the world. But they knew the Professor wasn't going to capitalize on it. When he made that decision, he was really making that choice for all of you. It was a unilateral decision. No one had a say in it."

She nodded.

"So in Chad's case, he felt slighted," Cyrus continued. "He felt he was sitting on the chance of a lifetime, and Meade wasn't going to let him or any of the others cash in. They were making their salary working on the project, but they didn't have a stake in the bigger picture. To me, that gives every one of them motive to do something stupid, just like Chad."

"But Walter would've taken care of them. He wasn't going to let them go uncompensated," she countered.

"Did they know that?" he asked.

She didn't know what to say.

"Did Walter ever make arrangements with the team? Did he ever give them a reason to think they'd be compensated in some way?"

"No," she admitted. "I guess he didn't. I never really thought about it until now."

Cyrus shook his head. "You didn't. It wasn't a concern to you. But it means that every one of the team members had a motive for trying to sell the technology before it was ready to hit the market. I've been getting a strong sense that we're dealing with two distinctly different groups vying for Meridian. When you think about it, we're lucky a dozen different groups aren't trying to take it from us."

Reese felt sick as she considered his logic.

"But first things first," Cyrus said with confidence. "I'm closing the loop on Bola Alvares tomorrow."

Reese stood and looked Cyrus over. Her patchwork was about as good as it was going to get. "Why don't you wash up? Okay if I warm up dinner?"

This brought a sincere smile to Cyrus's face. "Perfect!" he said. "Just give me a few minutes." He looked down at his jeans. They were caked with grime from the alley, blood, and who knew what else. Perhaps not so surprising, they had also torn at some point.

Chapter 31

Berton Springs, Colorado
Thursday, 8:52 pm

Walking down the hall, Cyrus pulled on a fresh t-shirt. He was already stiffening up. His body was fighting its self to relax; the adrenaline rush had left him, and he was now tired and numb. The house was dark. As he reached the living room, he found the fire restocked and burning brightly. A number of additional candles were lit around the room. A blanket was laid out before the hearth, and Reese had also laid out the reheated Chinese food.

She walked in from the kitchen holding a bottle of wine. She handed it to him, along with a corkscrew. "I thought a picnic would be nice," she said with a shy smile. "I wanted to surprise you when you got back…" She gently touched the darkening bruise on the side of his face. "It turns out you surprised me."

His pulse quicken with the warm touch of her fingertips. Her hand slid gently down the coarse stubble of his jaw. He looked at the blanket she'd laid across the floor, the pillows scattered around to make them comfortable, the warm fire, and the candles. She'd gone to a lot of trouble putting together an improvised, intimate setting for two. And he'd come back beaten up and bleeding. But she was rolling with it. The craziness of the last few days had knocked her down, but she was resilient. He admired that.

They took their places on the blanket in front of the fire. His legs didn't fold beneath him as easily as they should. The effort brought a renewed surge of pain that he tried to keep to himself. Thankfully Reese wasn't looking just then and missed his clumsy effort to get comfortable. By the time he pulled the cork from the wine bottle, Reese was ready with two glasses. He poured them each half a glass before setting the bottle aside.

Cyrus considered a toast, but he was at a loss for words. So much had happened in the last few days. The only positive thing to come from it all was her, as far as he was concerned. How the hell do you put something like that into a toast? He felt he had something to say but found no words to express what he was thinking or feeling. And lacking anything better, he simply raised his glass.

Reese smiled brightly and raised her glass in response. The ting of the tapped glasses was a virtual gong in the quiet of the room. Cyrus listened to the sound fade until all that was left was the snapping and popping of the fire. He took a deep swallow of wine, his eyes on hers the entire time. She took a sip as well, her eyes similarly locked on his. As she lowered her glass, a tight smile crossed her lips. It was that smile, he realized. Her smile and her eyes. They resonated through him, just as the sound of their glasses had filled the room.

He watched her smile stretch tightly across her lips. As if she were fighting herself not to smile more brightly, reigning in what she was thinking and feeling. But it was more than that. There was the light in her eyes that she wasn't able to contain. The hopefulness, the confidence, the desire. He was sure of it. She was falling for him, too.

So what he did, he did without thinking. He took her wineglass and set it aside along with his own. Sliding across the blanket, he moved nearer. Rising onto his knees, he pulled her close. Then, slowly and gently, he drew her mouth to his. She returned his kiss…delicate, caressing, and growing more passionate.

She pulled him more tightly against her. He was completely consumed, for once his thoughts only of this moment. She couldn't know that he had only ever given himself to one other woman so deeply. He had never felt his blood boil the way it did when he felt her touch. Until he met her, he had never expected to feel anything close to this again.

When they pulled away from each other for a moment of air, he felt her pulling his shirt free. He laughed and helped her, as she slid his shirt off over his head. But she stopped cold when her eyes fell on the bandage taped over his lower ribs.

"Oh! I forgot—" a hand went to her mouth. Cyrus put his finger under her chin and guided her eyes upward to meet his. He couldn't help but laugh. He was about to say something funny, but decided *to hell with it!* His mouth again found hers, and their entangled bodies went crashing to the floor.

By that point, they were both laughing. Neither one had any intention of stopping. A moment later, Reese freed herself of her tank top, which was followed shortly by the remainder of their clothing. The firelight grew dim while their dinner grew cold for a second time that night.

Chapter 32

Berton Springs, Colorado
Thursday, 7:11 am

Glaring morning sun shining through the front windows fought to warm the cold living room. The reflective light woke Reese as surely as a rooster on a country farm. A yawn and a stretch, she sat upright with the heavy down comforter pressed to her naked body with one arm. The fire had died out in the middle of the night, and the house had grown cold. She looked at the floor around her. It was covered with the blankets and pillows she had scavenged from the beds of the two guest rooms.

Cyrus lay on his back, still sound asleep. The comforter was pulled up halfway over his chest. She could just see the edge of the bandage on his ribs. She smiled, thinking with a small bit of pride that he had not let his injuries hamper last night's activities.

The scrapes on the side of his face were looking better. Her improvised medical attention appeared to be doing the trick. And the swelling on the side of his face was gone. Even the bruising seemed less pronounced than the night before. He was lying on his back, so the knot on the back of his head must've improved as well.

He was amazingly resilient.

She thought about his comment the night before. If he won the fight, what did the other guys look like? Had he killed them? He never elaborated on the details of the attack. Cyrus was a man of surprisingly few words—even in the gravest of situations.

She pulled the blanket back to take a better look at the bandage on his lower ribs. It had grown dark with blood seepage. Suddenly, she was feeling more modest about their lovemaking. He had clearly broken a stitch or two in the process. *On second thought, maybe I should consider it a point of pride.*

She was smiling somewhat sheepishly to herself when she looked up and noticed he was watching her. *Whoops.* She felt her cheeks flush in response.

"Good morning," Cyrus said with a grin.

She leaned over and kissed him. "Good morning," she said quietly. "You've been bleeding. I think you might've broken some stitches."

He chuckled. There was a fiendish glint in his eye, but he kept any commentary to himself. She had a feeling that their minds were following a similar line of thought.

"Do you want me to take a look at it? I can clean it up." She took a deep breath and drew up the courage. "If you need new stitches...I'll try to do less damage this time."

"No, don't worry about it. I'm not in any hurry to get up. Are you?"

She smiled. *Not at all,* she thought. She slipped under the blanket beside him and laid her head on his chest. "I could stay here all day." She meant it.

"That sounds just about perfect." She could sense he was smiling at the thought. "Unfortunately, I have an appointment with Agent Shaw later this morning. And then I'm going to have a talk with our friend Bola Alvares."

Reese rocked back onto her elbow and glared at him. "You're kidding?"

He shook his head. "It's gotta be done. The man tried to kidnap you, and he put a bomb in Alfie's truck. Until he's dealt with, none of us are safe."

Thinking for a minute, she wasn't sure she should ask the question, but she still felt compelled. "Then, when you say 'talk' with Alvares, you mean…"

"I mean talk," he said with a disarming smile. "Alvares knows about the platforms. Basically, they're the Holy Grail to smugglers. He won't stop until he gets his hands on the technology. Chad let that genie out of the bottle. There's no way to put it back."

"So you're going to *talk* with Alvares?" She was skeptical.

"I have to. He knows about the platforms. If he brought anyone in on the secret, I need to know. Anyone who knows is a danger to every one of us."

"And you think you can get a hardened drug lord to tell you what you want to know?" She knew he was smarter than to think it would really be that easy, but she couldn't imagine what his plan might be.

He considered the question. "Sometimes it's not the question that matters so much as the way you ask it."

So much for that. She still had no idea what he had in mind, but trusted he had a plan. She just hoped it didn't involve another beating like the one he had taken the night before. Oddly, despite what he had gone through in New York, he didn't seem troubled by the physical abuse his body had suffered. He really was unlike any man she'd ever met. It was no wonder Walter had spoken so highly of him.

The realization that her feelings for Cyrus were growing was a surprise. She had never fallen for someone so quickly. And last night? If she was honest with herself, last night meant something more to her on multiple levels. This, too, was unusual.

Though last night, after they had both fallen asleep, something had happened that was troubling her today. She was tempted to ask about it, but at the same time, it felt like an invasion of his privacy. Still, if the connection she felt was true, maybe it wouldn't be so out of line.

Running his hand through her hair, Cyrus broke the silence. "You've got something on your mind. Why don't you tell me what you're thinking?"

It was curious, he must have sensed her conflict. She took it as a sign to just go for it. Either he would be alright talking, or he wouldn't.

"You talked in your sleep. It sounded like a bad dream…a *really* bad dream," she said. She didn't move from where she leaned on an elbow. Only inches separated them.

Cyrus was quiet for a few beats. "That's funny, I don't remember dreaming last—" his voice caught and an awkward silence followed. "Oh… Ah, yeah. Well…"

He was clearly at a loss to explain, and Reese felt bad for putting him on the spot. "I'm sorry for bringing it up," she said. "I didn't mean to…"

Great. Now she didn't know what to say either.

The silence hung between them.

Cyrus took a long deep breath and seemed to be thinking something through. She turned and sat fully upright, holding the comforter tightly against her skin. A chill ran through her. *Damn, it's really cold in the house!*

"When you meet someone special, the worst thing you can do is dump all of your baggage on them," Cyrus said reluctantly.

"I don't want to pry. You were just very upset—I was concerned. I wanted to wake you. But you were so agitated, I was a little afraid of what might happen. You don't have to talk about it. I just want to make sure you're alright."

"No, I'm fine. And it's alright." He pulled himself upright so he was sitting on the floor with a blanket covering his lap and legs. "We just had a fantastic night together—something I take very seriously. But, in the middle of our first night together you hear something like that? I'm not sure what I said, but I know what I dreamt. I think it warrants some kind of explanation."

Reese found it hard to look him in the eye. She didn't want to press the issue. "You don't have to explain anything. You were just yelling for Natasha and you were *really* upset. Whatever you dreamt, it must've been horrible."

There was silence while Cyrus tried to find the words. "Natasha was very important to me. That last job I mentioned— the one in my former life?" He took a deep breath. "I saw her die… I couldn't prevent it. I'm not sure the nightmares will ever stop."

When her eyes found his, Reese was even more sorry she'd brought it up. She saw the hurt he held behind them, and it tore at her. She barely had a voice. *"I'm so sorry,"* was all she could say.

He offered a half-hearted smile. "No, there's more to it than that. That's why I say it's baggage. After I lost Natasha, I guess I closed myself off. I changed everything about my life. My job, my home, all my friends. I just needed to start over. But I lost a crucial part of myself along the way, and I resigned myself to the fact that I would never have it back.

"But meeting you changed that. I didn't understand it at the time, but I knew it the first time we spoke."

He dropped into silence again. She could tell he had more to say, but the words didn't come easy. The words were clumsy, and he was stumbling. She realized how strong he was for trying to get them out. This was obviously a subject very close to his heart.

"I know this sounds crazy and maybe even cliché," his smile showed his discomfort. "But when I look in your eyes, I get the feeling you understand. Meeting you sparked something in me…something that's been gone for a long time. Something I didn't even realize I'd lost."

Reese did understand. She could see it behind his eyes. He had loved Natasha very much. Whatever happened, it didn't matter. The woman had died, and that loss had left Cyrus deeply scarred. For all the strength, determination, and resolve she'd seen in him in the short time since they met, now she was seeing the sensitive side. He was as breakable as anyone else.

She wanted to tell him this, but words failed her now, too. Here he was, spilling his guts to her—baring his soul, and she was too choked up to explain how much she wanted to help, how much she cared, or how much she wanted to take his pain away.

Clearing his throat, Cyrus took another deep breath and lay back against the pillows. "I'm acting like a world class freak. Our first night together, and you get to see this..." He was shaking his head. "The truth is that I care for you, Reese. I care a great deal. I just don't want you to have the wrong impression based on what I might've said in my sleep. I haven't had that dream in a long time. And, I think that since I met you, I'm experiencing something I never thought I would again."

Reese knew. She understood just how he felt. It hurt to know he had that kind of pain locked inside. But as much as she empathized with his heartache, it filled her with hope to know he could share these things. It clearly didn't come easy to him.

She wanted to tell him these things—explain just how she felt. But when she looked into his eyes, the words just weren't there. Leaning over, she kissed him gently. A few moments later she pulled back and smiled. Her heart hammered in her chest and chill in the room had disappeared entirely There was no doubt in her mind, he could read the hungry gleam in the way her eyes locked on him. The same sentiment reflected in his gaze. She leaned over and kissed him again, this time more passionately and with abandon.

When two people are of the same mind, the best conversations can be had without words.

In one quick motion, she pulled back the blankets to make room for herself. She slid her naked body along his, even as his arms enveloped her. The blankets fell down around them and the room went dark. They made love again.

Chapter 33

Off the Coast of Santa Barbara, California
Friday, 9:18 am (10:18 am Colorado Time)

Anatoli had turned in another detailed report. Dargo sat at the desk bolted to the bulkhead of the small ship's main cabin. His eyes scanned the screen of the laptop as he scrolled through the latest update, a study in the movements of Nil Bayer. Though Dargo had worked for Bayer for only a short time, he already harbored distrust for the man. Not being one to blindly follow orders that could prove detrimental to himself or his team, Dargo had tasked Anatoli with tracking Bayer and reporting back.

The initial reports were strange. Bayer moved around Europe seemingly at random. One thing became apparent early on. The man shunned air travel. He traveled by car, or when possible, by train. This was a bonus, because it made Anatoli's job easier. Last-minute air travel was difficult and expensive. But last-minute travel by train or car posed no issue at all.

Bayer had no compunction when it came to spending large sums of money. He had outfitted Dargo's team with whatever equipment they required, with little or no fuss. Likewise, the man had shelled out large sums of money to pay Dargo's support staff. With operatives spread between California, New York, Chicago, Washington, D.C., and parts of Europe, this was no small financial concern. The man showed distress only for the timeliness of the operation, never the cost. Dargo was accustomed to working for the financially well off. They were the ones who could afford his fees. But Bayer's unconventional concerns had prompted Dargo to look more closely at his employer.

Such examination of one's employer was unprincipled, and that had troubled Dargo for some time. But as time had passed and the questions accumulated, so had his concern for the situation. Dargo was a professional. He didn't need to like an employer or agree with his ideology in order to take a job. It was the nature of the business. But this was also a vocation where few lived long enough to retire, let alone die of old age. Paying attention when things were off kilter had always served Dargo well. And, in all of his years on the job, he'd never had a greater sense that something was amiss. So he had set Anatoli on the man's trail. Initially with little result.

To Anatoli's credit, he was determined. He tracked Bayer day and night. As a result, Dargo had great confidence in the reports. Bayer had taken a number of meetings with industrial fabrication facilities in Germany and Switzerland. He had also talked with two prominent bankers in Switzerland. And even though Anatoli had complete audio recordings from each of these meetings, Dargo was no closer to understanding what Bayer was really up to. It seemed the man was seeking financing for a large scale manufacturing project. At the same time, he was looking at a number of facilities to produce his product. But no matter who he spoke with, he was never willing to go into detail concerning the product that was to be manufactured. Apparently the device was highly technical in nature, and Bayer considered it a proprietary secret of the highest order.

There was little doubt that Bayer's sub rosa project was directly connected to the mission Dargo had undertaken. It had something to do with the project the Americans called 'Meridian.' None of these things sounded a warning bell on their own. That had more to do with his overall impression of Bayer as a man. The real warning signs were the glimpses Dargo had at the sort of financing Bayer was working to secure. Bayer was already outrageously wealthy. Yet the man was making deals to borrow money and leveraging every asset he owned. Whatever Bayer's end game was, the man was dealing in sums of money that boggled the imagination. No wonder Bayer considered Dargo's operating funds to be pocket change.

The real problem was the sort of money Bayer was working to leverage. Dargo had seen such unadulterated sums before. Not personally, but he was a student of history. The sort of money Bayer was putting together could be used to fund a revolution. It was the sort of financing needed to fund a private army. And worst of all, Bayer seemed like just the sort of megalomaniacal asshole to do something like that.

As far as Dargo could tell, everything hinged on the acquisition of Meridian. Though Bayer was keeping him in the dark on the exact details of the technology, Dargo was no fool. He was putting things together. Even if what he was seeing made no sense. And since he had no trust for Bayer, he knew he needed to sort things out before they had their hands on

Meridian. If he didn't figure out Bayer's end game soon, he might find himself one of the loose ends that Bayer hired people like him to clean up.

No matter what he had done, Dargo was unable to connect the dots and find any clue to Bayer's larger plan. That was, until yesterday.

Over the last several days, Anatoli had repeatedly tried and failed to gain access to Bayer's laptop. On a number of occasions, he managed to gain physical access to the device, but each time he had failed to defeat the operating system's security. He'd had access to the computer, but he couldn't access the data. As far as Dargo was concerned, this was a major professional black eye. He had never come up against a computer system that he couldn't compromise, at least not in the field. Whatever Bayer had on his laptop, it used top-notch authentication and encryption. It was more secure than anything Dargo had ever encountered.

That led Dargo to take a closer look at Bayer's financial records. Bayer was a wealthy man who had done an amazing amount of traveling over the last year. As a result, Bayer's financial records were time consuming to data mine. But in the end, they provided a great deal of information about the man. Dargo had already searched that information for a clue to the man's motivation for attacking the Meridian team. He'd also looked for clues that might hint at what Bayer was looking to manufacture in Europe. Nothing had proven illuminating. But taking a fresh look at the financial documents from a fresh perspective, something struck him as tremendously useful.

One of Bayer's credit card statements held the key to accessing his laptop. A regimented and anal man, Bayer harbored great concern for the contents of his laptop. That much was clear in the level of security used to protect it. But the man was also concerned with the loss or theft of the machine. According to the credit card statement, Bayer subscribed to an online, cloud-based, backup service. Every time he connected his laptop to a network with Internet access, the backup service on his laptop would select the modified files and mirror them to the off-site facility for safe keeping.

Under normal circumstances, this would've been a good idea. It was ironic that Bayer spared no expense to secure access to the laptop itself while failing to select an equally secure off-site backup service. He was using a British backup service called DataSecure. Their technology had a major shortcoming. If the DataSecure servers could be considered a hotel, and each user account on the service the equivalent of a room in that hotel, it meant their security was like having every room unlocked by the same master key. More secure backup systems used an individual key for each user account, essentially a different key for each hotel room. Extremely secure systems allow the user to specify their own encryption key, ensuring that no unauthorized user anywhere would have access to the data—not even the people managing the servers. In the hotel analogy, it would be like letting each guest set a private combination for the door lock of their room. That way, not even hotel management could get in.

All of the data stored on the DataSecure servers was encrypted using the same cypher. While this meant the data on the service's system was encrypted and safe from prying eyes, it also meant that anyone with access to the service's master decryption key would be able to read any data on the backup servers, regardless of the uploading account.

Fortunately for Dargo, Bayer used DataSecure for his cloud backup solution. Dargo had simply contacted a hacker associate, and a few short hours later he had access to the decryption key, and with it, every bit of data on the DataSecure servers. Six hours later, he no longer had a need to access Bayer's laptop directly. He had retrieved an exact duplicate of the contents of the laptop's hard drive and restored it to a virtual machine on his own laptop. Now he had access to every file Bayer did. And best of all, Bayer would have absolutely no way of knowing his data had been compromised.

The last several hours had flown by for Dargo. He'd been examining the contents of Bayer's computer.

Even while a young man in school, Bayer had been gifted with an enormous ego. On his first day at the university he had started a journal. And to Dargo's astonishment, Bayer had maintained that journal ever since. In an effort to protect what he referred to as his legacy, Bayer had even gone so far as to digitize the entire archive. For years, the log chronicled nothing of intrinsic value. Just another college student trying to find his place in academia, intending to one day make his mark on the world. The tone of the journal changed shortly after Bayer graduated from the university, when he was recruited into the Soviet Academy of Sciences.

After joining the academy, being the low man on the totem pole, Bayer was passed from one project to the next, always acting in a support capacity. He participated in the development of a new type of rocket propellant, helped develop new deep-earth drilling technologies, and had had a part in many other projects of absolutely no importance at all. But eventually he'd become involved in energy research. According to the journal, that was where Bayer really had found his calling. He quickly rose through the ranks and was soon leading his own team in the study of different energy-generating technologies.

Bayer's team had worked with wind, hydroelectric, geothermal, solar, and even nuclear power sources. The goal was to develop a power source that would make Russia one hundred percent energy independent. They were to eliminate the need to import oil, coal, and natural gas. Russian leaders saw the requirement of resources from outside the country as a weakness. As such, it was critical to eliminate that weaknesses. Only then would Russia become the one true leader on the world stage.

About five years after taking the lead of his team, Bayer was reading through old state archives from the turn of the century. He believed he could draw inspiration for a new means of energy production if he looked to the past and considered how his country had grown through the use of more primitive energy resources. He also hoped to find support for his own programs by drawing on examples from Russian history to make his point. It seemed he was forever bickering with the administration and always needed new justification for the money spent on research. He had hoped that the study of the historic reports might help on at least one of those fronts.

What Bayer found was a report of a meteorite that had been discovered only a dozen miles outside of Moscow, in February of 1907. Apparently hundreds of city residents heard the strike. Many saw the light in the sky as the rock crashed to Earth. Fifty armed soldiers were immediately dispatched to the impact site, originally thinking it was a military attack of some sort. But in the end, the soldiers returned with only a strange stone twice the size of a loaf of bread. The soldier who had carried the rock back to Moscow had developed burns on his hands; blistering where he had touched the fallen chunk of stone. That might've been the end of Bayer's interest, had there not been one additional note at the end of the report, stating that the soldier with the burned hands also experienced burns up his arms as far as his shoulders. That was strange, because the man said he had never felt any heat from the rock, and the object had never touched him anywhere above the wrist.

The mention of the burns had piqued Bayer's interest. The burns were likely due to radiation, not largely understood in the early 1900s. Bayer had felt compelled to investigate further. According to the journal, it had taken him over a month to locate further information on the meteorite. It turned out that a pair of scientists had taken possession of the rock shortly after its retrieval from the woods outside of Moscow. No further mention was made of the soldier with the burns, but apparently the scientists worked with the meteorite for several months without incurring similar injury.

By Bayer's own admission, he was becoming more and more fascinated by the reports filed by the pair of scientists in 1907. Though the scientists of that day knew little about chemical analysis, they had discovered that the meteorite reacted in extreme ways when exposed to electrical current.

This was the part of the report that Dargo found impossible to believe. If the report was accurate, the scientists discovered that when a certain level of electricity was passed into the stone, the *weight* of the ore would change dramatically. Pushing only enough electricity to power a series of light bulbs actually made the stone completely weightless. For the weight to change, Bayer theorized in his notes, the mass of the ore must have changed when subjected to electricity. Either that, or some other fundamental change must have occurred in the object's density.

Though Dargo suspected that someone in the scientific archives was having fun at Bayer's expense, the journal entries made it clear that Bayer was buying into the idea completely.

Bayer had continued to dig into the state archives for further information regarding the experiments on the meteorite, soon to the detriment of his position at the Academy. Apparently, he was put on report after several unexplained absences from the lab. According to the journal, Bayer was spending that time in the archives.

For better or worse, that time must've paid off. After an arduous search—the journal didn't indicate exactly how many weeks—Bayer finally located a report suggesting the meteorite had been moved to a test facility located deep in the wilds of Russia. At first, Bayer wasn't sure he had picked up the paper trail of the same meteorite because the stone was now referred to by a new code name, *Alexander's Fountain*. Research was being conducted at a top secret, remote military lab that was entirely devoted to the study of the meteorite.

After confirming that Alexander's Fountain was indeed the same meteorite he was tracking, Bayer continued his research. Apparently Alexander's Fountain took its name from Alexander III, father of Nicolas II, then the Tsar of Russia.

At this point in the journals, Bayer became less specific when referring to the meteorite, or Alexander's Fountain, as he took to calling it. He seemed to be somewhat paranoid, concerned that someone might be reading his logs while he was away. All the same, it was clear that Bayer had found additional reports from the military installation, indicating that Alexander's Fountain was regarded as a powerful new energy source, electrical specifically, though implications were also made that the ore could also produce power in the form of vast amounts of heat. Depending on the current applied to the stone, the properties it exhibited were immensely different and could be harnessed in different ways.

Surprisingly, all at once, Bayer's access to the military and scientific reports dried up. At first he suspected he couldn't find the location where later reports were warehoused—likely the result of them being misfiled. But he soon found ancillary reports indicating some sort of catastrophe had taken place at the military facility in the wilds of Siberia. The reports had ceased because something had caused Alexander's Fountain to go critical, and somehow the accident had literally wiped the installation from the face of the map.

After that, the military machine had gone to considerable lengths to hide the fact that the military laboratory ever existed. But by this point, Bayer was not willing to let things go. These long forgotten reports held the key to fulfilling the goals of his project in the present.

In the months that followed, according to the logs, Bayer got himself in great trouble with his superiors. He became consumed with discovering what had happened to Alexander's Fountain. He lost his position as team lead and was later removed from the project entirely. After that, he was moved to less prestigious posts, conducting what amounted to busy work. The logs showed that this initially bothered Bayer, though he soon grew to see the reprimand as a chance to spend more time digging into Alexander's Fountain. His largest problem quickly became that there simply was no more information to be had. After the destruction of the facility, all reports entirely ceased. Though he thought the project might've been renamed or reclassified, Bayer found no evidence to support the theory. He found it strange, but it seemed the loss of the facility was a black eye the government wanted to expunge from history.

Sitting back in his chair, Dargo pulled off his reading glasses and rubbed his eyes. He'd read hundreds of pages from Bayer's personal journal, and after all that he'd seen, one observation stood out from all others. Bayer had started writing as a normal, if uptight, self-absorbed individual. But once he sunk his teeth into the meteorite research and the mystery of Alexander's Fountain, the man had grown steadily more obsessed and less stable. Dargo now believed his concern over his employer's motivations was well founded. This man was not to be trusted.

Still, he wasn't sure what to do about it. A wise man would simply walk away. But that was unprofessional, no matter how intelligent it might be. Plus he and his men had been paid, thus far, in good faith. Walking away would reflect badly on Dargo's standing in the professional community. Not to mention that walking away now could be unsafe. Dargo already suspected Bayer had murdered his predecessor.

But truth be told, Dargo had to admit he had concerns for the Meridian team should he pull the ripcord now. Bayer seemed to be teetering on the brink of doing something disastrous. What exactly, Dargo wasn't sure. But each time they spoke, Dargo had the feeling Bayer was on the verge of giving one foolish, bloodthirsty order or another. Bayer wanted Meridian so badly that he wasn't thinking straight. If Dargo were to leave, he feared the entire research team might pay the price. Not that he owed them anything. Certainly not Cyrus Cooper.

The fact that Cyrus was involved at all deeply troubled Dargo. Anger welled from the pit of his stomach every time he thought of the man. If it weren't for Cyrus, Natasha would be alive today.

Dargo clamped his eyes shut and tried to push away thoughts of his little girl. His little girl? Did he truly still think of her like that? Well, why not? She would always be his little girl, even though she had been twenty when she died. A grown woman by any standard. But still his little girl.

It pained him, even now, to think of the mistakes. So many mistakes. They seemed a lifetime ago. But he could still see her smile, still see the light in her eyes. She'd been precocious, a force of nature. There had been a stubborn streak in that girl that knew no boundaries. Still, he'd never seen her as happy as when she was with Cyrus.

The fact that she had been with Cyrus at all was a mistake. A cruel twist of fate had left Dargo's employer indebted to Cyrus. But complicated didn't begin to describe the circumstances leading to what had transpired. There was more than enough blame to go around. The Coalition was at the top of the list when Dargo attributed blame. The principals of that group had orchestrated all that had happened. And Cyrus had been Coalition—might still be, Dargo now reasoned. If that was the case, there would be a reckoning.

Still, he reminded himself, Cyrus hadn't been Coalition when Natasha first met him. That much he now knew for certain. And Dargo had to admit that she might have been better prepared for the threats she faced if he'd been more honest with her in the time before her death. There was more than enough blame to go around, he reminded himself once more.

It could have gone so differently, Dargo reflected. It had been a disaster that was decades in the making. With time, Dargo had gained painful perspective. He hadn't been the only man to lose a loved one to that foolish spy game. When all was said and done, there was no question that Cyrus had loved Natasha. For more than a year following that day, Dargo had watched from afar as losing her had nearly killed the young man.

Dargo snatched the glass from the counter beside his laptop and took a long slow drink. The stereotype was not lost on him, the angry Russian, sitting in the dark and drinking Vodka. He didn't care. Sometimes a stereotype was accurate. It didn't matter that he rarely touched the stuff these days. For some reason, over these last few years he found that, rather than relaxing, drinking only made him angry. Today it was fine. He was already angry. He missed his little girl.

Dargo took another drink and refilled the glass. He took a deep breath and looked at the freshly filled glass. His gaze was lost in the thick fluid for some time. He shook his head and set the glass back down. Then he pushed it across the counter, as far as his arm would reach.

Things used to be much simpler. When had that changed? He hated Cyrus! Well—perhaps he wanted to hate Cyrus. In some ways it made things easier. Things were complicated before Cyrus had come into the picture. Dargo had deep regrets that predated Cyrus. But there was no changing things now. If he were honest with himself, he would admit that Cyrus had actually saved Natasha's life on more than one occasion. Literally saved her life... Was it fair to blame him for her death, when she would've been gone long before, had it not been for him?

Damn it, he hated that boy!

When he took another deep breath, Dargo realized he'd been grinding his teeth. There was no doubt about it—it was time to get out of this line of work. Everything had gone off the rails. He was working for a man who, more and more, was proving to be unstable. At the same time, Dargo found himself running surveillance—more precisely, hunting—a man he somehow both hated and respected at the same time.

Dargo was not prone to complex emotion. What he sensed was a harbinger. Things were not right here. More and more, he believed that things were going to end badly.

Trying to push these thoughts from his mind, he went back to the notes he'd taken while reading Bayer's journal. The man had fallen from grace in the eyes of the Science Academy. He had used his increasing free time to widen his search of the directorate's archives. That was when he found a clue. They were records that were initially only tangentially related to Alexander's Fountain. But he followed the trail, and it was the thread that eventually led to Professor Walter Meade.

Bayer initially located a shipping manifest showing the transfer of technical hardware to the Alexander's Fountain laboratory less than a week before the facility was destroyed. Bayer was about to pass the shipping record by until he noticed the sheer volume of hardware being transported to the laboratory. It wasn't much of a leap to think such hardware was moved to the facility to conduct some kind of research on Alexander's Fountain. The only problem was that the manifest didn't detail the hardware being transported. And none of the documents Bayer found detailed a test within that timeframe.

On its own, this didn't help Bayer with his search, so he worked backward, using the shipping records as a starting point. He backtracked the shipment to the costal port where it arrived in Russia. From there, he tracked it back to the freighter which transported it. The freighter had no more detail on the shipment's contents, so he had continued working backward. This was where Bayer was truly surprised. He found that the shipment originated in the United States. New York City, to be precise. After New York, the trail became nonexistent. But Bayer was shocked that the technical hardware destined for a secret facility in Russia would have started its journey in the United States. Particularly at that time in history.

Lacking additional leads, Bayer had gone back to the records. Shipping records held no answers, so he widened his search to any records pertaining to the same timeframe and specific to the United States. It took him almost six months, but he finally found a tenuous connection. Bayer located reports indicating that, in the weeks leading up to the shipment's arrival in Russia, his country had conducted some sort of covert operation within the borders of the United States.

In this case the timing fit, but the information was incredibly scarce.

Again rubbing his eyes, Dargo reflected on how much easier the research might've been if the records were computerized back when Bayer was doing this research. The man had literally spent months searching through forgotten archives all over Russia. Bayer had started out as an intelligent and dedicated scientist. But this mystery became his white whale, and he had literally thrown away a promising career in pursuit of it.

From there, Bayer had visited the United States. A Russian making such a trip was virtually unheard of at the time. This would have been during the Cold War. Though, from the sound of the journal entries, it was likely the Soviet government would've been happy to be rid of Bayer by that point.

Nonetheless, Bayer followed the trail to the United States where he somehow located records detailing the warehouse facility from which the Russians had stolen the American equipment before smuggling it back to their shores. These records led to the name Rumsfeld Pellagrin, Walter Meade's predecessor on the Meridian project. So, naturally, somewhere along the way, Bayer had connected Pellagrin to Meade.

All of this brought the journal to the present day. The entries were nonspecific, but it seemed that over time, Bayer's pursuit of the miracle power source from the Alexander's Fountain experiments had led to the project Meade's team was developing. The project they called Meridian. Some kind of teleportation device.

Teleportation still seemed like science fiction, as far as Dargo was concerned. But he couldn't deny what he'd witnessed first hand. He and his team had sightings of Cyrus Cooper and Reese Knoland in California one minute and in Chicago moments later. As impossible as it seemed, teleportation was the most viable explanation. It was this technology that Bayer sought to control. But what was he trying to build in Europe? And why was Bayer, already a very wealthy man himself, setting up loans with some of the largest banks in Switzerland?

Chapter 34

Library of Congress, Washington D.C.
Thursday, 2:20 pm (12:20 pm Colorado Time)

It had already been a productive day, and it wasn't even noon yet. At least not on the West Coast. The constant shifts in time zone were wearing on Cyrus.

Taking a slow, casual look around the reading room, he made sure no one was paying him undue attention. Less than a half dozen people sat at tables scattered around the room, each engrossed in reading of their own. It took only a moment to locate a table near the window with a sweeping sightline, allowing him to keep every occupant in view. He had retrieved a packet of information from a dead drop on his way to the Library of Congress building. Against her better judgement, Special Agent Mindy Shaw had come through and left the files he'd requested. The records detailed the upper echelon of the Alvares drug cartel.

It had taken some maneuvering to convince Shaw that it was better for her not to ask questions. That was easier said than done because, when he requested the information on Alvares, he had specifically instructed her to ensure that nothing she provided could blow back on her. It didn't take a Washington insider to read between the lines. She had known Cyrus was taking some kind of action against Alvares and didn't want the provided intelligence back-tracked to her. She hadn't liked the arrangement, but she owed Cyrus so that loyalty had won out.

Shaw deserved credit. He'd put her in a difficult situation. She could've simply refused to help. It would've been completely understandable. Or she could've backed out gracefully, claiming that she couldn't get the information from the computer network. It was true that any records she accessed via the FBI's mainframe were tagged, reflecting her access. Therefore, pulling files via the mainframe was off limits. To avoid that, she had gone low tech. There was plenty of non-digital intelligence available to an agent who knew not only where to look, but how. In the end, she made a routine visit to the records room, ostensibly to review files from an unrelated case. While she was there, she copied what he needed pertaining to past and present investigations of Alvares.

She hadn't needed to explain to Cyrus how she'd done it. He knew how he would do it, if he'd been in her place. What impressed him was that she had come through. That, and she'd provided the information with nothing more than a request that he not get killed.

Now he sat at one of the library reading desks, leafing through the files. He considered Bola Alvares's summary report: male, Hispanic, six foot two, two hundred forty pounds. The man had a shaved head, stone cold dark eyes, and he was built like a wrecking machine. Alvares clearly spent a lot of time in the gym. That meshed with what Cyrus found in the man's psych profile. Alvares ruled his crew with an iron fist. He was known to be brutal both with the competition and within his own ranks. The man's physical bulk and reputation were powerful forms of intimidation. Cyrus wondered how the man would react to someone who didn't care about his looks or his reputation.

The main concern for Cyrus was a disparity in the files. One psych profile indicated that Alvares was a tightly wound sociopath who was quick to exact punishment on anyone who got in his way. But another report described the man as a calculating tactician, skilled at manipulation and savvy when it came to business. The two reports couldn't be more diametrically opposed. Cyrus needed to know which personality he would be facing when he made his approach.

Reading through a number of the included reports, Cyrus began to form his own picture of Bola Alvares. It seemed likely that a portion of each report was accurate. The truth between two opposing stories was often found in middle. As long as the man wasn't completely bipolar, Cyrus was confident he'd be able to work a more accurate profile of his own.

The Alvares cartel was known to be bloodthirsty and savage. Cartel enforcers were responsible for the mutilations and dismemberments of rival gang members. If Alvares was the crafty businessman indicated by one of the FBI profiles, his brutal and fearsome acts were theater, used to promote his reputation. A form of intimidation. Theater, but dangerous just the same.

But if the alternate profile was accurate, the man was nothing short of a sociopath with little impulse control. Not only did Alvares have a reputation for personally killing his rivals, but he was said to do it using their own weapons. If there was truth to the tale, it was believed that Alvares took his rival's weapon as a trophy after the kill.

Despite the contradicting personal profiles, both reports agreed on Alvares's rise to power. He'd started out as a street thug some twenty years back. An aggressive and brutal nature had helped him rise through the ranks of a local gang until he ran the outfit. After that he amassed more power, until he masterminded a small coup and ousted some mid-level drug lord, south of the border. From there, he quickly expanded his power base. After destroying a rival Mexican drug gang, he began spreading his reach through the southwestern United States. It hadn't taken long for Alvares to become *the* name in Mexican-American drug trafficking.

If Alvares got his hands on the teleportation technology, he would drown the United States in illegal narcotics. It would be a disaster. No one would be able to stop him.

The first step was to find out which members of Alvares's organization knew about Meridian. Step two was to make sure none of them ever shared that information. Anyone with knowledge of Meridian was a threat, and that threat had to be eliminated. Cyrus wasn't fooling himself. This would be wet work. It was one of the reasons he'd left the Coalition. But as a part of that outfit, he'd only ever had someone's word that what he was doing was the only solution to a problem. In this case, he knew for a fact this was the only way to eliminate the threat to his people.

It wasn't that his conscience had a problem with the work at hand. More generally, it was disappointment that the life he'd left behind wasn't dead and buried after all.

The next file had exactly what he needed: a list of Alvares's lieutenants. It was the key to discovering who knew about Meridian. In less than two minutes, Cyrus had the list memorized, including pertinent information relating to the organization's hierarchy. Next was a record of Alvares's movements over the past six months. This log would allow him to locate Bolo Alvares. It showed everywhere the man had been and how long he had spent there. People were creatures of habit. Even drug lords.

The last folder contained pamphlets detailing the different vehicles known to frequent each of Alvares's residences. The FBI and DEA used the information to help monitor and track the vast fleet of vehicles Alvares and his people used. Some of the information was important, some not at all. Cyrus memorized every bit of it. He would be walking into the proverbial lion's den. The more information he had, the better prepared he would be for whatever he faced. He had a plan, but, as they say, no battle plan ever survives contact with the enemy.

Almost ready to leave, Cyrus pulled up the left sleeve of his jacket and looked at his wrist. After studying his skin for a moment, he fished a small tube of superglue from his jacket pocket. He dabbed a bit of glue on the skin of his left wrist and blew on it to help the glue set. Once satisfied, he returned the tube to his pocket and pulled his sleeve back into place. He gathered up the files and headed for the library exit. Turning right when he reached the sidewalk, Cyrus became increasingly aware of his surroundings. The nagging tingle that had begun to pull at his senses when he'd arrived in D.C., only an hour before, had grown into an annoying irritation. He'd spent years avoiding situations that might land him on the radar of the Coalition. A confrontation with Alvares was virtually guaranteed to put him squarely in their spotlight.

He scanned the crowded street once more but still found nothing suspicious.

Of course not.

They weren't onto him yet, but he knew that wouldn't last for long. He was about to bring heat down on Alvares. By the time he was finished, Cyrus knew there would be no hiding from his old employers.

Chapter 35

Las Vegas, Nevada
Thursday, 4:55 pm (5:55 pm Colorado Time)

The afternoon had passed quickly for Cyrus. He'd teleported to Miami and collected a small satchel containing the gear Nathan arranged for him. Next, he rented a small two-seater Bell helicopter from an airfield just outside of Santa Barbara. The flight to Las Vegas took almost two and a half hours, but it was still faster than driving. Upon landing, he took a cab to the nearest low-rent used car dealership he could find. There he purchased an old, red Ford F150. It was a 4x4 that was jacked up on aftermarket suspension. He paid cash and drove it off the lot within minutes of making his selection. The salesman was more than happy to cut corners on the paperwork for a customer paying cash.

A few blocks from the car dealership, Cyrus pulled the truck into an empty parking lot behind a boarded up service station. Looking around to ensure he was alone, he triggered the hood release and hopped from the truck. He took the satchel with him and leaned under the hood. A few minutes of work with a Leatherman multi-tool and he was finished. Pulling an old Smith and Wesson 357 Magnum out of the bag, he double checked its load before sliding it into the back of his jeans. He made sure his t-shirt covered the gun. Last, he took a small device out of the bag. He flipped a switch on it before placing it inside the heel of his boot.

Once the satchel was empty, he stuffed it behind the truck's bench seat and climbed back behind the wheel. Then he pulled out onto the road and headed for the city limits. Fifteen minutes later, he was clear of Las Vegas and following a road that was virtually free of traffic. The four lane highway stretched out across the desert, disappearing with the endless sand and scrub at the horizon.

It took almost twenty minutes before Cyrus reached the entrance to an opulent upscale neighborhood, built squarely in the middle of nowhere. The housing development seemed a modern oasis springing from the middle of the open desert. A very plush, exclusive oasis, judging by the homes he passed as he turned into the neighborhood. Each home was two or three stories and extremely ornate in design. Every one of them was a mansion in its own right.

The neighborhood was laid out in ten-acre plots. Each lot an immaculate patch of green grass and thick plush foliage—not the sort of greenery common to homes of the region. The homeowners paid a high premium to maintain that level of gardening and lawn care. Most yards of Las Vegas homes tended to be covered with more gravel than grass. What was the point of trying to grow a lawn in the desert? Only the ultra-rich or the extremely foolish would fight nature in such a way. As Cyrus passed another sprawling estate covered in green grass and towering leafy trees, he considered that perhaps it required homeowners to be both ultra-rich and extremely foolish.

Nearing the back of the subdivision, his destination came into view. It was a double lot taking up the end of the cul-de-sac. This was the Alvares estate. The entire twenty-acre property was surrounded by a ten-foot-high security fence, lined on the inside by an expertly manicured hedge, which afforded those inside the grounds a fortifiable level of privacy.

About a hundred yards up the road, before he reached the gates leading to the Alvares estate, Cyrus saw a high aerial antenna set on the edge of a neighboring property. The top of the pole held a series of electronic devices. Several of them looked like weather sensors, the sort of high-end meteorological kits that people set up in their yards to transmit weather data to their computer or smartphones twenty-four hours a day. But Cyrus knew better. Some of the gear at the top of that pole was for evaluating weather conditions, but some of it was courtesy of a combined FBI/DEA task force that had been surveilling Alvares for the better part of the last three years. Cyrus knew the equipment contained several cameras that were filming and shooting still photos of people and cars approaching and leaving the Alvares estate.

As he drove past the surveillance station, he was careful to shield his face from the cameras. Showing up on the day's surveillance logs would lead to a lot of questions he didn't want asked. Luckily, thanks to the photos provided by Agent Shaw, Cyrus knew where the cameras were hidden. And, even if he didn't have the inside knowledge, it wouldn't have been difficult to guess. There was a high probability that Alvares was well aware of the surveillance as well. Such was the nature of drug enforcement at this level.

Once clear of the cameras, Cyrus dropped his left hand back to a comfortable position in the open driver side window. He drove up to the front gate of the estate without hesitation. Two guards were stationed at the pair of twelve-foot-high wrought iron gates. One guard remained in the small windowed shack beside the gate, while the other approached Cyrus's truck.

Cyrus explained that he was here to see Adreakay Escobar, and he said that Chad Brewster sent him. The heavyset security guard looked at Cyrus suspiciously but said nothing. The guard backed away from the truck while keeping a close eye on it. Pulling a walkie-talkie from his belt, he spoke quietly into it. There was a response that Cyrus couldn't make out. This was followed by a short, rapid-fire exchange between the guard and whoever was on the other end of the radio.

Cyrus watched the conversation, but no matter how he strained, he couldn't make out what was being said. He considered the information he'd been provided. If it was accurate, the man he had asked for, Adreakay Escobar, was not present at the estate. Escobar should be back in Mexico visiting his sick mother. But the lengthy exchange he was witnessing concerned him. If his information wasn't accurate, things were about to get complicated.

Finally, the guard seemed satisfied. He turned and headed for the guard shack. He spoke briefly with the man stationed there. A moment later, Cyrus heard the door open on the passenger side of the truck. The gate guard climbed in. Cyrus wasn't entirely surprised to see that the man had a Glock leveled at his gut.

Using broken English, the guard instructed him to drive up to the main house. The gates began to slide open, a section retracting into the fence on each side of the drive. As soon as the gates reached their rest position, Cyrus dropped the gear selector into drive and slowly advanced up the driveway. He followed the two-lane paved road along its winding approach and through a small grove of thick trees, before the main house finally came into view.

The house was three stories tall and fashioned after an Eighteenth Century, Deep South, plantation mansion. There was a deep-set front porch that spanned the entire front of the enormous white-washed façade. A third story veranda overlooked the front of the estate and was supported by a half-dozen enormous white pillars.

At the prompting of the armed passenger, Cyrus parked under the two-story-high portico immediately before the home's pair of massive French doors. He left the keys in the ignition and climbed down from the truck. Another armed Hispanic man was waiting to lead him to the front door of the house, where he was searched. They took his wallet and the Magnum. His hands were unceremoniously handcuffed behind his back, and he was led into the enormous entryway of the house.

Two armed men escorted Cyrus into a large library, just off the tiled entryway. The room was richly appointed with thick dark carpeting, while the walls were lined with beautiful oak bookcases reaching from the floor to the ten-foot-high ceiling, ringed with ornate molding. But while the woodworking of the bookcases was grand in craftsmanship and artistry, the shelves didn't hold a single book. Wide shelves were lined with precisely detailed, high quality models of sports cars and exotic aircraft.

The room was large, at twenty by thirty. An over-stuffed sofa and a pair of matching chairs sat in a group at one end of the room while a ten-foot-long conference table occupied the center. The other end of the room was dominated by a massive, antique oak desk that stood before a wide bay window overlooking the painstakingly manicured lawns.

The two armed men led Cyrus into the room but offered no explanation. He looked around, taking everything in. Given his current situation, the room's details might hold the key to his survival. Coming here was a calculated risk. Success was by no means guaranteed. He needed to be at the top of his game.

The toy models lining the bookshelves offered no help at all. There was nothing he could use as a weapon. The same could be said for the large conference table. It was completely empty. The six office chairs surrounding it were equally useless. While the large antique desk should've been the best place to find an improvised weapon, its surface held only two items, a small antique desk lamp and a closed laptop computer.

Cyrus looked at the guard standing to his right and the other guard off further to his left. They were both armed with Glock 9mm semi-automatics. All was not lost. They'd confiscated his .357 revolver, but that was to be expected. It was a throw-down gun anyway. With its serial number filed off, it couldn't be traced. He'd expected it to be taken as soon as he arrived. It would've been more conspicuous to arrive unarmed. No, there were plenty of weapons on hand after all. Liberating a sidearm from one of his escorts would prove little trouble. That sorted, it was time for Cyrus to start pushing some buttons.

"What's this all about?" Cyrus asked one of the guards.

The guard's cold stare was supposed to be intimidating. Maybe it was, when he used it on street thugs. "Señor Alvares will be right with you."

Cyrus did his best to look uncomfortable at the man's reply. "Alvares? That's not necessary! There's been a misunderstanding. I'm here to speak with Escobar."

A voice sounded from the far corner of the room. "It is strange that I should have a guest at the gate asking to speak with Escobar," the man said. Cyrus immediately turned to face the speaker.

Bolo Alvares was standing in the doorway on the far side of the room. A pair of additional security guards stood behind him. "Even more interesting, when I find that you were sent by Señor Brewster. You see, I have been having a great deal of trouble getting in touch with Señor Brewster. He and I have an arrangement, but he seems reluctant to make good on his side of the deal."

When Alvares walked into the room, Cyrus got a better look at the two men with him. They were both large. Very large. Maybe two hundred eighty pounds apiece. And they were built like they spent entire days in the gym. How either of them could turn his head was a mystery. Neither man appeared to have a neck! But as alarming as all of that was, what struck Cyrus as even odder was that the two men looked like mirror images of each other. *Brothers?* They had to be. Alvares was a very large man, but these two were gigantic. It was an obvious intimidation tactic.

Alvares hadn't asked a question yet, so Cyrus kept his mouth shut. He wanted to see where this was going. It was best for Alvares to start the conversation.

But Alvares didn't speak up…not at first. Instead, he dismissed the two guards that had brought Cyrus into the room. Before one of the guards left, he placed the .357 on Alvares's desk. As the two men exited, the brothers took up flanking positions on either side of Cyrus. He did his best to look uncomfortable with his circumstances. The brothers towered over him by at least eight inches. He wanted to look intimidated, when in truth, things were going remarkably close to plan. More or less.

Saying something in Spanish, Alvares sent one of the brothers to the door. The man leaned into the hallway and looked around. He stepped back into the room, shook his head, and closed the pair of French doors behind him.

Cyrus took this as a positive sign. The guards who just left spoke English. Apparently the twins spoke only Spanish. This was a sign that Alvares wanted their conversation to remain confidential. He didn't even want his own men aware of the details. Alvares would be sure to speak only in English, thereby keeping his henchmen in the dark. It meant the information was highly compartmentalized. Cyrus just needed to find out who was in the loop. Getting Alvares to admit such a thing would be the tricky part.

Alvares was quiet. His eyes moved slowly over Cyrus, taking him in. Cyrus knew the man was looking at what remained of the scrapes and bruises on his head, neck, and arms. But it was creepy. Alvares's gaze was disconcerting.

"So?" Alvares said, finally breaking the silence. "Chad Brewster sent you to speak with me?"

Cyrus shook his head. He tried to look confused. "No. Brewster sent me to speak with Adreakay Escobar. I'm only to speak with Escobar."

"Escobar works for me," Alvares said coldly. "Whatever you had to say to him, you can say to me!"

Cyrus considered what Alvares said. This was not the reaction that Alvares wanted. Clearly angered, Alvares leaned across his desk and snatched up the .357 revolver. He pulled the hammer back and pointed the gun at Cyrus's face. "Speak now, or I will mail you back to your friend in many small boxes!"

The surprise on Cyrus's face was the very best acting he could manage, but his quality time with Alvares's psych profile meant that none of this was truly surprising. And several reports from the FBI files indicated that Alvares had a proclivity for using his enemy's weapons against them. The fact that Cyrus would eventually be staring down the barrel of his own gun had been a virtual certainty. It hadn't taken long. That was why he had loaded it with blanks. It would afford him a small margin of error should he miscalculate Alvares's impulse control.

"Okay!" Cyrus relented. "Okay!"

Alvares lowered the gun and glared at him expectantly.

"Brewster said he hit a delay sneaking the platforms out of the lab, but he'll have them ready in a week. I was supposed to tell Escobar to wire the down payment and have the rest ready when he picks the hardware up on the twenty-second."

The confusion was evident on Alvares's face. It surprised Cyrus that it took the man a few moments to put it together. He was starting to grow concerned. Could he have been too subtle in hinting at Escobar's betrayal? He was beginning to worry that he had overestimated Alvares. The man might not be smart enough for the con to work. A sudden flash of anger in Alvares's eyes told Cyrus that things had finally clicked. The drug lord wasn't a rocket scientist, but he was finally catching up. How he had managed to rise to this level of power would have seemed comical to Cyrus under different circumstances. It also meant that his suspicion that Alvares's brutality was largely for show was now unlikely. The man lacked the intelligence for such forethought. Things could get sticky at any moment.

A surreptitious glance at the guards beside him told Cyrus that both men were equally troubled by their boss's display of emotion. *Good enough,* Cyrus thought. It was time for the next stage of his plan. His hands were cuffed behind his back. He needed to correct that injustice.

Taking great care not to draw attention from anyone in the room, Cyrus ran the tips of the fingers of his right hand along the skin on his left forearm, just above the wrist. He immediately felt the tiny lump of the foreign substance beneath his skin. Adjusting the position of his fingers, he felt the small dab of superglue he'd placed on his arm earlier in the day. He pulled the tiny fleck of glue away and let it fall to the carpet. It was too small to be noticed. Feeling around on the surface of his skin, he found the edge of the foreign object and applied pressure. When he pressed down on the far end of the object, he felt the close end strain against his skin. A little more pressure and the small thin wire pierced the surface of his skin. A little additional pressure and the wire was sticking out far enough to pinch between his thumb and finger.

After pulling the thin wire free from his flesh, he felt for the end. Before inserting the ridged wire under his skin and sealing the tiny puncture in his flesh with superglue, he had bent one end of the wire into the proper configuration. Finding the correct end of the wire by touch, he slid it into the keyhole on the first handcuff. Most people didn't realize how easy it was to pick the lock on a set of standard-issue police handcuffs. Even the more secure, double-locking cuffs could be picked with the same tool and required only an additional few seconds of effort, if you knew what you were doing.

Cyrus watched as Alvares paced back and forth behind his desk. A large vein along the side of the man's forehead became increasingly apparent. Soon he was pacing and clinching his fists over and over again. Cyrus had to look away to keep a grin from his face. It was as if he could see each thought slowly making its way through the man's mind.

Turning to Cyrus, Alvares's eyes flared with anger. He leaned over the desk and shouted at Cyrus. "This is not possible! I don't know what your game is, but Escobar did not do what you say!"

It was all Cyrus could do to keep from laughing out loud. The man really was a fool. "You don't believe that your right-hand man could betray you? Are you kidding? You're drug dealers! How much loyalty can the man have?"

Cyrus couldn't help himself, he shook his head and chuckled. The arrogance was incredible!

Some of the tension seemed to fade from Alvares's face. Cyrus saw this, and he felt a tingling. Something had changed. A moment later a smile reached Alvares's lips, and Cyrus knew something was wrong.

"You're very tricky, my friend," Alvares said with a broad smile. "I don't know your game, but you have gambled, and you have lost! Escobar could not betray me in this matter. He knew nothing of my arrangement with Señor Brewster. He knows nothing of this technology!"

Alvares shook his head and pointed at Cyrus. "Some secrets are too sensitive to share with even my most trusted advisor!"

And there it was, everything Cyrus needed to know. The people inside Alvares's organization had no knowledge of Meridian.

"Thanks," Cyrus said with a very relieved smile. "I had to be sure."

Without a moments hesitation, he tapped the heel of his left hiking boot stiffly on the floor three times. This brought a suspicious look from Alvares, but the look didn't last long. An instant later an enormous explosion detonated under the portico in front of the mansion. The explosives Cyrus had planted under the front end of his truck ignited in a devastating explosion that shattered the front doors of the home, rocked the house on its foundation, and sent shrapnel and flames flying in every direction.

While everyone was caught off guard, Cyrus made his move. Both hands were already free from the handcuffs. He had already spun the hinged clasp of one cuff silently into position, turning it into deadly steel hook. When the bomb went off, he attacked the first of the giant guards with the blunt, hooked end of the open handcuff. In a blinding swing, he slashed it across the man's throat, ripping a wide wound of cartilage and gristle. The giant's first reaction was to grasp at his throat with both hands. As he did, the gun flew free from his grip, already forgotten in the primal instinct to preserve his own life.

Cyrus snatched the guard's gun from mid air and racked the slide, ensuring there was a round in the chamber. He drew the sights of the Glock on the second brother, just as the man was raising his gun to fire.

The guard fired first, but he fired before he'd brought his gun fully to bear and the shot went wide. Cyrus didn't give him an opportunity for a second shot. A double-tap to the heart and a single shot to the head were fired off as fast as Cyrus could pull the trigger. But even as the second brother toppled to the floor, Cyrus knew that one threat remained.

His eyes turned to Alvares, who stood on the other side of his desk, drawing down on him with his own .357 revolver. Cyrus couldn't get his gun into position fast enough. He was at a disadvantage. The look in Alvares's eyes was feral. He was a rabid animal, frothing with rage. Baring his teeth, he pulled the trigger.

The .357 Magnum's distinctive report was enough to rattle Cyrus's teeth. It was not a gun to be fired without ear protection. There was even a short burst of flame from the barrel with the discharge. But still, Cyrus stood, staring Alvares down.

The confusion read clearly across the drug lord's face. Cyrus should have been dead right now. But the man proved himself not to be a deep thinker, just as Cyrus suspected. Alvares held the gun steady and pulled the trigger again. There was a near deafening blast from the gun, complete with a muzzle flash—but no bullet.

Cyrus thought the man would finally understand and give it up. That wasn't the case. Alvares cried out in a fit of rage and pulled the trigger three more times in rapid succession.

Cyrus wasn't sure if the report from the gunshots was echoing around the room or if the sound was reverberating inside his skull. He just knew that he wanted it to stop. Raising his liberated Glock in a relaxed manner, he fired a rapid double-tap to Alvares's heart, followed by a single round to the head.

Cyrus heard a hollow thud as Alvares's head bounced off the side of his desk before his corpse struck the floor. The interrogation had gone according to plan, but that jackass with the .357 had given him a splitting headache. Next time he tried something like this, he would be sure to use lighter loads. The .357 had been an educated guess. In reading the FBI reports, he knew that Alvares had a penchant for killing his rivals with their own weapons. And he suspected that showing up here today with an old fashioned wheel gun would only ensure that, should worst come to worst, Alvares would try to put him down using the Magnum. It had all worked out for the best, but Cyrus was left hoping he hadn't done any permanent damage to his hearing.

Retrieving the unused Glock from the second guard, he tossed the near spent Glock aside. He did a press check on the chamber and found the gun ready to fire. With the gun leveled in the direction of the door he'd used to enter the room, Cyrus stepped over the bodies and made his way to the pair of French doors Alvares had used to enter the office. Peeking through the doorway, he found the hallway beyond empty.

He made his way down the hall and stepped out into a large, modern kitchen furnished with the latest in industrial appliances. The room was deserted. He headed for the back door.

A glance through the window of the back door gave him a view of two men with automatic rifles kneeling behind the masonry work surrounding the patio outside the kitchen. The men had their backs to the house. They obviously expected any sort of attack to come from beyond the grounds, not inside the house.

Cyrus stepped out the door and onto the pavement of the wide patio. One of the armed men glanced over his shoulder and did a double-take when he noticed Cyrus. He nearly fell over trying to turn and bring his rifle to bear. Cyrus fired two shots, one to the chest and one to the head, felling the man where he knelt. This instantly spurred the other armed man into action. Cyrus dropped him with a similar double-tap before the man could gain a position and offer a threat. He felt no moral qualms about shooting these men dead. They were the enemy. They would have killed him, if only given the chance.

The estate's eight-car garage was forty yards away. Cyrus checked the area and found it clear, so he made a run for it. Inside, he hoped, was the car he'd seen in the FBI surveillance reports.

Ten yards from the garage, a man armed with an assault rifle stepped from one of the open garage bays. He was more surprised to see Cyrus than Cyrus was to see him. He had his weapon halfway to a firing position when Cyrus hit him with two shots to the head.

Not breaking his stride, Cyrus ran directly into the garage. There, spread out before him, were a half dozen, exotic sports cars and SUVs. The best a drug lord's money could buy. But Cyrus was looking for one specific car. And it was parked on the end. A black BMW 5 Series sedan with blacked out windows. The explosion and gunfire on the Alvares estate would have brought the FBI surveillance team to full alert. The blacked out windows on the BMW would get Cyrus past the FBI, without risk of being identified.

Slipping behind the wheel of the BMW, Cyrus found the key already in the ignition. A twist of the key brought the engine to life with a throaty growl. He dropped the car into first and popped the clutch, launching the four-door sedan from the garage like a wild animal loosed from its cage. The car left parallel patches on the concrete as he shifted into second, following the winding driveway around the central house.

The perimeter gate was three hundred yards out and still locked up tight. Cyrus was confident the drug gang wouldn't open fire on the BMW. With the dark windows, they wouldn't know if the boss was behind the wheel. Unless they'd already discovered his body, in which case they would be out for blood. Not wanting to take any chances, Cyrus picked up speed and shifted into third. He was closing the distance to the front gate at savage rate.

It was clear that the gate guards were not going to open up for him. Even if they thought their boss was driving the car, the guards had their backs to him. They had automatic rifles and were facing the street out front. Clearly the crew still thought they were under siege from an outside force. He supposed these guys didn't get into drug running because they had an abundance of analytical skills.

The gate was going to be a problem. Ramming it with a BMW would be like pushing a tomato through a cheese grater. Only in this case, he would be driving the tomato. Not a good plan. A quick glance across the dashboard brought him a glimmer of hope. His focus centered on the three garage door opener buttons built into the upper console, right beside the control for the sunroof. On a lark, he pushed the three buttons in succession. It was long odds that one of them would control the front gate, but it beat driving a tomato. To Cyrus's amazement, the front gates began to part!

Not wanting to sour his luck, he didn't waste time considering his fortune. Instead, he focused on the closing gap between him and the slowly separating gates. The timing was off. He downshifted into second, bringing the RPMs up and slowing the vehicle by a degree. The adjustment compensated for the slow movement of the gates and ensured he would have power at his command when he shot the gap. And, as he feared, the movement of the gates brought the attention of the four armed men beyond. They turned to face the oncoming BMW. Three of the men shouldered their rifles and prepared to open fire. The fourth man bellowed into a handheld radio. He would be communicating with the main house. It wouldn't be long before they received confirmation that their boss was not driving the BMW.

The gap in the gate was close to his needs, within inches, Cyrus was sure of it. He shifted, stomped on the accelerator and dumped the clutch. The car rocketed forward. Cyrus slid down in the seat, hoping the dashboard would block the onslaught of lead that was about to be unloaded into the car. But the surge of acceleration had taken place just as the fourth guard with the radio had given the order to open fire. The burst of speed and the close proximity of the car caused the men to flinch. That half-second was all the time it took for the BMW to blast through the gap in the still opening gates. One of the guards ducked to the side just in time to avoid getting hit; another wasn't fast enough. Cyrus felt the slight vibration of the car, as a body panel clipped one of the gunmen and sent him plowing into another man. Cyrus sat up in his seat and glanced into the rearview mirror. Only the radioman was still on his feet, and he could only stare as the BMW thundered off into the distance.

He had passed the FBI observation post, seeing it only as a blur. With luck, his escape would look the same way on film. Either way, the darkened windows of the car would keep the FBI from connecting him to what had transpired.

Downshifting and putting the car into a power slide, Cyrus left the opulent subdivision and pointed the car in the direction of Las Vegas. It would be a race against time now. If the FBI were on top of the matter, they would have contacted LVPD and scrambled at least one helicopter for air support. He dropped the hammer on the BMW. He needed to reach the city limits before that chopper was in the air. He wound the car up to one hundred and thirty miles an hour and closed the gap on Las Vegas in no time. The roads were virtually free of traffic, so the experience was more like a go-cart track than a straight shot down the highway.

Reaching the city limits, he dropped back to match the posted speeds. He didn't need to draw the attention of traffic officers this close to the finish line. Taking side streets, he headed for the heart of the city while being careful to avoid any potentially bottlenecking traffic.

Finally reaching his destination, he pulled into a multi-story concrete parking garage adjacent to one of the major casinos. Following the circling ramp, he took the car higher. Once he reached the correct level, he crossed the structure and found a nearly deserted area off in the corner. He parked the BMW and slid from behind the wheel. Aside from a remarkably small dimple in the driver side front quarter panel, the car was still in pristine condition.

Just as Cyrus stepped away from the car, an old Ford Bronco pulled up. He climbed into the passenger seat, and the Bronco pulled away.

"How'd it go?" Hondo asked from behind the wheel. He hadn't wasted time with pleasantries. They were already on the spiraling ramp headed for the garage exit.

"Pretty much to plan," Cyrus said with a smile. "The blanks in the Magnum were a good idea. But next time, remind me to pick something a little easier on the ears."

Hondo shot a glance at Cyrus and smirked. "So the SOB really tried to kill you with your own gun?"

"Just like the file suggested."

"It troubles me that you let him get the opportunity to pull the trigger at all!"

Cyrus couldn't deny that. But looking back, he wasn't entirely sure the man had gotten the drop on him. He knew Alvares had his gun. To be honest, he wanted to see the look in the man's eye when the gun fired and no one died. Childish? Sure. Unprofessional? Absolutely! Reckless? Okay. But how many people had Alvares killed in the very same way? It seemed fitting that he should die thanks to his own theatrics.

"I might've given him a little help with the opportunity," Cyrus admitted.

There were a few long beats of silence before Hondo burst out laughing. He shot Cyrus another glance. "That's more like the guy I use to know!"

They exited the parking garage and headed for the highway.

"How did things go on your end?" Cyrus asked, as they reached the city limits.

"Piece of cake. I disabled the surveillance cameras for the entire parking structure, so that won't be an issue. I dumped the old Cherokee I drove in with. I hot-wired the Bronco ten minutes before I picked you up. The thing had a nice solid layer of dust on it, and the battery was so near dead that it almost didn't start. No one's going to miss this crate. We're clean."

Cyrus nodded. He held up the palm of his left hand and looked at his fingers. Carefully picking at a fingertip for a moment, he peeled back a layer of glue. The small layers of glue applied to the pad of each finger had ensured he left no fingerprints at any point along the way. It was an old-school trick, but it was extremely effective.

Leaning back in the passenger seat, Cyrus relaxed for the first time all afternoon. They wouldn't be flying back to Santa Barbara. That sort of thing would show up in manifests, and he didn't want anything to connect him with what had just happened outside of Las Vegas. Even the helicopter he rented for the flight into town was covered by the use of a fake ID and a dummy credit card. They would be driving back. A solid five-hour drive, maybe more with traffic.

Cyrus wasn't entirely surprised that Reese was already on his mind. They had grown close over the last week. For some reason the realization that she was never far from his thoughts comforted him. He hadn't felt that way for anyone in a very long time.

Chapter 36

Berton Springs, Colorado
Friday, 11:22 am

Water ran from the faucet into the sink, which was filled with soapy suds. She scrubbed the plates and the pan from breakfast. It would've been easier to use the dishwasher but Reese preferred the distraction. Between the previous afternoon and earlier that morning, she'd finished the second of the two romance novels she'd taken from Cyrus's apartment earlier in the week. They had served to pass the time, but keeping her mind off the problems at hand was proving more of a challenge. And sitting idle while Cyrus dealt with the Alvares cartel had proven easier said than done. She was a proactive person. Sitting still, especially given the circumstances, was difficult.

The day before, Cyrus had been vague in his strategy, as he left to deal with Alvares. Had she known what he'd been planning, yesterday would've been pure torture. So far he hadn't explained what transpired in Las Vegas the day before, but if the online news reports had any truth to them, things had been violent and destructive. She'd watched a number of online news broadcasts. Basically no one understood what happened at Alvares's Las Vegas estate. The press was still not allowed on scene, but camera footage shot from beyond the front gate showed considerable damage to the property. According to news broadcasts, a confidential source described the scene as a bloody confrontation between rival drug gangs.

Casting a glance at Cyrus, she studied him sitting on a bar stool at the breakfast counter, still hard at work on his laptop. He hadn't said much, but he was clearly onto something. She'd never seen him so focused. His fingers would fly across the keyboard before settling into long periods of silence while he read whatever he discovered. This continued for the better part of an hour, ever since they'd finished breakfast. Reese tried to be patient. She knew he would explain everything when he had it sorted out. From what she was seeing, it appeared he was on a roll, and parts of what he referred to as 'the puzzle' were falling into place. It wasn't easy, but she would give him the time to work through it.

Instead, she focused her attention out the window over the kitchen sink and continued with the dishes. An overnight snowstorm had brought more than a foot of fresh powder. It was the first snow of the season. Though it seemed unusually early for such weather, given their high elevation in the mountains, it wasn't entirely unexpected.

The entire backyard was a blanket of virgin white fluff extending nearly fifty yards to the tree line. From there, dense forest clung to the steep incline of the mountain. The cabin was perhaps a half-mile from the peak. Pine and fir trees were laden with a thick coating of heavy white, which made them unique, foreign, and beautiful, all at the same time. She reflected on the wonderful location Walter had chosen to build his home. That he left it to Cyrus seemed fitting. She hadn't known Cyrus long but was coming to know him well, and the place suited him. He already seemed quite at home here.

Reese again regarded him. In many ways she felt she knew him—in others he was a mystery. He had basically gone off to war the previous day, with little concern for the danger he faced. Kissing her gently, he had given her a warm smile before stepping onto the teleportation platform and disappearing. But judging by the news reports, the situation he'd faced after that had been gruesome. Still, he seemed unfazed, even unconcerned. She was sure his thoughts were focused squarely on today and tomorrow. Reese had met many goal-oriented people while in school but Cyrus was something entirely different. He had an exceptional confidence that was paralleled perfectly by his ability. So far, she had yet to see him shy from a challenge. That was saying something, since the challenges of the last week had been life or death on more than one occasion.

Once again she thought, *who lives like that?*

How could someone face these things without flinching? What did a man have to face to develop that inner strength? There was no question Cyrus had a past. She'd seen shadows of it over the last week. It was clear that something terrible had happened to him. Something made him change his course and walk away from a very different kind of life. What it was, she had no idea. She wanted to ask, but she wasn't sure she wanted to know the answer.

She decided to put it out of her mind. It was out of her control, and it was more productive to focus on the here and now. She was more nervous the night before. She'd tried waiting up for him, but she hadn't known when he would be back, or if he would be back before morning. When she'd finally turned in, she'd found herself at a difficult crossroads. They had spent their first night together just the night before. And it was amazing. But it was only their first night. There'd been a strong connection from the very start. She felt it immediately, and she was sure he felt it too. But neither one had rushed things along. Until the previous night she had stayed in one of the spare bedrooms. But after last night, where was the right place to sleep? Was it presumptuous to wait for him in his bed? Would it be giving the wrong signal if she went back to the guest room?

It seemed silly now, but she'd agonized over the choice. So much so that she had been on the verge of falling asleep before she could make up her mind. Finally, throwing caution to the wind, she had slipped beneath the covers of his bed and instantly dropped off to sleep. The next thing she knew it was morning, and she awoke to find herself wrapped in his arms, as if it were the most natural thing in the world. She had no memory of him returning home. No memory of him coming to bed. And, to her relief, waking that way had just felt right.

For as messed up as everything was right now, at least one thing was right.

Cyrus looked up from the screen of his laptop and found her smiling at him. She felt her face instantly flush. She hadn't realized she was staring.

How embarrassing!

She further flustered herself with a small laugh that bordered on a giggle. Not knowing how to react next, and not wanting to prolong her self-conscious display, she turned quickly back to the sink. She drained it and rinsed her hands, then dried them on a dish towel. The entire time, hoping he wouldn't ask what she'd been thinking about.

She was saved by the bell, literally, when Cyrus's cell phone chimed. Glancing over her shoulder, she saw him snatch the phone from the counter. She had a feeling he had been waiting for a call. Apparently this was it.

The trill of the cell phone was magic to Cyrus's ears.

Finally!

He grabbed the phone from the counter, beside his laptop, and swiped his finger across the display to answer it.

"Hey, what'd you find?" Cyrus asked, forgoing any greeting.

"Just what you expected," Hondo said from the other end of the line. "Underwood's home was bugged. And whoever did it wasn't concerned with overkill. I found taps on every extension in the house, as well as bugs in his home office, living room, bedroom, kitchen, dining room—hell, I even found one in the hallway by the front door."

Cyrus massaged the corners of his eyes and took a slow deep breath. "I wish I was surprised. But that does seem a bit excessive."

"Excessive? It's bloody nuts. And, Cyrus? This isn't your normal off-the-shelf hardware. I've never seen tech like this. If I hadn't stopped to see Nathan before coming here, I don't think our normal gear would've picked this stuff up."

This meant they were up against people with skills and resources. Not a good combination. It was about what he'd anticipated after running into Yuri Dargoslav in that alley in Manhattan, but he'd hoped for better news. News of the high-end tech jived with the toxicology report Nathan emailed earlier that morning. Nathan had run a chemical analysis of the substance in the syringe Cyrus took off the team at his apartment. The drug was some sort of exotic compound that Nathan had never seen before. He could only guess at its prescribed effects. He was fairly certain the drug was not intended to kill, but even that was speculation. It could've been a sedative, it could've been a truth serum, or it could've been the latest designer stiffy prescription, Nathan had joked.

"What about his offices?" Cyrus asked.

"You're not going to like this. The locks at both the home and the office showed signs of being popped. Really skilled work, but they'd been messed with, no question. The home office wasn't a problem. Underwood didn't have anything relevant to the Prof or the project there. He said he was very regimented when it came to the information. The Prof was very specific. Said it was out of concern for Underwood's safety—and that of his wife.

"The office across town was another story. Good news there, though. Underwood kept everything in a hidden burn vault. I think it's safe to say that the location of the vault was discovered, but I'm certain the contents were never accessed. The problem is that Underwood is a civilian—he didn't know…what he didn't know."

Cyrus felt his stomach drop. "The copy machine?"

"Worse. The copy machine was also the office printer. Every document he copied, scanned, or printed went through the bloody thing. I pulled the drive and took a look-see. Everything Underwood has touched in the last two years was cached on the printer's hard drive. You can bet your last dollar, whoever broke in got everything they wanted, and they never had to open the safe."

There was no stopping the throbbing headache behind Cyrus's eyes. His worst suspicions had become manifest. For all of their work to keep their secrets secure, Meade and Underwood had made one of the more classic mistakes. They'd failed to realize that high-end multi-function copiers often included an onboard computer. That onboard computer utilized a hard drive to store documents, intended to accelerate printing, and even archive files for later reprinting or auditing. Such machines were an espionage goldmine.

Cyrus knew this was very bad for their cause.

"Clone the drive and dump a hardcopy of everything so we can do an assessment. Bring the clone, the original, and the hard copy back with you. Let the service guys earn their keep and replace the drive. It's like closing the barn door after the horses are gone, but it's the best we can do now."

"The clone's already in progress. Dumping a hard copy will take some time, but I'll get on it. Anything else?" Hondo's professionalism shone through. Always ready and willing to take orders, but not unwilling to think for himself and take the initiative. Working with people like Hondo was one of the only things Cyrus missed from his old life.

"Just one," Cyrus said. "Any signs of an onsite surveillance team when you popped in on Underwood?"

"Negative. If I had to guess, based on his peripheral involvement, the ridiculous number of bugs planted, and the fact that whoever is behind this already raided the printer's hard drive, I don't think they found him worthy of an on-site team."

Cyrus weighed the factors and had to agree. He would have come to the same conclusion if he had been tasked with surveilling Underwood and had access to similar resources.

"Alright. Do me a favor? While you're printing the hardcopy, can you start going through the cloned drive? There's one document I need above all else."

Cyrus went on to explain exactly what he was looking for, and then signed off. He set the phone aside and stared blankly at the screen of his laptop. His mind drifted as he considered the ramifications of Hondo's discovery. It was several moments before he realized Reese was standing on the opposite side of the counter, waiting to hear what had happened.

He explained how he had sent Hondo to Underwood's home first thing that morning. They'd been looking for any potential security breaches. Cyrus had phoned Underwood from the car on the way back from Vegas the night before. Underwood had insisted that Meade had devised the security protocols himself, and Underwood claimed that he was meticulous in obeying them.

While Cyrus hadn't doubted Underwood's integrity, evidence suggested there'd been a security breach. Something beyond the information Chad gave the Alvares Cartel. A team had ambushed Cyrus at his apartment in Chicago, and another was instantly on him when he made an impromptu trip to Manhattan. Both teams were comprised of experienced operators. They were all eastern European but their nationalities were incongruent. It had lead Cyrus to suspect they didn't have an affiliation with a specific government. They were likely independent contractors. Mercenaries. Yuri Dargoslav's presence supported that supposition. And if Yuri was on the job, it was likely his father, Dargo, was also involved.

That was troubling.

Cyrus had a complicated history with Dargo. They'd crossed paths before and things had ended badly. Dargo still harbored resentment toward Cyrus, and he couldn't blame the man. Cyrus, too, carried bad feelings from that mission. Ghosts that would haunt him until the day he died. It was the operation that had brought an end to his work for the Coalition. The mission left Cyrus unable, or at least unwilling, to ever trust anyone at the Coalition again.

If Dargo were here now, he would want to see Cyrus dead before his job was over. But Cyrus had to put that out of his mind. The more he thought about it, the more certain he became that Dargo was leading the opposing team. Right now Cyrus needed to figure out what Dargo was after and how to stop him. It was the only way to keep the Meridian team safe.

Chapter 37

Miami, Florida
Friday, 5:40 pm (3:40 pm Colorado Time)

This time Cyrus parked a block and half up the street. Once again, he fed far more change into the parking meter than was required. He pulled a duffle bag from the trunk of the rented Mercedes and slammed the lid. The car was flashier than he preferred, but it fit in among the other vehicles parked in this section of the upscale shopping district.

He walked to the nearest intersection and turned right. From there it was only two hundred feet before a narrow alley opened on the left. He reflected on the change in scenery. This alley was located in a high-rent part of Miami, and it was nothing like the last one he visited in Manhattan. This area was well maintained, free from trash, and there were commercial dumpsters evenly distributed between the windowless steel doors spread across the back of the block-long building. The presence of bright sunlight and the distinct lack of a urine odor also made the current venue a welcome change.

Moving silently down the alley, Cyrus watched the numbers stenciled on the whitewashed steel doors. Each was the rear entrance of a shop fronting the main boulevard. Locating unit 324 proved no problem at all. An electric meter hung on the wall a few feet from the door. A thick pipe was used as a conduit for the electrical service, running up the wall, before curving into the building above. A small access panel was on the face of the meter. Cyrus had been looking for it.

Laying the duffle at his feet, he pulled back the zipper and removed a Phillips-head screwdriver. A minute later, he'd freed the access panel from the face of the meter. Looking down into the device, he could see the heavy bolts that anchored the thick power leads, which supplied electricity to the store.

He cringed. This wouldn't be pretty, but it would work.

Pocketing the screwdriver, he pulled a lock-pick gun from the bag. It would have to do. He was out of practice, and time wasn't on his side. He needed to move fast. With the lock-pick gun at the ready, he returned to the power meter. He pulled one of the removable bits from the screwdriver's handle and took a deep breath.

Not pretty at all.

Stepping back as far as possible, Cyrus dropped the long screwdriver into the meter horizontally, bridging the gap between the positive and negative terminals. As soon as the metal dropped into place there was a thunderous bang, a blinding flash, and a whizzing sound. Cyrus had already stepped to the left and inserted the lock-pick gun's pins into the key slot of the door to unit 324. As the lock-pick clicked away at the deadbolt, he glanced at the smoking power meter. The face of the meter had a tear in its sheet metal housing. Glancing over his shoulder, he found the cause of the slash. The screwdriver was embedded in the cinderblock wall behind him. It had winged past, just as he had stepped aside to begin work on the door.

The last click of the lock-pick gun told him he was in. Without waiting a moment, he tossed the lock-pick away, moving through the door and into a dark hallway. Just as he stepped inside, a flashlight came to life in a room to his left. He headed for that room. As he reached the doorway, he came toe to toe with Nathan.

At first, Nathan could only look at Cyrus slack jawed. The man didn't know what to say. Cyrus knew Nathan could read the determination in his eyes. The man was in a profession where he couldn't succeed without being good at reading people. Cyrus watched Nathan's eyes as the man put it all together in the span of two seconds. Nathan's shocked expression switched to concern after he glanced up at the now extinguished ceiling lights. When his eyes met with Cyrus's again, he knew there was trouble.

"What?" It seemed all Nathan could manage as he struggled to understand what was happening.

Cyrus pointed back into the room, his expression deathly serious. "Have a seat."

Nathan knew better than to ague. Friendship only got you so far, and Cyrus could see the man knew he was walking a tenuous line.

Nathan went for his customary seat behind the desk but Cyrus stopped him. "No," he said and slid a tall stool over from the work counter, placing it on the opposite side of Nathan's desk. "You sit here."

After Nathan sat, Cyrus walked around the desk and sat in Nathan's office chair. The entire time Nathan's eyes were glued to Cyrus. A large battery-powered camping lantern cast the only light in the room. Cyrus had placed it beside the door, so the rest of the room was cast in murky half shadows. Nathan's eyes still watched Cyrus with great anxiety.

Cyrus was watching the man's expression carefully. Based on it, he had a pretty good idea what he would find. Without taking his eyes off Nathan's, he palmed the underside of the desk and pulled free a .45 caliber Colt 1911. Cyrus's eyes narrowed as he set the gun gently on the counter between them.

For several tenuous moments neither man spoke. This only served to raise the tension in the room. That was fine with Cyrus. Nathan would be wondering how far Cyrus was willing to take this. Truth be told, Cyrus was curious himself.

"I've done you a courtesy," Cyrus said finally, breaking the silence but not the tension.

Nathan took a visible breath. He nodded slightly. "When you took out the power, you took out the bugs," he said referring to the listening devices they both knew to be planted in the office. "For God's sake, Cyrus, why not just call and have me meet you somewhere?"

It was a fair question. There were two reasons. First, such a call would tip off the listening party, and the listening party might send a tagalong. Cyrus didn't need that. The second was that he wasn't entirely sure of Nathan's loyalties. Cyrus fished a small object from the pocket of his jacket. When he laid it down on the table beside the Colt, he never took his eyes off Nathan's.

The object was half the size of a dime. It was all black, and had the room's lighting been better, they would've been able to see the small lens on the device, which was no larger than the tip of a ballpoint pen.

The tension in Nathan's face flared. His eyes were locked on the tiny camera. After allowing a moment of silence to enhance Nathan's anxiety, Cyrus opened the palm of his hand and dropped over a half dozen additional tiny cameras onto the table beside the first. Now he could see that Nathan wasn't breathing. The man's eyes had stopped blinking. Finally, the man seemed to snap out of his trance. His eyes went to Cyrus, then back to the miniature cameras. His eyes flicked between the gun and the cameras once more.

"It's not what you think," Nathan said finally. His voice was hoarse and quiet.

"What should I think?"

Nathan was breathing again, but he didn't look well.

"I've helped you in every way you've asked. *I've done everything I could!*" Nathan looked like he was going to be sick. His face was covered in sweat. Granted, the air conditioning had gone down along with the power, but this wasn't the heat.

"I'm not the only one you helped," Cyrus said in a flat even tone. Since he'd arrived, he hadn't yet raised his voice. He found he could get further in situations like this by remaining calm. Sometimes a person acting calmly under extreme circumstance could be more unnerving than someone ranting and yelling. This way he had better control of the discussion. Still, Cyrus's voice had gone cold. He made no effort to hide that.

Nathan sat silently. He seemed to have a lot to say, but as far as Cyrus could tell, the entire conversation was going on in the man's head.

"Nathan, we go back a long way. Talk to me. You provided the tech to use against us, but you also gave us the gear we needed to find the bugs. If you hadn't suggested we take your detection gear, we never would have found this. Why are you working for Dargo?"

At that, Nathan's attention perked up. "Dargo? No! I sold this gear to *Yuri* Dargoslav. I sold this tech to him months ago, long before you were ever part of the picture."

Cyrus still didn't understand. His expression must have betrayed this, because Nathan took it as a sign that he should continue.

"Yuri came to me four, maybe five months ago. He needed some special tech. I'd just taken possession of these experimental cameras, so it seemed like a good opportunity to do a field test. Whoever Yuri was working for had deep pockets, and he could pay.

"It seemed like a great opportunity at the time. As I started pulling files and putting together reports for you, I started to see there was a chance Yuri's operation was related to what you were working on. But I didn't know for sure.

"You have to realize, for all I knew, Yuri's op was long over. He could be working on a completely different contract now. I didn't know. But I wanted to be sure. So when you were going to sweep for bugs, I thought you should take my latest hardware. If your op overlapped with his, you'd find those," he pointed at the cameras on the table beside the gun. "And I'd finally know for sure."

Cyrus took a deep breath and thought this through. His ongoing confusion was over everything Nathan had provided so far. The man had delivered all of the intelligence he'd requested.

As far as he could tell, all of the information was accurate. But Nathan was a free agent. By definition, he was in it for himself. Alliances were largely a matter of convenience in this field. While Nathan was a resource that had proven trustworthy in the past, no resource could be trusted blindly.

Nathan had provided surveillance hardware to Ian Dargoslav, by way of Yuri. He didn't deny that. And Cyrus was inclined to believe him when it came to the timing of the transaction. From what Cyrus was been able to put together, Dargo had been working his operation for several months.

With this in mind, the circumstances of his visit had now changed. In a way, intentionally or not, Nathan was playing both sides of the fence. Cyrus could bleed him for any information that might help get a leg up against Dargo, and more importantly, whoever hired Dargo. Tactically speaking, interrogating Nathan would be the smart play.

"Okay," Cyrus finally conceded. "I can see how that might happen in your profession. The fact is, you don't owe me anything more than you would owe Yuri or Dargo. In the end, we are just clients, and you're a business man."

Cyrus let the statement hang in the air. The confusion on Nathan's face appeared genuine. He still looked terrified.

With a nod of understanding, Cyrus realized the problem. He leaned forward and carefully lifted the Colt from the table between them. Rolling forward in the chair, he placed the gun on the edge of the table nearest Nathan. After taking a long look at Nathan, he rolled his chair back to where it had been and sat back comfortably.

"No trick," Cyrus said. "I believe you're being straight with me. You've provided me with everything I've asked. You've been professional and reliable. You're afraid I'm going to go all Gitmo on you. It's not gonna happen." He took a moment and considered what he wanted to say. "You've explained everything to my satisfaction. I appreciate that."

An awkward smile crossed Nathan's face. "Did I really have a choice?"

Cyrus shrugged. "We all have choices."

Nathan looked down at the pistol for a moment, finally exhaling. He was looking more himself by the minute. "I'm sorry. I wanted to tell you what I suspected… I just wanted to make sure I wasn't speaking out of turn. Giving Hondo the detection gear seemed like the best way to test the waters. Only you dropped in on me before I knew what he found. For what its worth, if he found any of my bugs, I was going to tell you all of this straight off."

Cyrus had to smile. He would like to believe that. But Nathan was a professional. He couldn't afford allegiances like that. "You don't have to say that," he said quietly. "I know the business you're in. Telling me about your deal with the Dargoslavs would've been bad for business."

Nathan considered Cyrus's words. His head bobbed back and forth as he thought. "Bad for business? Sure. One of the very few major 'No-Nos' in my profession, I suppose. I've known a lot of operators in my time, kid. I mean it—a lot! And not one of them has what you do. You've got integrity and a soul. And you were smart enough to get out of the game before those qualities were torn from you."

Cyrus didn't know what to say. He was good at reading people in times of high stress. It was part of the reason he'd gone for the high drama and blindsided Nathan. Even the best liars make mistakes when under extreme pressure. Nathan seemed truly sincere in his words.

"I mean it, kid. You've worked with pros over the years. Knowing what you did and given the circumstances, every one of them would've come down on me like a ton of bricks, and they would've cut on me until I said whatever they wanted. You could've gone that way. But you asked me… *Scared the ever loving shit out of me,* but you didn't start cutting. That's what makes you one of the good guys."

That was the problem. He didn't feel like one of the good guys. And, more importantly, he really had believed all of this was in his past. The last week had brought some painful feelings back to the surface. He gave Nathan a nod. It was the best thanks he could offer given the circumstances.

"Cyrus?" Nathan looked uncomfortable, as if he had something important left to say.

Almost afraid to ask what it might be, Cyrus just looked at Nathan and waited for him to continue.

"You look like you were in a car wreck. What happened?" Nathan finally asked.

Cyrus smiled. He kept forgetting he looked worse than he felt. Telling Nathan that he'd run into Yuri Dargoslav would explain his banged up appearance, but he knew that given the circumstances, Nathan would just feel more guilty. "Would you believe someone tried to mug me?" he asked finally. It was close enough to the truth.

The look on Nathan's face made it clear he didn't know whether Cyrus was joking. "Ah…if you look like this, do I want to ask about the other guy?"

That brought a chuckle from Cyrus. "No, you really don't," he said with a grin.

Stepping out of the chair, Cyrus headed for the door. After two steps, he stopped and looked back. "Sorry about the power. You're going to need an electrician to come out and get the service back up and running. I really did a number on it."

Nathan's laugh was genuine for the first time all day. "I'd expect nothing less!"

He followed Cyrus out into the hall.

"Oh," Nathan said suddenly. "I'm sure you haven't seen it yet. I talked with Hondo a few minutes ago. He said something about a list of compromised locations? I'm supposed to watch for his email. It's supposed to contain a list of properties. I need to pull ownership histories and look for anyone who has run a similar search recently. He was going to send you the email, too."

This was the news Cyrus was waiting for. Among all of the files recovered from the printer's hard drive in Underwood's office, Cyrus was hoping they wouldn't find a list of properties Meade owned. But since Dargo's men were waiting for him in Chicago and New York, Cyrus was betting some kind of list was on file. He needed that list. It should help him understand which transport sites were compromised.

With no power in Nathan's office, Cyrus resorted to checking the email on his smartphone. Sure enough, he had a message from Hondo. As they feared, the documents saved to the printer's hard drive had included a list of properties owned by Walter Meade. And at this point, it was a near certainty that the same list was in Dargo's hands as well.

The list included the apartment in Cyrus's building in Chicago, the group's office space in Santa Barbara, the apartment in Manhattan, an office space in Washington DC, and the house in Colorado.

Cyrus felt his stomach drop as he read the last line on the list of properties. *The house in Colorado!* They'd been so confident that location was secure. But if Dargo had access to the files, it meant he knew all about the house in the mountains!

Chapter 38

The phone rang for the third time. Cyrus could hear his heartbeat thundering in his ears. There was another ring, but still no answer. Why wasn't she picking up? He needed to let Reese know her location was compromised. She needed to get out of there immediately. Nathan still sat across the table from Cyrus, his face was ripe with nervous tension. Only this time he was reacting to Cyrus's near frantic response to the email message. Nathan didn't know what was going on, but anyone could see it wasn't good.

There was another ring of the phone. Cyrus was planning the fastest way back to the platform. He was twenty minutes away, even in the best-case scenario. Getting back to Colorado would take some time, and if Reese wasn't picking up, he had no idea what might be waiting for him.

Finally there was a click, and Reese answered. "Hey!" she said. "Sorry, I was just getting out of the shower."

The sound of her voice released the pent up tension from his body. With a sigh, he realized he'd been holding his breath. "We've got a problem," he said without preamble. "The location of the house might've been compromised. You have to get out of there now. Don't wait for me—leave immediately."

The pause on the line wasn't entirely unexpected given the bomb he'd just dropped. "Ah…" she stammered. "Easier said than done."

She seemed at a loss for words, but she finally continued. "We've gotten about two feet of new snow. I'm not sure I can drive out of here."

"That's not a problem. Take one of the snowmobiles and head for town. Wait for me at the general store."

"I thought you couldn't get the snowmobiles started?"

She'd asked the question so matter-of-factly that it confused Cyrus. They'd never talked about starting the snowmobiles. He had never tried to start them, let alone tried and failed. All at once, it clicked. He felt his heart skip a beat at the realization.

Shit!

"That's no problem," he said without letting his voice betray his discomfort. "I took care of it. They're all set now."

"Meet you at the general store? Got it," she confirmed.

"And, Reese? Be careful. This might be all for nothing, but I want to play it safe."

"I understand. I'll see you soon." She clicked off, and the line went dead.

Setting the cell phone aside, Cyrus stared blankly at the surface of the desk. Reese was something else. Her reference to a conversation that had never taken place was a warning. Dargo was already there. If Cyrus went back now, he'd be walking into a trap. The security of that damn house was the one thing that Cyrus hadn't questioned. He was sure Meade had kept its location secure. But the location of the house was part of the information cached in the copy machine's memory. If Dargo knew about the house, he certainly knew about Meridian.

All their secrets were compromised. The only things Dargo didn't know were the changes Cyrus had made since joining the operation. That at least meant the team was safe. The transport site in Australia couldn't be compromised because Hondo had taken the platform to that location personally. It also meant the platform setup in the storage locker in Santa Barbara was safe. But neither of these things helped with the present situation.

Something else occurred to Cyrus. Strangely, the Miami transport platform didn't appear to be part of the information entrusted to Allan Underwood. It meant that Underwood's list of transport sites was incomplete. While he didn't have an explanation for that, it made him wonder if there were other sites not included on Underwood's list.

Launching the Transport Control app Reese had put on his phone, Cyrus entered his security code and switched to the database of platform locations. He scrolled slowly through the list. As they'd discussed, the list wasn't terribly long. Meade's team had had limited resources with which to build their platforms, and thanks to the limited availability of Halon-Seven, they wouldn't be building any more.

As he reached the end of the list, Cyrus realized none of the listed locations helped with his current problem. He was certain to be walking into a trap. Alternatively, he could transport to Santa Barbara and then fly to Colorado. But even chartering the fastest available plane would take hours. And if he didn't get back soon, Dargo would sense the deception.

Frustrated, he scrolled back up the list. He reached the top and still had no better options. About to abandon his current avenue of thought in search of one more productive, he was struck by a sudden flash of insight and hope. There was one platform not on the list.

Beta II!

A plan was starting to form in his mind. He looked up at Nathan and was surprised to see a smile cross the man's face. Accordingly, he cast the man a questioning look.

"I know that look," Nathan said proudly. "You've got a plan!"

"That I do," Cyrus confirmed with a smile of his own.

"I don't know what's going on, but I can tell it's serious. Just tell me what you need."

This surprised Cyrus. He'd come here ready to take Nathan apart for his betrayal. It was something he hadn't wanted to do, but he was reacting to the situation as it developed. But watching Nathan, he understood. He wasn't just a professional, he was also a good man. A good man whose job required working with unsavory people. But after today Cyrus felt confident of something he'd never been sure of in the past. When push came to shove, Nathan was a man who would side with his conscience over his Swiss accounts. A quality far too rare in his, or any other profession.

"Thank you," Cyrus said with a grin. "I only need a couple of things." He leaned over the counter and detailed his mental shopping list.

Without so much as a sideways glance, Nathan set off to collect the requested gear. Cyrus was impressed. His confidence in Nathan was restored, but other concerns were beginning to weight more heavily. The moment he'd stepped off the transport platform in Miami, his apprehension toward the Coalition had resurfaced. That he hadn't encountered one of their field agents already was becoming a bother, and for the first time, he wondered who they might send. Certainly not Boone. Never again—he'd seen to that on their last encounter. And while rumor had it that the agency had suffered cutbacks following the disappearance of Monica Fichtner, he had no doubt that someone would eventually be sent to make an *approach*.

Chapter 39

Berton Springs, Colorado
Friday, 4:28 pm

There was a flash of light, and Cyrus felt his ears pop. He was atop the transport platform on one knee with his Springfield drawn, but the room was dark as pitch. Without making a sound, he reached up and lowered the night vision goggles from their rest position above his brow. They slid securely from his forehead and over his eyes. The goggles functioned by amplifying existing low levels of ambient light. Since there was absolutely no visible light in the room, Cyrus activated an infrared emitter built into the frame. The room immediately sprang into crisp, green-tinted detail.

Slowly scanning the room, he didn't move until he was confident he was alone. Not that he expected to meet resistance here. He stepped from the platform and walked slowly across the concrete floor. The file boxes and open cabinet drawers were exactly as he and Reese left them. And, as he'd hoped, the basement vault had hidden the flash of light that normally marked the arrival of a transport.

Looking back at the old prototype platform, Cyrus continued to wonder why Meade kept it online. It seemed likely the old man had kept it out of nostalgia, but why had it remained active? Based on all he read, it used older technology and required a massive amount of power to operate. That meant this platform either had a nuclear power source or it was retrofitted to utilize Halon-Seven. Either way, keeping the old prototype running seemed an unnecessary effort. So why would Meade have gone through the trouble? Could he have anticipated using it as some sort of escape route? Whatever the reason, there was no denying that it had come in handy today. Cyrus was inside the house. That was all that mattered.

He stepped up beside the vault door and tapped the release switch. The large vault door slid open with almost no sound. All the same, he had his gun up and at the ready. He peered around the edge of the thick concrete doorframe and scanned the darkened basement beyond. It was clear. Still, he kept his movements slow and deliberate.

Passing the server cabinet, he tapped the hidden button to close the vault door. As the wall slid shut, he watched the basement and covered the stairway with his silenced Springfield in the off chance someone might arrive to investigate.

When no response came, he relaxed slightly. He made his way quickly across the open floor, but he stopped short of the entrance to the enclosed stairway. Taking an extra moment to listen once more, he also reached out with his senses, feeling for any presence nearby. It wasn't a guaranteed method for assessing the situation, but it had worked in the past. The mind often picked up on subconscious cues, such as an odor or a shift in the air flow that would indicate the presence of another person. The conscious mind was often oblivious to these primitive tells, but paying attention to one's animal instincts often meant the difference between life and death.

Feeling nothing unusual, Cyrus tipped his shoulder and his gun hand around the corner and took a peek. The stairwell was clear. It was time for the next stage of the plan. He'd made successful entry. It was time to bring in reinforcements. He pulled his mobile phone from his pocket and tapped two buttons on the screen before hitting send.

Now he needed to wait.

He kept his position just outside of the stairwell and listened. Strangely, he couldn't hear any sounds coming from above. There should've at least been the normal sounds of a home. The small creak of the floorboards as someone walked from one room to the next. Or the sound of dishes being moved, things being disturbed. But there was absolute silence.

It was unnerving. Completely understandable if the house was empty, but the tingling feeling behind his eyes told him something was wrong. Nothing so mundane as an empty house.

The phone in his pocket vibrated silently.

Cyrus glanced up the staircase one last time before he doubled back across the basement to stop beside the hidden door in the concrete wall. He ran his thumb over the sensor on the security pad and touched the screen once the light went green. The massive door began to silently slide open. As soon as the door came to as stop, Hondo made a slow advance from the vault with his silenced H&K MP5 held high. He scanned left and right across the room, ignoring Cyrus until he was satisfied they were alone.

Their eyes met, two human-sized, mechanical-looking insects when wearing their high tech night-vision goggles. Hondo nodded silently. Cyrus triggered the door's mechanism once more and the vault closed behind them.

They advanced on the stairwell with organized precision, each man taking a position at a side of the empty doorframe.

Once again, Cyrus glanced around the corner and up the stairway. He could see the light shining through the gap under the closed door at the top. Sliding the goggles from his face and setting them aside, he waited for Hondo to do the same. They wouldn't need them from here on out.

They held position for several minutes allowing their eyes time to adjust to the darkness. Once satisfied, Cyrus led the way, climbing silently up the stairs.

Reaching the closed door at the top, he stopped and took a long slow breath. His heartbeat was calm and controlled, but he knew he would be able to hear better if he could slow down and focus. Sending all of his attention to his hearing, he listened for sounds coming from anywhere in the house. But as long as he waited and as patient as he was, he could hear nothing. Even if a group of men were lying in wait, sooner or later one of them would make some sort of noise. It was just a matter of patience. But for as long as Cyrus dared to wait, he heard noting. Nothing to betray a team waiting in ambush. For the first time, he began to wonder whether he might have misinterpreted Reese's comment.

It was unlikely, he reasoned. He would act accordingly.

Turning the doorknob silently and pushing, he looked into the hallway. He could see part of the kitchen and most of the dining room. The far end of the house, where the doors led to the laundry room and the garage, was also visible. He couldn't see anyone and nothing was out of place.

This ruled out the likelihood of a large-scale tactical team. It was a good sign. And, Cyrus reasoned, if they were here waiting for him, it meant they knew about the platforms. They would most likely be waiting in the spare bedroom, ready to grab him as soon as he teleported in. The plan was for Hondo to take out the team waiting in the spare room. He would be coming up on them from behind, a major tactical advantage. Cyrus would sweep the remainder of the house. No one knew about the prototype platform in the vault, so they should have surprise on their side.

Swinging the basement door open further, Cyrus stepped out with the silenced handgun held high and ready to fire. He would clear the living room, kitchen, and dining room, while Hondo took the back bedrooms. Leaving the basement door mostly open, Cyrus knew it would obscure the view, should anyone step from a back bedroom before he completed his sweep of his end of the house.

He glanced over his shoulder to see Hondo advancing slowly and silently in the opposite direction. This was it.

Just before Cyrus reached the end of the hall, where it opened to the living room on the left and the kitchen on the right, he heard the sound of movement in the living room. Someone was on one of the couches, and they had just shifted in their seat. *Crap!* Cyrus knew he wasn't as alone as he had hoped. The best-case scenario was that it was Reese, sitting there reading, and this was all just a misunderstanding. The worst-case? Well…he was about to find out. Glancing to his right, he confirmed that the kitchen was clear. Checking over his shoulder, he confirmed that the open door to the basement still blocked the view of the hallway beyond. He took a deep breath, readied his gun, and stepped around the corner into the living room.

Reese was sitting on the sofa, but she was bound hand and foot with white flex-cuffs. A swatch of gaffer's tape covered her mouth. Beside her sat Dargo, a hulk of a man wearing a black leather jacket, a black turtleneck, dark jeans, and boots. His face was weathered and mildly wrinkled. He'd aged since their last encounter, but his beard and hair were the same neatly trimmed gray stubble. The man had a .45 Colt resting in his lap.

Cyrus held the gun steady, pointed directly at Dargo's head. Dargo's gaze fell on Cyrus the moment he appeared in the corner of the room. There was no surprise in the man's eyes. Though his hand was still wrapped around the grip of the gun, he made no effort to raise it.

"Has been a long time," Dargo said. His English was still slightly broken, and there was only a mild Russian accent.

Cyrus didn't say anything. His eyes searched Dargo's for a sign of the man's intentions. Dargo had never cared for Cyrus, but after Natasha's death, Cyrus was confident Dargo wanted him dead. So confident, it fact, he wasn't sure why Dargo hadn't paid him a visit years earlier. Since the day Cyrus had walked away from the Coalition, there was one thing he believed with absolute certainty. Dargo would one day visit to settle a past debt. Cyrus just hated having Reese involved in old business.

But watching Dargo's eyes, Cyrus didn't see the hate he expected. Strangely, it wasn't clear exactly what he was seeing in the man's gaze. Was it possible Dargo didn't even know his own intentions here?

Cyrus considered this. If that were the case, Dargo wasn't here for the vendetta. He was here because of Meridian. He was here because he was on the job. This was something with which Cyrus could work. A man set on vengeance was unpredictable, but a man doing a job was a slave to the agenda of his employer. This increased the chances of getting Reese out of here alive.

"You're not happy to see me," Dargo said, finally breaking the unpleasant silence. "This is how you greet an old friend?"

"You made it pretty clear where we stood, the last time we spoke," Cyrus said finally. "Considering that conversation," Cyrus's eyes flicked to the gun Dargo still held in his lap. "Or the fact that you came strapped, I'm going with no. I'm not glad to see you, Dargo."

The Russian pursed his lips, making a show of considering Cyrus's words. He nodded in understanding. Finally, the man smiled. "What is the American saying? 'Fair enough?'"

Cyrus held his gun steady. There was no waver, no wobble to the sight picture he'd drawn on Dargo's head. Maybe 35 feet between them. It wasn't a difficult shot. In his peripheral vision, he could see Reese's eyes were large. Her eyes went back and forth between Dargo and Cyrus.

"Use two fingers," Cyrus warned. "Do it now." He didn't need to explain what his was referring to.

Showing no concern whatsoever, Dargo released his grip on the gun and picked it up between the thumb and pointer finger of his right hand. With a slow and gentle flick of the wrist, he tossed it to the carpet. It landed halfway between them.

"I intend no harm," Dargo said calmly. "But we must talk. Something has happened."

"You don't need a hostage to have a conversation, Dargo. Normal people use telephones. Cut her loose, now!"

"Da, da! Slow down," the Russian encouraged. "You're not exactly in the book. This last week, you have become a very difficult man to reach. Your friend Professor Meade, he died. You came out here and met Miss Knoland. Then you," he searched a moment for the words. "Then you drop from the grid. Not as simple as picking up phone, you see."

"Enough!" Cyrus said. It wasn't so much a yell as an end to the discussion. "Cut her loose. Once she is safely out of here, you and I can have that talk. But nothing happens until she's out of here."

Dargo raised both hands in a placating manner and nodded. "Da," he agreed. He reached over and peeled the strip of tape away from Reese's mouth.

The moment the tape came free, Reese's pleading look finally made sense to Cyrus. "There's two of them!" she bellowed.

Cyrus was already in motion, turning to his left. His eyes fell on a dark object already flying at his head, even as he spun. As the object came into view, Cyrus saw it spark with flashes of electricity.

A last minute pivot was enough for him to get his shoulder up. He felt a crush of pain course through his body as the Taser's 50,000 volts made a glancing impact. Luckily he rolled out of reach of the remaining jolt before he lost motor function. Still, the blast was enough to knock the gun from his hand.

Dropping to a knee, he grappled the wrist of the oncoming attacker. Using the man's momentum and weight against him, Cyrus recognized the bandaged face of Yuri Dargoslav as the man was launched overhead. The Taser was still crackling, even as Yuri crashed to the floor in a heap.

Cyrus didn't see his gun within reach. Oddly, Dargo still sat calmly on the couch beside Reese. He seemed content to let Yuri deal with the situation. That was fine with Cyrus. His gun nowhere to be seen, he went with plan B. A flick of his wrist and the telescoping baton he had just pulled from his back pocket extended to its full two-and-a-half-foot length. And just in time. Yuri recovered from his impact with the floor by rolling to his feet and drawing a semi-automatic pistol with his left hand.

Allowing Yuri time to take aim would prove fatal, so Cyrus instantly closed the gap. He brought the tip of the baton down on Yuri's gun with a snap that sounded like cracking metal. The gun winged across the room. The shock was evident on the young man's face.

This gave Cyrus his first good look at Yuri Dargoslav. The man's nose was heavily taped. It had clearly been broken in their last skirmish. His face was black and blue. It explained the aggression he now brought to his attack. The gun had only just fallen from the man's hand when Yuri batted Cyrus's baton holding hand to the side and landed a solid right hook to the side of his head.

The hit was more solid than Cyrus expected. Yuri's right hand was wrapped in a heavy plaster cast. It was another keepsake from their last encounter. Taking the shot to the head in stride, Cyrus wobbled on his feet and sagged a few inches toward the floor. But it was a feint. He wasn't woozy from the impact; instead he bent at the knees, turned his hip slightly and rose to deliver an uppercut, catching Yuri completely unprepared.

Yuri's head snapped back from the impact. He staggered backward. By the look on his face, the world around him was spinning out of control. But to the man's credit, he didn't drop. A decade of brawling had taught the young man how to take a beating as well as how to deliver one. Yuri stumbled backward several steps, but he promptly shook off the effects of the blow. With a snap of his wrist, he extended the blade on an eight-inch automatic dagger. His eyes narrowed on Cyrus.

"Enough!" Dargo bellowed.

The fight was escalating quickly and Cyrus didn't like the outcome he foresaw. He suspected that Dargo didn't either. Though he didn't know what Dargo wanted, Cyrus wasn't going to drop his guard with Yuri standing before him with a knife. The man was out for blood, and Cyrus knew Dargo calling him off wasn't going to be enough. Cyrus just wanted to get Reese out of here. If Yuri didn't obey Dargo's command to stop, Cyrus would put him down. But he would do it gently. Dargo had already lost a daughter. Cyrus couldn't bear to take his only remaining child from him.

When Yuri lunged with the dagger, Cyrus wasn't the least bit surprised. He parried the blade away with one hand and smacked the man in the throat with the side of his other hand. Yuri's knees folded like a cheap card table. A right hook to the head laid the kid out cold. Putting Yuri down gently was the basic idea. He would live, and the fight was over for the foreseeable future.

Turning back to the living room, Cyrus was surprised to see Dargo still sitting on the couch. Reese had fled the man's grasp and was now on the far side of the room, struggling in vain with her bindings. She was safe for the moment. Since Dargo was still stationary and not an immediate threat, Cyrus retrieved his gun and Yuri's knife. Reese arrived at his side, and Cyrus quickly cut her bindings.

"Just the two of them?" Cyrus asked Reese quietly.

"No," she said. Fear was still clearly evident in her eyes. "Three more in the back bedroom, waiting for you!"

He hadn't heard a sound from that end of the house. He glanced over his shoulder and down the hallway. Hondo was standing, gun at the ready. "Clear," he said simply. He'd taken care of the three men at the other end of the house, without so much as a sound.

"Check the perimeter?" Cyrus asked.

"Roger that."

Hondo walked quickly past them and disappeared out the door leading to the garage.

"Did he hurt you?" Cyrus asked Reese.

She took a moment to consider her answer. "No," she said quietly.

Cyrus read between the lines. She was trying to decide whether having the shit scared out of her constituted harm. She had decided not. He was more than a little impressed.

Since Dargo was not armed, at least outwardly, Cyrus kept his gun casually at his side. He just watched the man and waited for an explanation.

Dargo appeared to be regarding Cyrus as well. Finally, he seemed to come to a decision. He put both hands on his knees and looked squarely at Cyrus. "This makes the second time you could have taken my boy's life," he said.

It wasn't a question, so Cyrus didn't offer a reply. He waited for Dargo to make his point. The man wouldn't be here, if it wasn't to make a point. Had he wanted to kill Cyrus or abduct Reese, Dargo would've brought a full tactical team. Instead he brought only Yuri and enough men to subdue Cyrus when he got off the platform. There would be a reason for it. Cyrus chose to wait for the man to explain.

"Why?" Dargo asked finally. "Why let my boy live? You had him just now. Is a tactical mistake to allow reprieve. I know for fact you were taught differently. I also know you got the better of him in Manhattan. There too, you let him live. I wish to understand why."

Cyrus's eyes had never left Dargo's. Now that the question was asked, he took a breath. He glanced over at Yuri, unconscious and in a heap on the floor. With a slow shake of his head, he faced Dargo. "You've already lost your daughter. I'd do anything to change that."

Cyrus thought for a moment. "I won't be responsible for taking Yuri too," he said, this time more quietly.

The statement clearly had an impact on Dargo. The man looked unsure of himself. It was a mannerism Cyrus had never seen in him.

Cyrus glanced at Reese and could tell she didn't understand what was happening here. She knew they were walking a fine line, but she didn't understand the dynamic being shared.

"I've come to warn you," Dargo said, cutting to the quick of the matter.

The phrase 'no shit' came instantly to mind, but Cyrus maintained his composure. He responded by only raising his eyebrows. The effect was equivalent. It brought a wide grin to Dargo's face. It was the first real break in the tension.

"You have not changed very much," Dargo chuckled. "Natasha once described you as quiet—stoic. I see this now." He thought for a moment before adding, "She had much respect for you."

Reese's mouth dropped at the mention of Natasha. Her eyes went quickly to Cyrus and he tried to keep his attention on Dargo.

Cyrus didn't know where Dargo was going with this, but he didn't care to discuss the past—certainly not here or now.

Dargo slowly raised himself from the couch. The crackling of his weary bones was audible. He made a concerted effort to make his movements concise and deliberate. Cyrus felt Reese flinch at his side, but he wasn't seeing anything threatening in the man's behavior. If Dargo meant them harm, he would've arrived in force, and he certainly would've leveraged Cyrus's fight with Yuri to gain an advantage in the situation.

Cyrus tucked the pistol in the holster behind his back.

Dargo nodded in appreciation and walked slowly closer to Cyrus and Reese. He stopped when he could get a better look at Yuri. "Still young and impulsive. Not good at following instructions. He wasn't supposed to engage you in New York. He alerted you to our presence, no?"

Cyrus nodded. "You've had teams all over the place. I made a team in Santa Barbara a few days back. Then an outright attack on me in Chicago. I don't suppose you'll just come out with it and tell me what this is about?"

Again Dargo chuckled. "Actually, is why I am here. To warn you. You and your friends are in great danger."

"I've noticed that. I've had you breathing down my neck, and a drug lord trying to skin me alive. Don't tell me there's someone else looking to take a chunk out of my ass?"

"Alvares? An unfortunate coincidence. My understanding is that you have retired him. Is no loss there."

Cyrus didn't bite. He waited for Dargo to continue.

"Fine," Dargo said. It seemed he had decided to just say what he came to say. "My employer knows of your Meridian. He will do whatever is necessary to control the technology."

Cyrus considered this. Now they were getting somewhere. "Tell me about it. The body count is stacking up. I need to know... Did you kill Walter Meade?"

This brought an audible gasp from Reese. Cyrus felt her grip tighten on his arm. Reese still thought that Meade's death had been an act of God.

"Walter?" she whispered.

Dargo closed his eyes and shook his head slowly. "This was my predecessor," he said sadly. "From what I understand, Comrade Meade was truly good man. He had grand visions for the future."

The answer was a little too simple. Cyrus wasn't willing to buy into the explanation quite so easily. "Predecessor?"

"Da," the man said darkly. "Part of why I come here now. My employer wants Meridian, and he is not afraid to stack bodies, as you say, if it means getting what he desires. This includes all of you, but I suspect it will soon include myself and Yuri as well. Word is that he killed my predecessor after Comrade Meade died in his custody.

"Not a man to be trusted."

"And you are?" Reese said, barely containing her contempt.

Her outrage wasn't lost on Dargo. He considered her reaction, then bowed his head in contrition.

"So you're not here out of concern for my team. You've got a problem with your employer, and you want me to fix it."

Dargo laughed. "Nyet," he said with confidence. "That I would take care of myself."

The man grew silent as he thought about his words before he spoke. "Truth is, I harbored great hatred for you these years. Had you not left the Coalition, I would have tracked you down long ago. But you made good on the promise to leave that life after Natasha's death."

Cyrus wasn't going to interrupt the man. What he had to say was a long time coming. But having this conversation in front of Reese wasn't his first choice. He could feel her eyes on him. Not judging. But he was certain she had many questions. So much for sparing her his baggage.

"Then I took this contract," Dargo continued. "And you show up. I thought your retirement a lie, a trick to save your skin. I was furious. But as operation progressed, that did not tally. You did not choose this. You were pulled back in. You can thank Professor Meade for this. He needed you to see his work through."

There was no denying Dargo's assessment. It was as correct as it could be. The man had troublingly accurate information. "I did leave the game. It wasn't worth the price. And I never had any intention of coming back to this."

Cyrus looked at Reese, and he couldn't help but smile. His eyes fell back on Dargo. "But some things are more important than what I want. This isn't about me. If you know about Meridian, you know what Meade was trying to do. This project can change the world. Meridian can make life better for everyone."

Dargo considered this and nodded. "Da," he said simply.

"So tell me, what does your employer want with the technology?"

The shrug of Dargo's shoulders spoke volumes. He had clearly considered the question many times before. "I have no idea. He does not share such information. But whoever controls the technology stands to become wealthy beyond compare. Is not motive enough?"

That was Cyrus's concern. The situation was unprecedented. There were any number of motives. Whoever controlled Meridian would potentially have the ability to force change on the world at core political and economic levels. The right person could do tremendous good. The wrong person could impose untold suffering. This was why Meridian had to remain a secret until the moment it was ready for deployment.

"The key to sorting this out will be in learning everything there is to know about your employer," Cyrus offered.

Dargo pursed his lips. This idea clearly troubled him. "What you ask is unprofessional."

Cyrus couldn't help but laugh. He spread his arms to the house around him and looked at Yuri unconscious on the floor a few feet away. "No offense," he said. "But that ship has sailed!"

Reluctantly, Dargo agreed with a simple nod of his head. All posturing aside, it was why he had come.

Cyrus scratched idly at his jaw as he considered the situation. "One more question." He was looking at Yuri, still unconscious on the floor. "If you were here to talk, and you didn't mean any harm, why'd you let him have at me?"

A chuckle came from Dargo. Cyrus could even see the amusement in the man's eyes. Dargo smiled and slapped Cyrus on the shoulder as he walked by. The man headed for the kitchen. "Yuri has many unresolved feelings for you over the loss of his half-sister," the man said over his shoulder. "It seemed a good opportunity to work through them."

Dargo stopped walking and turned back to Cyrus. He regarded Yuri still on the floor. "Perhaps a poor decision on my part. I do not think his feelings for you will have improved after today. So much for therapy!"

When Dargo's gaze moved from Yuri and fell back on him, Cyrus would have sworn he saw approval in the man's eyes. "You have not changed, Cyrus. You will see this through."

Chapter 40

Berton Springs, Colorado
Friday, 6:05 pm

It had been a day Reese would never forget. Being taken hostage, only to see the situation reversed and have her captor and the hired muscle of their enemy, side with her protector. She still didn't understand the conversation she'd overheard between them, but she was aware the two men had a complicated history. Cyrus was grateful for the intelligence Dargo provided, but Reese could tell he didn't have absolute faith in the man. There was no doubt it was the reason Cyrus had chosen to personally escort Dargo, his son Yuri, and Dargo's three man team off the mountain. They had arrived on snowmobiles, which had been abandoned further down the mountain before approaching the house on foot. Cyrus didn't want to ask where they'd acquired the gear—Berton Springs didn't have a place that rented that kind of equipment. Despite Dargo's assurances that he intended his team no harm, Cyrus just wanted the men gone. He had admitted to being impressed by the way Hondo had disabled the men Dargo left guarding the teleportation platform. He'd taken them down without firing a shot, but judging by the men's bruised and bloodied faces, they hadn't gone down easy. Hondo, for his part, was no worse for the wear.

Hondo remained at the house with Reese, while Cyrus was away. After everything that happened, she was grateful for the company. The last week had been a roller-coaster ride in which she'd been taken hostage not once, but twice.

After scrubbing out the coffee pot, Reese filled the coffee maker with water and started it brewing. Hondo paced slowly across the kitchen. He hadn't stopped moving since Cyrus had left with Dargo and his men.

"You're worried about Cyrus?" she asked him finally, breaking the uncomfortable silence.

Hondo stopped mid-stride in the center of the kitchen. "I'm sorry?"

She'd pulled him from whatever intellectual concerns had kept him distracted. At first she was content to leave him to his thoughts. But the longer he remained zoned out, the more troubled she had become. Was there something more going on? Was she missing something? She had come to realize that Cyrus and Hondo, and Dargo by extension, operated on a level that was completely foreign to her.

"You've been on edge since Cyrus left with those men," she elaborated. "Are you worried about him?"

Hondo shook his head slowly as he considered the question. "No," he decided. He pushed the ubiquitous floppy bush hat back on his head. "Not at all. Not a worry when it comes to Cyrus and that crew. Can't say I'm excited to have Dargo in the picture, though."

"'Dargo,'" she said quietly. "That's an odd name. He's Russian?"

Resuming his pacing, Hondo nodded as he replied. "Ian Dargoslav, 'Dargo' for short. Retired Spetsnaz. Russian special forces."

Walking around to the far side of the breakfast counter, Reese pulled out a stool. "Hondo?" she said. When he looked up at her, she glanced at the chair. "Have a seat."

"That's okay, I'm fine."

She motioned at the stool. "I'm not. This may be all in a day's work for you and Cyrus, but my nerves are shot, and your pacing has me at wits' end. Please, take a load off. I'd consider it a kindness."

The self-conscious grin from Hondo made Reese feel better. She'd been reluctant to speak up, especially after all the man had done, but she was exhausted, and his constant movement was putting her increasingly on edge.

"Sorry," he said as he took a seat.

Reese rounded the counter and offered her thanks. She set out two coffee cups and poured the brew. The fact was, she had more questions for Hondo, but she wasn't sure how to ask them.

"You and Cyrus go back a ways?" she finally asked. It was an awkward opening, but she had to start somewhere.

"A bit," he confirmed. "We've worked together on and off over the years. Our paths crossed a few times when I was a Ranger. When I mustered out, we still managed to keep in touch. He's just one of those guys people naturally gravitate to, I guess. It's a rare quality."

"So Cyrus was in the Rangers with you?"

Judging by Hondo's expression, she'd missed her mark. But he didn't immediately reply, which Reese found disconcerting. He looked considerably more serious all of a sudden.

"No, not a Ranger," he said at last. "Wish he was though. We could've used a man like him."

A wave of guilt washed over her. She realized she'd put Hondo in a position he found uncomfortable. While she didn't understand why, his clumsy sidestepping of the question told her this was a subject better left alone.

"I'm sorry," she said somewhat meekly. "I didn't mean to pry. It just seems rather obvious that you and he work well together. I assumed you served together."

"No worries," Hondo said with a confident smile. "You're right, we go back a ways. But I served in the Rangers. A lot of good men there. It's just not a subject that comes up often."

"So you're American, but you're living in Australia?"

"Dual citizenship, actually," he chuckled. "I grew up as a boy in the outback and moved to the States when I was in my teens. Thought I was here to stay until I met the love of my life. She was here on holiday. Wouldn't you know it? She just happened to be from Down Under. I met her near the end of my time in the military. When I retired, I took her back home. To be honest, I'd forgotten how beautiful it was there. There's no better place to raise a family."

That brought a wide smile to her face. "So you're a family man! How many kids?"

"Just the one, so far," he said proudly. "But we're working hard for another. It shouldn't be long. The missus wants a whole litter of 'em!"

"That's really great!" Seeing the proud gleam in Hondo's eyes, she realized he wasn't just a proud father, but he was also a great dad. She was happy for his family.

So, Hondo had a family. And, as far as Reese could tell, his involvement in their current predicament seemed to be voluntary. That seemed odd. Why would anyone choose to put their life on the line in such a way? Especially with a family waiting at home?

Failing to find any tactful way of asking what she really wanted to know, Reese decided to just come out with it. "Can I ask you a personal question?"

After taking a long moment to look her square in the eye, Hondo finally nodded. "You want to know why I'm here—why I'm helping. Is that it?"

His question left her stunned. He had nailed it. For a moment, she didn't know what to say. But finally she found her voice. She gave him a weak smile. "No offense, but yes. You have a family at home—one you obviously care for a great deal. Why are you here, risking your life for a group of people you don't know?"

Her question brought a bright smile to Hondo's face. "You're asking the smart questions; I'll give you that. I can see why he's so taken with you. You've got a lot in common."

He sat back on the stool and looked decidedly more comfortable all of a sudden. "No offense taken," he said, as he considered how best to answer the question. "A ways back—in another life, really—Cyrus pulled my wife out of a rather tough jam. Saved her life, actually. Of course, she wasn't my wife at the time. He's the one who introduced us, actually."

As they'd been talking, Reese suddenly realized she was rubbing the marks on her wrists. The flex cuffs Dargo had used to bind her hands had done no permanent damage, but her wrists were raw from her futile fight with the binding.

Dargo's decision to take her hostage had been aggressive, even hostile, but strangely the situation had turned decidedly in their favor. That was where things were not making sense, and she realized that was also why she felt constantly uneasy. Why had Dargo warned them of his employer's intentions? From everything she'd seen, there was no love lost between Cyrus and Dargo. Cyrus clearly didn't trust the man, and they'd both referred to a dark shared past. So what was really happening?

"Hondo? Tell me about Dargo? I know he has a history with Cyrus. I just don't understand what it is."

Hondo considered the question. "In a word? Complicated."

"You've got to give me more than that! His men attacked us in Chicago. They later attacked Cyrus in New York. Then Dargo shows up here. But when you and Cyrus get here, Dargo lets his kid try to kill Cyrus? When that doesn't work, he warns us about his boss and then leaves peacefully? What the hell is going on?"

Raising both hands, Hondo signaled his surrender. "Okay, okay," he conceded. "It's not that I don't want to tell you—the fact is, I really don't know. Like I said, they've got a really complicated history. The last I knew—"

Hondo stopped mid-sentence. He didn't continue. He just proceeded to look increasingly uncomfortable with each passing moment.

"Last you knew, what?" Reese asked.

By the way the man fidgeted in his seat, Reese would have thought his chair was on fire.

"It's a complicated history," Hondo finally said quietly.

While Reese knew she'd made Hondo wish he could run for the door, she also knew he had been about to say something important. Putting her palms on the countertop that separated them, she met his eyes. While she didn't want to push, she sensed this was important. She needed to understand what was happening. Her life was at stake too.

"Last you knew, *what?*" she insisted.

Taking a deep breath, Hondo sat back in his seat. He let the breath out slowly and once again met her gaze. "The last I knew, Dargo was fixing to kill Cyrus. But he had his chance today, and he didn't try." He shrugged his shoulders. "So I don't know what's going on any more than you," he said with sincerity.

Standing up straight, Reese considered both the words and the meaning behind them. Her finger tapped absently on the counter as she worked through what she knew.

"This is about Natasha?" she said finally. It was a statement as much as a question. "Dargo blames Cyrus for what happened to her?"

The surprise wasn't hard to read on Hondo's face. He rested his elbows on the counter and leaned closer to Reese.

"You know about Natasha?" he asked in little more than a whisper. His voice made it sound as if she were in on some sort of conspiracy or privy to a monumental secret.

It was her turn to shrug. What did she really know? Bits and pieces, but she was putting them together with time. Today's confrontation with Dargo seemed like a rather large piece of the overall picture, but she didn't yet understand how the things she overheard fit in. "I know she was Dargo's daughter. I know she was someone special to Cyrus, and I know that she died."

Hondo's eyes narrowed slightly, as if seeing her suddenly, for the first time. His head tipped slightly as he looked at her more closely. "Cyrus told you about her?" His voice was still little more than a concerned whisper.

She nodded. "Not a lot, but yeah. I know he cared for her a great deal, and I know she died. From what I've gathered, I take it Dargo blames Cyrus for her death?"

Sitting back in his seat, Hondo nodded almost imperceptibly. "You're right about that." His voice and expression were finally back to normal, but he still seemed surprised at her knowledge of the subject. "Did he tell you what happened?"

The shock on Hondo's face had surprised Reese and left her off balance. Could what have happened have been that bad? Evidently, it was enough to make Dargo want to kill Cyrus. But surely that was just the reaction of a distraught father.

"No," she admitted. "To be honest, that's not the part that has me worried. I think Cyrus blames himself too."

Hondo gave that some thought. "Yeah, I'd say that's likely the case. I'd hoped he would work through that over time, but I think you're right on the money. If I had to wager one way or the other, I'd say he still blames himself. But it's rubbish! There was nothing he could've done. If he would just look at things objectively, he'd see that."

"I don't know what happened," she said. "Maybe some day he'll tell me the story. But my concern right now is Dargo. I'm afraid that if Dargo isn't on the level and he goes after Cyrus, Cyrus won't fight back."

"Not to worry about that, Reese!" Hondo laughed. "You saw what he did to Yuri. The man doesn't know how to lose."

Reese wasn't so sure. "That was Yuri. I could see something different in him when he looked at Dargo. Something I've never seen before. He wasn't going to let Yuri take him out, and he sure wasn't going to give up when you and I were in danger. But put Cyrus and Dargo in a room alone?" She grew quiet for several long moments. "In that situation, I don't know what he would do if Dargo turned on him. Whatever happened to Natasha, Cyrus carries a lot of guilt. I'm worried that Dargo could take advantage of it."

The conversation had Hondo back on his feet and pacing. Reese stood in the corner of the kitchen, forgotten coffee in hand and slowly growing cold. She suspected that Hondo's concerns were now very close to her own. But after their talk, she had decided something. She wasn't concerned with what had happened between Cyrus, Natasha, and Dargo. She was confident that Cyrus would share it all when he was ready. The only thing she wanted to know was whether Dargo was on the level. Was he sincere in his warning about his employer, or was he playing at some sort of revenge?

Chapter 41

Payton Street, Santa Barbara, California
Saturday, 9:05 am (10:05 am Colorado Time)

Having returned to the house adjacent to Alfie Ahmed's home, Dargo was looking forward to closing up shop. He knew Ahmed was safely sequestered, and more importantly, he had valid reasons for pulling up stakes should Nil Bayer question the decision. Every member of the research team had literally disappeared without a trace. They had clearly gone to ground. Ahmed was a low value asset anyway. Leaving surveillance on his home was a waste of resources.

And the new day held a new concern. The operative Dargo tasked with surveilling Bayer had contacted him late the previous night. He reported that Bayer was about to board a flight bound for Los Angeles. This was troubling for a number of reasons. Foremost of which was that, at the time, Dargo had not yet been informed of Bayer's impending arrival in the States. It suggested Bayer was up to something, and he was intentionally keeping Dargo out of the loop. If that were the case, Dargo was on treacherous footing. It was true, he didn't trust Bayer. This made his worst-case scenarios, unfortunately, all the more likely. The suspicion was supported by the fact that Bayer hated to fly. The man truly despised it. Bayer made every trans-Atlantic crossing by ship. *Always*. If he'd resorted to air travel, something of critical importance was about to happen.

Once more, Dargo chastised himself for ever taking this contract. He would be lucky if he lived to regret it.

He had contacted Bayer first thing that morning to report his progress. There was some relief when Bayer admitted that he was currently in California. Not entirely surprising, he was already in Santa Barbara. He wanted to meet with Dargo and discuss operations in person.

Maintaining control of field operations was now more important than ever. While Dargo didn't know what Bayer was up to or why he was really in the States, he knew he was likely to lose command of the operation. Bayer had been at a tipping point for some time. It was all Dargo could do to prevent the man from attacking Cyrus's people head on. Bayer honestly believed heavy-handed interrogation was the key to getting what he wanted. It didn't matter that Professor Meade had died as the result of such rash action.

Adding to Dargo's concern, there was the matter of his predecessor on the assignment, the man who had led the interrogation of Walter Meade. Following the failure of that mission, the man had never been seen again. Dargo was fairly certain Bayer had had the man killed. He had no intention of becoming another casualty of Bayer's ceaseless ambition.

With little time to prepare, Dargo had made a gamble and contacted Cyrus. It was his hope that together they might improvise a plan to keep Dargo's team in play and neutralize Nil

Bayer once and for all. To Dargo's satisfaction and relief, it had taken a single fifteen-minute phone call to devise a plan that would fulfill both objectives. Dargo had no idea how Cyrus would make the necessary arrangements within the confines of their aggressive timetable, but thankfully, that was not his problem.

Dargo's objective was to prevent Bayer from replacing him as head of field operations. The trick would be to present key intelligence and an operational strategy before Bayer could make his agenda known. That way, Bayer would have no reason to be suspicious of the plan or the carefully orchestrated timing.

With a glance at his watch, Dargo realized Bayer was already five minutes late. Like himself, Bayer was normally punctual to a fault. That got him thinking. What else might Bayer do like Dargo? Dargo made a custom of showing up to every meeting early, leaving time for reconnaissance prior to the rendezvous. That was a practice drilled into him thanks to years in the military. It wasn't a habit Bayer was likely to have developed in civilian life.

As Dargo set the last video processor inside its protective packing crate, he considered the situation. He snapped the lid of the case shut. Was he becoming paranoid in his old age? There was no doubt Bayer was a snake of singular order. Why was he in the United States? Dargo wondered if there might be more going on than he first suspected.

There were three knocks on the sliding glass door at the back of the house. The door immediately slid open, and a man stepped into the room. He was dressed in an expensive black suit and dark glasses. One of Bayer's bodyguards. He quickly looked Dargo up and down before scanning the rest of the room.

Without a word, he marched down the back hallway, only to return moments later, speaking into the cuff of his sleeve as he entered the room.

Nil Bayer stepped through the sliding glass door, accompanied by another bodyguard in a dark suit. The second bodyguard was a virtual duplicate of the first.

"Dargo!" Bayer said warmly. A little too warmly for Dargo's taste. It was out of character. "It's good to see you."

Dargo did his best to smile despite the circumstances. "You as well, Comrade Bayer. I am surprised to see you in United States."

A grave look crossed Bayer's face. "Yes," he said somewhat quietly. "I have business in Los Angeles. An unrelated matter. I do hate to fly, but the matter is most pressing."

Bayer looked around the nearly vacant room. All of the gear was stowed, the folding tables collapsed and now standing against the wall in the corner.

"I see you are—what is it the Americans say? Pulling up stakes?"

"Da," Dargo confirmed with a nod. "This is what I wish to discuss. I believe our opportunity has arrived."

The flash of excitement Dargo saw in Bayer's eyes appeared genuine. But Bayer said nothing and waited for him to continue.

"My son, Yuri, had recent run-in with Cyrus Cooper in New York. He allowed Cooper to escape, but not before planting surveillance tracker on him. We now know that Cooper has been using Professor Meade's teleportation system to move around the country. Our tracker relays the feed via satellite. There is delay, but most recent download suggests he has developed concerns for the safety of project data following trouble with Mexican drug cartel and multiple run-ins with my men."

"So he's moving the research data?" Bayer asked. "When and where?"

"The exact location is unknown. Yesterday morning he shipped a large container to Fairbanks, Alaska. I believe this container held one of the platform devices. I expect Cooper will use the platform to move the research to newly secured location, somewhere in Alaska."

"But we don't know the new location?"

"Nyet," Dargo confirmed. "We tracked the flight as far as destination in Fairbanks, but I was unable to get a man onboard prior to takeoff. But thanks to bug, we know Cooper has Meade's files hidden in a warehouse somewhere in Phoenix, Arizona. He will be there at 7:00 pm, local time, to start transfer of files."

"But you don't know the exact location of the warehouse?"

"Negative." Dargo confirmed. "But this will not matter. He does not have a platform on site. He has chartered a small cargo aircraft to Phoenix. He will be taking a device with him. My team will wait for him at airport and follow to the warehouse. Once there, we will put together strategy and capture Cooper, the platform, and all of Professor Meade's data."

Watching as Bayer digested the information, Dargo waited to see the man's reaction. Finally Bayer nodded. There was a hungry gleam in his eyes. "This is the break we've been waiting for. Are you sure you've enough men for the operation?"

"Absolutely."

Bayer smiled his reptilian grin. "Good. Then I can finally get my hands on Meade's Meridian and set the rest of my plans in motion."

While Dargo didn't know what the rest of Bayer's plans might be, he felt his skin crawl with the glint in the man's eye. Dargo had worked with some shady characters over the course of his career, but none made him more uncomfortable than his own countryman, Nil Bayer.

"I have one stipulation," Bayer said finally. "I wish to be on site when you capture Cooper and the Meridian technology. I want to make sure everything goes according to plan."

There it was. Dargo knew Bayer would mess with the plan, and he had desperately hoped the man would not let him down. "Sir, this is not advisable. Such an operation can be extremely dangerous. I cannot guarantee your safety."

"My safety is not your concern!" Bayer snapped. He wasn't allowing debate on the matter. "I will have my security detail. Your goal is the retrieval of the Meridian data. That information is your primary objective. The capture of Cyrus Cooper is secondary. If Mister Cooper proves too much of an obstacle, you will eliminate him."

Dargo felt his teeth grinding in response to his employer's demands.

Why had he ever accepted this damn job?

"Is that understood?" Bayer demanded.

"Understood," Dargo stated simply.

Chapter 42

"A personal question?" Cyrus laughed. "I think we've passed the point where you have to worry about asking me personal questions, don't you?"

Looking up from the box of files she was sorting, Reese smiled. "I'd like to think so," she said warmly. "But some subjects are more sensitive than others."

Sliding an industrial-grade tape gun across the top of the box, Cyrus sealed the cardboard file container. Once he was done, he stopped and held her gaze for a moment. He made a show of giving her statement consideration. "Fair enough. I think I know what you're going to ask, and the answer is, okay. I prefer not to share you, but if you really feel strongly about bringing another woman into our bed, I'm willing to make the sacrifice for you."

The stunned expression marking Reese's features made it almost impossible for Cyrus to keep a straight face. Her mouth hung open. He knew he'd caught her completely off guard.

"That's not— I wasn't— I'm not—" she stammered. The porcelain white of her cheeks had quickly gone past a blushing shade of pink on their way to red.

He couldn't contain himself. He burst out laughing.

"I'm sorry," he said, fighting his own laugh for a breath. "I really couldn't help it. You seemed so serious!"

It was a few moments before she could meet his eyes. But when she did, he could see that even through her embarrassment, she found the humor in his teasing. "You're willing to take one for the team?" she asked with a wide grin and a shake of her head. "Okay. I'll keep that in mind," she said suggestively.

Cyrus placed the sealed box on a pile and grabbed another. He began folding the top shut. "Okay. Now really, what did you want to ask?"

"Well, it's funny you went there with the question," she said with a playful smirk. "Because I wanted to ask about the shelf full of romance novels I saw back at your apartment. 'Bodice-rippers', I believe they're sometimes called?"

His eyebrows shot up, and he felt his stomach drop. "Ah," he stammered. "I had a lot of books back there. I don't recall any bodice-rippers. They're not really my style. I think maybe you're mistaken."

He went back to work on the box, pulling the tape gun across the top and sealing its contents tightly. Reese shoved one last folder into the box she was working with before pushing the box across the concrete floor, delivering it to Cyrus.

"Not much room for mistake," she said quietly, when they were on their knees, face-to-face and surrounded by the stacks of office filing boxes. "When we left your apartment, I grabbed three of them. I thought I might need something to entertain myself. Of course," she crawled up close to him. Close enough that he could feel the heat radiating from her body. "That was before I knew we'd be able to entertain ourselves," she whispered.

Cyrus smiled. He liked where this was going.

She winked, then stood up and walked back to the stack of files that marked her work location. "Don't forget to tape that one shut," she reminded him. Cyrus looked at her. He didn't understand. It took a moment for his brain to reengage. Momentarily slack jawed, he looked down at the box she had just delivered. It was his turn to be embarrassed. He hung his head. Ouch. She was a tease. There was no doubt, he had it coming. But he liked how she chose to get even.

He flipped the tabs shut on the box and quickly ran the tape gun over it. Hefting the box, he added it to the growing stack.

The two of them were alone in a large warehouse, located in a secluded industrial park. Cyrus didn't know the area; he had never even been to Phoenix before this afternoon. Now they were pretending to box 'top secret' information before it was teleported to Alaska for safekeeping. Cyrus had only rented the warehouse earlier that afternoon. He'd paid five thousand dollars for 48 hours of uninterrupted access to the building and the surrounding grounds, plus the temporary use of dozens of boxes containing old shipping manifests. It was all stage dressing—all part of a ruse to trap Bayer.

Glancing at his phone, he checked the live feed from the thermal display outside the warehouse. Dargo's men had taken up positions around the warehouse. They would be ready to move in at any time. As a precaution, Cyrus had set up the thermal imager so he could keep a better eye on the exterior of the warehouse. He didn't want someone changing the game plan on him at the last minute. While he had confidence that Dargo was playing it straight with him, he would never entirely trust the man. Dargo claimed to no longer harbor ill will for him, but Cyrus still suspected Dargo wouldn't be too broken up should he accidentally die of acute lead poisoning.

"Well?" Reese asked.

Realizing he'd zoned out for a moment, Cyrus returned his attention to her. "I'm sorry?"

"I said, 'you don't strike me as a fan of romance novels.'"

Not knowing whether that was a question, Cyrus countered with a safe reply. "I prefer thrillers or mysteries. Both with a splash of science fiction, if I have the choice. But truth be told, I'll read just about anything before I'm willing to watch reality TV."

She smiled. "I have to admit, I was more than a little impressed to find out you wrote the Alastair Rose books. And I was halfway through *Hot Vatican Nights,* when I realized how the romance novels were related to the Alastair Rose books."

That stopped Cyrus dead in his tracks. She found his thriller novels similar to romance novels? Had he misunderstood? "I'm sorry?"

She responded with a knowing glance. "Absolutely! Certainly nothing alike in content, but there was a remarkable similarity in the writing. It was almost like they'd been written by the same person."

Setting the tape gun aside, Cyrus sat back on the floor and took the pressure off his knees. "Wait. I don't understand. Now you're saying you don't believe I wrote the Alastair Rose books? You think Phoebe Bloome is Alastair Rose?"

This time Reese broke out laughing. "Ah, no! Nice try. I'm saying you're Phoebe Bloome!"

"Based on what? Because you think her writing style is similar to mine?"

"You're just not going to let this go, are you? Fine. I'll play along. The first clue was the writing style. I've read all of the Alastair Rose books, and I know his writing well," she gave him a sexy wink. "The wording and phrasing used by Phoebe Bloome was strikingly similar. Though, in fairness, Bloome uses a whole pile of flowery words that have never once appeared in an Alastair Rose book. The second clue didn't strike me until I considered the first clue more carefully. That's when it occurred to me that you had every Phoebe Bloome book ever written. Even a couple that I've never heard of!"

"You're a fan of Phoebe Bloome too?"

"Stay...on...topic! Fairly odd for you to be such a collector—but not conclusive in and of itself. Not until we get to my third clue."

"Quite the detective. You should write your own books. What's your third *clue*?"

"Not one of the Bloome books on your shelf has ever been read. They were all paperbacks. And we both know it's practically impossible to read a paperback without doing damage to the book's binding. Add it all up, and you are a collector of the Phoebe Bloome books because you are, in fact, Phoebe Bloome! Just as you are, in fact, Alastair Rose!"

He couldn't help it. Cyrus found the proud look on her face incredibly exhilarating. She hadn't solved the crime of the century, but she'd done a respectable job of deducing his shameful secret. That's when it occurred to him. Unlike the time he'd discovered that Meade and Underwood knew his secret, he really felt no shame in sharing this with Reese. It struck him as odd. He'd always dreaded a day when this came out. In fact, he'd gone to great lengths to hide any link between his pen name and his real name. It was odd that sharing a secret with Reese brought him no discomfort at all.

"Okay," he admitted. "You got me."

At his admission, she looked even more proud of herself.

"I'll make you a deal," she suggested. "I'll keep your sordid secret…if you better acquaint me with Johnny Rock and Abigail Lang's little trick with the ice cube and the peacock feather?"

Now Cyrus had a proud grin. "It's a deal!"

His mind spinning at the innuendo, Cyrus was pulled from his thoughts by the sound of creaking wood coming deep from the darkness of the warehouse.

Ah, that would be the signal!

He glanced at the thermal image on his phone's display. Dargo's men were still holding position outside the industrial park. And it was nearly 7:30. If things were going according to schedule, they should have had the warehouse surrounded by the time the signal was given. That didn't seem to be the case. The sound from back in the darkness was his cue; it was time to begin. If he was going to stick to the plan, he needed to investigate the sound. But the signal from the darkness didn't mesh with the thermal reading of the troop deployment he was receiving on his phone.

Something wasn't right.

"What was that?" Reese asked, moving smoothly to their script. Dargo would be listening. So would Bayer.

Climbing to his feet, Cyrus dusted himself off. "I don't know. Wait here while I check it out."

He thought for a moment. "If I'm not back in two minutes, don't wait, and don't come looking for me. Teleport out and don't come back until you hear from me."

This was complete play-acting on his part. Not only were the file boxes completely fake, but they didn't have a functional teleportation platform in the building either.

"Be careful," she said quietly.

He found sincerity in her voice along with the request. Clearly, she held some uncertainty for Dargo as well. He shot her a quick smile, grabbed his rifle and disappeared into the darkness.

Chapter 43

Phoenix, Arizona
Sunday, 7:24 pm (8:24 pm Colorado Time)

Walking slowly and silently into the darkness of the warehouse, Cyrus listened for any hint of the soldiers he knew to be there. According to the plan, two of Dargo's men would be lying in wait. But as he moved on, he was unable to find them.

The further he moved from the small work area he and Reese had set up, the murkier the warehouse became. It was a sprawling facility, and they'd engaged the overhead lights only in the section they were using. Still, Cyrus moved on. But with each passing step, an ominous suspicion was taking form, like a three-dimensional image in his mind. Something was wrong. The plan had already gone off the rails. He looked at the thermal readout on his phone. It showed that Dargo's men were still holding position around the warehouse. Given the time, that was wrong. Turning back, he would double-time the return trip. He needed to retrieve Reese and get the hell out of here.

"I've got a bad feeling," Cyrus said, as he stepped from the shadows cast by the last aisle of shelving. "Grab your stuff, we gotta—"

Cyrus froze in his tracks. A tall man wearing dark battle fatigues stood behind Reese. He had the muzzle of a Colt 1911 pressed against her head.

Two men swept in on Cyrus, one from either side. One relieved him of his rifle, the other took the Springfield from the holster behind his back. Once stripped of his weapons, one of the men pulled Cyrus's hands behind his back and secured them in flex cuffs. The entire operation took only seconds.

One of the two men beside Cyrus nodded to the man holding the gun on Reese. Cyrus mentally tagged Reese's captor as the man in charge and filed it away for future reference.

The man at Cyrus's right pulled out a small, hand-held radio. "Area secure. You can come in," he stated simply.

A moment later they could hear the squeaking sound of a distant service door. It was nearly thirty seconds before Dargo and four of his men emerged from the darkness, along with Nil Bayer and one of the men from his security detail. Bayer's security man was dressed in the same BDUs as the men who held Cyrus at gunpoint. This was unusual, because Dargo's men were dressed in less conspicuous street clothes.

"I don't understand," Dargo stated with some irritation. "This was not my assault plan. What is going on here?"

That was when Cyrus realized things had taken a terrible turn. His eyes flashed to Bayer just in time to see the man give a nod to the radio operator beside Cyrus.

"Now," the man mouthed quietly into his radio.

Simultaneous bursts of gunfire coughed from the shadows of the rafter catwalks high above. The four men that had accompanied Dargo spilled to the floor simultaneously. Dargo moved instantly to raise his assault rifle, but he was stopped cold when he felt the muzzle of a 1911 pressed to his temple. The security guard who had accompanied Bayer held the gun.

Though he now recognized Dargo hadn't betrayed him, the full weight of Dargo's loss had yet to grip Cyrus. Blasts of automatic gunfire were heard outside the warehouse. With a physical burst of pain, Cyrus realized the radioman's transmission was more than the signal to take out Dargo's men inside the building. It was also the cue to wipe out the exterior and perimeter teams.

The distant gunfire was over as quickly as it had started. Cyrus was seething. It meant nearly two dozen of Dargo's men were dead. Dargo, for his part, looked like he was ready to remove someone's head with his bare hands. Cyrus could see Dargo about to make his move just before he made it.

Bayer's bodyguard must've seen it, too. He fired a single shot into the flesh, just above Dargo's knee, a moment before the massive Russian vented his rage. Blood splashed across the concrete floor—but somehow Dargo managed to remain standing.

In the end, it didn't matter that he had held his feet. He'd lost his maneuverability and with it, any hope of a successful attack on Bayer. Blood coursed from the bullet wound in his leg. Still the big man stood, never even looking down at the injury. His eyes remained riveted on Bayer. Dargo was clearly gnashing his teeth. The bullet had brought only a brief reprieve. Soon one of them would be dead.

The man beside Cyrus secured his radio and fitted Dargo with a set of flex cuffs. It took two men to muscle Dargo into submission. In that time, Cyrus was afraid the trigger-happy guard might shoot the Russian again. But finally Dargo was cuffed, and the four soldiers seemed to relax as a result. That was interesting. Bayer's new team was comprised of operators who lacked the professionalism and experience of Dargo and his men. They were mercenaries. As soon as Dargo was restrained, every one of them relaxed and lowered their guard. They considered Dargo no longer a threat because his hands were bound and he'd been relieved of his weapons. It was a good sign. *They have no idea who they're dealing with.* Cyrus knew their ticket out of here when he saw it.

Cyrus had a simple plan. He needed to get everyone more relaxed, and ideally, more distracted. And he needed to buy some time in the process. If he could get free, he was sure Dargo could do the same. They would just need to make their move at the same time. There were four armed guards on the ground floor, plus Bayer. That wasn't much of a problem. It was the two additional guards located in the corners of the catwalk overhead who posed the real threat. Cyrus glanced over his shoulder. Scratch that. There were two additional men in the corners of the raised walkway behind him. Four on the floor and four up above. *Damn.*

The soldier who had bound Dargo finally finished, he approached his commanding officer. Cyrus was relieved to see the gun lowered from its position at Reese's head. Reese's hands were quickly bound behind her, and she was shoved toward

Cyrus. With some relief, she took up a position standing between Cyrus and Dargo. All three now faced Bayer and the mercenary in charge.

"What's this about?" Dargo demanded of Bayer.

"Consider this your exit interview," Bayer said with a dry chuckle. "Your services will no longer be required. I don't appreciate your betrayal."

A sound that could be described only as a low growl emanated from Dargo. It seemed that even bound and shot in the leg, he was more than a little tempted to attack Bayer. "You have murdered my men!"

"Oh, please. Give it a rest," Bayer said with some levity. "You would be dead now, too, if your son were here with you. Tell me, where is young Yuri? I want you to see him die before you are put out of my misery."

Cyrus considered the twist of fate that had spared Dargo's life. Dargo had benched Yuri, refusing to take the young man on this mission because Yuri was having trouble with the idea of working with Cyrus. Dargo had come to accept that Cyrus had had no fault in the death of his daughter, but Yuri had no such acceptance when it came to the loss of his half-sister. Plus, Cyrus had bested the man on two separate occasions. Since Yuri was a hothead, Dargo considered his son a potential liability and had left him out of the operation as a result. Had Yuri been present, both he and Dargo would surely be dead already. It seemed that, as long as Yuri lived, Dargo might as well.

Bayer had no idea the tactical mistake he had made. There was no doubt that Dargo had come to these same conclusions. Cyrus just needed to keep Bayer talking. He was pretty sure he knew how to do that.

"Two men have been sent to collect Yuri. He will be brought back here," Bayer continued. "You will watch him die, and then I will watch you die."

Cyrus wanted to change the subject. He took this opportunity to do it. "I know you," he said to Bayer.

Bayer's deep-set eyes focused on Cyrus. "I'm sure you do. But do you know that all of this would've been unnecessary, had it not been for you?"

"Yeah, yeah, yeah. Crush—kill—destroy—you're a gangster. Your checkbook has killed more people than second-hand smoke. But that's not what I meant. I'm saying that I know who you are. Nil Bayer. You're fantastically wealthy. You made the better part of a billion dollars after the fall of the Berlin Wall. What I don't understand is why you need more money. Of all the people I expected to come after Meridian, I don't understand why it's you. Meridian can make the world a better place. All you want is to make more money?"

The pulsing vein on Bayer's large forehead told Cyrus that his derisive words had scored the desired effect. For a moment, the man looked as though he might have an aneurism. This told Cyrus that the key to alienating the man was talking down to him.

Cyrus could recall reading a Forbes article about Bayer, years earlier. It was a classic rags-to-riches story. Bayer started out a low level scientist, working at the Russian Academy of Sciences. He'd likely been shown great disrespect by the military chain of command, to which, at the time, every department ultimately reported. Then, later, Bayer had made his mark and become amazingly wealthy. At that point, he would've finally gained power and influence. As a result, he was likely no longer accustomed to being challenged.

"Meridian has the power to remake global empires," Bayer corrected. "Professor Meade's plan had two fatal flaws. First, it was altruistic. Second, it lacked ambition. Why give Meridian to the world when the world will gladly pay for it? And why roll the technology out slowly? I have the manufacturing facilities standing by. I'll have the transport platforms in mass production in two months time. Plenty of time to stockpile the hardware for a *literal* global, overnight rollout."

Reese sputtered at the sound of Bayer's plan. "You can't do that! The technology *must* be deployed in stages. We've done simulations—an aggressive deployment will result in massive economic disaster on a global scale!"

The reptilian gleam in Bayer's eyes sent a chill down Cyrus's spine. "You are absolutely correct, Miss Knoland! Certainly not everyone would embrace the new technology overnight, but there would be enough acceptance to gain crucial momentum. That will be followed by a groundswell of support for the technology, which will force even the reluctant to follow suit. It will take two, perhaps three weeks at most, before the Meridian platforms gain critical mass. By that time, automobiles will have become antiquated technology. Airlines and shipping companies will have gone the way of the dinosaur. As a result, automakers, airlines, and dozens of other major industries will go bankrupt overnight. The demand for fossil fuels will plummet, causing massive economic unrest. These factors will snowball into a financial meltdown, as banks collapse and entire financial markets crumble."

Bayer's master plan left everyone speechless, but it struck Dargo particularly hard. He was appalled to have been a willing participant in such a plan. "You are insane!" he protested. "Untold lives will be lost in the chaos. This sort of thing starts world wars!"

"And you are correct as well, Mister Dargoslav!" Bayer was having far too much fun unveiling his plan. "Every person on Earth will look to their national or spiritual leader to show them a path from the chaos. But their leaders will have no salvation to offer."

Rolling his eyes, Cyrus could see where this was going. "Let me guess. You'll be the one with a turn-key solution ready to go. And you'll be happy to lend a hand, for a price."

"Precisely! By that point, I should think world powers will be willing to pay just about anything. Not monetarily, of course. By that point, conventional currency will be completely worthless. They will be forced to pay with what little they have left. I will unite a world vaster than even Alexander the Great! Disparate nations will unite under me, or they will see their people starve and freeze."

The confidence Bayer was displaying was chilling. Given his resources, what he described might even be possible. He sounded like a crazed supervillain from a Saturday morning cartoon, but the nut-job might just be able to pull it off, if he got his hands on the technology.

The shocked, wide-eyed look that Reese gave Bayer demonstrated her speechlessness. Cyrus couldn't blame her. The man was literally going for total world domination.

"How?" Dargo asked. "It is how the Americans say," he looked over at Cyrus. "You cannot unring a bell? The damage will be done. Once it is done, there is no going back."

At that, Cyrus nodded. He finally understood Bayer's plan. "He plans to profit from the chaos."

Bayer stood proudly with his arms crossed, and he waited for his captive audience to work things out. He looked like he was posing for the statue he believed would one day be made in his honor.

"It is not possible!" Dargo countered.

Tipping his head back and forth, Cyrus filtered the twisted logic in his mind. "Anyone sufficiently prepared for the chaos stands to profit from it. Given Bayer's means, I'm thinking that would include the stockpiling of tangible assets, things that will have substantial value following the collapse. In this case, weapons and ammunition. It also means he'll have fresh water processing plants standing by. Power plants, ready to go online. Massive stockpiles of canned and dried foods. Oh, and his own private army. You gotta have that, just to keep the Army, Navy, and Marines from stomping your ass from the get go. I'm betting that's where these thugs come in," his gaze moved from man to man, as he took in the team that had wiped out Dargo's men and taken them prisoner.

"But first things first, someone with Bayer's perverted sense of value would start with conventional investments above all else. On an intellectual level, he might understand what will be of value following the collapse. But he won't be able to deny his nature. I bet he's already begun stockpiling gold and silver. Once the necessities are covered, that'll be the currency he'll use to rebuild the markets."

"Rebuild them as I see fit," Bayer stated simply. That one statement confirmed everything Cyrus had put together.

Reese looked nauseated. "This technology has the ability to unite the world in a way never conceived! And you look at it as a tool for profit? You'll bring nothing but death and destruction!"

"It's all about power to him," Cyrus said sadly.

This made Bayer chuckle. "It's about more than power! It's about righting a long-standing wrong!"

By the glint in his eye, Cyrus could tell that Bayer was dying to explain, so he kept quiet and let the man have the floor.

"You refer to it as Halon-Seven," Bayer said. "If you think it was an American technology, you are sorely mistaken. Meade's predecessor stole the technology from Mother Russia. Your precious Meridian, at its heart, is Russian technology!"

Reese shook her head. She didn't understand. "Stole it?"

Bayer nodded. "In 1907, a meteor strike outside of Moscow resulted in the discovery of a new element. Russian scientists studied it at a secret laboratory. They discovered that the ore comprising a portion of the meteorite exhibited truly amazing properties. When energy was applied to the ore, the mineral would magnify the introduced energy by an untold factor. It was to be a technology that would change the world. Until, that is, an American agent infiltrated the laboratory in 1908 and stole the only known sample."

"You're crazy!" Reese said simply. She clearly wasn't buying his crazy tale.

"Not at all," Bayer countered. "All the information is there. It's a puzzle. You just have to be dogged in searching out the pieces and putting them together. You see, to cover the theft of the meteorite, an American agent detonated some sort of super-weapon and wiped out not only the lab, but hundreds of acres of Russian forest. The ore that was stolen from my homeland is now used to power your teleportation technology. You refer to it as Halon-Seven!"

This brought a spontaneous, heartfelt laugh from Cyrus. Bayer's twisted recitation of historic events was so flawed that he found it amusing. The laugh had come unexpectedly, but when he saw the glimmer of rage in Bayer's eyes, he recognized what amounted to an opportunity. He could set the record straight and run down the clock in the process. Bayer had clearly fixated on his messed up revisionist history of Halon-Seven. Cyrus thought that recounting the facts might buy the time he needed.

All the reports he'd read flashed through his eidetic memory. He'd read every note Meade had left behind. This included a number of classified documents secured in a burn safe hidden in the basement vault in Colorado. Cyrus hadn't even shared that information with Reese yet.

"You know, you get credit for solving a puzzle only if you put the pieces together correctly. All you've done is take a bunch of disparate bits of information and build a narrative that incorporates them."

"I assure you, my version of events is quite accurate!"

"Not even close, *comrade!*"

Cyrus had everything committed to memory. "A series of meteor showers began pelting the Earth sometime in 1902. The showers came in waves, on and off, over the next several years. In 1907, a meteor impacted 12 kilometers outside of Moscow. The meteorite was collected by the Russian military, at the time still under the command of Nicholas II, the last Tsar of Russia.

The meteorite was soon found to display unusual properties, one of which seemed to be the ability to amplify energy. A lab was set up in the wilds of Russia, where the Tsar thought the meteorite could be examined far from prying eyes.

"Interestingly, that lab wasn't built for the study of the meteorite. The facility was originally intended to be a prison camp for political prisoners. A gulag. Near the completion of the facility, it was repurposed for scientific research.

"Around that same time Rumsfeld Pellagrin, a brilliant American scientist, was working on a project in the United States. In a surprising coincidence, his work was based on observations made following a *separate* meteor impact in the United States. Pellagrin didn't know it at the time, but his meteorite led him to the discovery of what we now call quantum entanglement. Without a doubt, far ahead of his time, Pellagrin's study of quantum entanglement led to our principle understanding of quantum teleportation. Pellagrin believed it was possible to teleport anything from one point to another instantaneously, regardless of distance. All of this, gleaned strictly from his study of the ore that comprised his meteorite."

Bayer finally interrupted. "The American agent, Pellagrin—he stole the Russian sample to prevent Mother Russia from developing its own technology!"

"Not at all," Cyrus explained. "And, since I know you're not good with puzzles, try to keep up." He was needling Bayer. He just hoped that Dargo was taking advantage of the time he was buying.

"The American and Russian meteorites had a completely different composition. They fell to Earth in different meteor showers and exhibited entirely different properties. Pellagrin knew he was on to something groundbreaking. The science of his day was primitive by our standards, but his theories were sound and light years ahead of his contemporaries'. Pellagrin wholeheartedly believed that teleportation was possible. He knew that if he could perfect the technology, it would change the world. But every approach to quantum entanglement met with the same roadblock. The energy required to link more than a few particles was beyond the abilities of the day.

"All of that changed when a report reached the US Signals Intelligence Service in 1908. The report stated that the Russians had made a breakthrough. They had some sort of device with the ability to produce unheard of levels of electricity. If there was ever a chance of powering Pellagrin's teleportation platform, the Russian technology was the key. But in that lay the problem. The Americans couldn't just request access to secret Russian technology. Even admitting we knew of it would alert the Russians to a spy working in the Tsar's palace.

"So Pellagrin came up with a plan that would keep the spy safe and still provide access to the Russian power source. Stealing it was out of the question. The intelligence he had indicated the power source was delicate and experimental. It was also hardwired into the power grid of the military installation where it was being studied. Since Pellagrin couldn't bring the power source to his platform, he took his platform to the power source."

Taking a few seconds to gather his thoughts, Cyrus considered whether he should continue his narrative. If it bought him the time he needed, it would be worth exposing sensitive information. But if his gamble didn't payoff, he'd be helping Bayer, and that was unacceptable.

Ultimately he had no choice. If they failed, Bayer would cause untold destruction regardless of what he said or did. If he leveled with Bayer now and explained that there wasn't enough Halon-Seven to complete his plan, the man would likely kill them all right there. Then he would take the Halon-Seven he had and use it as a weapon. If the accident at the Fire Star lab had demonstrated anything, it was how the element could be weaponized. Cyrus opted to continue the story. He had to stop Bayer here and now, and that required buying a little more time.

"Pellagrin's transport platform was a large and complicated piece of technology," Cyrus continued. "There was no way he could sneak it into Russia, let alone into the secure Russian facility. So he had the Russians do the heavy lifting. He leaked information about a powerful new super-weapon that was being transported from New Mexico for a demonstration in Washington, D.C. Pellagrin made sure the cross-country trip included an overnight stay at a warehouse mid-trip, providing the Russians adequate opportunity to make their move. Sure enough, they took the bait.

"You should be proud," he said with a glance to Bayer and then to Dargo, since they were both Russian. "You guys pulled it off! The Russians stole several hundred pounds of gear that was to comprise a state-of-the-art super-weapon when fully assembled. After that, they secretly transported it back to Russia. And, wouldn't you know it? Just as Pellagrin predicted, the Tsar had the stolen hardware sent to the same secret military installation as Fire Star."

"Fire Star? What is Fire Star?" Dargo asked.

Cyrus had seen Bayer's expression change at the mention of the Russian code name.

"Fire Star is what the Russians called their power source, their meteorite. Anyway, the stolen hardware was to be examined by the finest scientific minds in Russia. So naturally, it was taken to the same base as Fire Star. But by the time the stolen hardware arrived, Pellagrin had already infiltrated the installation. After that, it was a simple matter of modifying paperwork. When the stolen American hardware arrived, it was promptly deposited in the Fire Star lab, where it was to be examined the next day."

The pulsing vein had retuned to Bayer's forehead. "You expect me to believe that a lone American scientist infiltrated a top-secret, Russian military base by himself?"

Chapter 44

Cyrus nodded. "Rumsfeld Pellagrin was something of a renaissance man. He was a scholar before he joined the Marine Corps. After his tour of duty, he returned to academia. The man wore many hats in his lifetime. He must've been truly extraordinary."

"Continue your story," Bayer ordered impatiently.

"Finding that these pieces fit together?" Cyrus pressed.

He didn't try to hide his satisfied smirk as he continued. "In the dead of night, Pellagrin snuck into the Fire Star lab and found the crates comprising the American super-weapon. They were stowed just as his forged work order instructed. He spent the rest of the night reassembling the device. But when he was done, there was no weapon. Pellagrin had tricked the Russians into delivering his teleportation platform to the very room that housed Fire Star!"

"And this is when your Rumsfeld Pellagrin stole the Fire Star meteorite and destroyed the facility, killing over a hundred Russian patriots," Bayer stated in a flat, cold tone.

"Not at all," Cyrus countered. "I'm afraid it was your *patriots* that pulled the pin on that grenade."

Cyrus decided that it would be an ideal time to resist continuation of the narrative. After all his years of research, Nil Bayer was desperate to know what really happened to the Fire Star lab. Cyrus knew he had the man's full attention, and the metaphoric clock was his to control.

Even the guards had become enamored with the story. He could see it in their faces and the way their eyes moved between him and Bayer as the conversation had moved back and forth. They were holding their rifles more casually as well. It confirmed Cyrus's suspicion. Bayer was relying on mercenaries. These men were loyal to his checkbook, not his cause. It also meant that, while these men knew how to handle weapons and were comfortable taking human lives, they weren't true professionals. All of these factors would aid Cyrus when it came time to make his move.

As it was, he'd already made progress with his flex cuffs. Keeping attention focused on his face was essential. While he was telling his tale, he was carefully working a lock pick free from its hidden location, slid up under the skin of his forearm. It was the second time in a week he'd used the trick. If he had to do it again, he would need to start using the other arm or risk developing obvious scars. That would end the trick's usefulness. The gag worked only if the guy patting him down missed the mark left on the skin.

All the same, having to do this in plain sight meant he had to move slow and deliberately. He needed to continue the story.

Bayer quickly grew short-tempered with Cyrus's delay tactic. "Would you prefer to continue, or should I have Miss Knoland shot in the leg as well? I doubt she will suffer it as stoically as Mister Dargoslav."

Cyrus rolled his eyes at the drama. *Fine.* "Pellagrin assembled his prototype platform in the Fire Star lab. There was a matching platform waiting to receive him at his lab back in the States. Unfortunately, by this point, the base guards had discovered that Pellagrin had locked himself in the lab. They tried to breach it but couldn't gain access. Ultimately, they attached a pair of explosive charges to the lab wall."

Cyrus gave Bayer a chance to suss out where this was leading, but the man remained silent. Either he wasn't seeing it yet or he wanted to hear Cyrus explain the series of events from beginning to end. With some frustration, he continued. "Anyway, Pellagrin fired up the Fire Star device and attached it to the platform. He crossed his fingers and jumped on the platform with what might've been only seconds to spare before the guards detonated their charges. Pellagrin was vindicated! The teleportation device worked flawlessly! The next thing he knew he was standing in his lab, back home with a contingent of shocked associates gapping at him. As you can imagine, he had literally appeared out of nowhere.

"It was over a week before Pellagrin heard of the massive explosion near Tunguska. No one knew what had happened, but reports came back stating that hundreds of square acres of forest were destroyed. To this day, there are still dozens of theories about what happened in the wilderness. Not one mentions a secret Russian laboratory. Apparently, every trace of it was obliterated by the blast."

Reese looked stricken by the story. "But what caused the blast?"

"Pellagrin was never certain. He suspected that the TNT charges used by the soldiers caused some instability in the Fire Star ore. It resulted in a catastrophic reaction, which vaporized the entire area."

Bayer thought for a few moments. "So you would have me believe the Fire Star meteorite was destroyed in the blast?"

Cyrus was genuinely pained at this part of the story. "It defies all reason," he explained, "but the meteorite was the only thing to survive the blast."

"How is that possible?" Reese asked.

"No one knows," Cyrus admitted. "But following news of the Tunguska event, Pellagrin snuck *back* into Russia. Surprisingly the Russians weren't in a hurry to examine the scene. Pellagrin suspected the Tsar was more concerned with covering up after the SNAFU. In any case, Pellagrin returned to the site. Not a trace of the installation had survived. But one thing stood out as obvious at ground zero. The old location of the base was still apparent, if you knew what to look for. Every tree for hundreds of acres had simply tipped over, like blades of grass in a windstorm. But, strangely, there a pattern to the toppled conifers. They tipped outward, radiating from a single central point. When Pellagrin backtracked the point of origin, he found the same baseball-sized lump of stone he'd seen in the Fire Star apparatus. It was the only thing to survived the blast."

"So the American spy did steal the meteorite!" Bayer concluded.

"Wow, you're like a dog with a bone," Cyrus snickered. "I don't know, at that point I think an argument could be made that he just found a rock in the woods. There was no sneaking or stealing involved."

"And you now use that meteorite to power the Meridian teleportation devices," Bayer accused. "Is it not your power source?"

"It is not," Cyrus said calmly. "It's true that the Russian meteorite is what we refer to as Halon-Seven, but it's not a power source."

"It seems a little late to lie," Bayer accused.

"It's not a lie," Cyrus explained. "The Russian scientists had it wrong. Halon-Seven isn't a power source. It's more like an amplifier and a battery rolled into one. A super-capacitor. But on its own, it produces no power at all."

"That's not true!" Bayer protested. "I have detailed reports from Russian scientists proving otherwise. You yourself explained that the meteorite was used to power the first Meridian platform!"

"I'm only saying that the scientists of that day didn't fully understand what they were dealing with. There is no question that they thought they'd found a powerful means for generating power. But they blew themselves up before they could figure it out. The ore was only releasing the energy stored inside it—the energy it had accumulated as it plowed through the Earth's atmosphere before making landfall. At that point, there was a massive amount of power stored in the ore's nano-lattice, just waiting to be released.

"The scientists just didn't know that the energy they were tapping was finite. It would eventually run dry, unless recharged in some way."

"That is not possible," Bayer countered. He had no evidence with which to counter but apparently rejecting the theory out of principle was enough.

"It's possible," Cyrus explained. "Halon-Seven is a necessary part of every Meridian platform, but not because it acts as a power source. It's used as a battery and a capacitor. Every time a platform is used, an excess of energy is released. That energy is channeled into a sample of Halon-Seven, where it's held in reserve to fuel subsequent uses of the platform. The Halon-Seven also amplifies the energy channeled into it, making it possible for the platforms to eventually function autonomously. Unfortunately, full scale production may not be possible in the foreseeable future," Cyrus said in conclusion.

"On the contrary!" Bayer took great delight in his opportunity to contradict Cyrus. Having been largely relegated to the role of observer during the summation of historic events, the return of Bayer's pompous demeanor indicated a power shift in the conversation. "I have the resources to put the platforms into mass production *immediately!*"

"You can build all the platforms you want," Cyrus said with complete confidence. "It won't do you a damn bit of good. Without Halon-Seven, those platforms are oversized paper weights."

"I have the resources to mine as much Halon-Seven as needed!"

"Dig as deep as you can. You won't find any more," Cyrus shot him down again. "Halon-Seven isn't indigenous to Earth."

Bayer looked at Cyrus with confusion. So did Dargo and Reese for that matter, though the look Reese gave him indicated she thought she understood where Cyrus was heading with this.

It was an opportunity for Cyrus to grind the pompous prick under his boot. "Hello? Remember? Meteorite? It comes from out there!" Cyrus glanced at the ceiling and the sky beyond. "Pellagrin didn't have the technology available to him in his day, but Walter Meade did. Meade was the genius who eventually replaced Pellagrin on the project. Once Meade knew the properties of the ore, he used satellite technology to search the surface of the entire planet. Do you know what he found? There have been only three meteor impacts on the planet that contain Halon-Seven. Three meteor strikes—*in the whole of Earth's history!* One in Russia, one in Australia, and one in South America. That's it! No more! Nowhere on the entire planet! There were only three meteorites that ever contained Halon-Seven!"

Now Reese was dumbfounded. Cyrus caught the shocked expression from the corner of his eye. "So what are you saying? It was just dumb luck, a one-in-a-trillion chance that someone actually discovered one of the meteorites and studied it?" she asked.

Bayer had broken into a hushed, rapid-fire conversation with his bodyguard. Cyrus took advantage of the opportunity and spoke quietly with Reese. "Long odds? I'd say so. Outrageously long odds. Too fantastic to calculate, if you ask me. But in the span of ten years, two meteor impacts made landfall, one in the United States and one in Russia. Both meteorites were completely different in composition. The one in the US changed everything we know about our world. The one from Russia is about to change everything about the way we live in that world.

"It's all there in Pellagrin's notes and further substantiated by Meade, in his notes and observations since. The two meteor impacts in the United States and Russia are the important ones. Each meteorite was distinctly different, but they were both virtual study guides to the universe. The one in the US was the cornerstone for our understanding of quantum physics. The one in Russia was the first of the three Halon-Seven samples."

"My God," Reese thought aloud. "If that's true, just think where we'd be as a people if our luck had been different."

The expression on Cyrus's face made it clear he was having trouble attributing it all to cosmic coincidence. "That's been bothering me ever since I found the last set of papers. I don't think luck had anything to do with it. Those cosmic study guides still wouldn't mean a thing unless they landed in the hands of people intelligent enough to interpret them."

"I don't understand," Reese admitted. "You're saying it wasn't a mistake that the meteorite ended up with Pellagrin?"

His eyes darted back to Bayer. The man was still having a quiet but heated discussion with his head of security. "We'll talk about that later," Cyrus said calmly. "When I make my move, I want you to duck into the aisles behind us and run like hell. Find a dark spot to hide, and don't come out until you hear me call."

He noted the confused expression on her face. He'd caught her off guard when the conversation changed gears. Her eyes snapped to his as she registered his meaning. He could see a steely determination coalesce behind her brown eyes. She gave him a crisp nod. She was ready.

Bayer called their attention forward. His expression showed a deep suspicion, but Cyrus could see the man was starting to see that his plan was not going to work the way he'd schemed. "You claim there is no cache of Halon-Seven," he said. "Then how is it your team has built dozens of transport platforms?"

"Fifteen platforms," Cyrus set matter-of-factly. "That's all there is. We can't build more than that."

He could see that Bayer wasn't satisfied with the explanation, so Cyrus elaborated. "As I said, there have been three meteor impacts. All three were tracked down and retrieved. All three samples were collected and studied. Professor Meade was able to split each of the three samples five ways. That left him with enough of the element to build fifteen platforms. It's simple mathematics."

Cyrus could see Bayer's jaw clamped in frustration. Corded muscles danced beneath the skin of his lower face. Though not entirely certain, Cyrus thought he'd seen a small facial tick at the corner of the man's eye. He decided to needle Bayer just a little more. "That's right. Your little megalomaniacal, super-villain wet dream is over before it started." He waited a beat or two for dramatic effect, then, "Wait, don't tell me. You haven't already invested all your money in bottled water and dried fruit, have you?"

That brought a chuckle from Dargo. Cyrus was quick to join in. After only a moment, both were laughing outright. Until, mid-laugh, Dargo's eyes met Cyrus's. Dargo was indicating he was ready. Cyrus gave him the slightest of nods. The men moved as one. Both were already free of their flex-cuffs.

Cyrus delivered a punch to the throat of the gunman closest to him. He gave it everything he had. The man's trachea collapsed, which made relieving him of his rifle a simple matter. Tucking the rifle to his shoulder, Cyrus unleashed a three round burst of fire that dropped the guard across from him, before the man could react.

At the same time, Dargo lashed out at the soldier nearest him. He slashed the man's throat using a short, thin blade he'd kept hidden through the pat-down. Dargo felled the man in one smooth motion, before taking up his assault rifle. The maneuver was grotesque but effective. A moment later, he unleashed a burst of fire that dropped the last remaining guard on the ground floor.

Reese was caught somewhat flatfooted by the brutal assault. The first burst of automatic fire had already left Cyrus's rifle before she turned and bolted into the dark confines of the warehouse.

Just as Cyrus and Dargo had jumped into motion, the first in a series of rapid crashing sounds echoed through the building. The rapid crashes stood out even over the brief bursts of automatic fire that sprayed from the assault rifles of Cyrus and Dargo.

Cyrus had loosed a burst of fire that stitched the body of the mercenary on Dargo's side of the room at the same moment that Dargo opened fire on the man. The body spun across the floor under the onslaught.

When his magazine ran dry, Cyrus dropped to one knee and snatched a fresh load from the combat harness of the man whose throat he'd crushed. He slapped the fresh magazine home and released the charging bolt in a single fluid series of actions.

Still on one knee, he brought the sights of the rifle up into the rafters, expecting to see one of the four armed guards above already drawing down on him. But as his sight picture settled on the sentry's position, Cyrus found only a corpse slumped over the railing.

He spun on his knee, searching out the next of the four men on the raised walkway. As he made a quick circuit of the rafters, he was relieved to find each of the four men heaped where they had once stood. Spinning slowly around the room, Cyrus found it clear of hostiles. Dargo was completing a similar circular maneuver.

Looking down at his feet, Cyrus saw the first guard he had taken out. The man's eyes were bulging. He was writhing in pain, clutching his shattered windpipe. Cyrus knew there was nothing he could do for the man. It would be a slow and painful death. There was no changing that now, and he wanted better for the man. Raising his rifle, Cyrus fired a single shot into the man's head, ending his suffering. Some would think him callous, but Cyrus understood, just as the dying soldier did. It was a kindness, given the circumstances. A slow suffocating death was a terrible way to go.

"Clear!" Dargo called out.

"Clear," Cyrus said with some sadness. He never wanted to take these lives. So much for leaving his old life behind.

Kneeling over one of the fallen soldiers, Cyrus retrieved his phone and confiscated Springfield from the man's battle harness. He secured his handgun in the holster behind his back before taking one more cautious glance into the dark confines of the warehouse and slinging the rifle over his shoulder. Two taps of the phone screen and he was connected with Hondo. "How are we looking?" he asked without prelude.

"Internals of the warehouse are clear," Hondo confirmed. He'd been shooting from the rooftop of a neighboring warehouse four hundred yards to the east. "I have one more on the move at the perimeter. I think he's making a run for it—" There was a lone, distant rifle shot. Part of it reverberated through the earpiece of the phone. "Scratch that. Tango down. Hold while I do another thermal scan."

Cyrus wasn't letting his guard down while he waited. His eyes probed the dimly lit confines of the warehouse. There were any number of places to hide. But there was no hiding from the thermal imaging device Hondo was using. Anything with a thermal signature greater than ten degrees over ambient would show up like a signal flare.

"Confirmed," Hondo concluded. "If I assume that rhinoceros next to you is Dargo and your last remaining tango is Bayer, he'll be hiding about thirty meters to the northwest. It looks like he's on his hands and knees. Be careful... I can't be sure without better magnification, but thermal shows what might be a puddle on the floor. I'm pretty sure he's pissed himself."

Cyrus laughed. He looked to Dargo. "We're clear. Bayer's thirty meters that way," he pointed. "Hondo says to be careful, Bayer soiled himself."

Dargo looked up at the fallen sentries still splayed on the catwalks above. "My perimeter team?" Dargo asked sadness filling his dark eyes.

"Negative. I'm sorry," Hondo reported from outside. He'd been listening to events as they unfolded inside the warehouse. "I had to take out two three-man-teams before I could get into position in the roost. By the time I was in place, they'd already eliminated Dargo's field team," he reported. The regret was obvious in Hondo's voice.

Meeting Dargo's eyes, Cyrus simply shook his head in disappointment. It was all the communication necessary to relay Hondo's report.

Dargo closed his eyes for a moment and mouthed a silent prayer for his fallen comrades. When he opened them again, Cyrus was surprised to see genuine and deep-seated pain. Cyrus followed Dargo's eyes to the holes high in the warehouse walls. Light from the sodium vapor perimeter fixtures was shining through. The four holes represented the four shots Hondo had taken to neutralize the sentries on the catwalk.

Dargo looked back at Cyrus. "It seems retirement has not dulled your suspicious nature. Tell me, was it Bayer you did not trust, or me?"

Cyrus chose not to answer the question. Dargo might feign resentment, but it was Cyrus's distrust that had put Hondo in a position to save their lives, and the man knew it. "You should contact Yuri. Bayer made it sound like he sent a team to pick him up."

Dargo nodded. "Da," he muttered and set out to retrieve Bayer.

"You should find Reese about 80 meters to the northwest," Hondo chuckled. "And Cyrus? Don't sneak up on her. From what I'm seeing in the thermal, she's about 10 meters off the ground. If I had to guess, she's gone up into the shelving and probably has a nasty surprise ready for the first person to come along. Quite a Sheila you've go there, mate!"

A relieved smile crossed Cyrus's face. "Roger that." He headed into the warehouse to retrieve Reese.

Halfway to the back wall, a single gunshot sounded from the other end of the building. The gun's report echoed through the confines of the massive structure. Cyrus would get no more useful information from Nil Bayer. In truth, he'd expected nothing less. Dargo had lost his entire team. Though he ran his outfit with military precision, Dargo considered those men his responsibility. The goal was to take Bayer alive. Still, Cyrus couldn't blame Dargo for his actions. Truth be told, had Cyrus felt strongly about bringing Bayer back alive, he would never have let Dargo be the one to retrieve the man.

Cyrus walked on in search of Reese.

Chapter 45

Airborne Out of Phoenix, Arizona
Monday, 10:14 am (11:14 am Colorado Time)

Cyrus, Reese, and Hondo were onboard a small private jet, making the short flight from Phoenix to Santa Barbara. Cyrus explained that one crucial component of Professor Meade's work remained unfinished. He said only that security was of paramount importance. To their disappointment, he wouldn't elaborate on the subject until they reached their final destination. Where that was, he would not say. Just that they would fly to Santa Barbara before using the platform for the final leg of the trip.

The three had spent the night in a motel while Cyrus arranged transportation for the this leg of their trip. He'd kept his explanation for the travel delay vague, saying only that preparations needed to be made in advance.

They sat in the spacious cabin with seating for twelve. Cyrus and Reese sat side by side on a small couch on one side of the aircraft facing Hondo, who was in a recliner on the other.

Aside from the low hum of the engines and a slight whistle of the slipstream outside, the cabin was surprisingly quiet.

"And Dargo just disappeared?" Hondo asked.

"It's not that surprising. His team was wiped out. He was supposed to be backing us up. If it hadn't been for you, we would've been in hot water," Cyrus explained. "Either way, his job was done."

The distant look in his eye told Cyrus that Hondo was trying to put himself in Dargo's position. "I suppose so. He did seem to take it personally. Losing your team? That's an awful thing for a C.O."

"It gets worse. Dargo thinks I had you on station as backup because I didn't trust him."

"He didn't know I was there? *You didn't tell him?*" Hondo took a moment to consider the new information. "You *didn't* trust him, did you?"

Cyrus didn't even need to consider his reply. "There are very few people I trust unequivocally. There was no percentage in sharing that part of the plan."

With a chuckle, Hondo leaned back in his seat. "You may be out of the game, but you haven't lost a step, mate. By the way, what about the mess we left back there?"

"I hired a pro to take care of it."

"You mean a cleaner? I didn't know you had the resources, being out of the game and all!"

Cyrus nodded. He tapped his finger on the side of his skull eliciting a loud thump. "Eidetic memory. I've got shit in here I can't forget, no matter how hard I try."

"And it included contact protocols for a cleaner? Current protocols? One you can trust? No offense, but most of those guys are wired wrong. And any one of them could sell you out to the Coalition." Hondo considered the situation. "I guess it's not like we had a choice. *It was one hell of a mess.* Only a pro could take care of something like that. Who'd you call?"

"Quinn."

A broad grin spread across Hondo's face. "Enough said. Good man. He's been through some rough stuff, if you believe the talk around the water cooler. But a dependable man, that Quinn."

"Yeah. Speaking of dependable, you took out the entire perimeter team back there and still had time to get into position to save our asses. I owe you big, my friend!"

Reese put her hand on Cyrus's leg. "*We* owe you big," she clarified.

He returned her smile. "Yes, *we* owe you. How many were on the perimeter team anyway?" Cyrus asked.

"Eight," Hondo said matter-of-factly. "That last one was the real bugger. I was having trouble nailing him down. I had their comms jammed, trying to keep the upper hand. But that last grunt was making rounds to different stations, and he kept finding his mates where I dropped em'. After that he turned into a damn jackrabbit. I'd picked my improvised roost while I was taking the sentries down. I finally had to leave the last guy be so I could get in position and cover you. It was a near thing, too. No sooner had I dialed in my windage when you and Dargo opened up on Bayer's boys. Discipline went right out the window—I just started popping the guys in the rafters."

That brought a genuine laugh from Cyrus. He looked at Reese. "Hondo makes it sound like he was up there taking potshots with his eyes closed and his fingers crossed. Makes it sound like it was all luck!"

He turned to make eye contact with Hondo. "But the fact is," Cyrus continued, "I counted four holes in the warehouse wall." He let the statement hang for several long beats. Reese looked at him. She didn't understand what he was getting at. "You might've been shooting by the seat of your pants, but by my count? That still means four shots and four kills."

No reply came from Hondo. His eyes were turned to the cabin floor. *I'll be damned*, Cyrus thought. *He's actually embarrassed!*

"Look," Cyrus said. "I'm just saying you haven't lost a step either. I'm damn glad I had you watching our backs. I owe you more than I can repay."

"The hell you do!" Hondo bellowed. His leveled his gaze on Cyrus. "You think I don't know what you did?"

Now Cyrus was confused. Reese must have been equally at a loss, judging by the look on her face.

"The account you set up for Emma?" Hondo clarified. "You didn't think we'd find out?"

Oh, Cyrus thought. He relaxed and leaned back in the seat.

"What's he talking about?" Reese asked. "Does anyone care to fill me in?"

"The daft bastard went and set up a bank account in my baby daughter's name!" Hondo sputtered. "Didn't think me or the missus would find out, I guess."

"I don't understand," Reese continued.

Cyrus shrugged. "Hondo helped me out with a story I was writing a little while back. He wouldn't let me pay him, so I set up a college savings account for his little girl." He turned his glare to Hondo. "He knows how I feel about paying my debts!"

"Wait, what?" This confused Hondo. "You set that up because of the Chicago job?"

"Of course, what'd you think?"

"Cyrus, that was a hell of a lot of money for me to watch you through a window for thirty minutes, then fly home."

"It wasn't about the half hour you spent watching my back. It was about you dropping everything to have my back in the first place. If things had gone south, you would've been in shit up to your elbows! But you didn't think twice. I asked you for help, and you were there. That's what the money was for. Not for the half hour you spent on a rooftop playing peeping Tom."

The sound of someone clearing his throat came from the front of the cabin. Without missing a beat, Cyrus and Hondo snapped their sidearms into position and drew a bead on the man standing there. Cyrus felt Reese tighten her grip on his leg in surprise. Cyrus had been aware of the intruder's presence and he knew Hondo was too. They'd been using the conversation as cover, while they surreptitiously readied their weapons.

"Wow!" the older man at the front of the cabin exclaimed as his hands went into the air in a gesture of surrender. "Guess I was wrong! I thought I'd gotten the drop on you boys. Suppose I should've known better," he chuckled.

The man went to lower his hands, but Cyrus stopped him. "Not so fast, Clayton. Keep them in the air!"

The man looked nonplussed but once again raised his hands. Thomas Clayton was in his late sixties and slightly overweight. He had short gray hair parted down the side. Not a hair out of place. He was government, the figurehead of the Coalition. As always, Clayton wore a three-piece suit, expensive, nothing off the rack. The man was about five foot eight, which meant he could stand upright in the cabin, while Cyrus and Hondo had to stoop to move around.

"Come now, gentlemen!" Clayton said in his most soothing voice. "I'm no threat to you."

Not willing to dignify the statement with a response, Cyrus gave the man his best 'don't bullshit me' glare. Clayton was the head of the Coalition. As such, he was a very dangerous individual. In so far as he was an overweight sixty-year-old man in a suit, he was little danger on his own, but his position in the organization made him a formidable threat, and both men knew it.

Obviously not pleased with the lack of response from either man, Clayton pushed the issue. "This is how you thank me, after all I've done for you?"

"Done for us?" Cyrus laughed. He replied before could catch himself. It was a struggle to tolerate the man when he had been with the Coalition, but since Cyrus was free of that group, he had no intention of listening to anything Clayton had to say. Cyrus didn't want to be on the same continent with him, let alone sharing a plane with the sonofabitch. And, if he listened to the little voice in the back of his head that was famous for keeping him out of trouble, Cyrus knew he should pummel the old man unconscious and throw him from the aircraft.

Clayton arched his eyebrows and waited for Cyrus to sort it out.

Dammit!

His mind immediately jumped to the pair of men dressed in black who had gotten Detective Franklin off his back following the incident at Reese's apartment. He'd hoped it had been Agent Shaw who pulled the strings for him. But the dogs had been called off before she'd had a chance to intervene. Looking back now, the men in black arriving in the middle of the night? The detective dropping his interrogation without so much as a follow-up phone call? That had Coalition written all over it.

Cyrus's frustration flared as he realized he'd been dogged by yet another group through the entire affair. The Alvares cartel and Nil Bayer hadn't been his only enemies here. The Coalition was there all along, waiting in the background. But why? And how? If they'd been maintaining surveillance, he would've picked up the tail long ago. There had been no sign of Coalition watchdogs.

What was Clayton up to?

With a resigned nod of understanding, Cyrus motioned to the plush recliner that faced the direction in which he, Reese, and Hondo sat. "Go slow, and keep your hands where I can see them at all times," Cyrus warned.

The barrels of Cyrus's and Hondo's handguns followed the old man as he walked forward, his hands still in the air. He slid into the seat facing them, before slowly lowering his hands and placing them on the armrests of the wide leather recliner.

As soon as the man was in his seat, Hondo was on him. A thorough pat-down produced only a Glock 30 semi-automatic, a cell phone, and a wallet, complete with false identification. After handing the phone and ID to Cyrus, Hondo pocketed the gun and again raised his weapon. Then he advanced on the front of the aircraft. Checking the galley and the lavatory as he passed, he next entered the cockpit. He returned a moment later and gave Cyrus a reassuring nod. No more surprises. There were no more unexpected guests aboard.

Clayton's appearance was troubling. Cyrus didn't trust him. He was pretty sure he knew what the man wanted, but this was an unexpected turn of events. And the thought of throwing him from the aircraft was more of a consideration than not. Cyrus kept his gun on the old man, while Hondo retrieved a pair of flex cuffs from his carry-on bag. When Clayton saw Hondo returning with the restraints, the indignant look on his face almost made up for Cyrus's inability to throw him from the plane.

Clayton held up his bound wrists and spoke to Cyrus through clenched teeth. "Is this really necessary?"

Returning his gun to his holster, Cyrus shrugged. "It's that or you leave, *right now*," he said coldly.

The old man regarded his bound hands once more, rolled his eyes and reluctantly placed his hands in his lap. "Fine," he muttered.

Finally relaxing in her seat, Reese took a breath. She hadn't realized she was holding it in the first place.

Cyrus looked at her. "Are you alright?"

"I'm fine, but who is this man? And why is he here?"

Raising his eyebrows, Clayton looked at Cyrus anticipating his response. If she had to guess, the man seemed curious to hear the explanation Cyrus chose to use. When Cyrus hesitated to answer, Clayton spoke up.

"Perhaps you wouldn't mind stepping up front for a few minutes so I might have a word with your friends?" he asked.

Her eyes shifted to Cyrus. Now she really wanted to know what was going on. What could this man want to discuss with Cyrus that he couldn't say in front of her? Whatever it was, Cyrus didn't look pleased.

"That's not necessary," Cyrus said, and laid a reassuring hand on her arm. He turned back to Clayton. There was a cold hard cast to his eyes. "I don't want to hear anything you have to say," he told the man. "I've heard it all before, and my answer hasn't changed."

"Yes, but your circumstances have," the old man explained. "You left four dead bodies in Santa Barbara, and I know the body count doesn't end there. If you come back to the Coalition, I'll make sure you're protected. No one needs to know."

"Needs to know what?" Cyrus said with a sneer. "What happened in Santa Barbara was completely justified. I'll stand by it. There were witnesses. You might've expedited my release from custody, but they couldn't prosecute me, and they knew it. What are you playing at?"

"I'm more concerned with your actions outside of Las Vegas last week," Clayton said with a smug grin. "Look, I've got an operation I need your help with. It's a simple matter, but it has to be you. It's a sensitive matter involving a cult operating out east. They call themselves The Order of Origin."

Whatever the man was up to, he clearly thought he had something on Cyrus.

"Las Vegas?" Cyrus asked calmly, without missing a beat. He ignored Clayton's comment about an operation to the East. "I know you're making a threat, but I don't follow."

"I'm offering to make all of your problems go away; it's as simple as that."

"Clayton, some things don't change. You're still an asshole, and I still won't go back to the Coalition! What part of *done* don't you understand?"

"I'm talking about a dozen dead drug runners killed outside of Las Vegas last Thursday! I don't know why you did it, and frankly I don't care. But when they figure out it was you, you're going to prison!"

Reese felt her stomach turn at the thought. How could this be happening? After everything they'd been through, everything they'd survived, could this man really bring them trouble now?

Cyrus nodded in understanding. "I read about that Las Vegas fiasco online," he said. "Some kind of gang war? They were fighting over turf, drugs, or God knows what. You think I had something to do with *that*?"

That brought color to Clayton's face. First the man's complexion flushed, then he started turning red. His blood pressure was skyrocketing. "Don't give me that! Damn it, Cyrus! I know you took out the Alvares gang! When the FBI finds out, you'll go down for it!"

Reese was doing her best to play it cool. To her relief, Hondo was sitting calmly in his seat. He didn't seem concerned. He hadn't moved a muscle since holstering his gun. But she couldn't help it. She found herself looking from Cyrus to the old man, and back to Cyrus again. It seemed to be some kind of standoff. She knew Cyrus hated his old life and had no intention of returning. Could this man really force him to go back?

Finally, Cyrus shrugged. "I'm flattered you think I could walk into a drug lord's home, start shooting, and still make it out alive. From what I've seen on the news, they figure it took at least a dozen men to storm that estate. And you think I did it all by myself?"

He laughed at the old man.

Clayton wasn't amused. "I know you can do it," he said coldly. "*I've sent you to do that sort of thing before.*"

The thought sent a chill down Reese's spine. Were they really having this conversation? Did people really talk like this? Did men really do these things and discuss them so casually?

"I don't know what you're talking about," Cyrus said flatly. "But hypothetically speaking, I'd wager a man capable of the things you're referring to would do them *only* to do right by his country. I'd also expect such a man to be sworn to secrecy. Hypothetically speaking."

"Oh, knock off the hypothetical bullshit!" Clayton spat. "You and I both know what you did! And when the FBI finds the evidence, it's over!"

Clayton was pissed. Actually, Clayton looked like he might have a stroke. Reese watched him carefully. The man was beyond angry. He wanted Cyrus to come back to work, and he seemed to be willing to do anything to achieve that goal.

"Let me give you one more hypothetical," Cyrus said calmly. If Reese didn't know better, she would think he enjoyed pushing the old man's buttons. "If I was the one who broke into a drug lord's home and shot the place up, killed the head of a major cartel, and fled leaving evidence that would lead back to me…" He stretched the statement with a dramatic silence. "Is that the kind of operative you'd want working on your goon squad? It strikes me as sloppy. And sloppy is unprofessional. You're the kind of guy who's only interested in running professionals. So, yeah, do what you have to do. But I want you to remember one thing. I quit. I left your bullshit behind. I did right by my country and by the Coalition. But I'm through with it, and I'm though with you." Cyrus's voice was flat and cold, his eyes locked on Clayton the entire time. "But if you come at me or mine again, I'll make sure no one ever finds your body. Remember, that's what you had me trained to do."

She could see the anger in the man's eyes. None of this had gone the way he had expected. But there did seem to be some positives. First of all, Cyrus wasn't the least bit concerned with the threats. And if he wasn't concerned, maybe she shouldn't be either. Secondly, Clayton didn't appear to know anything about Meridian or Halon-Seven. His interest in the events of the last week seemed to be limited to Cyrus and any way he might leverage those events to bring Cyrus back into the fold.

It was a relief. From what she'd been able to intuit, Clayton had resources and influence. If he'd found out about Meridian, he might very well be a greater danger to the safety of the team than Bola Alvares or Nil Bayer.

As Reese pulled back from her thoughts, she saw Hondo toss Cyrus a roll of duct tape. Cyrus stood and tore off a strip. "You were rude enough to stow away, but I'm going to give you a choice. You can go with this," he held up the flap of tape. "Or we can close you in the lavatory for the remainder of the flight."

For his part, Clayton looked genuinely amused. His eyes tightened on Cyrus with realization, and then he grew tense. "You'd better be joking!" he protested.

This brought no response from Cyrus. He stood his ground, figuratively and literally. The strip of duct tape was held high for all to see. "It's a basic rule of covert operations. You never walk into a place you can't walk out of."

A rattle moved through the aircraft, and the pilot's voice was broadcast from the overhead speakers. He announced they were beginning their descent toward Santa Barbara airport. While this was a relief to Reese, she was troubled by the curious look in Cyrus's eyes.

"What is it?" she whispered.

Cyrus's response was loud enough for both her and Hondo to hear. "He might be a bloated bureaucrat, but Clayton isn't foolish enough to board a plane where he's going to get himself stuck. He knew I would push back."

Cyrus glanced out the window, nodding with understanding. "He's got men waiting for us on the ground."

Clayton's troubled expression morphed into a look of triumph. The vindictive gleam in his eye couldn't be suppressed any longer. "That's right," he said smugly. "You know me, kid. I get my way, one way or the other! I have two-dozen men waiting on the ground. Either you take me up on my offer and come back to the Coalition, or your friends here get listed as enemy combatants and I throw them in a hole so deep and dark they'll never again see the light of day again."

Reese felt the sudden churn of acid in her stomach. This man wouldn't take no for an answer! No wonder Cyrus left the Coalition and never looked back. She glanced at Hondo. This time, even he looked concerned. She felt a new, more powerful wave of nausea. Could this man really make good on his threat?

There was one ray of hope as far as she could see. While Clayton looked supremely self-assured, Cyrus appeared completely unconcerned by the man's threat. Either he had one hell of a poker face, or he had a card left to play. All the same, she couldn't help herself. Her grip on Cyrus's arm tightened.

"He's just not going to be happy until I toss his ass out of this plane," Cyrus muttered to Reese.

He looked her full in the eyes. "I'll be right back," he said with a confident smile. Without a moment's hesitation, he kissed her. Not a peck on the lips but a slow, confident, nothing-else-in-the-world-matters kind of kiss.

Cyrus gave her a wink. Then he turned, grabbed Clayton by the strap that bound his hands and effortlessly forced him to his feet. Throwing an arm over the man's shoulder, he casually guided him toward the end of the cabin.

Reese couldn't help herself. "What's he going to do?" she whispered to Hondo—the whisper more out of concern than an effort to keep quiet.

Hondo shrugged. "You got me," he admitted. He knelt on his seat and looked though the window.

When Reese joined him, she could see what had drawn his attention. A dozen black SUVs sat at the end of the runway, their hideaway blue and red emergency response lights strobing in the distance. All the while, the plane was dropping closer and closer to the ground as the pilot prepared to land.

At the far end of the cabin, Cyrus was speaking calmly in hushed tones with Clayton. It didn't appear to be much of a conversation. Cyrus was doing all of the talking. Clayton wasn't reacting. He just listened without interrupting. After about two minutes of this, Cyrus must've finished what he had to say, because he became silent. He just looked at the short older man. For seemingly endless moments, Clayton stared back at Cyrus.

Finally, with great consternation, Clayton held out his hand. Cyrus handed Clayton his confiscated phone. The man tapped a speed dial key and waited only a moment. There was brief exchange with the individual on the other end of the line before Clayton disconnected and handed the phone back to Cyrus, who pocketed it. Clayton took a long look at Cyrus and exhaled deeply. Dejected and beaten, he slowly plodded back to his designated seat.

Cyrus walked back to Reese's end of the cabin and took his seat on the sofa. Hondo chuckled, and returned to his seat. Reese still didn't understand what had happened. Everyone suddenly seemed content with the situation. Well, except for Clayton. He looked like a child who had just been put in a timeout. But why? She knelt on the seat and looked back out the window in time to see the last of the black SUVs driving off the runway with its lights extinguished. Clayton's men were falling back.

She looked back at Cyrus. What had he done?

Cyrus smiled and shrugged. Reese couldn't imagine what he'd said to cause Clayton's about-face, but she looked forward to the story. For the time being, it seemed, things were back to normal. *Funny,* she thought. *When did all this become normal?*

Epilogue

There was a flash and a pronounced popping in his ears, and then the trip was complete. Cyrus held Reese in his arms. Once again, they had gotten used to teleporting together. He actually looked forward to it. Any chance to hold her close. It was the popping in his ears he could do without. However, this time it hurt more than ever. The others would have experienced it too, but only he would know the cause. They were standing in a fifteen-by-fifteen-square-foot concrete room, located four hundred feet below the Superstition Mountains in the southwestern United States.

The irony of their destination wasn't lost on Cyrus. Following the bloody confrontation at the warehouse, they'd flown out of Phoenix only to land in western California. From there, they'd teleported essentially back to where they had started in Arizona. Only this time, hundreds of feet below ground. The installation they had just entered carried a double-black security clearance that put it well above top secret. Even the venerable

Coalition wasn't aware of its existence. Cyrus wasn't able to share the specifics of their location with Reese or Hondo. The juxtaposition was reserved for his personal amusement.

Access to the facility had been arranged for him by Walter Meade, prior to the man's death. Meade truly had planned ahead and thought of everything. And Cyrus finally understood why. A thumb drive stashed in a hidden burn safe within the basement vault had finally fully put things in perspective. The data drive was in an envelope that also contained a hand-written letter, addressed to Cyrus. That letter had explained that only Cyrus could unlock the biometric encryption of the thumb drive, and Cyrus alone should be privy to the information it held. What he decided to do with the information after he considered it was entirely up to him. Meade had asked only that Cooper first review the data in private.

So Cyrus had, prior to the operation at the warehouse in Phoenix. The information on that drive had changed his perspective on everything: Meridian, Meade's work, even the way he looked at the world around him.

Moments later there came another flash of light, and Hondo appeared on the teleportation platform. His hands instantly went to his ears. "Bloody hell!" he grimaced.

Cyrus nodded. "It seems to be a shortcoming of the technology." He looked at Reese. "Is there any way to lessen the shocking effects on the inner ear?"

She considered the question. "We'll look into it. It's tricky but worth the effort. Where are we? There must be a serious shift in barometric pressure to make our ears pop like that."

He shook his head. "As much as I'd like to share, I'm afraid that's classified. But it's for your protection. And I need to be clear. What we're going to discuss must stay between the three of us, at least for the moment. Meade was very specific in requesting that this information not be disseminated—his words, not mine."

Hondo still had a finger in his ear, wiggling it to relieve pressure. "That sounds ominous, mate."

"You're telling me," Reese agreed.

Cyrus didn't respond. It was important to him that he be given their word, formally. He just waited for their response.

"You know me, I can keep a secret. I won't tell a soul. You have my word," Hondo confirmed.

Cyrus could tell by the look in Hondo's eyes that the man was somewhat unnerved by his need for a formal agreement on that matter. Hondo was realizing that the matter had gravity.

"I promise," Reese said simply.

Satisfied, Cyrus turned to the heavy steel door that was the only way out of the concrete chamber. He entered a twelve-digit code into the touchscreen panel beside the door handle and waited. A moment later, the light at the top of the LCD touch screen went green and there was a hissing sound, as the airtight seal around the door released.

When he pulled the door open, Cyrus could see the surprise register on both Hondo's and Reese's faces. They were both shocked to find that the door was nearly six inches thick and contained a powerful retractable pressure seal which had pulled back into the door when the lock had disengaged. Hondo was grimacing again and had his finger in his ear once more. The release of the door's seal had changed the pressure in the room. Cyrus felt his own ears pop again in response.

They stepped into a wide concrete hallway that was brightly lit with overhead fixtures. A man sat on a battery operated golf cart a few yards away. "Good day, Mister Cooper," the man said with a smile. "Room 16D has been reserved for you and is ready when you are."

"Thank you," Cyrus replied. He motioned for Reese and Hondo to step onto the golf cart. Hondo took a spot on the seat beside the driver, and Reese took one end of the front-facing rear seat.

The driver's mention of room 16D raised a question in Cyrus's mind. He had no idea how large the underground installation might be. He'd only been here once before, shortly after reviewing the life altering set of files that Walter Meade had left. Along with the files, Meade had included the access code for an undocumented platform as well as the communication protocols he needed to use prior to teleporting to the underground facility. Other than a few additional scraps of information, Cyrus knew precious little about the secret installation.

Cyrus stepped on board the cart and slid into the seat beside Reese. A moment later, the cart pulled away. It gained speed and went cruising down the seemingly endless concrete corridor.

Reese leaned in close to Cyrus. "I've been dying to ask. What did you say to Clayton that caused such an about face? One minute he thinks he has you over a barrel, and the next he's pulling his men back and walking away with his tail between his legs," she whispered.

Stifling a grin, Cyrus looked back at her and shrugged. "I simply reminded him that a man in his position would do well to think twice before blackmailing a field-proficient operative with an eidetic memory. In very nonspecific terms, I suggested that such an individual was likely to run across sensitive information, in the course of an operation, that might reflect poorly on the chain of command. I explained that such exposures are commonplace and often unavoidable. The problem is that an operative with a photographic memory can't help but file away every disparate bit of information. And sooner or later, he'll start to connect the dots. It's a hazard of the profession."

Reese's eyebrows raised in surprise. "You blackmailed him? You must have something nasty on him!"

Cyrus considered the still unexplained disappearance of Clayton's prior boss, Monica Fichtner. Though complicated, the bad blood Cyrus had with the Coalition could be traced back to her. To date, no one had discovered the location of Fichtner's body. It was believed by some that many of the improvements Clayton had since made to the organization were thanks to a healthy fear of a similar fate.

"Sometimes people just need a little motivation to do the right thing," Cyrus offered in cryptic reply.

The cart took another corner and stopped before an innocuous steel door with a nameplate marked simply *16D*.

"Here you go, sir," the driver said, and waited for his passengers to step from the vehicle. "When you're through, just dial the operator and another cart will be dispatched to return you to room 144X."

Now Cyrus really wanted to know how large the facility might be. It had a switchboard operator, apparently multiple golf-cart taxies, and at least 144 rooms. That didn't allow for the odd letter suffix to each room number, which could add nearly endless combinations and who knew how many additional rooms. What might other rooms hold?

Shaking his head, Cyrus pushed those concerns aside. Entering a code into the touch screen beside the door, he led Reese and Hondo into room 16D. He was about to reshape their understanding of the world. The mysteries of this facility would wait for another time.

Room 16D wasn't much larger than the room in which they'd first arrived. This room was about twenty feet wide and thirty feet long. There was a long rectangular conference table in the center, surrounded by comfortable office chairs. The far wall was dominated by a massive LCD flat-panel display. The remaining walls were bare concrete. The overhead light was modified. The lights projected brightly into every corner of the room. But there was a remote control at the near end of the table that allowed the lights to be dimmed for use in conjunction with the screen on the opposite wall. Beside the remote were a series of cables extending from the surface of the conference table. Cyrus immediately set about connecting his laptop to the cables.

Reese took a seat to his right and Hondo at his left. More than half a dozen empty chairs surrounded the rest of the table.

"Are we expecting guests?" Hondo asks after regarding the empty seats.

"No," Cyrus confirmed. "It's just us. But we need to discuss this here. The data on this USB drive can be accessed only while connected to the network at this facility. It's a proprietary failsafe."

A moment later Cyrus had his laptop booted up. He dimmed the lights and powered up the wall-mounted flat-panel display. Taking the USB thumb drive from the pocket of his jeans, he pressed a button on the device that caused the USB port to extend from the end. He put his thumb on a small sensor on the surface of the tiny drive. There was a chirp and a small LED strobed green. Then he plugged the drive into the side of his laptop.

"I don't know how to preface this, so I'm just going to jump in. Reese knows some of these details, and I covered some of this back at the warehouse with Bayer. While some of this is a refresher, some of what I'm about to explain will correct points we didn't fully understand earlier. Other parts are entirely new. Meade's flash drive has changed my perspective on everything," Cyrus explained.

With a tap of his keyboard, the first image arrived on the screen at the end of the room. The photo was a very old, poor quality, and black and white. "This is Rumsfeld Pellagrin and his team of three assistants, shortly after Pellagrin recovered a particularly interesting meteorite along the east coast of the United States in 1903. The meteorite came to be known as sample J-189D. Pellagrin was just 23 years old at the time."

A new slide appeared showing Pellagrin and a number of others at work in what now looked like an antiquated lab. Pellagrin was studying the recovered meteorite. "The specifics of the discovery are too much to get into right now, but the properties and characteristics observed from the study of this meteorite led to our current understanding of physics."

He changed to the next slide. It showed Pellagrin again in the lab, this time with a man whose head was ruled by a wild shock of unkempt hair. Both men appeared to be in deep examination of a pair of meteorite fragments. "Pellagrin and his friend here, Albert Einstein, worked closely for a number of years. It's not common knowledge, for reasons that are about to be made clear, but Einstein did not develop his famous theories of physics in a vacuum. His theoretical work wasn't entirely theoretical after all. Many of his theories were the result of real-world observations, and the study of the meteorite Pellagrin discovered in 1903.

"Of particular importance to us, the study of this meteorite led to our understanding of quantum physics and quantum teleportation. Both sciences necessary to make Meridian function."

Noting the slack jawed expression from Hondo, he knew this was all news to his friend. The surprise in Reese's eyes was likely due to the enlightening bit regarding Einstein. While she knew of Einstein's involvement in the early days of Pellagrin's work, J-189D's effect on science was only beginning to fully sink in. *Just wait*, he thought. They were just starting down the rabbit hole.

"In 1907 another meteor impacted twelve kilometers outside of Moscow. The strike was witnessed by dozens of people. The Russian military immediately recovered the meteorite and, appropriately enough, it ended up in the hands of Russian scientists." He switched to a slide showing three Russian scientists posing behind an unremarkable looking fragment of rock. In the background of the image, they could see a woman who appeared to be setting up a piece of scientific equipment.

"After a great deal of study, the outer layers of the meteorite were deemed unremarkable and were later stripped away. But at the core, they found something very different." He presented the next slide showing an entirely different, irregularly shaped chunk of stone.

"They began testing this piece of ore and quickly decided it was capable of emitting massive amounts of energy. When they briefly applied heat to the meteorite, the stone would become superheated and continue to emit that heat until forcibly cooled. When electrical current was passed into the ore, the charge pulled from the stone was many times in excess of the charge applied to it."

He loaded another slide showing the meteorite attached to a single small power lead on one side and a primitive voltage meter on the other. The voltage meter was pegged, and smoke was rising from the device. "It wasn't until Rumsfeld Pellagrin gained access to the Russian research that he realized what the meteorite was truly capable of. Unfortunately, by that time the Russians had already suffered a mishap with the meteorite that resulted in a massive release of energy that wiped out their entire research facility and all of its personnel.

"Though interesting, the specifics of the accident aren't what we need to focus on, if we are to understand the larger picture. What is important, is that following the Russian mishap, Rumsfeld Pellagrin secretly traveled to Russian and was able to recover the core of the meteorite the Russian scientists were studying."

Hondo raised a hand calling for a stop in the monolog. "Wait a second," he said. His face was scrunched in confusion. "You said that Pellagrin went to Russia following the explosion and retrieved the rock that caused the explosion? It wasn't destroyed in the blast?"

The question brought a smile to his face. "No," Cyrus clarified. "Pellagrin discovered that what they thought was a detonation was actually a massive unbridled release of the energy stored in the meteorite. There was no conventional explosion—though the entire research facility was simply wiped from the face of the Earth.

"Pellagrin took the meteorite and returned to the United States. It was the study of the ore that consumed the rest of Pellagrin's life. But as Pellagrin aged, he took on a protégé. A young man named Walter Meade. Meade formally took over Pellagrin's work when the man passed away in 1957."

Reese nodded in understanding. "That's when Walter came into the picture."

"Yes. At that point, Pellagrin had built a pair of prototype teleportation platforms and tested them only once. He'd only been able to generate enough power to fuel the devices a single time. With the power requirements so high, the platforms had been mothballed until decades later when Meade went back to work on them, this time powering them with a pair of nuclear reactors.

"Still, a nuclear power source for each platform was out of the question. At least if they were to be deployed as far and wide as Meade intended. And so the project stalled once more. By this time, Meade had put years of research into the Russian meteorite, in addition to the American sample J-189D.

"Meade based his work on that of Pellagrin, who took his initial cues from the Russians. And they all took the detonation in Russia as a warning for just how careful they needed to be with the ore."

Cyrus's eyes gleamed as he thought about a particular revelation. "One of the most crucial discoveries was made in 2006, when Meade performed a scan of the Russian meteorite using a new Benzol-based scanning technology. He discovered that inside the chunk of ore was a single, perfectly round sphere, about the size of a marble or a ball bearing."

Cyrus put another slide up showing the meteorite as a before image.

"This confirmed what Meade had concluded, based on earlier tests. Despite the odd characteristics exhibited by the ore, its composition was not altogether unlike most rock structures found on Earth. He'd never been able to explain how or why the meteorite exhibited the properties that it did.

"But once he had that scan, he knew that the rock's outer composition was just a shell. The orb on the inside was what he was really after."

Cyrus put up the next slide. It showed a single black orb with a lusterless matte black finish. The object was a fraction of the size of the original meteorite, and it was absolutely uniform in shape.

"This is what was at the center of the meteorite. A perfect sphere—no seams and no markings of any kind. Ultimately, this is what Meade referred to as Halon-Seven."

Cyrus gave them a few moments to take in the strange object. The two just sat there staring at the screen. Cyrus knew what they must've been thinking. The object was a perfect sphere, unblemished in any way, even after traveling through space and ultimately crashing to Earth.

"When Meade was able to split the sphere into five separate sections, he began to wonder whether it might be possible to integrate them into the design of the platforms. That was when he started to consider using the ore to deal with the power problems of the platforms."

"Hold on," Reese said. "You're saying Walter cut the orb into five sections? I have a hard time believing he would do that, especially after what happened in Russia. Even more so after he found out the object inside the meteorite was this sphere. That raises so many additional questions! A perfect sphere doesn't happen in nature."

Cyrus took a moment to consider his next words. "This is actually where things get far more complicated. Meade didn't actually cut the sphere. According to his notes, he made a discovery while performing a battery of experiments. After he cleared away the detritus that was the outer layers of minerals, he had unfettered access to the sphere at the core. He started all of his tests over again from scratch. All new scans and tests of the object, as if he were looking at it for the first time.

"In one of his most important tests, he was sending different voltages and wattages into the orb to measure its output response. He found that the orb could not only store the energy passed to it, but it could amplify it. Essentially, he found a sort of control interface for the orb. He would send specific ultrasonic bursts into the object, and based on those harmonic frequencies, the orb would react differently to the power he fed it."

Judging by the look he was getting from both Reese and Hondo, Cyrus could tell he was in danger of losing them. But this was a crucial bit of information. He had to make this part clear.

"It was as if the orb was not a rock but a *manufactured device*. A device that could be controlled with ultrasonic audio commands."

Cyrus changed to the next image and showed the meteorite on the left side of the photo. On the right of the photo were five equally sized spheres, each the size of a BB from a BB gun.

"In response to one frequency, the orb split into five identical but smaller versions of itself. Each with exactly one fifth the mass of its previous configuration."

Reese stared at him, apparently stunned. Each time she tried to speak, she stopped short, seemingly tongue-tied.

Hondo found the words more succinctly. "What the bloody hell is that thing?"

Reese nodded absently. "He's right," she mumbled. "There's no way that orb is naturally occurring."

"That was Meade's conclusion as well," Cyrus confirmed. "As you said, a perfect sphere is virtually impossible in nature. Add to that the characteristics exhibited, and there could be no other conclusion. Halon-Seven must be a manufactured device."

Sitting back in his chair, Cyrus gave them both several minutes to think about the implications. Similar thoughts had been on his mind since reviewing Meade's files. There was some catharsis in sharing the information with his friends.

The pale look on Hondo's face betrayed his concern with his next question. "Manufactured by whom?"

"Let me ask you a question, Reese." Cyrus said, and he waited a long moment for her attention to return from the overhead screen. Her mind was clearly reeling from the implications.

A barely coherent "Uh huh?" was all she could manage.

"Did Meade ever explain why he called it Halon-Seven?"

She thought for a moment and finally shook her head. Her eyes sharpened and met his. She was back to focusing on the conversation rather than the far-reaching implications of the orb.

"No, I guess not. It seems odd now, but I never thought to ask. I don't think any of us did."

Cyrus nodded. "I suppose it's understandable."

He tapped a key on his laptop, and a new image appeared on the screen at the end of the room. A massive, seemingly endless sequence of 1s and 0s filled the screen from edge to edge, top to bottom.

"One of the harmonic tones Meade sent into the orb caused it to emit an audible signal of its own. He put the tone through heavy analysis and discovered that the tone could be equated to binary code. This binary code," Cyrus clarified.

Both Reese and Hondo looked back at him, shocked once again.

"The orb played a sound?" Hondo clarified.

Cyrus nodded. "The sound was translated into what turned out to be binary computer code. That binary code was resolved into ASCII text. It's the same word, repeated over and over again in seven different languages. Mandarin, English, Spanish, Russian, German, Portuguese, and Arabic.

"The seven most widely spoken languages in the world today," Cyrus elaborated.

"Seven languages?" Reese muttered, her voice a mere whisper.

"What was the word?" Hondo asked.

"Halon," Cyrus said with a smile. He once again sat back in his chair. "When Meade named the—substance—he was using the name provided to him, *by the orb*. He called it Halon-Seven, because the meteorite, or the device we now know it to be, told him the name 'Halon' in seven different languages."

The silence of the room seemed to stretch on forever. It was clear that neither Reese nor Hondo knew what to say. Cyrus was right there with them. Where they were simply shocked, he had moved on to the point where all of this made his head hurt.

"I have to ask," Reese said finally. "Are we sure that Pellagrin confirmed that this was a meteor? Was he absolutely certain this object came from space? Keeping in mind that this meteorite came to us by way of the Russians?"

"He had conclusive documentation," Cyrus confirmed. "And Meade further confirmed it. The outer layers were comprised of minerals at concentrations not native to Earth. In fact, there were elements never before discovered."

"But if that's true, and the device contained seven Earth-based languages…"

"It would mean that we're not alone after all," Cyrus confirmed.

"Bullshit!" Hondo laughed. "Very funny."

Cyrus pushed on, undeterred. "Shortly before he died, Meade got access to a state of the art, next generation, electron microscope that was being tested by a German corporation. It has the most powerful magnification optics manufactured to date. He used the microscope to examine one of the Halon-Seven orbs. The description he used for what he found was what he called a 'micro-lattice.' Something he described as being manufactured at a nano-scale. His conclusion was that we don't have the technology to fully examine the composition of the Halon-Seven orbs, let alone manufacture them. Wherever Halon-Seven came from, it wasn't here."

When the silence stretched on again, Cyrus decided to continue.

"This also explains why we won't be able to find any more Halon-Seven. All we have is what Meade collected from the three meteor strikes."

"That's right," Reese said. She seemed to snap out of her state of awe and back into the moment. "Back at the warehouse, you mentioned two additional meteorites."

Cyrus nodded. "Once Meade knew the characteristics of what he was looking for, he conned the White House into getting him time on several satellites. He didn't go into great detail due to the sensitive nature of the satellites utilized, but he was able to search the entire surface of the planet for any additional signs of Halon-Seven. He found two more impact sites and immediately had the meteorites retrieved. Each of the other two contained an orb that was a duplicate of the one Meade already had. He was able to split each orb into five separate pieces. Together with the samples he already had, those orbs are now used to regulate power in the Meridian teleportation platforms currently in service."

"And where did those meteors make land fall?" Hondo asked.

"Russia, Australia, and South America," Cyrus confirmed.

Reese cocked her head. She'd thought of something. "Walter's scans—did they include the oceans, or just dry land?"

"He was able to scan 100% of the Earth's surface. Land, sea, and even the ice caps."

"I don't know," Hondo said with a chuckle. "What are the odds that the only three meteor strikes made landfall? Isn't three quarters of the planet covered with water? I think there's a good chance the Professor missed something."

"Four," Cyrus corrected.

This brought questioning looks from Reese and Hondo.

"There were four crucial meteor impacts to make landfall. All four of them had a payload with the potential to change our world forever. You should include the first meteorite, the one Rumsfeld Pellagrin discovered. It was different from the three containing Halon-Seven, but it was every bit as significant— maybe even more so. That's actually where all of this started. Had it not been for what we learned there, we wouldn't have the science necessary to understand the secrets of the subsequent meteor impacts."

"Fair enough," Hondo admitted. "I think you just proved my point. Those are really long odds. What are the chances of people actually finding those meteorites, let alone understanding what they had once they did?"

Cyrus tapped a button on the keyboard, bringing up a new slide. This one showed the surface of the planet as a map. Each meteor impact location was marked, along with its impact date.

"It was those odds that haunted Meade," Cyrus explained. "He believed that those meteors didn't arrive here by accident. He thought they were sent to those locations."

Reese's jaw waggled as she struggled for something to say. "Sent by whom?" she finally asked.

"He had no idea," Cyrus said sadly. "And that bothered him more than anything. Pellagrin recovered the first meteorite. Together, Pellagrin and Einstein discovered that it contained secrets of the universe. Later, Meade cracked the code of Halon-Seven and found two duplicate meteorites. He knew the three meteorites could be the key to solving the world's energy problems as well as allow him to perfect the teleportation technology that Pellagrin pioneered at the start of the twentieth century.

"He believed these resources were sent to us intentionally, but he never knew who sent them or why."

"Based on the evidence, I'm inclined to believe him," Reese admitted. "But I'm afraid we may never know the who or the why."

Cyrus leaned forward in his chair. He was personally excited about this part of the presentation. "Walter Meade never realized it, but I think the explanation was right under his nose."

He brought up another slide showing a photo of the Russian scientists standing in their lab in 1907. Another tap of a key added a new photo to the screen. This image showed Rumsfeld Pellagrin's lab team working in 1932. Another image popped up showing Professor Meade standing in a lab with a very old Rumsfeld Pellagrin. That photo was dated 1955.

The three of them sat there in the darkened room with the three photos glowing larger than life on the far wall. Finally Cyrus hit one more button, and a photo of Meade and his current research team joined the set. Four images showing the progress of the Meridian project over the last century.

"Meade wanted answers for so long," Cyrus explained. "He had all of these photos in his archive, he must've looked at each a hundred times. But I think it's what all four have in common that will answer so many questions."

Each looked across the four images for several long moments, but no one spoke up. Finally Cyrus tapped another key. The image collage on the display was replaced by a duplicate of the first. But the new image had a red circle around one face, which appeared in all four of the photographs. It took several long beats, but when he heard a gasp escape Reese's mouth, he knew the connection was made.

Cyrus tapped one more key and a new photo was added to the edge of the screen. The large overhead display now showed five photos in total, taken over the last one hundred years. The one he had just added was taken the day before, in Australia. It was a solo shot of Tracy Clark. Her hair was different in each of the photos, but the characteristics of her face made for a match.

Hondo's voice sounded like gravel. "That's not bloody possible!"

"I don't believe it," Reese muttered, almost to herself.

Looking across the four primary photos, the face of the young woman they called Tracy could be seen in the background of the photo showing the Russian science team. She had been setting up some sort of device behind the lead scientists when the photo had been taken. But she was a primary member of the photograph showing Pellagrin's team in 1932. In the photo of Meade and a very aged Rumsfeld Pellagrin, Tracy was caught at the edge of the frame, with a clipboard in her hand and wearing a thick pair of glasses. And there she was again, as they knew her today, standing alongside Reese and Professor Meade, in a recent photo taken in the California lab sometime in the last year.

The same woman, wearing different clothes and differing hair styles was in every one of the photographs. But most shocking of all, Tracy Clark had not aged in the years between photos.

"I don't believe it!" Reese stammered.

"Seeing is believing," Cyrus said simply.

"But how?" Hondo asked. "How can that be? And for what possible purpose?"

"Those are the million dollar questions," Cyrus admitted. "If I had to guess, I'd say that it was her job to make sure we stayed on track."

"I don't understand," Reese admitted.

"You lost me," Hondo confirmed.

"Someone went to a lot of trouble to point these, quote unquote, 'meteorites' at specific parts of our planet. Like you said, Hondo, it makes for some pretty long odds that they would be discovered and land in the hands of the right people. But those odds improve if you have someone on the inside, making sure to nudge people in just the right direction. The right suggestion here, an advantageous accident there, who says whether it's serendipity or happenstance that shapes our future? Maybe it's a more corporeal presence."

Sitting back in his chair, Cyrus watched his two closest friends take in the most earth-shattering news of their lives. This changed everything they ever believed about the world around them. They had proof that some guiding hand was, at least in some way, responsible for the most significant scientific breakthroughs in human history. And if our race was urged, leveraged, or coaxed in a given direction, in such a way, over the last hundred years, how might we have been influenced over the millennia prior? How might human history have been influenced by an unseen intelligence?

There was no doubt in Cyrus's mind that he had considered many of the questions that were now blasting through the minds of his friends. He tapped one more key on his laptop and brought up his last slide. "Professor Meade may not have discovered Tracy, but he had a pretty precise idea where the four meteors originated. All four came from this part of space. He provided precise vectors."

The screen showed a constellation of stars not unlike any other section of the sky visible on a clear night.

"I think it's time we had a talk with Tracy Clark."

Cyrus Cooper will return in...

Surviving Origin

A Note from Xander Weaver:

Thank you for reading "Halon-Seven." I hope you've had as much fun reading it as I've had writing it. If you did, you're encouraged to show your support by posting a review with your online retailer of choice. Those reviews make a big difference to new readers, and are a definite aid when it comes to spreading the word about my work. Just a brief statement explaining what it was that you enjoyed is all it takes.

Your time and effort are sincerely appreciated.

Thank you!

—Xander Weaver

Acknowledgments:

Some believe that writing is a solitary endeavor; the result of a single author slaving over a keyboard until the story that needs telling has been told in its entirety, but this has never been the case for me. I do my best work when receiving feedback and input from trusted friends and colleagues. My wife, for example, is the first to read all that I write. She makes the first round of edits, even before I hand the manuscript off to the editor. Why? Well, when you've married someone as talented, intelligent, and genuinely interested in your work as I've had the good fortune to do, it would be foolish not to make use of that valued resource.

Then there's my editor for this manuscript: Kane Gilmour. A gifted bestselling author, a professional editor with a killer resume and an all-round great guy, Kane is more than just a professional resource. He's a friend. With tremendous demands on his time these days, I'm thankful for the opportunity to work with him on a project that means so much to me.

The cover art for *Halon-Seven* is once more the brilliant work of Lee Roesner, a longtime friend and proprietor of Paradigm Graphic Design. Lee has the sort of talent and artistic sense that makes great design seem effortless. I couldn't be more thrilled with the cover of this book and the way its theme is perfectly meshed with the rest of the series.

As in the past, I'm also fortunate to have a support team of fact checkers, proofreaders, and general enforcers who raise the quality of my work. For both their time and effort, I want to give special thanks to: Wayne and Terri Manke, Tom Nielsen, Wenzel Roessler, and Jake and Julie Dresser. Jamie Dresser, in particular, championed this book from its roughest draft through to its final proof—truly a level of support that goes above and beyond. He read this manuscript more times than anyone, tenacious in his will to see it in print.

With friends and colleagues like these, the writing process is anything but solitary. I am extremely fortunate to know the true meaning of "friendship."

Newsletter:

Want to hear about the latest book release, contests, and giveaways?

Join the newsletter:

XanderWeaver.com/newsletter

About the Author

Thank you for reading *Halon-Seven*. This is the fourth book in the "Cyrus Cooper" series, and in many ways it was my favorite to write. Cyrus is a far more complicated character at this point in the game. Having left the Coalition—where he'd been a major part of thrilling covert schemes—behind, his hope of leading a simpler life quickly seems not meant to be. If anything, he's thrown into a world that's more chaotic than any he has ever known. Now he's forced to deal with wounds from the past, while searching for his rightful place in the present. And the future is coming...whether he likes it or not.

As is my way, this story is a mix of thriller, espionage, and science fiction. Like many authors, I am first a reader at heart. I write the genre of stories I *want* to read—that I *love* to read. I desire action, mystery and suspense—I want to be thrilled! A book should make me think, even while taking me on a wild ride that sticks with me long after the tale is finished. Learning things along the way is a great deal of fun, but at the core of it all I thrive on characters. Whether I love them or hate them, the greatest characters ever written are those that spark an emotional response that makes reading, and writing, fun. *Halon-Seven* is my attempt to capture these qualities.

If you would like to be notified of future book releases in advance, I welcome you to join my newsletter at: www.XanderWeaver.com. Rest assured, your personal information will never be sold or traded.

While I'm working on the next thrill ride, I frequently post updates to Facebook (Weaver.Books) and Twitter

(@XanderWeaver). Please follow the progress and join in the fun!

Other books by Xander Weaver:

Book One: *Dangerous Minds*
Book Two: *Rogue Faction Part 1*
Book Three: *Rogue Faction Part 2*

For more information, please visit:
www.XanderWeaver.com

www.ingramcontent.com/pod-product-compliance
Lightning Source LLC
Chambersburg PA
CBHW030538020726
47494CB00005B/1418